THE HOOKER AND THE HERMIT

RUGBY SERIES BOOK #1

L.H. COSWAY

PENNY REID

THE HOOKER AND THE HERMIT

RUGBY SERIES BOOK #1

L.H. COSWAY

PENNY REID

COPYRIGHT

This book is a work of fiction. Names, characters, places, rants, facts, contrivances, and incidents are either the product of the author's questionable imagination or are used factitiously. Any resemblance to actual persons, living or dead or undead, events, locales is entirely coincidental if not somewhat disturbing/concerning.

Copyright © 2015 by Cipher-Naught; All rights reserved.

No part of this book may be reproduced, scanned, photographed, instagrammed, tweeted, twittered, twatted, tumbled, or distributed in any printed or electronic form without explicit written permission from the author.

NO AI TRAINING: Without in any way limiting the author's and publisher's exclusive rights under copyright, any use of this publication to "train" generative artificial intelligence (AI) technologies to generate text is expressly prohibited. The author reserves all rights to license uses of this work for generative AI training and development of machine learning language models.

Made in the United States of America

ISBN: 978-1-960342-03-4

PRINT EDITION

DEDICATION

In no particular order: baked goods, Colin Farrell's eyebrows, and the thighs of rugby players everywhere.
And to the city of Edinburgh, where a love story was born.

ONE
ANNIE

The Email Checker: *When one pretends to be checking his/her email on a smartphone, but is instead actually taking a picture of a person/the people directly in front of him/her.*
Best for: *Most situations where it is socially acceptable to be checking email, e.g. coffee shops, while dining alone at a restaurant, waiting for public transportation.*
Do not use: *In locations with no cell phone or Internet reception.*

I'm not going to pretend that I have pristine intentions. But to be fair, when he initially entered the restaurant, I was already checking my email.

In fact, I didn't look up from my phone until I heard the kerfuffle and squawking of excited females. These sounds—giggling, squeals, *oooohhhhh*, whispered *Oh, My God!* and *Is that really him?*—typically accompanied the arrival of a male celebrity. I'm especially tuned into the signs and symptoms for two reasons: my job and my hobby.

I am the primary project lead of the Social Media Marketing division at Davidson & Croft Media. My specialty is transforming reputations in the court of public opinion. Give me a disgraced celebrity, politician, or public figure—sex-tape scandal, DUIs, arrests, the great rehab escape, sexting an intern (what I call "Donkey Donging")—and I will transform that person's image.

I will make her sparkle. I will make him shine. I am legendary in my field. I am the best at what I do.

And I admit this as truth with absolutely no conceit or vanity because I'm terrible at almost everything else in life. Take walking or talking, for instance, never mind attempting both at the same time. Or smiling. Or not being weird. Or not creeping people out. Or not being the cause of every awkward silence in a five-mile radius.

The only other things at which I excel in life are: 1) responsible financial planning, 2) my hobby blog, and 3) eating.

Which brings me to now, Tom's Southern Kitchen, and the group of ladies molting feathers left and right as they try to dry-hump the remarkably attractive and muscular man who has just entered.

I'd lifted just my eyes, peering at him and the women as I tried to place his face. He was standing in profile, and his handsome mouth was curved in a patient, polite smile. I couldn't tell if he was enjoying the attention or if he just had exceedingly excellent manners.

Regardless, he looked quite a lot like the Irish actor Colin Farrell, except a Colin Farrell who'd been working out nonstop, had thighs like tree trunks, and was ten to fifteen years younger. So, maybe a Colin Farrell just back from a visit to the plastic surgeon and a CrossFit boot camp. This glorious specimen of maleness had dark brown hair, spiky and short. His nose was perfect, almost adorable, but it somehow fit his face. His jaw was angular and strong. He even had the actor's high cheekbones, dark brown eyebrows, thick lashes, and doe eyes.

I couldn't decide if this guy was a doppelgänger or if he was the real deal, but it didn't really matter. He would be perfect for my Saturday Celebrity Stalker post. It was, without fail, the most popular post every week.

Which leads me to my greatest and most closely held secret. The truth is that I, Annie Catrel, am The Socialmedialite, the owner and purveyor of the blog *New York's Finest*.

That's right.

I'm The Socialmedialite.

I'm that girl, the most influential infotainment blogger in the world.

And, because I am meticulous about my security protocols, no one knows who I am…that I am she…that she is me.

Never mind. You know what I mean.

Anyway, Saturday Celebrity Stalker is my weekly post dedicated to celebrities or their look-alikes wherein their physical features are picked apart John Madden style (John Madden being the famous American football coach-then-announcer who loved to draw on the home viewers' TV screen with circles, arrows, and random lines to demonstrate errors in football plays).

Except I do this to celebrities (almost exclusively male celebrities) and question their judgment regarding grooming, makeup (yes, makeup), clothes, and accessory choices. And if they're walking a dog, I do it to their little dog, too.

The degree to which I pick apart the celebrity's lack of judgment depends on several factors, and I'm the first to admit I'm a good deal easier and/or nicer to those people with talent than I am to celebriturds (people who are famous because they're famous/rich but with no redeeming qualities to offer society) and celebritrash (celebriturds who are also fame whores).

However, I try not to comment too much on bodies or facial features. Personally, I feel like we—Western culture—are so body obsessed, there's no need for me to add to the hysteria. Especially since these famous people already give me so much fodder with their ridiculous million-dollar fanny packs (made in third world sweatshops) and their gold-plated floss holders.

Why does anyone need a gold-plated floss holder? Tell me. Why? Why? Why?

I don't know. I don't get it.

Most men *loved* being featured on my blog. My posts typically resulted in emails of praise and thanks from publicity-hungry agents and celebrities. Sometimes they'd make a donation to charity in the name of the blog or respond with a self-deprecating parody on YouTube.

I took care to focus on satire, poking fun at the extremes, playfully objectifying these untouchable gods among men. Women, especially females of notoriety, in our society had to suck up and swallow daily doses of criticism about *everything*—too fat, too skinny, wearing the same outfit twice in public, having an opinion—from fake TV personalities and tabloid vultures.

In comparison to these self-esteem vampires, I provide a public service. So I make fun of these famous-people-specific idiosyncrasies on a blog followed by twenty million people. It's all in good fun.

The look-alike continued to smile and sign napkins for the group of ladies. He might not have actually been the Irish actor, but he was definitely a somebody. Luckily for him, it was 3:30 p.m. on a Thursday afternoon; that meant Tom's Southern Kitchen was virtually empty of customers. Surreptitiously, I angled my telephone and clicked out of my email, pulling up my smartphone's camera.

I then took about forty or fifty shots over the next two minutes until my view of the hubbub was blocked by a waiter bringing over my bag of takeout. I didn't quite make eye contact with my server as I paid for the food, collected my belongings as leisurely as I could manage, and left the small restaurant.

Eye contact is difficult for me. I know that seems strange; it is strange. For the longest time, I assumed I was just very shy—that is, until I started engaging with people online. That's when I discovered in-real-life-Annie might be introverted. She is reclusive and quiet. She observes. She seldom speaks. She dislikes attention of any kind.

But The Socialmedialite, my online handle, is gregarious and silly. She is opinionated. She craves interaction and attention. She is clever and witty (mostly because, online, wittiness is not a factor of time; in real life you have to be *quick*-witted in order to be considered witty).

My bag slung over my shoulder, I carried the takeout in one hand and held my phone in the other. I was eager to thumb through my new pictures on the short walk back to my apartment. I hadn't taken notice of much while sitting at my table, pretending to check my email, except for the guy's resemblance to the Irish actor.

Therefore I was anxious to analyze what he was wearing, what he was carrying, and any other potentially remarkable external manifestations of eccentricity. I turned the corner, now just a half block from my building, and studied the shots.

Initially, all I saw was a guy who looked like Colin Farrell with a strange-looking, albeit small, apparatus strapped to his back, his feet in those godawful toe-shoes that make the wearer look like a hobbit. His shirt was lime green, skin tight, highlighting his impressively muscled physique, and appeared to be made of Lycra; his thighs were corded and thick, plainly visible because he wore spandex—black spandex, not lime green.

On 99.9% of people, this outfit would have looked completely ridiculous. But not on this guy. He looked hot. Really, really hot.

However, during my second, third, and fourth perusals—and especially in the pictures where his face was turned toward the natural light of the windows—I noted something remarkable about his eyes. Though his mouth held a wide, welcoming grin, his eyes struck me as sad. Terribly, terribly sad. And when I say "struck me," I mean his eyes made my steps falter and slow, and caused a sudden involuntary intake of breath.

Here was this guy, physical perfection, obviously living a charmed life, walking around with mesmerizingly sad, soulful eyes. They were the kind of eyes that pull you in, ensnare you, bind you, hold you and your focus and your priorities hostage.

They took my breath away.

Some strange, long-dormant, and heavily suppressed instinct urged me to run back to the restaurant and wrap him in my arms. My heart gave a little twist. I wanted to kiss away his hurts…or at least make his hurts some cookies.

I shook myself, forcing my feet to move purposefully forward toward home, where I intended to bury these arresting and unwelcome instinctual reactions.

The critic in me reassessed the image and couldn't ignore the toe-shoes, the lime green workout shirt, or the spandex—SPANDEX!—shorts. Even the top 1% of good-looking men should know better than to wear spandex shorts outside of a sporting event.

Just…no.

Sad and soulful notwithstanding, this man needed an intervention.

Although, spandex is nice for highlighting....

Struck by sudden curiosity, and because I am a red-blooded woman, I zoomed in on the area of his groin.

That's right, I'm a reclusive pervert, and I make no apologies for it. And, giving the matter some thought, a reclusive pervert is much preferable to an extroverted pervert. I might also be a tad sexually starved, since I avoid all physical, real-life human interaction.

Just a tad.

I walked past my doorman and into my building, keeping my attention fixed on the phone as I studied the bulge in the man's spandex running shorts. Tearing my bottom lip between my teeth, I boarded the elevator and tried another picture; in this one, he was angled toward the window, half facing the camera. I zoomed in a bit more.

"Whatever you're looking at must be *really* interesting."

I jumped back and away from the voice, sucking in a startled breath, jostling the bag of takeout in my hand, and clutching my phone to my chest. I hadn't realized that I was not alone on the elevator.

I found him, my companion, looking at me with an amused smile. His blue eyes were suspicious, but good-natured, slits. I recognized him immediately as my very tall, very nice-looking, ambiguously single next-door neighbor.

Ambiguously single because he always had a date, but it was never the same lady friend twice.

I didn't blame him, not at all. By all outward appearances, this guy was a hot commodity. Impeccably tailored designer suit and Italian leather shoes that announced both power and wealth; a chiseled jaw beneath perfectly formed lips framing stunningly white teeth; strong nose, bright blue eyes, expertly spiked and shaped blond hair. He looked like the type that subscribed to a beauty regimen. I was pretty sure his eyebrows were plucked and shaped by a professional.

I guesstimated his age as just cresting thirty; hard to tell with the meterosexualizing of his appearance. Add to all this a body that reminded me of a cyclist or a runner—lean and well-maintained—and he was a well-groomed wolf in wolf's clothing, and the females in Manhattan were helpless sheep.

After two seconds of stunned staring, I ripped my eyes from his amused half-lidded gaze and blinked around the mirrored space, trying to get my bearings.

"Sorry," he said, not sounding sorry; in fact, I was pretty sure he was trying not to laugh. "Sorry I scared you."

I shook my head, my phone still clutched to my chest, and fixed my attention on the floor of the elevator.

"It's fine. I was just startled," I said, swallowing.

We were quiet for a beat, but I could feel his eyes on me. I glanced at the display above the floor buttons, trying to gauge how much longer I was going to have to share the elevator with Mr. Ambiguously Single.

To my dismay, he spoke again. "You're Annie, right?"

I nodded, my eyes flickering to the side to glance at him and then back to the display.

"I'm your neighbor Kurt." In my peripheral vision, I saw that he'd turned completely toward me and offered his hand.

I glanced at him again, at his friendly, easy smile and friendly, easy eyes. Then I glanced at the takeout bag in my right hand and the phone held to my chest. I seriously debated whether or not to shrug and say nothing.

See, the problem with being a really well-paid hermit is that you have no incentive to ascribe to social niceties and norms. My company loves me (most of the time); the clients love me—they love the magic I work. I seldom go into the office—only Wednesdays and Fridays. I have an office; I just prefer to work from home.

I'm not agoraphobic. I go out in public, I walk five miles in the park every day, I love the Natural History Museum and visit once a week; as well, I frequent places where celebrities are typically spotted, so I can get shots for the blog. Being a lurker doesn't require social interaction. Yes, I often people-watch, but I've long since learned to bury the feelings of envy at seeing scenes of human connection, like clusters of women, close friends, sharing an afternoon of compassion and confidence, or a loving couple holding hands through the park.

Therefore, if I speak—in person—to more than ten people during any given week, then it's been an above-average week.

Nevertheless, some part of me rebelled against being rude. I might contemplate becoming a wackadoodle recluse in my brain, but I could never fully commit to the role. Therefore, I shifted my belongings, placed my phone—with the crotch shot—in my bag, and accepted his hand for a quick shake.

But it wasn't a quick shake. His fingers tightened around mine until I lifted my eyes to his and relaxed my hand. His gaze was expectant, interested, his smile soft and really very attractive. I was wary as to why he was wielding both in my direction.

"It's nice to finally meet you, Annie." He sounded like he meant it.

I returned his smile as best as I could, felt my eyebrows lift on my forehead. "You, too, Kurt."

"We should get together some time. Get to know each other." He said these words in a rush, almost like he was afraid I might disappear before he finished speaking.

"Yeah." I nodded, trying to mimic his intonation of sincerity. "Sure. We should do that."

Thankfully, the doors opened. I took advantage of the distraction to pull my hand from his and dart out of the elevator. Of course, he was close behind since we both lived on the same floor.

"You know, we've lived next door for going on two years, and this is the first time we've spoken to each other?" He asked this conversationally with a lilt of humor in his voice.

"Hmm," was all I said, placing my takeout on the floor and digging in my bag for my key.

I did know it. But I didn't think it was all that remarkable. He was a good-looking playboy who likely spent more on one bottle of moisturizer than I did on all my hygiene products over the course of a year.

I did my best to be a mousy, low-maintenance eremite. The chances that we moved in similar social circles or had similar interests were not good. Not good at all. Why talk to a person if you had nothing in common with them? What would that accomplish, other than a painfully stunted conversation?

Successfully unlocking the door, I tossed the keys back in my bag and picked up the food. Kurt hovered at my side, leaning against the wall. Again I could feel his eyes on me. Rather than ignoring him and ducking into my apartment, I turned slightly and gave him a small wave.

"Well, I'm going to go inside now and eat this food." I held the bag up as evidence. "See you around."

"We should trade numbers," he said, reaching into his back pocket for his phone, "so we can arrange dinner."

My smile morphed into a frown, and I stared at him, my next words slipping out before I could catch them. "Are you serious?"

Kurt's eyes flickered to mine, a crooked smile tugging at the corner of his mouth. "Of course I'm serious. I never joke about dinner."

He said the words so smoothly, like words should be said, like an expert in banter and flirtation. My heart gave an uncomfortable twist then took off at a gallop. It was one thing to trade polite chitchat in the elevator with my beautiful neighbor when I was certain it would lead nowhere. It was quite another to give aforementioned beautiful neighbor my telephone number and, therefore, permission to contact me for a shared meal.

I couldn't do that.

I couldn't.

My table manners were terrible. I'd never been taught.

I sucked at conversation and therefore always ended up tongue-tied, silent, and beet red.

I cussed like a sailor.

My heart-shaped face was very pretty; I knew this. I'd been reminded of it frequently as I was growing up—no one wanted me to forget how blessed I was to have such a pretty face. My eyes were quite large and light brown, rimmed with thick lashes; I had a cute nose that suited my features; my cheekbones were high, my lips were full, and my chin ended in an *adorable point.*

Which was why my wardrobe consisted of black, gray, or brown pants, skirts, and tights as well as oversized black, gray, or brown sweaters.

I was trying to be wallpaper. This was purposeful. The clothes, my lack of makeup or hairstyle, my quiet and withdrawn demeanor were all typically sufficient to deter interest.

I stared at his phone in helpless panic—confused, horrified. I waited a beat for him to say, "Just kidding!"

But he didn't. Instead, he lifted his gaze to mine. It moved over my face then back to my eyes—his were still easy and friendly—and I was paralyzed.

His smile widened. "You are too cute…." He said these words like he was talking to himself.

I started, flinched, my eyelashes fluttering at the unwelcome compliment, and I gave into the panic. Looking everywhere but at him, I darted into my apartment, saying lamely, "Uh, my phone is broken or needs repair or got lost, so I'll just give you the number later, when it's fixed or I find it. But it was really nice meeting you. Goodbye."

And with that, I shut the door in Kurt's face.

* * *

New York's Finest
Blogging as *The Socialmedialite*
March 8

If Sporty Spice married a hobbit, had a three-way with a leprechaun, and then gave birth to a sexy, bizarre baby (paternity unknown).

Guess who was spotted this week looking equal parts hot and ridiculous in every kind of synthetic fabric currently manufactured by the miracle of chemical engineering? None other than Colin Farrell (or his doppelgänger) down near the Village. Obviously, no one loves him. Friends don't let friends dress like this (unless it's cosplay or part of a bedroom role-play fantasy). If you take a look at the pictures above, you'll certainly understand my horror at finding anyone willing to wear lime green Lycra and Speedo running shorts. The only explanation I can think of is that he was drunk (you know how those Irish enjoy their whiskey…and beer…and any and all alcohol).

I could have forgiven the spandex, but I can't forgive the freaky feet. Toe-shoes are never okay. They're weird and disturbing and really, really pretentious. And, as an aside, for those of you who are interested in looking like a hobbit, this particular brand of toe-shoe will set you back $635. That's right!

You too can look like a weird little man for the very low price of six hundred and thirty-five dollars!!! WTF?

Also, for the record, Colin needs to invest in a cup. Yes, I enjoy the occasional bulge, but this bulge was verging on concealed weapon status. If he continues to run around in these spandex shorts, he will only have himself to blame for the gropings. Goodness, if I'd been within arm's reach, I definitely would have copped a feel. Amiright, ladies? You all know how I like my bangers and mash, and there's nothing more Irish than sausage!

Booyah!
<3 The Socialmedialite

TWO
RONAN

Calories: *4,000.*
Workout: *4.5 hours in total.*
Eggs: *Could go to my grave quite happily without ever seeing another one.*

I'd just finished doing fifty chin-ups when the phone started ringing.
And if that wasn't the opening line of a narcissistic arsehole, then I didn't know what was. I'd spent way too much time around privately educated, privileged rugby brats, and their ways had finally rubbed off on me.

At least I didn't say I was getting my pump on.

Anyway, I'm not a narcissistic arsehole. However, I might be a bull-headed idiot with too short a fuse who lets his temper get the better of him when there just so happen to be paparazzi hanging about, but that's a story for another day. Or you could go out and pick up a tabloid.

Yeah, I was going through a bitter patch, but I had every right. I was sick of my private life being splashed all over the papers. Somehow, I'd never connected the idea of being good at a sport with the possibility of becoming a "celebrity."

I understood my role; I did my best for my league and for the sport. I knew what rugby needed from me, and I wasn't planning on letting anyone down. But if there was one thing I hated in this world, it was people who wrote about other people's personal lives for a living. Those people could all do with taking a dive off a very high building, in my opinion.

You see, bitter.

Picking up a towel, I wiped the sweat from my neck then went to pick up the phone. My little sister Lucy's face was flashing on the screen which made me less hesitant to answer. I thought it might be my publicist, Sam, with some new instructions on how I could clean up my public image, and I was in no mood for that shite.

"Luce, how're you doing?" I said as I held the phone to my ear and looked out at the Manhattan skyline before me. Some people might have been well up for living in a penthouse apartment in the center of New York, and yeah, it was my choice to come here; but I hadn't anticipated there would be nowhere to drive. Driving was one of the only things that kept me sane. Me and my 1969 Chevy Camaro and the open road. No stress, just miles and pure freedom. Ah, that was the life.

I should have done my research.

In order to make up for the lack of driving, I'd been working out more than usual, which was always a good thing when you played professional rugby for a living. Well, technically I was suspended from the team; but fingers crossed I'd be back in a couple of months, and I wanted to return fighting fit. You wouldn't think it to see the dark, moody eyebrows I was sporting, but I was a silver-lining sort of bloke. It wasn't my intention to be irritable; life had just dealt me a crap hand lately.

"Morning, bro. You sound out of breath. Did I catch you at a bad time?" Lucy replied. There was something about her tone that put me on edge. Usually she was cheerful and upbeat. The girl was full of sunshine. Right now she sounded hesitant, and, almost as if I was having a moment of foresight, I knew I wasn't going to like the reason why.

"Timing's perfect. How's everything at home?"

"Oh, you know, the usual. Ma's still spending too much money on clothes. I'm trying to teach her that material possessions don't equal happiness. It's a work in progress."

Ever since I'd made the big time, my mother had acquired expensive tastes. I didn't mind. My mother and my sister were the only real family I had. If my money could give them a good life, then I was all for it.

I chuckled softly. "It's not like she's snorting cocaine, Luce. She likes dresses. What woman doesn't?"

"There are so many things wrong with what you just said, I don't even know where to start, Ronan."

My smile grew. I always enjoyed baiting her. "What? Girls like pretty things. It's a known fact."

"You know what, I don't even feel bad about what I have to tell you now. Take out your computer. There's something you need to see."

My smile vanished and was instantly replaced with a frown as I walked through the penthouse to find my laptop. I flipped it open and brought up a new window. "What is it this time? Has Brona been spreading her lies again?" I asked.

"No, no, it's nothing like that. It's actually kind of funny. I read this blog all the time because I love the girl who writes it. At least, I think it's a girl. It could very well be an old bald fellow in a basement with a pet rabbit. It's called *New York's Finest,* and you were featured on Saturday. Only get this, she thinks you're Colin Farrell. How hilarious is that?"

My frown slowly disappeared as I typed in the name of the website and brought it up. Being mistaken for a famous Irish actor when you were in fact a famous Irish rugby player was positively whimsical when compared with some of the PR disasters I'd experienced of late. Then the article popped up, and I was frowning again.

There was a picture of me standing by the bar at my mate Tom's restaurant last week, signing autographs for a couple of women. It looked like it had been taken from a low angle, as though the person who took it was sitting at a table. It was a completely unexceptional picture until you factored in the plethora of red arrows that surrounded it, each one pointing to some perceived flaw in my appearance.

Apparently, I chose my outfit while drunk, my footwear was disturbing, and my cock and balls were on display. I scowled and tried not to get pissed. I was going to give myself high blood pressure if I didn't quit getting so worked up about the media. Still, it was irritating how this blogger had totally ripped into what I was wearing. Clothing for me was all about function. I wore what was best for training purposes and gave not one iota of shit what I looked like.

Scrolling down, there was a short article written by someone who referred to themselves as The Socialmedialite, who called me both a leprechaun and a hobbit, and then went on to suggest I invest in a cup. Well, when I say "me," I mean Colin Farrell because that's who this person thought I was, which is ridiculous because I barely even look like him.

"Oh, you *so* look like him, Ronan," Lucy disagreed down the line, and I realized I'd said that out loud.

"I don't. This blogger is an idiot if she can't see how much I don't look like him. I bet she does her research on flipping Wikipedia, the amateur."

I scrolled down the page to the next post to see she'd snapped a photo of Bradley Cooper getting out of his car in workout clothes. There was a wet stain on his pants that was obviously sweat or spilled liquid. Nevertheless, The Socialmedialite had composed an article containing a list of possibilities as to how the stain had occurred. Some of the stories were way too detailed which made me think she was in serious need of a life. A number of readers had even commented below with their own scenarios. One person thought his personal groomer had tried to foist a bottle of clove oil on him to shave his face, and Bradley had swiped away the offending article, stating he would never shave off the source of all his sexy power, thus resulting in the stain.

Seriously, some people.

"This site is ridiculous," I muttered while Lucy snickered in response. "It's not even funny. And sausage is more German than Irish."

"What are you talking about? It's hilarious. It objectifies men in the same way women have been objectified for centuries. Turnabout is fair play, you know."

"It's stupid. And anyway, I'm way too tall to be a hobbit." I stood up and walked over to look at myself in the mirror. At five feet eleven inches, I thought I was a decent height for a man.

"Oh, wow. Vanity, thy name is Ronan. She's already getting to you, isn't she? And she called you a hobbit because of those godawful shoes you were wearing."

"My trainer suggested them," I grumbled. "Don't you have your yoga class to be getting to this morning?"

"Yes, I do, cranky. You're obviously taking this all the wrong way. Don't you know that the ability to laugh at oneself is the most desirous quality of all?"

"Not really in a laughing mood these days, Luce," I replied gloomily and pulled a bottle of water from the fridge.

I could hear her sigh down the line. "I know. I'm sorry. I was trying to cheer you up. Promise I was. How is everything in the Big Apple? You settling in okay?"

"Don't apologize. I'm a grumpy old bastard. And yes, I'm settling in fine. My car arrived yesterday which was kind of a cruel joke since all I can do here is sit in traffic. I should never have let Tom talk me into taking time off in New York. I wanted to go to Canada, get lost in the mountains or something."

"Yeah, that would've been cool. But at least this way you get to go see the naked cowboy."

"I don't know who or what that is, but I think I'll pass."

"Spoilsport. I was looking forward to a picture of the two of you. Anyway, I'd better get going."

"Okay, take care, Luce. I love you."

She made a kissy sound into her phone that nearly deafened me. "Love you, too!"

The moment I hung up, my phone began ringing again, and this time it *was* Sam, my PR agent. I briefly considered ignoring the call but knew he'd have a fit if I didn't answer. The man was more highly strung than Margaret Thatcher on the rag, God rest her.

"Sam, what can I do for ya, bud?"

"Oh, it's more a matter of what I can do for you, my friend. But first, did you see you were featured on *New York's Finest* Saturday?"

Seriously, I felt like I was stuck in Groundhog Day, and that film always got on my tits. "Yeah, my sister already had the good grace to inform me."

"Well, I don't know why you sound so glum about it. This is a big deal, Ronan. You're virtually unknown over in the States. This could be the thing that helps you crack America. I can just see it now, a picture of you reclining in a pair of tighty whiteys advertising for Calvin Klein on the side of a skyscraper."

"Fuck, man. Are you a psychic? How did you know that's my one true dream?"

I could practically hear him pursing his lips in irritation. "I'm going to ignore your sarcasm because I have more news, and I don't have time for your pissy attitude. I have a friend who works for Davidson & Croft Media there in New York, and they're just itching to meet you. They think they can re-brand you. Clean up your image. You know, turn you into the David Beckham of rugby."

"Again, do you have a crystal ball, because this shit is positively clairvoyant."

"They want to meet you today at one. I'm emailing you directions," he said impatiently.

I glanced at the clock. "It's already half past eleven. I have to shower, and the traffic in this city is a nightmare. Can we re-schedule?"

What I really wanted to say was, *Can we forget about it altogether?* But I still had some sense of professionalism, and yeah, I guessed working with this agency could probably do me some good. It would be like pulling teeth, but I knew anything worth doing was usually difficult. I ended the call and went to hop in the shower. I was in and out in less than ten minutes and made quick work of getting dressed. When I walked by my computer, I noticed that the website was still open, and I had a sudden urge to vent.

It seemed like my life was being controlled by faceless people sitting behind computers writing stories about me, and I was sick of it. Sam always coached me to have a "no comment" policy on this kind of thing, but I wanted to have my say for once.

Months of silence meant I had a lot to get off my chest, after all.

So I sat down in front of my laptop, opened up a fresh email, and began to type. Fuck it if I was late to the meeting. If these people were so eager to see me, they could wait.

March 10
Dear Socialmedialite,
Just thought I'd enlighten your vacuous little mind as to a few things.

1. *I'm not Colin Farrell, I'm Ronan Fitzpatrick. Go look me up. It'll make for some colorful reading.*
2. *Your fixation on the minute details of the male form leads me to believe that one, you have no life, and two, you have not been laid in a loooong time.*
3. *I think that if you're going to make these kinds of judgments on the appearance of others, then you should at least be open about who you are. Anonymity is the choice of cowards.*

My suggestions:

1. *You actually do your research and make sure that when you think you're getting a picture of Colin Farrell, it's actually Colin Farrell. FYI: Ear-wigging on the conversation of a group of giggling women does NOT constitute research.*
2. *Go out and have a drink. Talk to a guy. Let somebody fuck you. You'll be amazed by what clearing those cobwebs can do for your frame of mind.*
3. *Put up a picture. Tell everyone who you are. Let's see if you can handle people criticizing your looks the same way you criticize theirs.*

You're welcome.
Ronan Fitzpatrick

And send.
That felt good.

I quickly made a note of the address Sam had sent me and then went to catch a cab. Arriving at the agency's building, I stared up at the high-rise before walking in and announcing my presence to the receptionist. She was a slim, attractive blonde and immediately gave me the glad eye after she took in my appearance. If I was the same guy I was at twenty-two, I'd have been in there like swimwear. Unfortunately, I was a cynical, disillusioned twenty-seven-year-old with no patience for women and their wiles. Right now, all I was on the market for was no-strings sex. For years I'd been faithful to Brona, and then she'd gone and shoved my fidelity in my face by shoving my teammate's cock down her throat.

But maybe Brona did me a favor. My vision was now remarkably clear. These women were all glittery, seductive eyes and shallow propositions. All I could see was another version of her: superficial, dim-witted, materialistic fame-whores, looking for a place to hitch their star, only out for what they could get. Not surprisingly, that was enough to deflate even the most determined hard-on.

"I'm looking for Davidson & Croft. Can you help me out" —I glanced at her name tag before finishing— "Stephanie?"

She smiled, all white teeth and glossy lips, before giving me instructions to take the elevator up to the twelfth floor. When I finally reached the busy offices, a handler was waiting for me—more glossy lips and white teeth. I checked out her arse as I was led to a room where several people were sitting around a table, dressed in smart business clothes. I looked completely out of my place in my dark brown leather jacket, boots, jeans, and a plain black T-shirt.

They all stood the moment I entered, and a short woman who, I shit you not, looked like Danny DeVito in drag came and offered me her hand.

"Mr. Fitzpatrick," she said in a voice that was surprisingly feminine, given her appearance. "It's a pleasure to meet you. I'm Joan Davidson, and these are my associates, Rachel Simmons and Ian Timor. Come, have a seat."

I sized her up quickly. She was definitely the one in charge; there was just something imposing—almost intimidating— about her despite her size.

"Same to you, Joan. And you can call me Ronan."

I nodded hello to Rachel and Ian before sitting down as instructed. A moment of silence ensued as I cleared my throat, leaned forward, and steepled my fingers in front of me on the table.

Joan tapped a finger on her chin as she contemplated me. "So, Ronan. I have to say, I'm very interested in working with you. I've been in this business for a long time, and I love a challenge. I've been acquainting myself with the details of your career, and what I've learned leads me to believe we could make a big difference working together. So, what would you like to achieve with us? I want to know your vision so that we can help you actualize it. We like to tailor the experience here at Davidson & Croft to the individual."

I let out a long sigh. "I'll be straight with you, Joan—my agent back home sprang this meeting on me just over an hour ago. Publicity isn't my thing. I'm an athlete, and I don't get the whole media circus that's been surrounding my life lately. I just want to play rugby and be left alone."

"Well, that's positively boring," Joan chuckled, soliciting grins from the thus far silent Rachel and Ian, and a glower from me. "And being left alone isn't an option, I'm afraid. You're the bad boy of rugby, the one all the girls swoon over."

I grimaced. "Yes, I understand what's expected. I'm aware of what the league is hoping to accomplish through me, but I'd like for it to be about how I play the sport *on* the field."

She continued as though I hadn't spoken, "The problem is you're a little *too* bad right now. We need to make you clean bad, acceptable bad. We want you to be Mark Wahlberg, not Charlie Sheen. We want to reform you. Think Robert Downey, Jr., but younger and without any prison time."

Rubbing at the back of my neck, I replied, "You see, this is the problem. All of what you just said went right over my head, love." I was playing dumb, and it seemed that Joan was shrewd enough to sense that.

"You hospitalized one of your teammates, Ronan."

My jaw tightened. Who did this woman think she was speaking to? "So what?"

"That's not a good thing."

"That's rugby."

"Usually it's supposed to be an opponent, isn't it? Not one of your own."

I shrugged. "Usually. But this time I made an exception because he slept with my fiancée."

She waved me away. "There's no need to be defensive. I'm here to remedy you, not incite you."

I blinked at her. She was here to *remedy* me?

Joan smiled. "Look, what you did was bad, but it's not the worst thing you could've done. The more time that passes, the more people will forget. And you'd be surprised how easily that can be done. We get you seen going on a date with a much-loved actress, maybe giving a donation to a charity or two, and the tarnish on your reputation will begin to disappear. What do you say?"

I frowned at her and worked my jaw. This whole thing was making me itch, and I needed to get out of there. "I say I need to take a piss."

Joan didn't bat an eyelid at my harsh response. "Very well. The bathrooms are located at the end of the hall, the blue door on the right."

The one named Rachel stood like she was going to escort me to the head. I glared at Joan, who apparently understood my irritation because she waved at Rachel to sit and shook her head.

I swiftly rose from my chair and left the room. Stomping down the hallway, I stopped midway to the end and ran a hand over my face. I was ridiculously tired. I wasn't sleeping like I used to. I thought that spending a couple of months in a place far from where I came from would work, help me to detach from everything that had happened. Too bad my brain didn't know how to shut off.

Finding the bathroom, I quickly relieved myself and then began to make my way back to the meeting. I was passing by what looked to be the staff break room when I paused, considering ditching this whole thing and heading out to Tom's place for a while.

Glancing through the door, I saw a dark-haired woman sitting at a table. I noticed she had a cup of tea in front of her as she brought a cream cake to her mouth for a bite.

Her full lips curved to one side in a pleased smile laced with blatant anticipation. I'd never seen someone look so hot for a confectionary before. It was kind of sexy; and I'm not sure why, but it made me smile the first full-on smile I'd had in weeks.

Then she opened her mouth, setting the soft, sweet cake on her pink tongue, and I nearly groaned. *Kind of sexy* transformed into *fucking hot*. I didn't know this woman at all, but I briefly wondered if she was up for a bit of no-strings fun.

I must have made some movement to alert her to my presence because she looked up quickly, big brown eyes widening when she saw me. She swallowed just as a glob of cream fell from the cake and plopped right onto her top.

I chuckled, mostly to mask my voyeurism, and took a step into the room. "Messy bastards, those éclairs."

She just kept on staring at me, her eyes getting bigger and bigger by the second. I waited a few beats for her to say something, but she seemed stunned to silence. Fuck, I could tell she recognized me.

Of its own accord, my gaze wandered over her form, or what I could see of it: lush hips, full-figured but not fat. She wore a brown skirt, black tights, and a big gray top, her dark brown hair in a neat bun. Her clothes were plain. As I took in her face properly, though, I realized that she didn't need any glitz. She was incredibly striking in a very natural way. Especially since her cheeks and the ridge of her pretty nose were turning bright pink.

Lowering her eyes, her black lashes a stark contrast to her peachy skin, she picked up a napkin and began furiously rubbing the cream from her top. She was just making matters worse. I walked over to her, knelt down, and took the napkin from her hand. She actually flinched when I touched her. Jesus.

"Let me help. The idea is to dab, not rub," I said, getting all up in her space. I sneaked my hand under her top to pull out the material so that I could clean it. My knuckles brushed against her stomach, and I heard her suck in a harsh breath. Her skin was beautifully soft. I dabbed at the fabric, and the air in the room seemed to thicken. It lasted only a moment before she tentatively pushed my hand away from her, grabbed the napkin, and pulled back.

"I can manage on my own, thank you." Her tone was impeccably polite, her cheeks now full-on red. She was definitely embarrassed. I *had* gotten a little too close. When I was drawn to someone, though, I often forgot about boundaries.

"I'm Ronan," I said and presented my hand. Her gaze flickered to it for a brief moment, and I watched as she gathered a deep breath, almost like she was summoning courage. She fit her fingers in mine quickly, giving me a firm shake.

Her hand was soft and warm. It also shook as she withdrew it hastily.

"Annie," she said, so quietly I almost didn't hear. Her eyes barely settled on mine before she looked away again. Her lovely, pale throat was working without swallowing.

"It's nice to meet you, Annie." Christ, she was pretty. It was too bad she looked like she was going to have a heart attack if I didn't leave soon.

Her skin was flawless, radiant. But her clothes became a source of irritation; she might as well have been wearing a tent. I wanted to see the shape of what lay beneath.

She also seemed a tiny bit apprehensive. Perhaps she thought I was a psycho who beat up his friends and put them in hospital. I never knew what people had read about me or what they believed.

When she had gotten most of the stain out, her eyes shot to mine, and there was something guarded and defensive in them, almost like she was bracing herself for a fight. "Can I help you with something?"

Deciding to hell with it, I went all in. I hadn't felt an attraction to anyone in months, so I wasn't going to let her slip through my fingers. "Your number would be a good start," I said in a low voice.

Her eyes widened again, and it was obvious I'd caught her completely off guard. Quickly, the vulnerability was gone; it was replaced first with flustered confusion and then hardened resolve. "No."

Her single-word denial made me frown. Before I could ask Annie if she was already seeing someone, Joan walked into the room. "Ah, Ronan. I thought we'd lost you on your way back from the bathroom."

"Just getting to know your lovely employee here," I said, giving Annie a flirtatious wink. She looked like she wanted to flip me the bird, but she couldn't since her boss was standing right there.

"Oh, Annie is our brightest and best," said Joan with an expression that showed she truly respected the woman. Then she paused for a second as though struck by a thought. "You know, tell me if this sounds crazy, but I just had an idea." She glanced at me. "Ronan, you said you were clueless when it comes to publicity, and Annie here is a whiz at cultivating a popular online presence for our clients. I think I need to pair you two up. Annie can teach you the social media ropes, show you how to play the game, while our team gets to work on revitalizing your public image."

"You know what, Joan, I think that's a brilliant idea." I beamed at her. Of course I did. If it meant spending time with this gorgeous Annie, then I'd suffer through the nausea that social networking presented. And honestly, in a way, her rejection was refreshing. Most women saw my wealth and my fame and instantly had dollar signs flashing in their eyes.

Annie didn't seem so keen on the idea of teaming up, and okay, maybe I could understand her hesitation. I'd practically groped her under the guise of helping her get out a stain, but still, she looked like she found me about as appealing as second-hand underpants.

She cleared her throat, which I noticed was still red with embarrassment, and spoke up. "I'm very busy at the moment, Joan. Perhaps somebody else could help."

Joan waved away her protestations. "Nonsense. Tell Rachel to take some of your workload, free up your schedule. I think you two will work well together. I just have a feeling."

There was something in Joan's expression that brooked no further argument, and Annie seemed resigned as she nodded her acquiescence, her big brown eyes flickering to mine and then to her teacup.

Joan clapped her hands together. "Wonderful! Come with me, Ronan, and we'll figure out a schedule." As the tiny woman led me from the room, I gave Annie one final heated smile.

This day was looking up already.

THREE
ANNIE

The Kinnear: *When one surreptitiously takes a picture of another person (usually a celebrity) without anyone else realizing the photographer is using his/her phone. Typically, the phone is completely hidden.*
Best for: *In crowds, e.g. airports, restaurants, while shopping.*
Do not use: *In quiet areas or in situations where movement is restricted.*

Ronan Fitzpatrick.
His name was Ronan Fitzpatrick, and his hand had just been up my shirt.

The back of his fingers had brushed against my bare skin, sending really, really delicious spikes of awareness to the pit of my stomach and up my chest, neck, and the top of my head. My brain had been momentarily paralyzed.

I'd been alone, eating my feelings after my alter ego, The Socialmedialite, had received a truly heinous email. I'd read it less than an hour ago; it was from the asshat I'd mistaken for Colin Farrell last Thursday and written about on Saturday, but who was actually a disgraced Irish rugby player…named Ronan Fitzpatrick. And I'd just met him. In person.

I must've read the email three times.

Okay, I'm lying. I read it no less than twenty times.

Then I Googled the shit out of him. He was right. It made for colorful reading. Ronan Fitzpatrick, of the exceedingly posh and pretentious South Dublin Fitzpatricks, was Irish rugby royalty. His father had been a famous rugby player until his death in a car accident some twenty years ago.

As well, his father's family was stinking rich. Old, old, old money rich. The kind of old money that Americans can barely comprehend. Like, hundreds of years of old money and aristocracy. My stomach hurt. I didn't even know who my biological father was, and this guy could trace his family tree back over three hundred years.

Adding to his apparently charmed life and silver-spoon upbringing, Ronan was—if the papers were to be believed—the best hooker to come out of Ireland maybe ever. And by "hooker," I don't mean prostitute. Hooker is a position—a very pivotal position—on the rugby field. Based on my quick research, it appeared to be the rugby equivalent of an American football team's quarterback.

Ronan was apparently the best hooker that ever was and ever will be, amen.

However, more recently, Ronan's infamy stemmed from allegedly hospitalizing one of his teammates during an on-the-field brawl. Also recently were several pictures of Ronan sharing the front page of tabloids with a distressed-looking bottle blonde. She was labeled as an actress, singer, and Ronan's ex-fiancée, Brona O'Shea. The photos were split screen style, like they'd been ripped in half.

I felt both judgey and vindicated as I took in her appearance. She'd obviously had several elective plastic surgeries. Just to be sure, I searched for pictures of her over the last five years. As I suspected, her appearance had changed dramatically over time.

At first she was a fresh-faced Irish rose: pink cheeks, sandy-blonde hair, clear blue eyes. The most recent shots made me grimace. Fake tan, fake tits, lipo, lip injections, Botox, nose job. God, what kind of hell must it have been for her to be with someone like Ronan? Had she changed herself so completely to please him? And he just dropped her after proposing marriage? I was disgusted.

After my glutinous Google-fest, I read his email once again.

At first I was shocked all over again, stunned, actually. Then I was outraged. Likely this was because his assessment of my cobwebs and cowardice struck a nerve.

He was right, of course. I was cowardice covered in cobwebs. But that didn't make me any less pissed off by his insulting personal attack.

Most people could see the silly in my blog posts, laugh at themselves, handle it gracefully.

Mr. Ronan Fitzpatrick, it seemed, was not most people. He was obviously a privileged douchenozzle, used to getting his own way and everyone else be damned. I knew his type. His type was why I preferred to be confused with wallpaper. His type was why I was cowardice covered in cobwebs.

After receiving the email—reading it *ad nauseam*, working myself up into a knot of outraged and hurt fretfulness even though I knew I could never respond to it—I decided to cool off. I decided I needed food therapy.

The first thing I did was send a message to my best online pal.

@Socialmedialite to @WriteALoveSong: I just received the douchiest email of all time. Remind me to never write about male sports figures again. Their meaty heads are impervious to jokes.

I took a walk, my feet carrying me to my favorite French bakery two blocks away and then back to the offices of Davidson & Croft. I made a detour for the break room, intent on brewing my special peppermint tea; I'd never met a problem that couldn't be fixed with pastry and tea. Just as I sat down, I read my friend's response.

@WriteALoveSong to @Socialmedialite: Oh no! It's just like I always tell you: jocks are cocks. Sorry. :-

This made me smirk. I could always count on her to make me smile.

But then, one minute I was smirking about my friend's joke, quietly enjoying the closest thing to an orgasm I experienced these days—éclairs from Jean Marie's on Fifth Avenue—and the next minute he was there.

I was assaulted by the sight, smell, and sad, soulful eyes of Ronan Fitzpatrick.

The paralyzation-athon was not what discomfited me, nor was it how my heart rate skyrocketed at his proximity. The source of my discombobulating anxiety was that, even after my brain wheels started spinning again, I hadn't pushed him away. His hand was up my shirt, his face mere inches from mine, and I didn't push him away.

I couldn't.

He smelled so freaking good, like clean man and soap, just the tiniest hint of aftershave and mint. I stared at him, at his lips tugging to the side in a seductive smile; at the collar of his leather jacket where it touched his neck; at his jean-clad thighs, thick and muscular and powerful; at his heavily lashed eyes, sad and soulful. Every one of my nerve endings was on fire.

Holy heathen in heaven, it wasn't even his looks.

He was…overwhelming and magnetic. Sensual and in-your-face sexual. Also not helping matters, he had no concept of personal space.

I finally managed to remove him, but my effort was half-hearted and done with shaking hands. The rest of our conversation had been a blur, right up until Joan walked in and promptly paired us up.

I stared at the empty doorway where they'd just departed, my mind working without purchase, trying to absorb all that had just occurred. Slowly but surely, my foggy irritation gave way to the earlier outrage and hurt I'd been feeling since reading Ronan Fitzpatrick's nasty email.

No way.

There was *no way* I would pair up with this guy—the epitome of a privileged and entitled beefcake. He was everything I loathed rolled up into a tight, luscious, muscular, heady, and quixotically alluring package. My social phobias aside, I needed alone time with Ronan like a car needed a swim in the ocean.

I was standing, gripping the back of the chair I'd been sitting in, my tea now tepid, my éclair half-eaten, when Joan waltzed back into the break room. I glanced behind her, searching for him, a renewed spike of panic hitting me in the chest. I noted gratefully that she was alone. I also noted that she was grinning.

Joan never grinned.

She charged toward me like she was going to mow me and my chair down, but then stopped three feet from my table. "I didn't know you were coming in today, dear." She said these words cheerfully, her little eyes narrowing as her grin widened.

I returned her squint but not her grin, as I was too busy trying to determine the best course of action. Maybe I could feign a brain tumor and request a six-month leave of absence. She would see through any such attempt, of course. Joan was shrewd in the way other people were tall; it was in her DNA.

"Joan," I began, quickly clearing my throat and deciding that honesty was the best policy because I'd never be able to out-maneuver or manipulate her, "I really, really do not want to work with that man. I understand if you need to assign me to his campaign, but pairing us up would not be beneficial to anyone." My heart hadn't quite recovered yet from Mr. Fitzpatrick's hand up my shirt; therefore, I tried to surreptitiously even my breathing.

"Dear, pairing you up has already been beneficial to everyone." Her grin became a small, knowing smile, and her black eyes glittered. Abruptly, she turned and called to me over her shoulder, "Follow me."

I heaved a resigned sigh, swiftly gathered my tea and pastry, and followed her through the maze of hallways to her gigantic office.

She was waiting for me at her door and shut it after bellowing to her secretary, "Hold my calls, and tell everyone to go away until we're done." Then she turned to me and tugged on my elbow until I was sitting in one of the chairs that faced her desk. "You sit and eat. I'll talk."

Once I was deposited where she wanted me, she moved behind her giant desk and claimed the high-backed red leather chair. Behind her was an enormous window displaying downtown Manhattan. As ever, she was in the power position.

"Let's get to the point, dear. Mr. Fitzpatrick gets what Mr. Fitzpatrick wants.

And, having eyeballs, it took me less than three seconds to comprehend that Mr. Fitzpatrick wants you."

If I'd been drinking my tea, I would have choked on it. As it was, I wasn't drinking my tea; therefore, I choked on my tongue, but the effect was the same. I was coughing and sputtering; I felt my eyes widen to saucer size.

"Are you—are you suggesting—are you saying—"

Joan waved her hand in the air like she was flicking my half-formed thoughts away with her fingertips, "No, no, dear. Nothing so lascivious. Let me see how to put this...." She tented her fingers and peered at me over them. "Let's start with the basics. Do you know who he is?"

I hesitated. I could recite all the details I'd just learned while cyberstalking him via Google news, or I could play dumb. But if I pretended to be oblivious, Joan would certainly see through my pretext of ignorance.

I decided to reveal only the most basic thread of my knowledge, so I answered, "He's a rugby player."

Joan nodded, "That's right. But do you know *who* he is?"

I blinked slowly and gritted my teeth. "How could I? I just met him."

"He is the brightest shining star of rugby. He has the potential to be the face of the sport all over the world—think David Beckham for soccer, just infinitely more masculine, dirtier, grittier, and with a fouler mouth. And he is on the precipice of greatness."

She paused, maybe waiting for me to express my understanding of her inferred explanation, but I was lost. I typically had minimal contact with clients. My reports and presentations were usually handled by Rachel, the VP of Projects, or by Joan directly. I didn't see why this guy was any more of a VIP or deserving of my undivided attention than the rest of our A-list.

Realizing my lack of comprehension, she took a deep breath. "Annie, the rugby people, specifically the RLIF, are ready to throw money at us for taking him on. They're convinced he's the one who will pull the sport into the limelight—specifically, bring interest and appetite to the USA—and they want us to cultivate him. Now do you get it?"

Feeling stubborn, I frowned. "Of course I understand why you want the client, and I'm happy to help lead the social media group cleaning up his image, but—with all due respect, Joan—I don't understand why you would suggest that Mr. Fitzpatrick and I *pair up*, as you put it."

Joan leaned forward, resting her slight weight on her elbows. She was typically four inches shorter than my five-foot-five, but from her scarlet perch, she appeared to hover from a substantial and menacing height. I wondered briefly if her feet touched the ground or if she'd used a stool to ascend to that impressive altitude.

"We need his cooperation." She said these words slowly, her eyes moving over my gray sweater and brown skirt and then back to my eyes. "Before seeing you, Ronan Fitzpatrick wasn't going to give us two minutes, let alone the months we need to set his image on the right path. But the moment I mention pairing the two of you, he's smiling. He's suggesting another visit to the office—he's asking when we can get started."

I swallowed, a growing dread unfurling in my stomach. I worried briefly that Ronan had somehow figured out who I was, that he knew I was The Socialmedialite, that he remembered me from the restaurant, that he saw me taking pictures of him, and that he was looking forward to our pairing in order to exact his revenge.

But I quickly dismissed the thought as preposterous. When he came upon me in the break room, he demonstrated no sign of recognition, just interest.

Just heated, intense, determined, pointed, carnal masculine interest.

Joan must've perceived the extent of my anxiety because she assumed a less oppressive posture, leaning back in her seat, and shrugged. "Again, I'm not suggesting that you return his attentions. I'm simply asking you to come into the office when he is here, discuss our plans with him in person, take him out for client lunches and dinners, personally assist him with the intricacies of navigating his launch onto the world stage—you know, precisely what I would ask any other member of the team to do. No more, no less…."

I closed my eyes, gathered steadying breath through my nose; I was clenching my jaw so tightly my temples ached.

I completely comprehended Joan's not-so-subtle point, which was that I was frequently on the receiving end of special treatment. I was the only one who was absolved from meetings, excused from conferences, lunches and dinners, think tanks, presentations, et. al.

Basically, I did my thing. I did it alone. I had almost complete autonomy. I didn't have to be a team player. Aside from intermittent infographic emails, I'd never had to schmooze a client.

But now she was calling in my hermit card. This was Joan reminding me how good I had it here. I had to admit, she was right. I had it easy. I had it great.

Unclenching my jaw, I opened my eyes and found her staring at me. Again, she was grinning, her eyes glittering.

She nodded slowly. "I see we understand each other."

I pressed my lips together, rolled them between my teeth to keep from screaming in frustration, and returned her nod. Never mind the fact that every fiber of my being wanted to run away, maybe find a cabin in Maine, maybe become a true recluse who ate only canned beans.

I wouldn't last three hours without Internet access, let alone the deprivation of New York's cuisine. No éclairs from Jean Marie's, no arepas from Flor's Diner, no shrimp and grits from Tom's Southern Kitchen, no kung pao chicken from Mr. Hung Dong. I would die of food tedium.

"Good," she said lightly, obviously pleased. "We start tomorrow."

I nodded stiffly, and gathered my cup and accoutrements from the little table next to my seat. Holding my pastry and cold peppermint tea to my chest, I turned to go, my thoughts in turmoil. But Joan's voice stopped me just as I reached the door.

"One more thing, Annie. Use your business account to buy some new clothes. I think you wear that same outfit every time I see you. You're a representation of the company. If you're going to be taking Mr. Fitzpatrick out, you'll need to look the part."

I stiffened and turned to face her; knowing there was no point in arguing, I decided to stall. "That's fine, but it'll have to be next week. And, if I'm taking on Mr. Fitzpatrick's account, I'll have to pass over *The Starlet* to Becky."

Joan looked thoughtful for a moment. *The Starlet* was one of our biggest individual clients and was our code name for Dara Evans, four-time Oscar nominee with a perpetual image problem. She had an image problem because she was a raging bitch.

We kept her looking like flowers and sunshine; she kept us on our toes with DUIs and assault charges. Her most recent debacle was from this last weekend. An amateur video shot with a cell phone showed her at a Yankees game, wherein she snatched a foul ball out of the hands of a crippled five-year-old boy (who had rightfully caught it). Then she made fun of his handicap and held the ball just out of his reach.

Yeah, so…raging bitch.

"Fine." Joan nodded.

I immediately turned and left, assuming the "fine" was in reference to both handing over Dara Evans to Becky as well as delaying any new additions to my wardrobe.

I hurried down the hall, nodding politely to my co-workers but not stopping long enough to chat. I'd been working at Davidson & Croft Media since graduating with my master's degree twelve months earlier; in that time, people had come to expect my behavior and very rarely tried to draw me into conversation.

Finally, I was back in the haven of my office. I shut the door and crossed to my chair, dropping into it and depositing my éclair and teacup on the desk. I tried to wrap my mind around how I'd gotten into this mess. Then I again briefly thought about how I might escape from having to spend any time with Ronan. Then I again pushed those thoughts away.

If I wanted to continue at Davidson & Croft Media—and I did want to continue at Davidson & Croft Media because no one else would pay as well and put up with my eccentricities—I would just have to suck it up and live through the next few months.

I unlocked my computer, planning my message for Becky, trying to find the words to break it to her that she would be taking over social media containment for The Starlet. I felt a measure of guilt. Becky seemed like a nice person. I wouldn't wish Dara Evans on a dog I didn't like.

When my screen awoke, I flinched. I'd left open The Socialmedialite's email account, and Ronan's odious message was mocking me. I stared at it for a moment, my fingers tapping impatiently on my desk.

Under usual circumstances, I would *never* respond to a message such as his. I would delete it, ignore it, and put him on my celebrity blacklist (those who are never discussed, referenced, or mentioned again). I knew the worst thing that could happen to a celebrity was to be made irrelevant. Society's ambivalence is the death of notoriety.

But now—now that I was going to have to suffer through actual in-person interactions with Ronan—I couldn't contain my desire to lash out at him in some way and return his insufferable message with a response worthy of my angst and aggression.

Annie might have to be nice to Ronan, but that didn't mean The Socialmedialite had to take any of his crap. Without really thinking it through, I opened my alter ego's email account and quickly typed out a message.

March 10
Dear Mr. Fitzpatrick,
Please accept my humblest apologies.

If I'd known my benign little blog post was going to get you all hot and bothered, I would have sent it to you directly and arranged a rendezvous to our mutual satisfaction. Despite your propensity to dress like the love child of a hobbit and a leprechaun, I can't deny—toe-shoes notwithstanding—I wouldn't be opposed to your dipping into my pot of gold, especially if that bulge were au naturel. Though, with your superiority complex, I suspect it was a tube sock. Let me guess, you drive a fast car...right? Maybe something with a lot of cylinders to compensate for other deficiencies?

Also, thank you for proving every Irish stereotype 100% correct. Now I know for certain your people's predisposition for hysteria and dramatics has not been exaggerated. Well done, you. Keep up the good work.
Sincerely, The Socialmedialite

FOUR
RONAN

Calories: *4,500.*
Workout: *5 hours in total.*
Steamed chicken: *Starting to fantasize about frying, roasting, sautéing, grilling, braising, barbecuing...*

Six-thirty in the morning, and I'm staring at the screen of my laptop, pissed. The only reason I had the thing was so that I could email Lucy and Skype with her and Ma from time to time. Other than that, I wasn't much of an Internet sort of bloke. When people asked me if I was on Facebook and I told them no, they looked at me like I was an alien from another planet.

I liked face-to-face interaction, wanted to be able to see, smell, and gauge people in the flesh. Screens to me were just flat black mirrors. They wiped out all of the most vital and exciting things about a person, giving you a bland, one-dimensional representation instead.

I made the concession of emailing Lucy because of the time difference when I was traveling. If I was somewhere like Australia, we were on opposite ends of the globe, and it was nearly impossible to find a decent hour that suited us both to talk over the phone.

Which brings us to the present and why I was looking at a highly offensive message from The Socialmedialite that had made its way to my inbox. I'd been under the assumption that the virtual pimp-slap I'd given her would be my triumphant last word. (Virtual pimp-slaps were allowed in my book; real-life ones, not so much.)

Within the space of two short paragraphs, she'd managed to squeeze in a cacophony of insults. I was yet again a hobbit/leprechaun, I stuffed my jocks with a tube sock, I drove a fast car to compensate for a small dick, and I was a fitting tribute to the short-fused, temperamental Irish stereotype.

Almost of their own accord, my hands were moving over the keyboard, clicking on "reply," and furiously venting the anger I felt inside. Somehow I was channeling all of my hatred toward the media at this one faceless person. I didn't think I'd ever typed so fast in my life. I'd written a long, meandering tirade of a paragraph when I looked back at it, immediately highlighted the entire thing, and then hit "delete."

I wasn't going to let this blogger know she was getting to me. I was going to be just as cutting as she was without conveying the fact that I gave a shit. Of course, strangely, I did give a shit, a whole lot of a shit. It wasn't just my legendary quick temper, either, but I wasn't going to give her the satisfaction of knowing that.

So I took a deep breath, composed myself, and started from scratch.

March 11
Dear Socialmedialite,
It's obvious that you live in a fantasy world for the following reasons:

1. *You believe in hobbits and leprechauns.*
2. *You call your vagina a pot of gold.*
3. *You think I'd ever be interested in your pot of gold.*
4. *You believe a tube sock looks like a cock.*

Ronan Fitzpatrick
   P.S. Your xenophobia truly knows no bounds. Stereotypes are bullshit, but I guess it makes sense that you'd spout them, being the peddler of excrement that you are.

I sat back, flexed my hands, and hit "send," feeling a rush of satisfaction as I wondered how she would react to my response. Trying not to delve too much into the notion that I might actually *like* fighting with this person, I quickly shot a message off to Lucy. I included a few things I thought she would potentially be interested in, mostly how I hated having to work with this PR company, but that there was a pretty girl named Annie who they were going to pair me up with, so it wasn't a complete loss. Ever since Brona, Lucy had been trying to encourage me to get back into the dating scene, so I mentioned Annie purely to keep her happy. Thus far I'd had a couple of sordid one-night stands, and, as I said, that's all I was after.

A brief memory of the soft, silky feel of Annie's skin against my knuckles struck me, and it was a welcome distraction. The recollection was so visceral in its simplicity that I felt myself harden.

It had officially been too long since my last shag.

As I made my way into the gym and pulled my iPod from my pocket, I wondered how long it would take to lure Annie into shedding her clothes. They disguised her well, but I'd noticed the subtle curve of her waist and breasts. She would be exquisite when I got her bare, such a contrast to the plain, dowdy way in which I'm sure she thought most people perceived her. And despite the fact that it frustrated me, there was something about her timidity that appealed to me on a very base level. I could just imagine how easily she'd...submit.

My thoughts were making me way too excited for 8:00 a.m. I briefly considered a long shower instead of a workout, but I struggled onward. Perhaps hitting the treadmill extra hard would work off some of the sexual frustration. Firing up my iPod, I selected my favorite workout playlist and started at a slow jog. "The Final Countdown" came on, putting me instantly in the zone.

Mullets and questionably tight pants aside, the best music in the world was '80s rock, and I had no qualms about admitting it. I didn't want music that was maudlin and depressing—I wanted music that put me in a good mood and made the world look a little bit brighter.

Two hours later I was showered, dressed, and on my way to my second meeting at Davidson & Croft. Joan had scheduled it with me yesterday, assuring me that Annie would be there. And yeah, I had kind of made it a requirement for my participation and attendance. I mean, the only reason I was doing this was because I wanted to get to know her. If I could clean up my rep while getting into Annie's curvaceous knickers, then I'd be one happy, sexually sated camper.

Much to my irritation, when I arrived at the offices, I was ushered into a small conference room with Rachel and Ian, and there was no Annie in sight.

"Where's Annie?" I said, folding my arms and leveling my stare at Rachel. She seemed to be more open to chatting than the stern-faced Ian.

Rachel shuffled her papers. She looked a little nervous. "Oh, she might be in later. Annie doesn't always work at the office."

I leaned forward, eager for more information. "Where else does she work?"

"From home. Aside from Joan, none of us really know her that well, but from what I've heard, she's a bit of a hermit. The brilliant ones are always a little odd, you know."

"Brilliant ones?"

"Well, yeah, Annie can singlehandedly turn your public image around. Remember that Oscar winner who nearly ran over an eighty-year-old lady when he was drunk?"

"Eh, no...."

Rachel grinned. "*Exactly*. Annie buries the bad and either exalts or manufactures the good, placing accomplishments on a bright, shining pedestal—with a spotlight no one can ignore. I've never seen anything like it, and I've been in this business for a long time."

I briefly wondered if Annie thought it was ethical to cover up stuff like that or if she just did it because it was her job. Something about her made me think that, unlike the privileged and distinguished background I was reported to have, Annie was a lot like me. Coming from nothing but trying to build a solid place in the world, willing to do things she didn't necessarily agree with in order to survive. I bear the name Fitzpatrick, but I have never been accepted by my father's family. They didn't approve when my dad married my mother, a girl of no means and no social standing. So, when I was just a kid and he died in a car crash, they basically disowned me and Lucy.

I kept my voice disinterested, conversational, and pushed Rachel for more information. "Where'd she learn to do that?"

"She graduated top of her class at Wharton." Rachel's grin widened, like she was proud of Annie's accomplishments.

"Wharton? Isn't that Ivy League in the States? Like those twats from Cambridge and Oxford?" I knew I sounded unimpressed. I was disappointed at the thought that Annie was a blue blood.

Rachel shrugged, though she looked amused, like she was trying not to laugh. "Something like that."

I scowled. "So, she's a bit of a snob, then? Comes from a rich family?"

She vigorously shook her head. "God, no. Not at all. I think she grew up in Scranton." Rachel wrinkled her nose as though the word "Scranton" tasted like piss. "She just likes to keep to herself, and like I said, she's completely brilliant at what she does. She had her pick of firms around the world trying to win her over, but she chose us. That's why Joan allows her eccentricities. We all know we're lucky to have her."

I stared at Rachel, thinking about all of this.

Growing up, we had very little. Ma had to work hard to put me through Belvedere, the same school Dad had attended, and I'd always be grateful to her for that. I wondered who had worked hard to help Annie go to Wharton.

"So, Mr. Fitzpatrick," Ian began, all business, "Rachel and I have put together the preliminary proposal, and I'd like to run through it with you if that's all right?"

"Sure, go ahead," I replied, shrugging, and that was my cue to zone out.

Ian seemed to be slowly losing his temper as I continually clicked a pen while he spoke. He could get as angry as he wanted. Joan had promised me Annie would be here today. So I was feeling a little bit conned with the whole "no Annie" situation.

"We'd like you to attend a few high-profile film premieres and awards ceremonies over the coming weeks. Having you photographed on the red carpet will get you featured in magazines and on websites, put you on the radar, so to speak," said Ian before glancing down at the papers in front of him and continuing under his breath, "so we should look into vetting potential dates for you."

"Oh," Rachel said excitedly, "I'm on good terms with Taylor Swift's people. Perhaps I could get you an intro." She glanced at Ian. "Is she single right now?"

Ian shrugged. On the inside, I was pissed at the idea of being set up like that; on the outside, I took the piss.

"You know who I've always had a thing for, that Rosie O'Donnell. You think she'd be up for a bit of the young stuff?"

Rachel obviously didn't understand sarcasm because she gave me a confused look. "Um, I'm pretty sure she's a lesbian. And that's not really the image we're going for. You need to date someone young and attractive, someone the press really likes."

At that moment the door swung open, and Joan stuck her head in. "Hello again, Mr. Fitzpatrick. Are you being well taken care of?"

I cocked my head to her. "I thought Annie was going to be here."

Joan frowned for a moment. "She was supposed to be." She glanced at Ian. "Didn't Annie show up today?"

"I haven't seen her," he replied.

"Well...isn't that curious." And with that she left the room.

I looked back to Rachel and Ian. "I think we're done here."

"But Mr. Fitzpatrick, we still have to go over the rest of the preliminary proposal. We haven't even covered the social media front and the planned press releases, and I would like your input at some point, too."

I was already standing up. "Yeah, yeah, I'll go to the premieres and all that. Just give me a few days' warning so that I can make sure I'm available."

"Of course," said Rachel.

Ian didn't argue further. To be honest, I thought he was glad to see the back of me. As I was making my way to the elevators, I was cut off by Joan. It was funny how a five-foot-nothing woman could come across so foreboding. I stopped and looked down at her. I wasn't glaring, and I wasn't scowling; but I was definitely emanating hostility.

"We made a deal, Mrs. Davidson."

"That we did, and the deal is still on," she said and handed me a small white business card. "This has all of Annie's contact details. She's been unexpectedly busy today, but said she'd like you to give her a call so that the two of you can arrange to meet."

I took the card, momentarily pacified, and stuck it in the back pocket of my jeans. "I'll be sure to do that. You have a nice day." I nodded and walked by her, continuing to the elevators. It was a long walk down the hallway. When I finally reached the corner, I saw a familiar figure wearing a gray coat hurry inside a car. She was mumbling to herself, but I couldn't quite catch what she was saying. I jogged forward and slipped into the elevator just as the door closed.

When Annie saw I was the person who'd just entered, her eyes got all big, the same as they did yesterday. Then she looked away and studied the floor. She stood in the corner, and I stood about a foot away from her. She appeared to be wishing I'd give her some space, but somehow I wasn't feeling charitable.

I'd ask myself what it was about her that made me want to get so close, but I already knew. She was incredibly beautiful and a perfect candidate to explore my baser needs with.

The elevator stood still, neither one of us having selected a floor yet. I stepped forward and hit the button for the lobby, hearing her exhale in relief and mutter indistinct words to herself again.

"Good to see you, Annie," I said, smiling amiably. Not that the smile was having much effect since she wouldn't look at me. The elevator started to descend.

"Yes, you, too," she replied, lifting her eyes to me with a concerted effort.

I felt like I'd just been given a gift. Those eyes were unfathomably big and brown, like melted chocolate. I even thought I could see flecks of gold. After having spoken to Rachel, I was now beginning to understand that Annie might be a little bit socially phobic. Why else would she choose to work from home most of the time? And why else would she be so uncomfortable talking to me? It made something in my stomach tighten. Simultaneously, I both loved and hated her coming across so hunted just to be standing alone in an elevator with me.

The protector inside me was frowning while the predator soaked up her discomfort with glee.

Still, I wanted her to be relaxed. Okay, that was a lie. I wanted her to lose control, and I pondered how I might coax her into doing that. She was looking away again as I glanced at her sideways, considering. What I did next might have been a bad idea, but I had to see if pushing her boundaries would work. Since she was leaning against the wall in the corner, she was in the perfect position for me to cage her in.

Brazenly, I hit the "stop" button, and the elevator came to a shaky halt.

"What are you doing?" Annie asked, a hint of nerves causing her voice to rise.

I turned and stalked to her, placing my hands behind her on the wall of the lift over either side of her shoulders. My gaze wandered over her features—luscious lips, sweet nose, long lashes, fucking beautiful eyes that rapidly flickered between mine. I heard her breathing escalate.

Bending down a little so we were almost level, I lifted a hand from the wall and rubbed my thumb along her chin.

"I like you," I stated.

She swallowed, her voice sounding rough and uneven. "Mr. Fitzpatrick, that button is only supposed to be pushed in case of an emergency."

Obviously, I knew that, but I figured I'd deal with the consequences after getting a little taste of her. I wanted to sample those pretty lips.

"I'm living up to my bad-boy reputation, then, aren't I?" I murmured, dropping a hand to her collarbone, the flat of my palm against her sternum. Her heart was racing. "Is your heart beating fast because you like it when I touch you or because you don't?"

There was a momentary flash of temper in her expression. "Obviously, the latter."

"Have dinner with me," I said, ignoring her answer. My gaze wandered to her mouth, where she very briefly wetted her lips. I wondered if she was attracted to me but was trying to hide it.

"Of-of course we'll be having dinner together." She cleared her throat, and her eyes finally settled on mine. "Davidson and Croft frequently schedules client dinners."

"I'm not talking about client dinners."

She swallowed. "We're going to be working together, so non-client dinners would be unprofessional."

I brought my mouth closer to hers, and our breaths mingled as I said quietly, "Let's be unprofessional together, Annie."

Her eyes seemed to glaze over a little after I said it, making me grin, because it looked like she was imagining what that would be like. I wanted to be so fucking unprofessional with her, it wasn't funny. Quickly, she righted herself, brought her hands to my chest, and pushed. I caught them, holding them in mine, my thumb brushing her inner wrist. She shivered. Her hands were shaking.

"Nothing can happen between us, Mr. Fitzpatrick." She didn't sound convinced.

"It's already happening, Miss...." I paused, let go of one of her hands, and pulled the card Joan had given me out of my back pocket to read it. "Catrel."

She focused on the business card, and panic flickered over her features before they hardened. "Who gave you that?"

"Joan," I happily replied. "She wanted to make sure I'd be able to contact you directly, seeing as you were missing from the meeting today. I was very disappointed when you didn't show."

She tried to grab for the card, but I stepped back and held it out of her reach.

"Give that to me. You don't need it. I'll contact you if we ever have to meet," she said desperately.

I chuckled as she advanced on me until I was the one backed into the opposite corner of the elevator. Her chest pushed into mine as she went up on her tiptoes, still swiping for the card. "Look at you, Annie; you're all over me," I teased.

Immediately, she backed away, scowling and folding her arms over her chest. "I don't want you calling me unless it's work related," she said in defeat.

My devious smile told her I had absolutely no intention of sticking to that rule.

"Oh, I wouldn't dream of it," I purred, lazily scanning her figure. Her coat was long and bulky, covering everything up. It was a good thing I had an active imagination.

"I bet you have a killer body under all those layers," I said huskily, still in a teasing mood.

She blinked, and her mouth straightened into a firm line. "Some of us don't feel it necessary to flaunt our looks, and I'm very happy with my layers."

The remark was obviously aimed at me, and I didn't know why she seemed so against being friendly. I wasn't that bad of a guy. Well, not really. "That's not what I meant. I was trying to pay you a compliment, Annie."

My words were low, tender; my sincerity seemed to elicit a reaction in her. Her previous disgruntlement deflated. It was true. For whatever reason, I thought she was the perfect combination of genuine, beautiful, and sexy. I wasn't used to genuine. She glanced at me, opened her mouth to say something, but then snapped it closed again.

Just then a voice crackled through the speakers, requesting to know why the elevator had been stopped.

"It's nothing. We're fine," Annie said, clearing her throat again and talking into the speaker. "Can you start it back up, please?"

Seconds later, we were moving again. I took a step toward her, but the look she gave me said it would be a good idea to keep my distance. People started to get on and off, and once we reached the ground floor, Annie quickly scurried by me, rushed straight out of the lobby, and into a yellow cab. I didn't mind her scarpering as I glanced down at the card I still held in my hand.

I had her number now, and I had every intention of using it.

FIVE
ANNIE

The Creeper Selfie: *When one takes a selfie with the express purpose of including some person or action in the background. Usually only part of the photographer's face is present in the photo—usually the eyes, but sometimes half of a face—in order to display shock, excitement, or disgust.*
Best for: *Chaotic situations, when others are focused on the action the photographer is trying to document. Also, airplanes.*
Do not use: *In restaurants or near mirrors.*

I followed the email exchange between my administrative assistant (Gerta) and Ronan Fitzpatrick on Wednesday morning for about two hours. It spanned a sum total of thirty emails before I finally stepped in to end the debacle.

Poor Gerta. All she was trying to do was set up a meeting with him for this week, and he turned it into a debate on James Joyce, under-age rugby, and whether Clongowes Wood College in Clane, Co. Kildare, was ultimately responsible for *Ulysses*. I made a mental note to give her a raise. Gerta deserved it. She really was a saint.

It appeared Mr. Fitzpatrick was not exaggerating when he'd said that he wanted to contact me directly. I didn't know what to do about his persistence because I didn't think anyone had ever been so determined to get in touch with me.

In the end, I sighed heavily, opened a window in Infographicsgenerator.net, and drafted my email to Mr. Fitzpatrick.

When communicating with clients, I use infographics almost exclusively. I find that most of our clients—as they are extremely busy and lack patience—do not respond well to text emails (i.e., emails containing only words); they prefer the shortcut of pictures. A graphic representation of my thoughts and/or the information I need to communicate allows the client to absorb the information faster and remember it for a longer period of time.

Infographics as a Means to Effectively Transfer Knowledge Reducing the Bias of Consumer Interpretation was the title of my Master of Science thesis at Wharton. The idea came to me when my master's thesis professor mentioned that my emails and written correspondence often came across as terse and condescending.

The great thing about the pictures within infographics is that they're always positive images. The images are not open to tone, inflection, or word-choice interpretation because they're intrinsically happy. I don't have to worry about people understanding the multisyllabic syntax. Not to mention the little illustrated people are always smiling, even when I'm not.

Think of it like sending someone a smiley-face emoticon instead of typing the words "You make me happy."

Or sending a thumbs-up emoticon instead of "I agree." Or "I like that." Or "Good job."

Since graduate school, I've found text-less emails to be invaluable as both a timesaver and as a means to ensure all business correspondence remains positive and strictly professional. It works for me. It works for my clients. It works for my co-workers. Everyone wins.

The only person I interact with at work who disallows my infographics is Joan. I assume it's because she's a bit old-fashioned in her consumption of data. Eventually, however, she'll have to make the switch. As a society, we're moving away from the written word. We want the shortcut. We don't want to have to think about the meaning of words—ours or someone else's—and how they affect us or those around us. We want to feel good.

I quickly assembled the graphic I needed—basically, a clock with a question mark, a picture of a calendar, and a series of food choices—and opted for a green, orange, and white color scheme. I felt that the subtle inclusion of the Irish flag's colors would make Mr. Fitzpatrick feel good which might encourage his cooperation.

I saved the file and then forwarded it to Mr. Fitzpatrick.

Inexplicably, my heart thudded in my chest, and I pressed my palm against my ribs. I also found I had a lump in my throat when I hit "send." This acute anxiety was likely attributable to the fact that the last time I saw Ronan, he was touching me, telling me he liked me, and suggesting we engage in unprofessional behavior.

And I kind of really, really liked it.

Ronan—that is, Mr. Fitzpatrick—had the uncanny ability to get under my skin and steal into my thoughts. I hadn't stopped thinking about him since rushing out of the elevator less than twenty-four hours ago. Granted, I'd been thinking about him quite a lot since The Socialmedialite had received his first angry email.

Since our first in-person encounter and our initial virtual email exchange, I'd done a significant amount of research on him. Usually I would leave this type of task to a junior staff member and review a summary report. But not this time. This time, I wanted to make the calls myself.

I contacted his university, where he'd studied physiotherapy, and spoke with his major professor, and then I requested a transcript. I'd also chatted with his agent, coach, the team's offensive coordinator, two of his teammates, his physical trainer, and his nutritionist back in Ireland.

They all had similar thoughts regarding my Mr. Fitzpatrick.

First, he had a temper, but not like it had been portrayed in the media. They'd all credited his short fuse to passion—for his mother and sister and the people he cared about—and not mindless or childish temper tantrums (like the media suggested).

Second, Ronan was dedicated and honorable, if a tad overly serious and a bit of a wet blanket. This description of him—provided by his teammates and confirmed by his university coach—made me laugh, mostly because it was so completely unexpected and at odds with the flirtatious man who'd cornered me in the elevator.

It seemed Mr. Fitzpatrick took his physical health and competition readiness to the level of near obsession. When the rest of the team gathered after a match to drink at a nearby pub, Ronan was always the designated driver. His nickname was *Mother Fitzpatrick*.

Third, everyone in Ireland—according to my contacts—knew the reason Ronan had lost it on the field and pummeled his teammate, and her name was Brona O'Shea. There was a YouTube video of the fight that had garnered millions of views. Even though he was the one doing the damage—and boy, did he know how to throw a punch—I felt bad for Ronan as I watched it. There was a sort of pain in his eyes that struck a chord with me. When I spoke to his nutritionist (Jenna McCarthy) about Ronan and Brona, she made it sound like they were the popular celeb golden couple, and all of Ireland followed their every move. As well, no one in the whole of Ireland (all five million people) understood why Ronan Fitzpatrick put up with Brona O'Shea.

"Why, I was just talking to my husband about it last night," Jenna had said, sounding far too invested in Ronan's relationship status. "I said I hoped Ronan doesn't take her back this time. She's a snake, an absolute snake, and she's holding him back."

"This time? Have they split before?" I'd pushed, telling myself I needed to understand the history of Ronan's relationship with Brona in order to craft a comprehensive image profile for our social media team.

"Ah, yes, but it hasn't been quite so public before. This time she crossed a line. Instead of dallying about with some rock star, this time she slept with his teammate, his flanker—Sean Cassidy."

"She—" My mouth moved, but I struggled to find words. I was shocked. "Ms. O'Shea cheated on Mr. Fitzpatrick?" I made a mental note to Google image search Sean Cassidy. In fact, I did it surreptitiously as I spoke to Jenna. He was hot in a blond, pretty boy sort of way.

"Of course! What do you think we're talking about? She's a woman of easy virtue, that Brona. Ask anyone. Ronan's the most loyal person I know, oh!" Jenna made a sad sound, and I heard her sigh before she continued, "I think Brona having it away with his flanker was the last straw. He put up with her changing the way she looked, helped her with her joke of a music career, and all of her other garbage. If you ask me, the man deserves a medal."

"So…." I'd paused, mulling this information over before asking, "So Mr. Fitzpatrick isn't responsible for Ms. O'Shea's altered appearance?"

"Eh? What's that? You mean her plastic surgeries and the fake tits and the rest of it? No, no. Those were all her doing."

"What about his family? What do they think about his relationship with Brona O'Shea and her behavior?" I'd asked this question to everyone, and they all gave me more or less the same answer.

"Oh, the high and mighty Fitzpatricks? They won't even talk to Ronan, never have. His ma raised him and his sister by herself. The Fitzpatricks won't even acknowledge him. He's better off without them, in my opinion. They're the posh society types. They think everything they do is brilliant and everything he does is shite. But he won't speak a harsh word against them. He's too good for them, if you ask me."

Going to the source certainly had given me a lot to think about, such as the unfair assumptions I'd made.

I knew better than anyone that information found on the Internet was suspect at best, and I reprimanded myself for believing—even for a short time—the rumor magazines' depiction of Ronan. It certainly did explain his anger and overreaction to my article on *New York's Finest* last Saturday and his emails to The Socialmedialite; he'd been exploited by money-hungry gossipmongers. He hated the media.

I'd decided to put off responding to his latest email, where he'd called The Socialmedialite xenophobic. I didn't know what to say. I didn't want to fight with him or add to his aggravation. But I also didn't like that he'd lumped *New York's Finest* in with the trashy, infotainment garbage that had been tearing him down.

No person is ever truly their online or media persona. For better or for worse, the human condition, desires, and faults are so much more robust than pixels on a screen or words beneath a caption.

Nevertheless, robust isn't my job nor is reality.

My job is shortcuts and sound bites and manipulation of perception. But it's so much nicer when the image I create is representative of the real person. I never enjoy putting the shine of perfection on a piece of shit, à la *It's not poop, it's chocolate…just don't try to eat it because it's full of E. coli.*

I couldn't decide if I felt better or worse after talking to Jenna and the others. In addition to my inconvenient and forceful physical attraction to Ronan Fitzpatrick, I also found myself liking him—specifically the him painted by my calls to his acquaintances and teammates—which was possibly even more inconvenient.

As I waited for Ronan—I mean, Mr. Fitzpatrick—to respond to my infographic email and meeting request, my mind drifted and then landed on the memory of being trapped in the elevator with him. I wasn't surprised. I had difficulty thinking about anything else.

He was so…present.

When he looked at me, I felt so entirely *seen*. But it was more than that because I got the impression he wasn't just *looking* at me when we were together. Yes, he watched me, but he also touched me and felt me. He listened to me and not just my words; he listened to the sounds my body made as it moved, as though searching for a clue or a tell.

I wondered if this—this being present and focused on more than just the superficial—was a learned skill, part of what made him a world-class athlete.

I also had the distinct impression that, when he'd leaned into my space, he'd tried to smell me, and he'd managed to do it without coming across as a creepy creeper.

Admittedly, if he were less epically good-looking, he might have come across as a creepy creeper. But, as he had the body of a gladiator and the face of a movie star, I felt flustered, flattered, and turned on. The fact that I felt flattered made me feel like an idiot. I hated this about myself. I hated that, even though I knew better, good looks negated odd behavior.

His odd behavior being that he was attempting to use all five of his senses to experience me while trapping us in an elevator; I didn't doubt that, if I'd given him any indication that I was in favor of his advances, he would have tried to taste me as well.

I shivered at the thought, a wave of warmth spreading from my chest to the pit of my stomach, stinging and sudden, like a hot flash. I lost my breath a little, imagining what it would be like to kiss him. He was so confident in real life, in a way that was a complete conundrum to me, and appeared to excel at everything he attempted. If he tried to use all five senses when speaking with me in an elevator, I expected his kisses would also be of the world-class variety.

I got up from my computer, took a lap around my apartment, then opted to run some cold water over my wrists to cool down. As I was working from home, I was still in my yoga pants and the Shark Week long-sleeved T-shirt from my workout earlier in the day.

Inside the bathroom, I glanced at my reflection in the mirror, finding my eyes bright and excited, my skin flushed. I grimaced. This was not good. I was going to have to interact with Ronan—*ack! Mr. Fitzpatrick! His name is Mr. Fitzpatrick, and I will call him Mr. Fitzpatrick*—over the coming months.

Keeping my distance had always been easy for me because the alternative held no allure. Or rather, since high school I'd never met someone alluring enough to make me question keeping my distance.

My phone dinged, alerting me to a message. I glanced at the screen and saw it was from my online BFF, @WriteALoveSong.

In truth, I didn't know much about her. I was pretty sure she lived in New York and worked in some field related to the music industry. Her blog, *Irony For Beginners*, focused more on the indie scene, whereas my posts were more mainstream. She seemed to enjoy her anonymity almost as much as I did.

Yet, we checked in with each other every few days, if not every day. She shared news stories with me, and I'd send her pictures of independent artists or anything that might be related to her content focus. As well, we'd message back and forth about our days or the blogs or life in general—always careful to never reveal too much.

I had several other online friends, but she was my closest friend. I looked forward to her messages. In this one she wrote,

@WriteALoveSong to @Socialmedialite: Is the cocky jock still giving you shit? I'll beat him up for you.

I quickly responded,

@Socialmedialite to @WriteALoveSong: I'm ignoring him. I'm hoping he'll disappear if he thinks I'm indifferent.
@WriteALoveSong to @Socialmedialite: Good luck with that. Hey, why did the hipster leave the ocean?

I braced myself as I typed,

@Socialmedialite to @WriteALoveSong: Why?

WriteALoveSong (how I thought of her in my head) sometimes liked to send me hipster jokes. They were always cheesy and silly. I kind of loved them.

@WriteALoveSong to @Socialmedialite: Because it's too current... ba-da-da-dum.

@Socialmedialite to @WriteALoveSong: I sea...

@WriteALoveSong to @Socialmedialite: Oh no! Not an ocean pun! Now you're just being shellfish.

I laughed and clicked off my phone. I loved that WriteALoveSong and I could have so much fun yet never have met in person. We worked, our friendship worked, because we didn't push each other for more. We didn't need to see each other to know each other. We were happy in our shadows of anonymity.

Whereas Mr. Fitzpatrick might be a nice guy, a serious guy, a loyal, generous, wet blanket of a man, but he also lived his life in the spotlight. He was always pushing. I took great pains to fly under the radar and blend in with furniture. I'd been born introverted, and life experience proved my natural instincts were actually a blessing.

In real life, I could count on me. I could rely on me. I would never abandon myself. I would never go back on my word or lie to myself or let myself down. The way I saw it, everyone else was a wild card, and that included Mr. Fitzpatrick.

I also didn't like how disordered and reckless he made me feel, how aware of my body and the beating of my heart. He made me want...*things*, things that I'd learned to bury and forego. My life was about control—over my thoughts, emotions, environment, and therefore—over my destiny.

My pulse had calmed to a nice, steady beat; I took one more calming breath then returned to my computer, intent on ignoring these clamoring feelings and desires. Instead, I would focus on preparing my portion of Mr. Fitzpatrick's proposal and then write a new blog post that had nothing to do with cocky jocks.

The chime of my email pulled my attention to a new message waiting in my work mailbox. It was from Mr. Fitzpatrick, and it was a response to my infographic meeting request. I held my breath, intent on controlling my body's alarming insta-reaction to anything related to the gorgeous rugby player.

Despite my best intentions, I clicked the message and devoured its contents. It read:

March 12
Annie dearest,

If you insist on sending me images, I'd prefer they be of you.
See you tomorrow at 8.
Affectionately, Ronan
P.S. I can't eat any of that stuff you sent. Again, if you'd sent a picture of yourself, then it would be a completely different story…

Unsurprisingly, my pulse quickened at the double meaning in his last line. He couldn't eat any of the food, but if I'd sent a picture of myself, he'd…he'd….
 I groaned.
 Then I ran back to the bathroom. This time I opted for a cold shower.

* * *

New York's Finest
Blogging as *The Socialmedialite*
March 13

Have you noticed that the ratio of supermodels in Jason Carter's entourage to number of Jason Carters has been steadily declining over the last twenty-four months? The number of Jason Carters has remained constant at one (or two, if you count his custom-made Louis Vuitton fanny pack as a separate sentient being), whereas the number of supermodels has decreased from seventeen to six in just two short years.

Exhibit A (picture 1) was taken nearly twenty months ago as he and his harem of seventeen left Tiffany's.
Now look to Exhibit B (picture 2). This picture was taken nine months ago. Here he is down to twelve.
Now look at Exhibit C (picture 3). This was taken last week. Again, we have Jason Carter and his fanny pack, but an entourage of only six.
WHAT IS GOING ON, PEOPLE?!?!?!
Why the diminishing number of models?
Doesn't he know he is the primary source of fame for these women? Doesn't he care we're going to have poorly dressed supermodels if he and his fanny pack don't step up and foot the bill for their Jimmy Choos and Louis Vuitton handbags??
I thought I could count on three things to never change in life: death, taxes, and Jason Carter's (and his fanny pack's) entourage.
Is nothing sacred? What's next? Will George Clooney date someone his own age?!?!?

THE HOOKER AND THE HERMIT

Feeling a tad out of sorts today....
<3 The Socialmedialite

* * *

I WAS UNCOMFORTABLE.

And that was putting it mildly.

I tried to cross my legs, but the sky-blue silk skirt—which fell just above my knees—felt too short; I opted for crossing them at the ankle instead. I also tugged, I hoped surreptitiously, at the V-neck of my long-sleeved, cream-colored shirt because it showed cleavage. It showed my cleavage. My cleavage was showing. As well, the shirt was formfitting and plainly exhibited the shape of my stomach, back, shoulders, and chest.

It was a nightmare.

I wanted to run to my office, grab my Snuggie (which is basically a blanket with armholes), and cover myself up.

Unfortunately, Joan was sitting across from me, watching me like a hawk. I was a mouse, and she was a peregrine falcon. Resistance was futile. I'd arrived at the building and found her in my office at 7:15 a.m., five garment bags full of clothes lying on my couch. She was drinking a cappuccino from my machine and smiling at me like she'd just won something.

"I know you're busy, so I had one of the shoppers buy you a new wardrobe," she'd said, holding up an outfit. "Change into this one now."

When I opened my mouth to object, she added, "Looking professional is no more than I would ask of any of my employees."

Objectively, I knew the clothes the shopper had handpicked were lovely. They were stylish, well made, very expensive, and undoubtedly professional looking. It's just they weren't brown or navy or gray. They weren't baggy. They fit, and they fit too well, like they'd been made to highlight my curves and... assets. I looked *pretty* in them, like a girl. Like a feminine girl. And, adding to my horror, there were shoes! Little kitten heels and spiky stilettos and everything in between, one pair for each outfit.

People had stared at me when I walked down the hall. I could feel their eyes following me, though I kept mine on the hallway carpet. I distinctly overheard one of the associates from Printed Media say, "Is she new? Who is that?"

When I walked into the conference room, all conversation stopped. My team gaped. Rachel gasped. Ian stared. And Joan smiled. I felt like a sideshow act at the circus, the kind where people stare and point.

Again, it was a nightmare.

I shuffled and thumbed through my stack of papers. I turned to Gerta, attempting to ignore her stunned perusal, and asked whether she'd made enough copies for the team. I purposefully sat near the door just in case I needed to make a quick escape. Worst-case scenario, I could pretend I had gastrointestinal distress.

I was still forming my escape plan and trying to fight my blush of intense discomfort when Mr. Fitzpatrick arrived.

He was five minutes early.

"Bollocks, bitches, and Battlestar Galactica," I mumbled.

I have a bad habit of mumbling curse words when I'm aggravated; honestly, I think I might have a mild case of Tourette's. To soften the string of foul language and make me feel like less of a freak, I try to throw in a pop culture reference at the end. It usually works, but not today.

I closed my eyes briefly, gathered a slow, steadying breath through my nose, and tried to wrestle the spike of adrenaline into submission. People moved around me, crossing to the door and shaking his hand, introducing themselves. I stood slowly, my jaw clenching so tightly I thought I might crack a tooth, and turned.

But I couldn't quite bring myself to lift my eyes to his. So I waited, using my hair as a curtain, dipping my chin to my chest, and pretending to read the papers I'd brought and knew by heart. I waited until everyone was introduced and had reclaimed their spots around the conference room. I waited and listened as Joan invited Mr. Fitzpatrick to take the seat next to mine.

I waited until he drawled, "We keep having this breakdown in communication, Joan. I was under the impression that the *entire* team would be here."

I lifted my chin just as Joan's eyes flickered to mine, a pleased smile on her face. She began, "I think, Mr. Fitzpatrick—"

But I interrupted her with, "I believe everyone is here."

Ronan glanced at me and did a completely ridiculous, cartoonish double-take complete with wide eyes, agape mouth, raised eyebrows, and three blinks. His confusion didn't last long, maybe two full seconds, before his eyes traveled down and then up, quickly appraising my body like I might be an apparition and magically disappear. When his eyes met mine again, they were pleased and half-lidded. A lazy smile claimed his lips and did terrible things to my state of mind.

His gaze scorched me; my body ignited in a flash until I was sweating between my thighs, under my arms, on my stomach, and down my back. I was burning up.

I was officially a lunatic.

Pressing my lips together and averting my eyes, I motioned to his chair—the one next to mine—and cleared my throat. "Please, Mr. Fitzpatrick, won't you sit down?"

"Yes," he said a little too hastily, with a touch too much enthusiasm.

I basically fell into my seat, my knees no longer cooperating, but covered the clumsy bit of discomposure by scooting myself closer to the table and straightening the stack of papers in front of me unnecessarily. I did my best to ignore the way my shirt was sticking to my abdomen, never mind the fact that Ronan—I mean, Mr. Fitzpatrick—was still blatantly staring at me. I could see him in my peripheral vision.

As a countermeasure, I released my sheet of hair from where I'd tucked it behind my ear, essentially blocking my face from view. If I had to sit through this meeting—and maybe a hundred more like it—dressed in these damn clothes, then I deserved a coping strategy. Hiding behind my hair would have to be it.

"Yes, well—let's get started." Joan sat on the other side of Mr. Fitzpatrick, her voice cutting through the chatter. "Ian, can you take us through the progress to date?"

I still felt Mr. Fitzpatrick's eyes on me, but mercifully Joan had decided to start with Ian's status update rather than my part. I barely heard Ian. It didn't really matter; I'd already read his memo, so I knew the team was vetting actresses, models, society types, and athletes in their search for suitable women to act as his "red herring" dates.

Part of me was glad. I would pale in comparison to those women, and Ronan's attention would surely focus elsewhere.

Another part of me couldn't think about Ronan attending a red carpet event, a supermodel draped on his arm, without wanting to stab something. I think I was a little infatuated with him after talking to his teammates.

After Ian, Rachel was next. She covered tangible media—so both print and television—and took the team through planned magazine spreads in *Sports Illustrated*, *Men's Health*, *GQ*, and *Playboy*.

"I'll say no thanks to the *Playboy* idea," Ronan scoffed then continued humorously, "at least until after I've had my tits done."

I tried not to smile. Rachel chirped a laugh, and Ian narrowed his eyes.

"Mr. Fitzpatrick, our aim is to make as many people aware of you as possible, and *Playboy* has a very large audience."

Ronan folded his arms and stared at him coldly. "I thought we were supposed to be improving my image, you know, clean me up."

"Yes, of course. But we're not out to make you an altar boy, either."

"I hope not. All the altar boys I knew are now heroin addicts."

"Annie...." Joan paused, waited for me to meet her eye, and then said, "Help us out here."

I nodded once and slipped Ronan one of my packets, withdrawing my fingers before he could make contact. If he touched me, my mind would blank, and I'd be even more of a spectacle. I placed my hands on my lap; they were shaking.

This was the part of the presentation Joan or Rachel usually did. I prepped the materials, and one of them would deliver the spiel. But not this time. No, no, no...not this time.

I cleared my throat and glanced quickly around the table. All eyes were on me. My heart beat faster, drumming uncomfortably in my chest. Everyone gathered had already read the proposal and signed off on the details of the mission statement, the ideal image sketch, and the social media campaign. They all knew it was my work. Nevertheless, it didn't make speaking in front of a crowd any easier.

"I, uh...." I blew out a shaky breath, willed my mind to focus and cooperate, but it was no use. I could feel the panic rising, choking me like flood waters. I swallowed, the paper in front of me blurring.

Suddenly, Joan's voice cut through my downward spiral, firm and steady. "Well, look at the time. I'm sorry, Mr. Fitzpatrick, but the team has another meeting. It looks like we'll have to leave you and Ms. Catrel alone to discuss the specifics of the ideal image sketch. I hope you don't mind?"

"No...." He answered almost absentmindedly at first, his voice sounding preoccupied, and then he responded in his normal tone, "No, not at all. I completely understand. I'm sure Ms. Catrel and I can take it from here."

I came back to myself as the sounds of chairs being vacated and people leaving the room provided a backdrop to my breathing exercises. My clothes were sticking to me. I was sure my upper lip and forehead had broken out in sweat. I was hot and sticky and uncomfortable, but at least I wouldn't have to give my presentation in front of the entire team.

No. Just Ronan Fitzpatrick.

"Fuck, fuck, fuck, fuck, Fred Flintstone," I mumbled.

The last sounds of my departing teammates were punctuated by the click of the door closing at my back, yet I didn't look up from the table until several additional seconds had passed. I allowed myself a brief glance at Ronan and was surprised to find him reading the packet I'd placed in front of him.

Without looking up, he asked, "What does 'ideal image sketch' mean?"

A wave of gratefulness washed over me, and with it my heart stuttered then slowed. I didn't know if Ronan was focusing on my work in an effort to disarm the tension caused by my near panic attack or if he was actually interested in the content of the plan. I guessed the former. Regardless, I breathed a silent sigh of relief and straightened in my chair.

Before I could respond, he continued, "Who put this together?"

"I did."

His eyes darted to mine, a small frown creasing his brow, and then back to the packet. "I didn't think you were all that involved so far."

"I have been involved with the proposal, Mr. Fitzpatrick, even if I wasn't present for the initial meeting. The preliminary details were discussed with you on Monday and Tuesday, and what Rachel and Ian reviewed today includes basic, common-sense strategies. Now, the work I do is much more focused on details, on shaping the message and creating your ideal image."

"My ideal image?" His voice lacked inflection. He still wasn't looking at me.

I lifted my chin, tossing my hair over my shoulder, facing him. "Yes. The version of you we want the public to see."

"What's wrong with my current image?" Ronan's brown eyes met mine, and they held a challenge; he faced me, pushing his chair back a bit, placing our knees about a foot apart. His mouth curved into a slight frown as though I'd offended him.

I swallowed my nerves, fisting my hands on my lap. This was another area where I completely failed: one-on-one, tactful communication with clients. I didn't know how to tell clients the truth—that the public doesn't want the *real* Ronan Fitzpatrick, that we needed to make him a different version of himself in order to maximize the exploitation of his talents and move him forward in his career—without pissing the clients off.

"Please understand that I am not suggesting that I tell you how to live your life, your real life. I'm not at all qualified to give advice on living life, and I am in no way judging you *at all*." I took a calming breath and added under my breath, "In fact, I'm the last person on earth who should ever give anyone advice about real life."

"What was that?"

"Nothing, sorry." I glanced at the proposal then back to his penetrating stare. "What I'm talking about here is your public image. I am an expert on perception, of how to use social media to achieve gains in public opinion. There is nothing *wrong* with your current image, it's just—"

"So, you like my image?"

"Of course I do, I mean—"

"Specifically what do you like about my image?" Now the corner of his mouth tugged subtly upward, and his eyes were dancing, dark pools of amusement.

I pressed my lips together, trying to stifle my answering smile, knowing I'd walked right into that. "Well, I like that your teammates call you *Mother Fitzpatrick*."

I was gratified to see his eyebrows hitch slightly at my use of his nickname, his mouth open with equal parts smile and surprise. "I see you've been doing your research."

"Of course. If I'm expected to shape your image, I need to understand the raw materials with which I'm expected to work."

"Raw materials...." His eyes were positively dancing, and his grin was growing, like he knew something about me or he suspected something and liked it. "Who did you talk to?"

"Well, to start with, Jenna McCarthy, your nutritionist."

"Hmm…." He didn't look pleased or displeased, obviously schooling his reaction. "Who else?"

"Your major professor at university, your coach, your physical trainer, and two of your teammates."

He stiffened at the last mention, and his eyes narrowed. "Which teammates?"

"Mr. Flynn and Mr. Leech."

"Ah, they're good blokes." He nodded and added as though as an afterthought, "They're all good blokes, but sometimes they make shite decisions."

I thought that was awfully generous of him, considering his fiancée had *had it away with his flanker*, as Jenna put it.

Ronan appeared to be lost in his thoughts, so I took the opportunity to study him. I felt my expression soften as my gaze traveled over his forehead, nose, cheeks, and lips. He had a few scars I hadn't noticed before: one at the corner and beneath his right eye, about two inches long with a zigzag near the middle, like it had been the result of a jagged cut. He had another, much smaller and fainter, also slightly to the right under his full bottom lip.

He was so handsome, but more than that, there was an aura of feral sensuality about him, something powerful, magnetic. He wore his sexuality openly. He was so blunt and honest about his desires, about who he was. And if his friends and co-workers were to be believed, he was also intensely honorable, driven, and intelligent with a good, loyal, and generous heart.

Yeah…I'm a little infatuated.

"Why didn't you come straight to the source?"

His question startled me, and I blinked at him, trying to make sense out of the jumble he'd just spoken. When I realized I couldn't recall the question, I said, "I'm sorry, what was that?"

He gave me a small smile, his eyes telling me he was delighted. Leaning toward me, Ronan hooked his fingers behind my knees and pulled me forward between his legs. He then placed his hands on my thighs—resting them above the material of my skirt—and bit his lip, peering up at me like he wanted to know all my secrets, or at least borrow them.

I didn't protest. At first I was too surprised. Then I was entirely too mesmerized by the way he was biting his lip.

"Annie…." he said.

"Yes?"

He paused until my gaze lifted from his mouth, met his eyes.

"Why didn't you come straight to the source?" The question was a low, masculine rumble, almost a whisper, and his thumbs were moving back and forth over the silk of my skirt, sending lovely spikes of awareness and delight to my pelvis.

"The source?"

"Yes. If you wanted to know about me, why didn't you just ask? I'll tell you anything you want to know."

"Uh…." I said dumbly.

His eyes flickered to my mouth and seemed to darken. I wished then that I knew what he was thinking.

Then I cursed myself for wishing because he said, "I wonder what you taste like…."

SIX
RONAN

Calories: *3,500*
Workout: *3 hours in total.*
Porridge: *Cannot be redeemed by dried fruit, cinnamon, or copious amounts of honey.*

Her thighs felt good in my hands—too good, actually, all shapely and soft and everything I loved about a woman.

Seeing Annie in the clothes she was wearing today, I actually hadn't recognized her for a second. The contrast between what she'd been in the last two times I'd seen her and now was striking. I kind of wished she was wearing the old clothes because seeing her like this was testing my willpower. She was all luscious curves. It was a wonder I managed to keep my hands to myself all through the meeting.

It was a relief when the others left us to talk things out alone. I knew my attention made Annie nervous, but at least now she could manage to get a few words out. Before, when her colleagues were in the room, I could tell she was having a hard time finding her voice. Her helplessness in that moment made me want to rescue her. Be her hero.

And now I was gripping her thighs, running my thumbs back and forth over the fabric of her skirt, and wishing it was her skin. In a heartbeat, I'd gone from savior to predator.

"Say again?" she asked quietly, and I repeated my previous statement.

"I said, Annie dearest, that I wonder what you taste like."

Our mouths were only inches apart, and I felt the air move when she sucked in a soft breath like she was bracing herself. We stared at one another for a long moment, trapped in silence punctuated only by the sound of our breathing. I smiled when her body moved forward by the tiniest fraction as though she was drawn to me against her better judgment.

I could kiss her now.

Shifting in her seat, she swallowed and finally spoke. "Isn't that kind of an intimate thing to say to a stranger?" Her tone betrayed her. I knew how to read body language, and hers was telling me that she was interested. I'd more than piqued her curiosity.

"Ah, we're not strangers, Annie," I whispered against her lips. "We've already shared a cozy elevator ride, I've cleaned your top, and you've sent me a very odd a picture of a question-mark clock. We're practically dating."

"I don't date, Mr. Fitzpatrick."

"No?" I murmured.

My thumbs were still caressing her thighs; and if she was feeling me like I was feeling her, I knew she had to be a little bit wet right now. The thought practically made me groan, and I couldn't hold back any longer.

Decision made.

Gripping her tight, I brought my mouth to hers and kissed her hungrily. When our lips met, I heard her make a tiny sound. Her body went rigid, and she wasn't reciprocating. I thought it might have been down to shock, though, because when my tongue slid past the seam of her lips, she opened them willingly and trembled against me.

My fingers dug into her thighs, and I pulled her closer. I was on fire, felt like I was melting into her. Never before had a single kiss gotten me so worked up. She tasted like chocolate and mint. Annie rocked forward, and then I felt her tongue move experimentally against mine. Of its own accord, a groan emanated from deep in my chest. When I brought my hands to her neck and massaged her throat, she whimpered. I was hard as a rock already. Her hands were fisting my shirt, almost as though she didn't know whether she wanted to push me away or pull me closer.

Then the cutest noise in the world came out of her when her stomach rumbled very loudly. Immediately, she drew away, her cheeks coloring. She could barely look me in the eye.

"Mr. Fitzpatrick, I...."

I cut her off. "It's Ronan, Annie. Call me Ronan."

She looked at me then, and we stared at one another for a long moment. I wanted to kiss her again. My heart was racing. I could still taste her.

"I can't call you Ronan...." She said this, and I didn't know if she was talking to me or herself; her fingers absentmindedly moved to her lips, touching them lightly.

"Yes, you can."

"It would be too familiar." Again, she sounded like she was speaking to herself.

"I like familiar." I inched closer.

"It would be a mistake." Her eyes were unfocused.

"Sounds like fun."

"I can't risk it...."

She was definitely speaking to herself, and the words had a sobering effect. I stilled and leaned back a bit, searching her face, remembering her earlier statement.

"Annie, why don't you date?"

I was curious. I didn't do relationships anymore, not after Brona; so I wondered if, like me, Annie had some deep-seated reason for not dating.

"Huh?" She blinked at me, dazed. She yanked her fingertips away from her mouth like she'd just realized what she was doing and shook her head.

I grinned because the kiss seemed to have made her foggy headed. "You said before that you don't date. Why is that?"

"I just don't." Her eyes fell away and then lifted back to mine like she was trying to be brave. I thought that the way she spoke in short sentences was more down to her social anxiety rather than not having more to say. It was like the words were there, but they got stuck in her throat.

"A beautiful woman like you should be dating. It's a damn shame to waste all that pretty skin." I leaned forward, her sweet lips too tempting; but her eyes flashed, and she flinched away.

She rolled her chair back and away from me. "I don't see how not dating is wasting my…skin." Annie frowned and tugged on her sleeve, sitting up straighter now and obviously trying to regain an air of professionalism. It was way too fucking late for that.

I only raised an eyebrow at her in response, at how she'd pulled away, because I knew she was playing dumb now. I stared at her, trying to figure out how we'd gone from kissing to this. I wasn't ready to talk business again, not yet—maybe never with her. Not when we'd just been wrapped around each other and I wasn't sure why we'd stopped.

A second later her stomach rumbled again, and her cheeks grew redder.

I saw my opening, and I took it. "You're hungry. Let's go get some lunch." I stood up, holding my hand out to her.

She glanced at me and then focused on my fingers. She was looking at my hand like it might bite her. "I told you I don't date."

"Somebody thinks very highly of themselves," I teased, wanting to ease the tension. "I'm not asking you on a date. This is work. We still need to finish up here, and you're clearly too hungry to continue." Obviously, I was full of shit given that I'd just been feeling her up, telling her I wondered what she tasted like, and kissing the hell out of her. But I wanted her to feel comfortable enough to spend time with me so that I could—well, so that I could get into her pants. And surprisingly, despite myself, I kind of wanted to get to know her better, too, but I refused to analyze why.

Self-consciously, she wrapped her arms around her middle, still flustered. "I can grab something here. I've got some Snickers bars in my office."

I stared at her, frowning. She mumbled something under her breath about pricks and Pepé le Pew.

"I'm not letting you eat Snickers bars for your lunch. You need real food. I'll take you to my mate's restaurant. You know Tom's Southern Kitchen?"

Her eyes widened in a weird way and lifted to mine, and there was a beat of silence. "Yes, I know it. I really like the food there," she admitted, almost reluctantly.

"Well then, how can you refuse?" I asked, still holding my hand out to her. She looked at it again, her mouth making a firm line, and then she turned and gathered her things, standing up without my assistance. She hesitated at the door, glancing at me over her shoulder. I hurried forward and opened the door for her, and she seemed surprised by the gesture.

She gave me a little glance from under her long lashes and then continued walking. I followed, liking my view of her backside as we left the offices.

"Did you drive here, Mr. Fitzpatrick?" Annie asked as we stepped into the elevator. Unfortunately we weren't alone; three other working professional types stepped onto the lift with us.

I noticed that Annie was still insisting on addressing me formally, but I wasn't going to let it get to me. Truth be told, her calling me Mr. Fitzpatrick was a bit of a turn-on. I could imagine her beneath me, submitting, begging *Mr. Fitzpatrick* for more. Just being around this woman got me all worked up, got the dirty part of my brain working overtime.

"Because if you did, I can catch a cab and meet you at the restaurant," she continued as the doors opened to the lobby, everyone filing out.

I rested a hand on her lower back and felt her flinch at the contact, her spine straightening. But then she relaxed and let me guide her through the lobby.

"No, I didn't drive today. Although I'd love to take you for a ride sometime. It'll be a real experience for you." I put a hand on her elbow just as we went through the doors and wondered if she'd picked up on the innuendo. She stopped when we got onto the street, and I saw her throat working. When she looked back at me, her gaze was heated as it moved from my eyes to my hand on her arm, and her cheeks and neck were a delightful shade of pink.

I guessed my offer to give her a ride was putting pleasant thoughts in her head.

"In the meantime," I said with forced nonchalance, trying to school my smile, "we'll catch a cab together. That way, we can share the cost." I winked, having no intention of letting her pay.

She stared at me mutely but seemed to approve of splitting the bill. I made a note of that. Despite her apparent timidity, Annie struck me as the fiercely independent type. I thought it might be a matter of pride to her never to let a man (or anyone for that matter) carry her.

Christ, I knew how to pick them.

She flagged down a taxi quickly enough and didn't protest when I slid my hand into hers to help her into the car. I sat beside her, spreading my legs wide and taking up as much room as possible. Her brow was furrowed all the while, and I rattled off the address to the driver. Gathering herself, she opened one of the folders she was carrying and began to flick through some pages.

"It'll take us a couple of minutes to reach the restaurant. We should use the time to cover some things before we get there."

I leaned closer, my arm brushing hers. "I'm all ears."

Swallowing, she ran a finger down the bullet points on the page. "So, I think we should start you off with a Twitter account. It's straightforward enough and will give you a feel for connecting with people online, engaging your audience. We can connect the Twitter to both Instagram and Tumblr."

"No, thanks. I'm not a Twatter sort of bloke."

Her lips twitched like she was trying not to smile, but then she flattened them into a stiff line. "It's Twitter. Please don't discount every idea before I've even had the chance to explain it to you, Mr. Fitzpatrick. I'm only trying to make life easier for the both of us."

The exasperated way in which she spoke made me feel bad, so I replied, "Fine. Go ahead. Tell me all about this Twatter."

"It's not...."

"I know," I interrupted, smiling warmly. "I'm only pulling your leg, hon."

She shook her head and settled her eyes back on her papers, though I had a feeling she was using them as a safety blanket as opposed to actually needing them. After all, I'd been intentionally trying to get into her personal space as much as I could since we first met.

"In a nutshell, Twitter entails sending little nuggets of information about what's going on in your life out into the world in the form of 'tweets.' Each tweet can be no longer than 140 characters. I suggest checking out the profiles of some other famous sportsmen to see how it works. It's easier to learn the ropes as you go rather than my giving you a lesson because I'll just bore you."

"Oh, Annie, you could never bore me."

Our eyes met, and she went quiet then, her lips parting like she wanted to say something but couldn't. A couple of minutes later, the taxi came to a stop.

"That'll be twelve-ninety," said the driver, and I quickly pulled out a twenty, telling him to keep the change, while Annie rummaged in her little pocket bag. I put my hand on hers to stop her, and her body went still.

"I've got this. Next round's on you."

She glanced at me, frowned, nodded, and then made her way out of the vehicle. The lunchtime rush was in full swing when we stepped inside Tom's restaurant. It wasn't a fancy place, but it was always busy; and given that it had only been open for two years, it was doing pretty well. Tom and I had gone to school together, and even back then he'd been obsessed with becoming a chef and opening his own restaurant. I don't think either of us ever expected him to end up running one of the most popular kitchens in New York, but then again, neither did we expect I'd become rugby's reluctant bad boy.

And yes, I do cringe every time I have to say that.

Placing my hand at the base of Annie's spine—this time without her flinching—I ushered her in as a waitress led us to a table and handed us two menus. Annie took the seat across from mine and didn't even open her menu to take a look.

"Not hungry anymore?" I asked, lifting a brow.

She pulled out her phone and ran her finger down the screen, her attention on her messages or whatever she was checking. "I am. I just know what I want already. I've been here before a few times."

I grinned. "Ah, I knew there was a reason I liked you."

Her new blush was minuscule, but it was definitely there. I heard Tom approach before I saw him. "Well, would you look who it is, Mr. Muscles. I hope you don't think you're getting any of that steamed broccoli bullshit again. I refuse to cook food without a taste."

I stood and patted my auburn-haired friend on the shoulder. "You'll make what I ask for."

He only snorted in response before his attention fell on Annie. "And who's this fine young lady?"

"Annie, Tom, Tom, Annie," I said, making the introductions.

Annie smiled widely, her attention no longer on her phone. In fact, she seemed overjoyed to be making Tom's acquaintance. "It's a pleasure to meet you, Tom. I eat here all the time. You're an amazing chef."

Fuck me. Was she fangirling him?

He winked, took her hand, and brought it to his mouth for a kiss, the chancer. "The pleasure is all mine." Then he turned back to me and shook his head.

"Look at you, dressed up to the 4 ½'s. Couldn't you have made more of an effort for beautiful Annie here?"

I glanced down at the jeans and T-shirt I was wearing.

"Oh, we're not on a date. I'm...."

"She's teaching me how to twatter," I interrupted.

"Sounds dirty," Tom chuckled. "Well, I'd better be getting back to the kitchen. The world can't wait any longer for my culinary genius."

He left, and Annie was still smiling at his retreating form.

"You little flirt," I declared, leaning my elbows on the table and grinning. "So, is that what it takes to bring out your coquettish side, a chef?"

Her expression quickly sobered. "I was being polite to your friend."

"Uh-huh."

The waitress returned to take our orders, and Annie asked for the jambalaya. I made a special request for mashed potatoes without the butter and cream, two steamed chicken breasts, and a raw spinach salad. Tom always liked to slag me off about my OCD meal plans; but if I wanted to reach my physical goals, then I couldn't afford to slack. Yeah, sometimes the food was boring as hell, but my nutritionist tailored my diet to fit my lifestyle perfectly.

Annie was on her phone again, so I reached across the table and touched her wrist. "Hey, I don't know about you, but in my book, it's rude to ignore someone when you're having a meal together."

Her eyes were on my hand rather than my face when she replied, "Our food hasn't arrived yet."

"That's beside the point, Annie. Put down the electronic tit for half a second, and talk to me. That's what we're here to do, isn't it?"

She set her phone down on the table, and I withdrew my hand. "I apologize, Mr. Fitzpatrick. I was emailing my assistant, Gerta—I believe you two have made one another's acquaintance via phone and email—about your Twitter account. She's going to forward you the login information alongside a tutorial on how to use the site."

"I bet that'll be riveting stuff."

She ignored my sarcastic comment and continued to detail the ins and outs of social networking. The topic bored me, but fortunately I was mesmerized by the way her mouth moved when she spoke and the soft, melodic quality of her voice. Plus, it definitely wasn't a hardship to look at her.

She'd gotten a good ten minutes of talking in when our food arrived, and then she was quiet as she ate. I found myself sitting back and watching her. Similar to when I'd spotted her with the éclair that first time, she was so completely into her food, and it was too fucking sexy. I had no idea why I found it sexy, but there you had it.

Before I met Annie, I'd never really noticed much about female eating habits—probably because my ex, Brona, ate a diet of black coffee and garden salads.

Yeah, that's right; she took her coffee black to match her heart, I mused bitterly.

"So, what's with the wardrobe change?" I asked. "Let me guess—those first two times I saw you were laundry days?"

She suppressed a smile, and I was pleased that I'd amused her.

"My boss, Joan, is trying to get me to dress more appropriately at the office. Apparently, my lack of style isn't good when dealing with...clients." She seemed a little bit distressed by this which made me think she wasn't too happy with the idea.

It irritated me because Annie was clearly a beautiful woman, and I thought Joan might be trying to capitalize on that appeal by sexing her up. Despite the fact that I wanted her in my bed, the thought of other male clients being more amenable to working with the firm because of Annie made me clench my fists under the table. My angry protectiveness was a little unexpected, but then again, I'd always hated when people who were too timid to stick up for themselves got taken advantage of.

"Don't let Joan bully you. You should only ever wear what you feel comfortable in."

My words seemed to surprise her. "It's fine. Joan's just, well, Joan."

I reached forward and took her hand in mine, and she let me. "I can have a word with her if you want, tell her to back off. Just because she's a woman doesn't mean she can't be accused of sexism in the workplace. I doubt she's ever told Ian to stop wearing those shapeless brown slacks to work just because they aren't stylish."

"That's not necessary, Ronan. I can handle Joan."

I tried not to show my surprise when she used my first name. She pulled her hand out of mine and held her chin high. I didn't push further, sensing she didn't want to talk about it anymore. Still, I was going to say something to Joan, with or without Annie's consent. Making the girl wear things she didn't want to was fucked up.

I finished my food, and the next time I looked up, I found Annie staring at me. It was unexpected because usually she went out of her way to avoid eye contact. A slow smile spread across my face.

"Having a good look, are you?" I said and ran a hand down my chest. "This is what you're missing out on, Annie. I bet you wish you'd said yes to *dinner* now." I put extra emphasis on the word to convey that, by "dinner," I did not mean dinner.

"How did you get your scars?" she blurted, completely changing the subject, and it sounded like she hadn't meant to ask the question.

I raised a brow and pointed to the one below my eye. "This one I got from falling off a horse when I was a teenager, believe it or not. The family who lived next door to me would have horses every now and again, and like the stupid shit that I was, I thought I'd have a go. Could've broken my neck."

"Ouch." She winced and then continued, "That must have been a pretty fancy place, to have horses."

Immediately, I burst out laughing.

She frowned at me. "What's so funny?"

"There's nothing fancy about where I grew up. Where I come from, horses in the countryside are fancy; whereas horses on a housing estate are there because some scumbag bought them illegally from some other scumbag, and they thought it'd be fun to go galloping around for a while."

"Oh." Her brow furrowed. "I didn't pick up on any of that from my research. From what I could gather, you come from a…." She hesitated as though she were choosing her words. "Your family was privileged."

Now it was my turn to frown. "You really need to start coming to the source for your information, Annie. That's the only way you're going to get a clear picture."

She leaned forward and clasped her hands together. "Okay then, I'm coming to the source now. Tell me about how you grew up."

"First of all, my family wasn't privileged. My ma worked her arse off to send me to school."

"But your father's family, aren't they the well-to-do type?"

I could tell she was fishing, looking for something in particular. I had no desire to talk about my father's family because they were all fucking bastards, the lot of them. And when I spoke about them, about how they'd left my ma and sister and me to starve, I typically lost my shit.

I scratched the back of my neck, a nervous gesture, and shook my head. "I don't talk about the Fitzpatricks," I said, knowing my voice was cold and steely.

Her eyebrows lifted a notch, and her gaze searched mine. I could see her curiosity, her interest, but was relieved when she let the topic drop. "Then, if you don't mind, tell me more about your childhood."

And so I did. We sat there for next half an hour, and I told her about my strange background of contrasts, attending a school for posh boys and then going home to a shithole council estate every evening. How I used to wish Ma wouldn't push me to emulate Dad's education because walking through the estate wearing that uniform every evening meant I quickly had to learn how to fight. Annie was rapt by my story, hanging on every word.

"The local kids would accuse me of thinking I was better than them, and then at school most of the students thought they were better than me. It was a joke." I shook my head at the memory.

"I'm sorry you had to go through that." Her expression had gone soft, concerned.

"Nah. Fighting is good practice on and off the field. In a match, you can't hesitate to get rough."

"It sounds violent."

"Maybe," I conceded, trying to see my childhood and the sport of rugby from her point of view. "But it's real, you know? When you fight with your fists, it's real; it's not mind games and manipulation. I don't mind the violence so much. It's insincerity, lack of honesty I have a problem with."

She nodded fervently. "Yes. Yes, precisely. Trusting people is impossible because you never know, you can never know, what their intentions truly are. Sometimes they don't even know."

"That's not what I said, Annie. Trusting people isn't impossible. I trust my ma and my sister, my family. Sometimes I didn't even know where Ma was getting the money to pay the tuition fees, but she managed it somehow. I guess now that I can give her a good life, all the struggle was worth it."

When I finished talking, she sat back and folded her hands in her lap. "You're lucky to have such a supportive mother. I'm sure she's very proud," she said and then went quiet for a long time as though lost in thought.

Trying to lighten the mood, I added, "Well, in the end, I had a good deal to do with my own success. It wasn't all Ma's doing. Careful, you'll wound my delicate male ego."

Her eyes flickered to mine, and she laughed softly. It was a gorgeous sound.

"See, I can make you laugh. I'm not so abhorrent, am I?" I murmured.

"No," she whispered. "Not abhorrent at all."

"Even with all my gruesome scars?"

Her eyes flickered over my features as though cherishing each of the rough lines, and when she spoke, she sounded distracted. "I like your scars. Your face would be too perfect without them."

"Perfect? You mean like your face?" I loved how much she was talking.

Her nose wrinkled automatically, a completely natural and genuine response to my compliment—such a refreshing display of casually honest modesty. God, she was so different from the birds I usually got with. She was fresh air. She was perfect.

She's what you need.... The thought came from nowhere, and it was sobering. This wasn't a girl I would be able to fuck and forget.

"There is nothing perfect about my face."

I cleared my throat, trying to force the teasing back into my tone. "Your lips are perfect."

"No."

"Yes."

"No." She rolled them between her teeth.

"You forget—I've kissed those lips, so now I'm an expert."

I startled her. The look on her face betrayed that she was remembering our kiss. She seemed abruptly embarrassed again. I was enjoying talking to her and her company more than I'd enjoyed being with anyone for a very long time. I didn't want her to leave yet, so I quickly changed the subject.

"But enough about your gorgeous face. I feel like I've given you a muddled view of my childhood. Growing up wasn't all about fights. There were some really good times, like the Christmas when I was fifteen. It had been a tight year for us because Ma lost one of her jobs at a café in town. She always put paying for my schooling first, so we ended up eating beans on toast most nights. I felt bad because my sister, Lucy, went without just so that I could go to a fancy school. A couple of months previously, I'd started working a paper route, and I'd saved up almost all the money I earned. Then, the day before Christmas Eve, I went shopping. I bought Ma a bottle of her favorite perfume, and I got Lucy a jewelry-making set she'd been wanting all year. Then I went to the supermarket and spent every last cent I had on the fanciest food I could find."

Annie was again absorbed in my story, her eyes large and interested. "What did you get?"

"All kinds of things. I swear to God, I felt like Willy fucking Wonka when I got home, loaded down with bags full of treats. And the look on Lucy's face when she saw all the chocolate—I'll never forget it. Although, the problem was, when you're used to so little, your stomach doesn't really know how to deal with indulgence. We both ended up lying on the living room floor with stomachaches, and we hadn't even eaten that much." I chuckled.

Annie was nodding like she agreed, a smile on her face. "That's so true! I remember this one time a family brought me to dinner at this really fancy restaurant and told me I could order whatever I wanted on the menu. I planned on eating every last crumb of all four courses, but by the time I'd gotten halfway through the second, I was way too full for anything else. I went home all disappointed in myself."

I looked at her curiously. "A family? You mean, *your* family?"

It took her a moment to answer, and she wouldn't make eye contact when she did. "Oh, uh…it was just a, uh, a friend's family." For some reason, I had a hard time believing that answer, and I couldn't pinpoint why. She turned to the side and pulled a credit card out of her pocket, avoiding my gaze.

First, there was definitely something off with her explanation; I would have to press her on this issue later. And second, she had her shit in bucketfuls if she thought I was letting her pay.

"The meal's on the house. Tom lets me eat here for free," I lied.

Her brows shot right up into her forehead. "Really?"

"Uh-huh."

"Wow, I'm actually jealous." She put her card away, and then it seemed our little heart-to-heart was over because she was all business again. "Okay, well, I need to be getting back to the office now. Please check your email when you get home, and Gerta will be in touch with more information over the next few days."

She stood, and so did I, blocking her path out of the restaurant. "Why Gerta?" I asked, voice low. "Why not you?"

"I'm…it's just that I don't usually work directly with clients, Mr. Fitzp—"

I put my finger on her lips before she could finish the sentence, and she went utterly still. "What will it take to get you to call me Ronan all the time, huh?"

She inhaled deeply and then took a step back so that I was no longer touching her. She leaned forward as I retreated but then caught herself.

"I can't call you Ronan all the time. It would be unprofessional."

"But you want to. You'd like very much to call me Ronan all the time."

Her large eyes settled on my lips and then dropped to my neck. "We have a business relationship. What I want is immaterial."

"Not to me. I'd like to give you everything you want."

Annie's gaze jumped to mine, and she blurted her next question like she hadn't really meant to ask it. "Why?"

"You're very real, Annie. I like that you're without pretense. I like that you're both smart and sexy as hell without a lot of fuss. I like who you are."

"You don't know that. I could be terribly fussy. You don't know me."

I felt my mouth hook to the side. "Then tell me."

There seemed to be a conflict in her eyes, and I knew she was struggling to remain reserved. I could have killed to know what she was thinking.

At last, she glanced away. "As I said, Mr. Fitzpatrick, Gerta will be in touch." Her voice was low, soft, and trembled a little. With that, she quickly sidestepped past me and shot out of the restaurant.

I stood there, indecisive, considering whether or not I should go after her. I didn't want to be pushy, though, so I slumped back down into my seat. I decided that I should wait for her to make the next move. I had kissed her. She knew I wanted her now, so the ball was well and truly in her court. The problem with this plan was that Annie was so skittish, I could be waiting a hundred years for her to make a move.

What I needed to do was figure out a way to entice her without pushing. Pulling out my phone, I found a new email from my sister, Lucy, telling me about her day. There was another from Gerta with all the Twitter info, but I thought that could wait until tomorrow.

When I got home, I worked out for a while and then ate dinner. I was lonely, and my fingers itched with the urge to call up Annie. It would have been pointless, though, because Gerta was always the one to answer, and Annie was always conveniently busy. That evening my phone pinged with an email alert, and I almost didn't even bother to check. Being as bored and lonely as I was, though, I found myself having a look eventually.

What I found surprised the shit out of me. The Socialmedialite had decided to reply to my last message, and it was nothing like what I expected.

March 13
Ronan,
Can I call you Ronan? Ronan, you need an intervention. Sorry in advance that this email is so long.

I'm going to be blunt: you need to chill out, Ronan. Relax. You are seriously overreacting. Take a step back, and really, really think about what's actually going on here. Since you like numbered lists, I will use that format.

1. Being featured on my blog—especially how I featured you on my blog—is not a bad thing. It's a good thing. You could have used it to send me an email to highlight a charity near and dear to your heart; instead, you sent me hate mail. :-
2. You should know better than to email random, faceless bloggers. I could be a 67-year-old shut-in, male, ex-postal worker in the Bronx with a penchant for ginger cats. I could be a vindictive nut. What if I'd taken your email and posted it online? That would have made you look completely crazy and added to your woes.
3. I'm not going to post your email online because I'm not a nut, and you seem like (despite your short temper) a nice person, if perhaps a little too honest and earnest about your feelings. Sometimes it's best to keep your feelings to yourself. You don't need to share what you're feeling every time you're feeling it. Keeping your emotions circumspect will keep you from getting hurt by the cruelty that is most people.
4. You need to relax about all this media bullshit. Do as the song says and Let. It. Go. Just, let it go. Focus on the positive, and IGNORE THE NEGATIVE. Sorry for shouting at you, but—like I said—from the research I've done about you, you seem like a nice person.
In summary, let me know if you want me to highlight any charity in particular, never send emails to people you don't know personally, share your thoughts and feelings only with those you trust, and let go of the negative, focus on the positive.
I sincerely hope you take my advice.
All the best, The Socialmedialite

The first time I read it, I was angry. The second time, my anger slowly began to deflate because, although she was coming across a little bit high and mighty, I could also see that she was trying to be kind, and I didn't know how to handle that. She had given me advice. Good advice. Under normal circumstances, I would've left our correspondence where it stood. But it was late, and I was lonely for company.

I was homesick, but at the same time, I couldn't go back yet. There were too many bad memories there, too many painful feelings. And Brona was there. I didn't want to be in the same country as her, not yet anyway. It was sad, but I think I would have replied to the Devil himself right then, I was so desperate for someone to talk to. I wanted it to be Annie, but I'd settle for this online blogger.

March 13
Dear Socialmedialite,
Thank you for your advice. You didn't deserve to bear the brunt of my anger. It was simply a case of bad timing. When I saw your article, I had been holding my tongue for weeks, allowing people to write lies about me and never once fighting back.

I guess you're not as bad as I made out, are you?
Believe it or not, I am trying to let it go. In fact, I'm in what you would call media training at the moment. So this is progress, yes? It's boring as fuck, but at least I'm trying.
Regards,
Ronan Fitzpatrick
P.S. Are you really a 67-year-old ex-postal worker shut-in from the Bronx? Because that visual is totally killing my buzz. I'm imagining you as a sexy librarian dominatrix type. I don't care if you're not. Picturing you that way is what makes me happy, so you'll just have to live with it.
P.P.S. Any charity for disadvantaged children works for me.

I knew my response was overly friendly and personal, flirtatious even. What was I on? I was feeling reckless and hit "send" before thinking it through; then I regretted it. I went back and forth on this until I saw a new message come up in my inbox.

Ronan,
Feel free to visualize whatever you like. It doesn't change the fact that I have a scruffy beard, beer belly, and a gigantic tattoo of a topless mermaid on my arm.
SML

I laughed and immediately hit reply.

SML,
Just out of curiosity, what cup size is the mermaid?
Ronan

I went and made my night time protein shake. When I returned to my laptop twenty minutes later, I saw her reply.

Go to bed, Ronan.

And so I did.

SEVEN
ANNIE

The Fake-out: *When the photographer pretends to be taking a picture of one thing (perhaps a group of people or a tourist attraction) but is instead taking a picture of something or someone else.*
Best for: *National monuments, locations of interest/note.*
Do not use: *If there is nothing interesting nearby.*

The first gift arrived in the afternoon on March 14th.
 When the building concierge called, I was still in my pajamas.
 "Ms. Catrel, it's Tony from downstairs. Sorry to call but you got a special delivery, and the guy here won't let me sign for it."
 "Oh.... Are you sure it's for me?"
 "Yep. It says 'Annie Catrel' on the front."
 "Um...hmm." I frowned, not sure what to do. I didn't know anyone, not really. I had no friends in real life. Though I had some online friends and colleagues with whom I was friendly as The Socialmedialite, none of them knew who I really was or how to contact me, let alone where I lived.
 "Do you want me to escort him to your apartment? Or do you want to come down here?"
 "I guess I'll come down."
 "Okay. Sorry to bother you."
 "No problem, Tony. 'Bye."
 I stared at the phone for a few seconds after clicking off and then rushed to dress in jeans, flip-flops, and a T-shirt, pulling my hair into a ponytail.
 Downstairs I found Tony glaring unhappily at a courier who was holding a

medium-sized box. I noted the man—really, a teenager by the looks of him—was wearing a T-shirt with a logo that read *Tea and Sympathy* over the left breast.

"Annie Catrel?" he asked.

"Yes." I glanced at the young man then at Tony.

"Here, this is for you." The courier held out the box and placed it in my reluctant grip.

"Do I need to sign something?"

"No. I just had to make sure I gave it to you directly." He gave me a boyish smile that told me that he'd enjoyed ruffling Tony's feathers and then turned on his heel and walked out before I could question him further.

I gave Tony a compassionate look then escaped back up to my apartment. Once safely inside, I considered the package only briefly before cutting it open. Inside I found a glass-topped tea box filled with delicate little hand-filled and -labeled bags of tea. The box was teak or some other beautiful, rich wood. The teas ranged from Earl Grey to a special Tea and Sympathy blend.

I marveled at the lovely little pouches, smelling each. Soon I found I was smiling with wonder. I searched the box for some note as to who had sent it and then turned my attention back to the package it came in. At the bottom of the cardboard box was a card. It read:

Dear Ms. Catrel,
I hope this makes you hot.
Warmest regards, Ronan Fitzpatrick

My mouth fell open at the cheeky, albeit very succinct, note. I couldn't help it. I laughed.

He was…he was so…he was such an unabashed flirt! And yet the tea was such a thoughtful gift. The fact that it was so perfect for me, something I would have wanted but never would have purchased for myself, gave me such a forceful buzz of delight.

Despite myself and my carefully honed instincts to never want or expect anything from anyone, I promptly went to the kitchen and put the kettle on for tea.

I also wanted to say thank you, but reaching out to Ronan as Annie Catrel could only lead to trouble. Therefore, as I waited for the pot to boil, I shot him a quick email from The Socialmedialite.

March 14
2:14 p.m.
Dear Ronan,

I see that you're on Twitter now. I followed you; be sure to follow me back so we can interact.
Also, I came across an article on online engagement. It's entitled "Social Media Campaigns for the Beginner." The link is in the attached document. I hope this helps.
-The Socialmedialite

It wasn't a thank you, per se, but it was something small I could do to help him. In the karmic scheme of things, it would have to suffice. I hit "send" just as I heard the kettle whistle.

The tea didn't make me hot. But it did warm me up, and it did make me smile.

* * *

March 15
12:32 a.m.
SML,
Thanks for the article. It was enlightening, but this still feels like a monumental waste of time. I'm sitting on my arse in front of a computer, staring at twatter, instead of actually doing something.
-R

March 15
12:45 a.m.
Ronan,
It's Twitter, not "twatter."
Twatter sounds like a very specialized vibrating tool of some sort. ;-)
-SML

March 15
12:52 a.m.
Twitter, twatter, fudder, motherfucker, I don't care what it's called.
I could be interacting with real people instead of this pretend interacting. How do you do this all the time? I would lose my mind.
-Ronan

March 15
7:18 a.m.
Dear Ronan,
I honestly enjoy it. I love interacting with people online. I feel like it's a safe haven where people are free to be who they really are.
-SML

March 15
8:15 a.m.
Explain, please.
Why can't you be who you really are at a doughnut shop or in the park? Why do you have to be online? I'm myself everywhere I go. It's not limited to a pretend world created by nerdy perverts masturbating in their parents' basements. You know the Internet was invented by porn-mongers, right?
This shite makes no sense.

* * *

THE SECOND GIFT arrived mid-afternoon on March 15. This time, Tony didn't call. He just showed up at my door with the gift in tow. Rather, I should say *gifts* in tow.

"There's a lot more downstairs." Tony gave me a confounded look then surveyed the inside of my apartment. "I don't think they're going to fit."

I glanced between him and the five men behind him, all with armfuls of flowers. Daisies, roses, lilies, sunflowers, irises—every kind of commercially available stem was represented. I gaped at the scene then turned my stunned expression back to Tony.

"What-who-where—"

"There's a note." He clumsily pulled a card from his pants pocket, dropping a magnificent arrangement of peonies and hydrangeas.

I picked up the felled flowers then took the note, ripping it open and scanning the contents. Of course, it was from Ronan. It read:

Dearest Annie,
Roses are red.
Violets are blue.
I'm using my hand
But I'm thinking of you.
- Ronan
P.S. Just to clarify, I'm using my hand to write this note…get your mind out of the gutter.

I choked and then choked a startled laugh. Then I choked again as the hallway full of flowers came back into focus.

Ronan Fitzpatrick was completely crazy.

"What do you want us to do?" Tony shifted uneasily, his black eyebrows pulling together in a plain display of anxiety.

"Um...." I struggled, glancing from left to right as I searched my mind. It was no good. Everywhere I looked, I saw flowers. I squeezed my eyes shut so I could think. "Just—just give me a minute...."

Tony was right. Just the armfuls of flowers in the hall would never fit in my cozy little apartment. Plus, it would be such a waste, having a jungle of flowers to myself. Really, they needed to be shared....

"Wait! I have an idea." I opened my eyes and gripped Tony's forearm. "Do you think there is any way we could have these sent to Memorial Sloan-Kettering? Distributed to the patients?"

He nodded thoughtfully, slowly at first but then with more conviction. "Yeah, yeah. I can make that happen."

"Let me know how much it costs. I'll be happy to reimburse you."

He gave me a relieved smile. "Thanks, Ms. Catrel. I'll let you know." Then he turned back to his compatriots. "Okay, guys, back down stairs. We're sending these to Sloan-Kettering. Come on."

I watched them march back to the elevator. It wasn't until the doors closed behind them that I realized I was still clutching the peonies and hydrangeas to my chest.

* * *

March 15
10:55 p.m.
Dear Ronan,
LOL! @ "porn-mongers."
You are very funny.
In a way, your last email is correct, but in another more accurate way, you are wrong.
The online environment is unique, and that's a very good thing.
Rather than be judged by what they look like or their ability to speak in front of a crowd, people are judged by the merit of their ideas and words.
-SML

March 16
12:02 p.m.
Dear Slovenly Miss. Lazybones,
People should be judged by what they look like—not 100%, but it should be taken into account. If you work hard on yourself, take care of yourself, then it's a reflection of the person within.
People are more than just their brains. Like it or not, assuming a person has control over their personal appearance, the body is just as important.
If you ignore your body, you are ignoring an essential part of yourself.

-Ronan

* * *

THE THIRD GIFT arrived late in the afternoon on March 16.

I was just returning from my walk in Central Park when Tony called to me before I could make it to the elevator.

"Ms. Catrel! Wait—wait a moment." He jogged over. I'd never seen him jog before.

"Oh, hi. Thank you again for your help with the flowers yesterday."

"No problem at all, Ms. Catrel." He made me a little polite bow then glanced over his shoulder. I followed the path of his eyes and found a very pretty lady in a very nice suit walking toward us. "So, this lady here"—Tony lowered his voice and threw a thumb over his shoulder— "she's from Cartier, and she—"

"Ms. Catrel?" the woman asked with a wide smile. "Are you Ms. Annie Catrel?"

I nodded, shrinking back a little. She was so very pretty, sleek even. Her makeup was impeccable in a way I'd never mastered, even when I'd dabbled with eye shadow and lipstick in the past. She was also very tall, with very black hair, and very blue eyes, and very white, straight teeth.

"This is for you." She reached into an attaché case and withdrew a red velvet box, pushing at me until my hands automatically lifted to grab it.

"For me? What is it?"

She gave me a very nice smile. "Compliments of Mr. Fitzpatrick."

Then she turned and left, her heels clicking and echoing on the stone floor.

I glanced from Tony to the box. He shrugged then sighed, "So…this guy, this Mr. Fitzpatrick, is he going to keep sending you gifts? I mean, not that it's any of my business. But if he is, we should maybe set up some kind of system for receivership if you're not in the building."

I shook my head. "Sorry, Tony. I honestly don't know what's going on."

"Really?" He sounded both skeptical and amused. "Ms. Catrel, let me spell it out for you: I think you're being wooed."

My eyebrows jumped, causing Tony to chuckle. Then he turned and left me, too.

I gripped the box tighter and made my way to the elevator, feeling a buzzing sense of unease. In my hands was a velvet box from Cartier, hand-delivered by the store, compliments of Ronan Fitzpatrick.

Back in my small living room, I placed the box on the coffee table and went to my room to change. I decided that, whatever it was, I had to send it back. Part of me didn't even want to open it. What was the use of opening it when I couldn't keep it?

But curiosity eventually overcame the better part of valor. I sat on the couch, took a deep breath, and then opened the box.

There was a note. I picked it up. Beneath the note was a delicate gold necklace with an attached gold and diamond pendant. It was breathtaking. The pendant was comprised of a series of intricate knots; I recognized them as Celtic, but I had no idea what they meant. A larger diamond was set very tastefully within the center of the knot; as well, several smaller stones were set in highlighted relief along the outside border.

It was really quite magnificent. Refined, understated, subtle, and yet must have been outrageously expensive. I quickly closed the box, setting it back on the table, then turned my attention to the note.

It read:

Dear Annie,
I saw this today, and it reminded me of you. Do not even think about trying to give it back to me; I'll not take it. You'll have to donate it to charity if you don't want it. It is freely given and comes with no strings attached. Though, if you decide to mode

l it for me while naked, I'll not complain.
   -Ronan

* * *

March 16
   7:30 p.m.
   Dear Ronan,
   I cede your point about the physical being an important part of self; it's important to be healthy, I agree. But I don't understand spending hours primping or spending hundreds of dollars on clothes that go out of style after two months. Extremes—in either direction, ignoring the physical or giving it too much importance—I think are counterproductive and dangerous to overall well-being.

   Though, you must admit, in-person interactions are fleeting. But online the interaction is preserved (basically) forever. Nothing is fleeting because it can be revisited anytime you wish.

   Give it a chance!
   - Slovenly Miss. Lazybones

March 16

11:15 p.m.
Dear Secretly Miss. Lonelyheart,
If you want to preserve in-person interactions, all you need to do is record them…. I've done this in the past, each time with stellar results.

It sounds to me like, as much as I need lessons in social media, you need lessons on how to truly live. When's the last time you experienced any kind of in-person interaction that left you breathless or excited? Nothing online can come close to experiencing the touch of another person, a kiss, a caress—or the anticipation of these things.

Nothing in this make-believe world comes close.

I would send you a link to an article on the subject, but that would really undermine my point. You need to actually experience it. Take your own advice and give it a chance.

-Ronan

EIGHT
ANNIE

March 17
1:14 a.m.
Dear Ronan,
I'm not ignoring your last message, but I'm writing you now because I wanted to be the one to tell you before you found out from someone else. This article (attached) hasn't been published yet, but it will be in tomorrow's newspaper, and shortly after that all over the gossip sites. As you read it, you'll see that your ex-girlfriend is accusing you of domestic violence and years of emotional abuse. I have a friend at the paper who sends me celebrity stuff before it's in print. Please don't react! You should probably make a few benign posts on Twitter today, maybe about your boring diet (take pictures) or about your friend Tom's restaurant. I will also be happy to tweet back and forth with you about something related to your charity.
Just...don't react to it. She sounds completely crazy. If you react, you'll be playing right into her hands.
Sincerely, Secretly Miss. Lonelyheart

My internal debate lasted from the time I went to bed at 1:30 a.m. until I awoke from a fitful sleep at 7:13 a.m.
Then it lasted two minutes more. I could stay at home and work and ignore my worry about Ronan and his spiteful ex-girlfriend, wait to be contacted by the office once the story was printed; or I could go into work, break the news to Joan, and have him called in for a damage-control meeting.
Ultimately, I gave into the urge to seek out Ronan. I justified it to myself by

recalling that he wasn't just any client. We'd been partnered, and Joan wanted me to be more present in the office. Plus, I could use it as an opportunity to return the necklace.

When I arrived at the office Monday morning, the streets were already crowded with people setting up for New York's St. Patrick's Day parade. I wasn't scheduled to be in the office until Wednesday and may have been checking both my work account and my Socialmedialite email account obsessively on the way in, hoping he would email one of us. I was also checking his Twitter feed, hoping he didn't plan to retaliate publically.

As soon as I arrived, I went to Joan's office. Her assistant told me she'd arrived an hour ago but was currently in a meeting. I asked that she call me as soon as she had a free moment and then I retreated to my office.

I was able to get some work done. Focusing on the beginnings of an action plan to counter Brona O'Shea's propaganda was a good way to channel my restless energy, but I continued to check my emails.

At 9:00 a.m. on the dot, my cell phone chimed. I grabbed it and saw that the number listed was the phone line from the main conference room.

I stood as I answered it. "Uh, hello?"

"Annie, are you online yet?" Joan's voice arrived with a slight echo; I knew I was on the speakerphone in the conference room.

"Yes, I'm online."

"Good. Listen, the *Times* is running a story today on Ronan Fitzpatrick, and it's...well, I'll let you read it. It'll be all over the place by this afternoon. The point is we need to come up with a plan. I'll need you in the office today."

"Oh, well—"

She cut me off. "You should know I'm sitting here with Rachel, Becky, Gerta, and Ian. Mr. Fitzpatrick is on his way. How soon can you get here?"

I cleared my throat, a ripple of excitement running through me at the news that Ronan was already on his way. I'd be spending time with him today. I wished it were under different circumstances, but I couldn't deny that I was excited to see him. My hand smoothed down the length of my knee-length black dress. Like the other clothes Joan had purchased, it fit me like it was made for my body yet was completely appropriate for the office. I'd paired it with a cropped pink cardigan and black velvet heels.

"I saw the article early this morning. I've put together a basic action plan and can send it to the team. Basically, my take on the situation is that we need to pair him up as soon as possible. We need an appropriate and steady date for him, and we need to step up the public appearances, both with the date and without."

"I agree." This came from Ian. "Those were my sentiments exactly. We need to pair him with someone the media will love, someone with credibility and the opposite of Brona O'Shea, and give them plenty of romantic photo-ops. A new love interest will bury this story. We're going to have to scrap the earlier plan for multiple partners, at least for now."

I swallowed a sudden bitterness in my throat and tried to focus on the plan, the good of the client. "Ronan is interested in charities for disadvantaged children. I know the program director for *Sports Stars*, and I know she'd love to have Ronan for events." This was mostly true. The Socialmedialite knew the program director for Sports Stars. Either way, the charity focused on pairing sports celebrities with at-risk youth, and The Socialmedialite had orchestrated several introductions in the past. The program director owed me a favor. The group was great for photo-ops and positive press.

"We need a final list of candidates by the end of the day, Ian." Joan's voice held an edge, and I could almost see his pained expression. "And no actresses or models or spoiled, rich brats. We don't want any drama. Profile women in sports or a professional type who is looking for career advancement. We need someone serious, so this Brona will look frivolous in comparison. Maybe check with the district attorney's office, see if they have any up-and-coming legal stars with an eye on politics. But she's got to be gorgeous because no one will care if she isn't gorgeous."

"So a smart, serious, gorgeous professional woman who doesn't mind pretending to date a foul-mouthed, obnoxious Irish rugby player whose trashy ex-girlfriend is accusing him of domestic violence…did I get that right?" Ian's sarcasm was so heavy I wondered that we weren't all crushed by the weight of it.

"Just get it done, Ian. We need someone now." Then Joan turned her attention back to me, and her voice softened. "Listen, Annie. I really need you in the office when Mr. Fitzpatrick arrives. If you can head him off and assure him we have a plan, I think it will go a long way toward easing the Rugby League International people. The story broke last night in Ireland. It was all over the evening papers, and to say that they're having a meltdown is an understatement."

"Yes." I nodded, pacing my office. "Yes, I can do that. I'll speak with him when he arrives."

"Thanks, Annie. Send out your action plan to the team, and Ian will fill in the blanks for the candidates," Joan said and then clicked off the call.

I pulled the phone away from my ear and scrolled through my Socialmedialite email account again, looking for a message from Ronan. Still nothing.

My stomach growled just then, and I realized with some fascination that I'd skipped breakfast. This was highly unusual. I loved breakfast food. I especially loved waffles. I never got twisted up and distracted by client drama; but then, I'd never kissed a client before, and I'd never emailed back and forth using actual words instead of infographics.

I allowed myself to think about the kiss. My fingers drifted to my lips. I touched them, recalling the feel of his mouth against mine, his hands on my legs, my fingers fisting in his shirt, the way he smelled, how he tasted.

The kiss.

My body warmed at the memory, and I leaned against my desk because my knees felt a little wobbly and—double doughnut dammit—that man was an excellent kisser.

But more than that, we'd connected in some rudimentary way last Thursday over lunch. Hearing about his childhood, listening to him speak, how open he was, how guileless and willing to trust…he made me want to trust. I hadn't wanted to trust anyone since I foolishly entrusted my virginity to the high school quarterback on prom night. The night had been so stereotypical in its tragedy and disappointment, thinking about it now made me both laugh and cringe.

I'd been so stupid.

People couldn't be trusted.

Waffles, however, never let me down or dumped me the morning after. I could count on waffles.

I decided all at once that I needed waffles…or an éclair…and peppermint tea. Maybe I would message WriteALoveSong and see what she was up to…

I grabbed my black clutch wallet and bolted for the door, not really paying attention to the occupants of the hallway as I made my way to the elevators. I pressed the call button, then checked the messages on my phone again. Peripherally, I was aware of the *ding* of the elevator. Without glancing away from my email, I took a single step toward the lift.

"Annie."

I stopped short, recognizing Ronan's voice immediately, and glanced up just as he stopped directly in front of me. He was coming off the elevator and he looked…awful. He looked upset and irritated and frayed. His hair was wet, but he hadn't shaved. The dark shadow of his stubble mirrored the worry shadows under his eyes. He was wearing a white T-shirt and jeans and his black leather jacket.

He looked just as yummy as an éclair but with an aura of dark vulnerability that made me want to cuddle him and make him tea and kiss him a lot. These feelings were alarming as I'd never done these things for someone, nor had anyone—well, since I was six—ever done them for me.

"Ronan…." I breathed, automatically reaching for his hand and searching his gloomy expression. "Are you okay?"

He grimaced. "You saw it, then? You saw the story?"

I nodded as he exhaled an audible breath.

"Don't worry, we're going to—"

"It's all lies! I would never do that; I would never fucking—"

I covered his mouth, holding his gaze for a beat, then walked him backward onto the elevator, grateful that we were the only ones in the lift.

When the doors slid shut, I lowered my hand and pressed the button for the lobby. He caught my fingers, and his eyes never left mine.

"You have to know. I would never do those things. I would never hurt a woman. I would never lock someone away in a room and…fuck, she is so fucking crazy!" His growly exclamation and expletives betrayed his obvious frustration. He looked like he wanted to tear something or someone apart, but I reflected that big, strong, powerful guys like him must always look that way when they're angry. His body was made for force and action, but that didn't mean he would actually do anything.

Except, my brain reminded me, *he did beat the crap out of his teammate and does regularly beat the crap out of guys on the rugby field….*

I squeezed his hand. "You're right—she is crazy. But don't worry. We have a plan."

He frowned at me, giving me a sideways glance laced with suspicion. "What kind of plan?"

Before I could answer, the doors parted and announced our arrival to the lobby. He looked away from me, and I saw that his eyes were rimmed with sorrow and something else, something like helplessness.

Maybe it was because of our amazing kiss last week, or maybe it was because of the emails he'd been trading with me as The Socialmedialite, but I felt protective of him, possessive. I wanted to keep him safe; I wanted to cheer him up. But I was clumsy at real-life interactions. I didn't know what to do, what to say, how to be anything other than quiet, because when I spoke my thoughts, disaster and weirdness were usually close behind.

Acting on instinct, because I wanted to give him comfort, I tugged him out of the elevator, slid my hand into the crook of his elbow, and walked close to his side.

"Come with me, and I'll tell you about it. I haven't had breakfast yet, and I'm starving."

He glowered at the glass doors leading to the street, the set of his jaw stern and surly. "I've already eaten."

"Then you can watch me eat." After I finished making the suggestion, I grimaced, and my cheeks warmed. That sounded really strange. Why would he want to watch me eat?

He moved just his eyes to mine. They were almost completely hidden beneath his thick, dark lashes, and I was pleased to see his expression soften with curiosity. "What are you going to eat?"

"Uh, I was thinking about an éclair." My words were quietly spoken because they were somewhat embarrassing.

The first time he saw me, I was eating an éclair. He was probably going to consider me obsessed with éclairs, which was true. I was obsessed with éclairs.

His mouth crooked to the side. "Yeah, okay. That might be fun."

His answer was surprising; his assent sounded completely genuine, like he actually thought watching me eat would be fun. I couldn't help my small answering smile.

"Okay. Good."

"Good." He grinned, his eyes moving over my face.

I was so busy being lost in his truly magnificent bone structure and gently curving smile and warm eyes that reminded me of chocolate fondue and chocolate ganache and chocolate everything that I tripped as we exited the building.

"Gah—shit!" I lurched forward, stumbling and reaching out with my free hand.

Ronan caught me before I could make a cement face-plant and turned me toward him; he held my upper arms to keep me steady.

"Whoa, are you all right?"

I nodded, scowling at my clumsiness. "Sorry, I'm just obviously.... I'm not good at walking...sometimes."

"Well, you can't be good at everything," he teased.

I felt my scowl give way, and I rolled my eyes. "Yes, of course it would be too much to expect that I'd be a proficient walker."

"Luckily for you, I'm quite gifted at walking. Here," he said, sliding his arm around my shoulders and pressing me close to his side, "if I hold you like this, then you can share some of my mad walking skills."

I scrunched my face, my arms feeling awkward at my sides as we walked in this position. I tried tucking my hand into my dress pocket, but that just made me elbow him in the stomach.

"What are you doing?" he asked. "Why are you wiggling around like that?"

"Where do I put my arm? It feels weird just hanging here."

He threw his head back and laughed. Eventually he glanced at me as his fit of humor tapered off. He looked at me like I was adorable and hilarious and enchanting. It made me feel less and more awkward at the same time.

"Put it around me, like this." He pulled my arm around his middle so that my hand rested on his opposite hip. A heated flush spread from my chest to my throat at the way I was touching him. It felt entirely too intimate, like we were embracing while we walked.

Ronan was so strong and solid and *male*. I tried to swallow away the dichotomously wonderful and alarming sensations being so close to him elicited. My stomach twisted and fluttered. I tried to even my breathing and failed.

"What's wrong now?" he asked. I found him watching me with narrowed eyes.

"Nothing."

"Yes, something is wrong. You're breathing funny, and you're really tense. If you can't loosen up, we're going to stop here, and I'll make you relax by giving you a back massage...or an orgasm."

I snorted a surprised laugh and then covered my mouth with the hand that wasn't currently touching his hip.

His answering laugh—a shocked bark likely caused by the sound of my inelegant snort—made me laugh even harder.

"What is that sound? Are you snorting?" He squeezed my shoulders as we crossed the street, his voice thick with amusement.

I snorted again—because when I laugh, I snort like the love child of a pig and an alligator unless I hold my nose, in which case I sound like I've got a terrible case of the hiccups—which made him laugh even harder. Soon we were in a perpetual laughter loop, and we had to stop in front of a bike shop to catch our breath. I couldn't look at him without bursting into a snorting fit of giggles, so I kept my eyes on the sidewalk until he pulled me forward and hugged me to him.

I was paralyzed by my own merriment and didn't push him away; instead, I buried my head against his chest, gripping the lapels of his jacket and enjoying the rolling, rumbly cadence of his laughter as it receded. He had a great laugh, a sexy laugh. My laugh was the mating call of the Yeti.

"You have…." He paused, sniffed, lifted a hand to wipe his eyes, and waited until I looked up at him. "Ah, God…." He shook his head, smiling at me. I knew he was trying to collect himself, so he wouldn't dissolve into another bout of uncontrollable hilarity. "You have the most astonishing laugh I've ever heard."

I let my forehead fall to his muscular chest and pressed my lips together; my words were muffled when I finally trusted myself to speak. "This is why I don't laugh around people. I have the worst laugh. It's the worst."

"It's wonderful."

I tilted my chin upward and glared at him. "It sounds like the sound a pig would make if it were having sexual relations with an alligator."

Ronan threw his head back, and—surprise, surprise—he laughed.

I allowed myself a smile but swallowed my giggle before it could bubble beyond my lips.

"Come on." I tugged on him. "I'm hungry, and we still have two blocks to walk."

"Good." He pulled me backward against him then threaded my hand around his waist. He placed it on his hip and me once more under his arm. "That'll give me time to tell you some of my favorite knock-knock jokes."

*　*　*

I DIDN'T REALIZE that I was relaxed until I'd already been relaxed for over an hour. True to his word, Ronan had fun watching me eat, maybe too much fun.

The bakery was quite small and had only two tables, both pressed up against the glass storefront and overlooking the sidewalk. He claimed the only vacant table while I ordered my food. I joined him, sitting across from him like it was the most natural thing in the world, while he picked up a terrible knock-knock joke where he'd left off before we'd separated for me to order.

I ignored his eyes, which were dancing with challenge, daring me to laugh, and instead set a cup of water in front of him, arranged my tea, and then stuffed my face with the sweet, soft, creamy éclair.

I might have moaned. I know I closed my eyes while I chewed. It was…it was heaven with cream filling.

When I opened my eyes, I found Ronan watching me. His elbows were on the table, and he was leaning slightly forward, sitting straight in a chair that looked too small for his athletic form. One of his thumbs was brushing against his lips, and his eyes were trained on my mouth like it had just cured cancer.

I stiffened. "Do I have something on my mouth?"

When he spoke he sounded a little dazed. "Not yet.…"

I lifted an eyebrow at him as his eyes refocused on mine; they were hot and…interested. Almost predatory. Actually, they were definitely predatory. Definitely.

I swallowed unnecessarily, my stomach fluttering, and I looked at him sideways. "What?"

"I could watch you eat that all day."

I lifted my eyebrow higher but was silent.

"It's true. I could. We should do that. I should have you over to my place. I'll provide the éclairs, now that I know where you get them, and you provide the entertainment."

"No, please, no. Based on your gift-giving track record, you'd buy every pastry north of 59th Street."

"Liked the flowers, did you?" His grin reminded me of a very wicked and very pleased little boy. "I like the idea of filling up your place with treats."

"Wow, that's a very tempting offer." I endeavored to sound both unimpressed and demure, but really, an apartment full of éclairs was right up my proverbial alleyway of bliss.

"But you should know.…" Ronan leaned close and glanced over his shoulder like he was making sure no one else was listening. I sipped my tea and tried to look bored as he continued, "You'll have to do it naked."

I spit out my tea.

I spit out my tea right in Ronan's face.

It was horrible. I was horrible, even though it wasn't at all purposeful.

A terrible moment of shocked and mortified paralysis passed where I could only belatedly cover my mouth and gape at him and what I'd done. Meanwhile, after his initial flinch of surprise, he sat motionless, his eyes closed and my warm tea all over his face and white shirt.

"OhmygodIamsosososorry!" I jumped up, grabbed at the napkin dispenser, and pulled out at least ten paper napkins in quick succession; then—because I didn't know what else to do—I began mopping his face and neck and shirt. But I was so focused on the mess I'd created, I didn't notice where I'd placed the cup of tea until it was too late.

That's right. I knocked it over with my elbow just as he opened his eyes, and it rushed across the table, splashed on his shirt, and puddled on the front of his pants. Ronan sucked in a sharp breath then stood abruptly, his chair falling in his haste to stand, and he cursed (likely because the tea was still hot).

"Oh, my God!" I stepped back and away, lifted my hands to cover my face, and held perfectly still because, if I was still and silent, then I could cause no more damage. I still clutched the damp napkins.

I've always been slightly clumsy, but this was ridiculous. The trip and slight stumble earlier were more my *modus operandi*. I was always tripping over my own feet or colliding with things because I wasn't looking up. Spit-takes and drenching people with hot tea were well beyond my normal. I closed my eyes and willed myself to disappear.

Then I heard his laugh.

I opened one eye and peered through my fingers; I found him leaning against the window, holding his stomach, laughing uncontrollably. I watched him for a few moments, wondering if he was laughing because he was frustrated or because he was actually finding my abuse of him funny.

Seeing my reticence, he gave me a big smile. Shaking his head and exhaling an audible breath, Ronan looked the opposite of the furious and tortured man I'd encountered about an hour ago. He looked befuddled, yes, but he also looked merry and happy and maybe a little overwhelmed.

I dropped my hands to my sides and took a half step forward. "I am so, so sorry. I am so sorry."

He waved away my apology as the lady from behind the counter came over with a towel and asked if he was okay.

"I'm fine," he said to both her and me. He closed the distance between us and placed his hands on my upper arms. He must not have liked my expression because he dipped his chin to his chest and repeated, "Really, I'm fine. I am."

"I can't walk, and obviously I have difficulty swallowing."

He *tsked*. "That's too bad...."

My eyes widened at his statement, but my mouth dropped open when he added, "I prefer a woman who swallows, but spitting doesn't bother me much."

"Ronan!" I hit him on the chest. I had no idea when we'd crossed that line, the line where I felt comfortable hitting him for his naughty taunts, but there we were.

Another laugh rumbled from his chest, and he didn't look at all ashamed. "Oh, the tea was totally worth it. I'd take it a hundred times for the expression on your face right now."

I flattened my smile, determined not to subject him to my snort-laugh again, and surveyed his clothes. He was a mess.

"At least, I don't know, let me help you somehow...." I dabbed at his soaked shirt, quite liking how this close I could see the muscles of his chest and stomach. Distractedly, I patted the front of his pants.

"Annie...."

"I know; I remember. I'm supposed to dab, not rub." I recalled his words from our first meeting.

"Annie...."

"Am I rubbing?"

"No...but, God, I wish you would."

I stared at him for a beat, understanding the implication of his words, then groaned and closed my eyes. "You have to stop doing that. You can't say those things."

"I know you like it."

"Maybe so, but that's how you end up with tea spit in your face."

"It's not so bad."

I peeked at him, found his eyes on me, warm and appraising.

"You're a bit of a tornado, aren't you?" He said this good-naturedly, and his warm and appraising gaze turned hot and interested. "After all this, I think the least you can do is give me a kiss to make it better."

I stared at him, nonplussed. Movement over his shoulder caught my attention, and I glanced at the woman cleaning up after my mess at the table. She was watching us furtively and obviously eavesdropping on our conversation. I cleared my throat and took a step closer to him, lowering my voice so it couldn't be heard.

"How can you want me to kiss you? I've just assaulted you with my tea...twice."

"I'll take your tea assault any day...if..." —Ronan leaned forward, lowering his head but stopping just a hair's breadth from kissing me. He continued on a whisper— "...if it's followed with a kiss."

His action drove the breath from my lungs, and I felt myself swaying forward. Even tea-soaked and messy, he made my stomach flip and my heart flutter. And, dammit, he was entirely too charming, too sexy, too...glorious.

Before I could catch it, a desperate-sounding half moan, half sigh escaped my lips. He took this as permission—which, basically, it totally was—and he captured my mouth with his.

And I kissed him back.

We touched only with our mouths and tongue and teeth, and, like him, it was wonderful. He kissed like he flirted, aggressively, with complete expert abandon. My breasts felt heavy and full, and I wanted him to touch them, touch me, do something other than tease me with his mouth. But he didn't. And when I would have stepped into the kiss, he lifted his hands and caught me, holding me away. I gave a small frustrated groan and lifted my head.

He looked pleased and content.

Meanwhile, I was feeling frustrated and disoriented and hot.

He pressed his lips to mine once more and then stepped away, his delicious chocolate gaze cherishing. "I don't want to mess up that pretty dress." His tone was soft as he explained, and pointed to his tea-stained shirt.

I stared at him, feeling a little lost in Ronan Fitzpatrick and his epically warm smiles and hot kisses and scorching looks.

I was completely out of my depth. My feelings were all tangled up, and I had no right to be tangling feelings with Ronan.

Studying him now, really looking at him, I saw that—whatever we were doing, this dance we'd started—for him, this wasn't a dalliance, a quick flirtation. He was actually *interested* in me. He liked me, or at least what he knew of me.

And he deserved better, and I didn't think this because I had chronically low self-esteem. I thought this because it was the truth. I was a mess. I was inexperienced. I was a broken, control-freak hermit. My issues had issues. My hurts had hurts. I knew how to run away. I was really good at running away; I didn't know how to stay.

Nothing could happen between us. Nothing could ever happen, and the sooner he realized this truth, the better.

I didn't know what to say, so I said, "I'm so sorry."

"Stop apologizing."

"Not for the tea, but I am sorry about that."

"It's fine, no big deal."

He reached for my hand. I pulled it away, stepped back, and crossed my arms over my chest. His forehead wrinkled, betraying his confusion, and his eyes scanned me.

"Annie—"

"No, really, I'm sorry. I, we…this can't happen. The gifts, it's too much. Everything was wonderful, and your notes, they were so…and I can't tell you how much I love—but this, we, us…it just isn't ever going to happen."

His eyes narrowed on me; and I could see that he was preparing to argue, so I cut him off.

"It's because I'm a mess, okay? I'm a complete mess."

"Everyone is a mess."

"Not like me. This" —I pointed to my face— "I am crazy. I have severe abandonment issues and daddy issues and mommy issues. I'm not just shy. I'm petrified. And I don't want to change. I like my life. I like having control over everything. I don't want…." I swallowed and looked away, no longer able to meet the burning intensity of his gaze. "I don't want you."

"I know that's a lie."

"I don't want you, Ronan," I whispered harshly. "Not enough to change who I am."

We stood there in silence, and I could feel his eyes on me. I watched the rise and fall of his chest as a war within me raged. I wanted to touch him, and I wanted to never see him again.

Just when the moment grew unbearable, Ronan turned away. He shuffled to the table we'd abandoned, pulling a bill from his pocket and placing it on the table. He paused there, obviously collecting his thoughts, then walked back to me. With measured slowness, he reached for my hand.

"Ronan, don't—"

"I'm not asking you for anything. I just want to hold your goddamn hand, okay?"

My gaze flickered to his face, found his expression hard and determined. I nodded once and fit my fingers in his, ignoring the spark that traveled up my arm and the deep, fathomless swelling of want that choked my throat, making it impossible to speak.

He led us out of the bakery, down the sidewalk, across the two blocks, and back to my office building. We didn't speak, and his hold on my hand was firm but not tight. If I'd wanted to, I could have removed myself, but I didn't. When we stopped at intersections, he'd brush his thumb over my knuckles and between my fingers in a sweeping circle. The movement sent spikes of fluttering awareness to my lower belly.

But I couldn't speak, and I could barely breathe. I still had the necklace in my bag, and I was still intent on returning it; but I knew now was not the time.

He didn't let go of my hand until we were in the elevator, on our way up to the office. He stood on the opposite side of the carriage and wouldn't look at me. The fury was back, the tortured and sorrowful rim around his eyes, and I felt like the biggest jerk on the planet because I had a part in putting it there.

When the doors opened, he waited for me to exit first. I walked in front of him, trying to figure out what to say, how to move us back to a professional space and away from Annie and Ronan. We needed to be Ms. Catrel and Mr. Fitzpatrick; we needed to work together.

I paid no heed to the receptionist as I walked past, but she stopped me.

"Oh! Ms. Catrel! Mr. Fitzpatrick! They're all waiting for you in conference room two. You need to go there now, like, right now!"

I glanced at Ronan over my shoulder. His gorgeous face was marred with a scowl.

"Why?"

"It's about the pictures," she said, jumping to her feet. She looked at him, then at me, then at him again. Clearly, she expected us to know what she was talking about.

"What pictures?" he asked after a pause. "Did Brona publish pictures?"

"What? No. Not Ms. O'Shea. It's the pictures of you and Ms. Catrel from today...." The blonde receptionist *tsked* then waved us over.

I shared another wary glance with Ronan, then walked around her desk, and leaned over her shoulder to see the computer screen.

Her next words were whispered. "See, outside the building. His arm is around you, and you're laughing. And then these" —she scrolled farther down — "where you're...well, you're kissing."

"What?" Ronan flinched then joined us behind her desk.

Sure enough, clear as day, there were pictures documenting my last hour with Ronan—well, everything leading up to and including the kiss. There were no pictures of us walking back to the building. I had to wonder if they just hadn't been loaded yet.

But I couldn't think.

I couldn't process what this meant.

Dumbly, I asked, "And Joan? Joan has seen these?"

She nodded, "Oh, yes. That's why they're waiting for you in conference room two. You both need to go there right now."

I straightened, my mind a mess, and blinked at Ronan.

He appeared to be baffled but not upset. Mostly just perplexed and surprised.

Meanwhile, I was twisting my fingers together and worrying my bottom lip and trying to plan a graceful exit strategy from Davidson & Croft. There was no way, no way on a cold day in Hawaii, that I was going to keep working here. Not after that. Not after my co-workers had seen pictures of me kissing a client. I was.... It was the worst kind of unprofessional behavior.

"There you are." Joan's voice roused me from my panicked planning. I didn't even get two seconds to prepare before she was on us. "You two need to come with me."

Insinuating herself between Ronan and me, she grabbed both of our elbows and pulled us forward down the hall.

"Joan," I croaked, "I can explain."

"No need, dear. It was brilliant. You are both brilliant." She glanced at me and gave me something resembling a smile. "I'm so proud of you."

"What?" I blurted, my wide eyes moving from her to Ronan. I found him looking at her in plain confusion. He was obviously just as befuddled as I was.

"The pictures. The laughing, the hugging, the kissing. It was all brilliant, though I wish you'd talked to me before putting your plan in action. But it's fine. You're perfect. You're exactly what we want for Ronan's image. Ian can't believe he didn't consider it before now. It makes complete sense, given your background. You're the perfect candidate—you meet all the criteria."

It was my imagination, I know for a fact it was; but I felt the world tilt, pitch to the side, and I heard the sound of a thousand screaming tea kettles in my ears.

"Wh-what?" I breathed, shaking my head, trying to bring Joan and Ronan and the hallway into focus.

Joan had no choice but to stop because my feet had stopped moving. She glanced at me with an expression that displayed her bemusement and gave me a once-over.

"Are you feeling well?"

"What do you mean I'm perfect? Perfect for what?"

She blinked at me. Her gaze flickered to Ronan and then returned to move over my face in a shrewd examination.

At length she said, "I mean that little act you two put on over the last hour was perfect. You, Annie, are perfect to act as Ronan's fictional date, partner, and love interest for the foreseeable future…obviously."

NINE
RONAN

@RonanFitz: So this is Twitter. Can't say I'm impressed.
@Tomsouthernchef: @RonanFitz Oh, go drink some prune juice, Granddad.

For the second time in the space of a week, I felt like kissing Joan, and it wasn't because she was such a handsome specimen of a woman. Seemingly, she was becoming my very own fairy godmother; I wasn't yet sure if this was her intention, but I'd roll with it anyway.

Annie had gone very, very quiet ever since Joan announced her misunderstanding that we'd planned and staged our earlier interactions, that we'd planned for Annie to pose as my fake girlfriend. Her worry was written all over her face. In a way, I could understand her obvious reluctance since I'd been sending her gifts all week, and she probably thought I was some sort of obsessive psycho.

I'll admit I'd been coming on a bit strong, but I was in New York all alone and had a lot of time on my hands. For some reason, over the past few days my mind had kept wandering to Annie, hence the gifts. So yeah, it was a combination of boredom and spending way too much time thinking about her lips and that lush little body of hers. I wanted in, and my dick thought presents would be the way to get there. God, I could still taste her on my tongue, could still hear the tiny moans she made, the way her breathing stilted and became sexy little pants.

I could also still taste the bitterness of her rejection. It hadn't just caught me off guard; it had pissed me off. She didn't want to change; she said she liked hiding in her comfortable little world, and yet the way she kissed me said otherwise. Now all I could think about was rattling her cage.

We followed Joan into the conference room where Rachel and Ian were waiting. Rachel wore a big, encouraging smile while Ian's face was schooled into an expression of grudging respect with a dash of cynicism. Perhaps he suspected those photos of me and Annie weren't so much staged as they were perfectly real.

I sat down on a chair, and Annie took the one beside me. Her movements were slow and awkward like she was in a daze, and when she placed her hands in her lap, I could see that they were shaking. I didn't like seeing her like this. I knew she was reeling from the fact that pictures of us shoving our tongues down each other's throats were currently making the rounds on the World Wide Web. And now I wanted to kill the Internet just for making her feel that way. I'd always been protective of the females in my life, but this was coming on so quickly it was almost disconcerting.

Reaching over, I tried to take one of her hands in mine to soothe her, but she quickly pulled away. The glance she gave me was a very clear communication: *No*.

"So, we're a little ahead of the game with this," Joan began as she sat down at the table. "Brona's story won't be going live on this side of the world until this evening, and already the Internet is abuzz with these pictures. Everyone loves it when a celebrity starts dating a non-celeb. It gives them hope that it could one day happen to them. I swear, you two" —she paused and waggled her finger between me and Annie— "this was a stroke of pure genius. Annie, darling, I may need to give you a raise."

"There's no need for that, Joan," Annie said softly. "In fact, about those pictures…."

"We're very surprised how quickly they got online. Shocked the fuck out of me, pardon my French. We were only at the café twenty minutes ago," I cut in, sensing that Annie had been about to confess everything.

"Yes, Mr. Fitzpatrick, the wonders of modern technology continue to astound and amaze," Joan replied. If I wasn't mistaken, there was a touch of sarcasm in her voice. Then she clapped her hands together. "There's lots to do, lots to do, but first, the uncomfortable part. I need to ask you a question, and you need to answer me honestly."

I leaned forward, resting my elbows on the table. "Go for it."

"Is there any truth to your ex-fiancée's claims? Or, I'll put it more bluntly, did you ever beat your ex?"

Annie sucked in a shocked breath while Rachel and Ian stared on blandly. A knot of anger tightened in my stomach at being reminded of Brona's most recent antics. Spending the morning with Annie had made me forget for a time, but now all the frustration and fury were easing their way back in.

"No, there's no truth to her claims, Joan."

"So you were never violent with her?"

I tightened my jaw and flexed my hands. "No."

"Well, I'd like to say I'm surprised, but sadly there are a lot of ambitious sycophants out there with dark and vivid imaginations, imaginations that allow them to dream up all kinds of titillating stories. Unfortunately, the press eats these stories up like cockroaches at a restaurant in New Jersey."

I winced both at her analogy and also at the fact that, well, in a way I *was* lying. Don't get me wrong—I never once lifted a hand to Brona in physical violence—but I suspected where her story was coming from. And, quite frankly, if she did have proof, then I was well and truly fucked. I could actually feel myself sweating just thinking about it.

Joan was still talking about strategies, and I was staring at Annie, trying to gauge how she was reacting to all this. I felt certain she would not be pleased about being my girlfriend—pretend or otherwise. Only a half hour ago, she was quite fervent in proclaiming that she didn't want a relationship with me. That she was too messed up.

"So what do you think, Annie?" Joan asked as she came to the end of her spiel.

"I...." Annie began hesitantly and cleared her throat. "Of course, yes. I'm so pleased to help."

At her words, I felt electricity shoot through me. She wanted to give this a go? I wanted to high-five the fuck out of myself then do a victory dance. But I didn't, because, you know, manly.

"Well, obviously. You *did* come up with it, didn't you?" said Ian with a derisive chuckle and a hint of impatience. I didn't like his tone. In fact, it made me want to smack the prick.

Annie swallowed. Ian's comment had clearly made her even more anxious than she already was. Without thinking, I put my hand softly on her thigh beneath the table; surprisingly, it seemed to calm her. At least her hands stopped shaking.

She continued, her voice still quiet but with a flat matter-of-factness, "I match the majority of the criteria, and my past makes up for any deficiencies in physical appearance. I'll be a sympathetic figure with the public."

I couldn't help but give her face and body a quick up-down-sweep, nor did I try to stop my single-eyebrow raise. Deficiencies in physical appearance? She must not own a mirror or be at all aware of the wolfish stares that followed her around the street...and the office.

And what was this about her past making her a sympathetic figure?

"Oh, don't be so modest," said Joan. "You match all of the criteria. Now what we have to do is continue to have you both seen in public. A romantic rendezvous here, a stolen glance there, perhaps a passionate clinch or two along the way, and you're all set. I'm taking it you both possess the acting skills to pull this off."

Annie quietly nodded, and I grinned at her, running my hand down her thigh and squeezing her knee before letting go. I knew for a fact that neither one of us needed acting skills. Hell, the sexual tension between us could almost be considered another entity, it was so thick. Every time I looked at her, all I wanted to do was bury my face in her neck and lose my hand up her skirt.

The fact that she was now wearing clothes that highlighted her supple figure, rather than disguised it, made not touching her that much more difficult. Then I remembered the reason why she was dressing this way, and I frowned. I needed to have a word with Joan.

Thankfully, the meeting was brief, and while I'd been scanning Annie's body, everyone stood to leave. Annie was the first one out of her seat. I caught her by the elbow before she could escape and murmured in her ear.

"Don't leave without me."

All she did was nod and then hurry out. Once Rachel and Ian were gone, I told Joan I'd walk her back to her office. She seemed surprised but walked with me anyway.

"First off, I'd like to thank you for being on the ball with this. It might be hard to believe, but when I first met Brona, she was actually quite a sweet girl. A little dim, yes, but still sweet. Then things began picking up with my career, she got a couple modeling jobs, and all of a sudden fame was the crack in her crack pipe. Nowadays she'll do anything for a bit of attention."

"I'm well acquainted with the likes of Brona O'Shea," said Joan, giving me an understanding look. "You don't need to explain her behavior to me."

"I appreciate that," I went on. "Annie's a sweet girl, too. She's not dim like Brona—"

"No. She's bright like the sun," Joan cut in, giving me a sharp smile. "Don't underestimate her, Mr. Fitzpatrick. Annie is highly intelligent."

I raised an eyebrow at this interruption but continued my thought, "She is also extremely timid and vulnerable to being taken advantage of. Understand, I'm not trying to tell you how to run your business, Joan, but I will tell you upfront that it doesn't sit right with me how you've been treating her."

We'd just reached the door to her office when she stopped and looked up at me, eyes slightly narrowed.

"Pardon?"

"You've been telling Annie she needs to dress differently. More sexy, or whatever the fuck, and I don't like it. You don't have to remind me that she's incredibly intelligent and amazing at her job, and you don't need to capitalize on her beauty just to make clients more amenable. It's sexism in the workplace, pure and simple."

Joan blinked at me, was silent for a beat, and then let out a yip of laughter.

"First of all, I would never mandate that my employees dress 'more sexy,' as you state. That would be highly inappropriate. I reminded Annie that we have a dress code and then saved her the time of having to shop for it by purchasing a wardrobe for her. All the outfits are stylish, tasteful, business casual, and high quality. Nothing about Annie's new clothes is meant to tantalize, Mr. Fitzpatrick."

I scoffed, curling my lip, my disbelief of this last bit plain on my face.

Still, Joan continued, "I'm very fond of that girl, but she's been living in a shell; and I'm just doing my bit to help her out of it. So if you feel the need to protect her, you have nothing to fear from me. I want to protect her just as much as you, if not more so."

Well, that put me in my place. I didn't know what to say right then, so I simply furrowed my brow, cleared my throat, and gave her a gruff, "It's good we're on the same page, then."

"Yes, very good," said Joan, opening the door to her office and walking in. "Until next we meet, Mr. Fitzpatrick."

Turning on my heel, I went in search of Annie's office and found her drinking a cup of tea and chatting quietly with her assistant, Gerta. I stood in the doorway for a moment, watching her as she set the tea down, then bent to open a drawer, and fished out some folders. I might have been a little mesmerized for a moment as I took in the sight of her shapely backside. It was incredible. I just wanted spank it and bite it and worship it and completely fucking defile it.

Gerta was the one to see me first, smiling at me wide and friendly. "Oh, Ronan, I didn't see you there. Is there anything we can help you with?"

Gerta and I had become well acquainted over the phone after I made a point to apologize for jerking her around last week, thus the familiarity of her addressing me by my first name. In fact, I'd been purposefully using charm to win her over. I needed her on my side in the Annie v. Ronan phone-call-avoiding wars. Annie quickly stood and spun around, looking a little frazzled as she tucked an errant strand of hair behind her ear.

"Yes, I was actually wondering if I could have a moment alone with your boss," I said, eyes leveled on Annie.

"Of course," Gerta began, getting up from her seat, but Annie stayed her with a hand.

"It's okay, Gerta. I was just about to head home anyway. *Mr. Fitzpatrick* can walk me out."

The way she emphasized addressing me formally made me want to grin. I thought that maybe, just maybe, my Annie was getting a touch territorial and didn't like the camaraderie Gerta and I had struck up.

She stuffed the files in her handbag, slung it over her shoulder, and led the way out of the office. All the way to the elevators, she kept at least a foot of space between us. It made my inner predator growl with satisfaction to know she felt the need to distance herself for fear of what might happen. I prayed for an empty lift, and someone answered that prayer because when we stepped inside, there was no one else. I stood close beside her as she hit the button for the ground floor.

"So, looks like we'll be spending a lot more time together, baby." I grinned and tilted my head down at her.

She scrunched up her face. "Don't call me that."

"What?" I winked. "We're a couple now. Couples give each other all sorts of nicknames."

"Not all couples do that. And if you've forgotten, we're a fake couple, so there's no need for nicknames."

She was all stoic and together now, nothing like the Annie of this morning. The one who snorted and laughed with me, the one who made my heart stop when she smiled.

"Damn, I was looking forward to your calling me puddinchops," I joked, trying to break down her barrier. It worked a little because I saw her lips twitch in a smile.

"Christ, that's awful," she replied with a little shudder.

I nudged her with my shoulder. "What would you suggest, then?"

"I already told you that I quite like Mother Fitzpatrick," she reluctantly teased.

"Oh, fuck no. That's not happening," I said and let my voice drop as I moved closer so that our arms were touching. "Though I won't object to your calling me Daddy."

Her eyes got really big then, and I burst out laughing. "I'm joking, Annie; relax. I'm joking."

We were stepping out of the lift when she exhaled, "Thank God."

"I know." I chuckled. "I think I might have even creeped myself out with that one."

When she looked at me then, there was a smile on her lips, and I thought I saw genuine fondness in her eyes. Beyond the lobby, I could see that the streets were absolutely crowded, and I remembered it was St. Patrick's Day. I wasn't crazy about crowds, and when I saw Annie looking nervous, I could tell that she liked them even less than I did.

Placing a hand on her lower back, I said, "Hey, I was thinking of taking a drive today. Get out of the city until all the festivities are over. You want to come?"

"You want to go for a drive…in your car…with me?" she asked, swallowing.

"Sure," I said. She hesitated, and I guessed she was struggling because of the line she'd drawn between us while we were at the bakery. So I tried to ease her concerns while also attempting to encourage her to say yes. "Listen, no hard feelings about earlier, about what you said in the bakery. I heard you loud and clear. But this…no need for things to be tense between us. This can be our first fake date as a fake couple. I might even take a picture and post it to Instagram."

It was too bloody cute when her eyes practically lit up that I'd mentioned Instagram and actually knew what it was used for.

"You've been studying the material I sent you?"

I gave her a sincere look, hoping she got the double meaning. "I'd do anything you asked of me, Annie."

It took a while for her to reply. Her eyes lost focus as they moved between mine, and when she spoke she sounded a little dazed and a little afraid. "I guess going for a drive could be productive…?"

"Don't sound so frightened." I laughed. "I'm not a maniac; and besides, there'll probably be paparazzi following us, so I won't be able to try anything *too* crazy."

As soon as we stepped out onto the crowded street, the lack of space seemed to stress her out because she was breathing agitatedly. I moved my hand from her back and pulled her close, keeping my arm around her shoulders like a barrier.

"Got a touch of claustrophobia?" I asked, guessing.

She nodded, pressing herself to me. I enjoyed how her soft curves fit against my body, how she felt under my hands.

"Just a touch," she admitted.

"I won't let anyone get to you, okay? You stay close, and we'll be fine. Is there any point hailing a cab, or will it be quicker walking?"

"Quicker walking," she said sharply, and it seemed she was having trouble getting the words out.

Soothingly, I kept rubbing my thumb back and forth over her shoulder.

"Deep breaths, yeah?" I said, coaching her.

She breathed in deeply and nodded. "Yeah."

It took a while for us to get to my apartment building, and we walked in silence. I even had to sweet-talk a female cop into letting us jump a barrier blocking one side of the street from the other. When Annie pulled herself up on the bars and climbed over, I had to work not to openly stare at how her dress rose, revealing her shapely thighs.

By the time we got to my place, I needed to have lunch. Going to change out of my stained shirt, I told Annie to take a look around if she wanted and help herself to the food in the fridge. She said she wasn't hungry and seemed content to wander through the penthouse. I knocked back a protein shake and then shoveled down the salad and cold cuts I'd prepared earlier this morning. I was just eating the last bites when Annie pulled up a stool next to me.

"I think I'd die of boredom if I had to eat what you eat every day. I've just been looking in your fridge, and there isn't a single dessert in sight."

I shrugged and pushed my plate away. "You get used to it. Well, okay, sometimes it's a struggle; but mostly the sugars get flushed from your system, and you stop craving them all the time." I paused and looked her over. "So, this drive we're taking, you got any suggestions on where we could go?"

Her eyes met mine then darted away, her cheeks blushing pink. She laughed softly, but I detected a note of anxiety. "Let's just try to get out of the city first. If we even manage that, then we'll decide."

TEN
RONAN

@RonanFitz: @Socialmedialite I'm not having fun and I hold you solely responsible.
@Socialmedialite: @RonanFitz Have you checked out @dirtyrugbyjokes yet? ;-)
@RonanFitz: @Socialmedialite My earlier statement stands firm.

As it happened, we did make it out of Manhattan. It took us a while, but I was finally on the motorway heading toward Poughkeepsie. Man, they did roads so much better here than they did back home. Sometimes it felt like there were a million lanes going each way. Also, there was something deeply satisfying about having Annie sitting beside me while I drove. It had been almost ten days since I'd been on the road, so I was obviously in dire need of a fix.

I heard Annie let out a quiet laugh and turned my head to look at her. "What?"

"I was just thinking that I've never seen anyone so *fixated* on a car before," she replied, her tone surprisingly playful.

I held back a smile, quiet for a moment, before I teased, "Yeah, well, I never saw anyone perform fellatio on an éclair until the day I met you, love."

She gasped and proceeded to slap me on the arm. "Ronan! I can't believe you just said that."

"Hey, I think you should own it. The way you eat is sexy as fuck."

I glanced away from the road to look at her and saw that she was blushing again. She fiddled with the hem of her pink cardigan and stared out the window. I wanted to touch her so much in that moment that I was practically white-knuckling the steering wheel. It would be so easy to just slip my hand under that silky dress, feel her skin, see how quickly I could get her wet....

I pushed those thoughts away because I was suddenly having difficulty focusing on the road.

"I've never owned a car before," she said, breaking the quiet.

I looked at her. "No?"

She shook her head. "Never. I've always wanted one, though. Something fast, like this one. It's gorgeous. But I've never had a reason to buy one, and I don't know how to drive. Also, highways feel so…I don't know, intimidating."

"Ah, once you get over the learning part, it's as natural as walking. Believe it or not, you're sitting in my very first car. To this day, she's still my favorite."

She gave me an incredulous look. "This was your first car? This is a classic! Did you fix it up yourself? It must have been so expensive."

"It was, but I scrimped and saved for it. It wasn't until I made it onto a professional rugby team that I could finally afford it, though."

"Wow," she breathed. "Well, all the scrimping and saving was definitely worth it. I'd love a car like this." She leaned back as though luxuriating in the comfort of the seat and classic lines of the muscle car, and I had to admit, it was a bit of a turn-on. Like I needed to be any more sexed up around this woman.

A couple of minutes passed before I could speak again. "Hey, Annie."

"Mm-hmm?"

"What did you mean back in the office when you said people might find you a sympathetic character because of your past?"

There were several beats of silence, like she was considering whether or not to answer me. Finally, she did. "You know how in movies sometimes, they'll have this cliché where a parent leaves their baby on the steps of a church or a hospital or something?"

I nodded and glanced at her. She was smiling, but it was the most heartbreaking smile I'd ever seen.

"Well, that cliché is me."

I frowned at her, dividing my attention between her and the road. "What do you mean?"

"My mom abandoned me at a fire station when I was six."

Jesus. Fuck.

I blinked at her, stunned. "Christ…." I exhaled the word and refocused on the road.

I wanted to ask more but didn't know how to proceed, so we sat quietly for a few minutes.

She surprised me by volunteering, "Then I was sent to a group home and… well, eventually, following that, I was in and out of foster homes. See, I know this business, and if people love anything, it's a sob story. Why else would they continue to highlight the contestants with sad backgrounds on all those reality talent shows? It helps the audience to relate, to sympathize and, in turn, show support. So, when the press digs into my background, sees how I dragged myself up from low beginnings, it could work to our advantage." She tilted her chin up, a stubborn tilt, like her professionalism was her armor.

I didn't respond. I didn't know what the fuck I was supposed to say. Instead I drove, thinking about what it must've been like for her, a beautiful little girl with big brown eyes, a little girl given more brains than affection, a little girl who no one loved.

When I considered her innate tendency toward introversion paired with her childhood, it really was a wonder her past hadn't completely destroyed her, made her withdraw into herself completely.

She was brave, but it was buried deep under layers and years of neglect and loneliness. She had *no one*.

Honestly, her story and the bland tone she used when she related it made my stomach hurt like I'd been sucker-punched. I felt queasy. She spoke about her past like it had happened to someone else. It made me want to hit someone.

While I appreciated that she was doing this fake girlfriend act to help me, I couldn't care less about all that. I cared about her, and I was struck by how much.

Oh, Christ.

I *cared* about her.

This was not supposed to happen. I'd promised myself I wouldn't let anyone get close again after being taken for a fool by Brona, and now Annie was already burrowing under my skin. I wanted to know all about her, and it unsettled me. I also had a feeling getting Annie to open up, *really* open up, wasn't going to be an easy task, especially now that I knew the basics about her childhood.

She broke the silence. "With Brona's story coming out, even though it's all lies, you need to be prepared for people to turn against you. Having me as your girlfriend allows us to balance out some of that negativity."

I realized that, unlike me, during the last few minutes she hadn't been thinking about her childhood; she'd been thinking about how to exploit her childhood to help me, how her past was going to work to *my* advantage. I was used to other people using me, but I'd never had someone voluntarily offer to be used *by* me. My protective instinct flared, like a beast, fierce and strong. But still I said nothing.

She turned an introspective smile to me, one that I caught out of the corner of my eye. I glanced at her as she suggested, "I could plant a nickname for Brona around social media—*The Harpy* has a nice ring to it. No one would be able to trace it back to me."

I let her attempt at humor lighten my black mood, and I gave her a half smile. "My mates call her The Hag."

She chuckled softly and shook her head. "Name calling…it's like we're in elementary school."

"She started it," I said, hoping to make her laugh again. It worked.

Eventually, the silence lightened, grew oddly comfortable. About twenty minutes passed before we reached a town. I noticed a small, old-timey-looking ice cream parlor as we drove by, so I did a quick U-turn and parked outside. Annie looked out her window.

"We're going in here?" she asked curiously.

"I figured it was about time you ate. You haven't had anything since breakfast," I told her, reaching out to tuck her hair behind her ear. She didn't protest at my touching her, so I ran my knuckles along her neck for a second, savoring the silky feel of her skin. She trembled. Yeah, she wanted me just as badly as I wanted her. She was just better at hiding it, and now I knew why.

"You know, despite evidence to the contrary, I don't actually eat dessert for every meal. You'd make a terrible parent. All you'd feed your children is sugar."

"Ha-ha. Come on, let's go inside."

"I'll go in, on one condition," she said, holding up a hand.

"Does that condition include eating you out? Because if so, you don't even have to ask," I replied, filthy flirting.

She sucked in a breath. "Ronan, you are…."

"Hush. I know. I've got a dirty mouth. Continue with your condition, honey."

Shockingly, she gave me a playful scowl even as her cheeks blushed scarlet. "I'll have the ice cream, but only if you have some, too."

"Oh, will I be licking it off you then?"

I could tell she was trying not to smile now. "God, you're insufferable. No, you won't be licking it off me. You'll be eating it from a cone, like a normal person who eats food for pleasure every once in a while, rather than only for fuel."

I really, really didn't want to eat the ice cream, mainly because it would fuck up my regime. However, I thought that maybe I could use this deal to my advantage. "Hmm, I'll eat the ice cream—like a normal person—if you'll let me ask you five questions about yourself. And you have to answer honestly, and you can't talk about work for the entire duration of the conversation."

She narrowed her eyes at me. "Two questions."

"Three and it's a deal," I said, holding my hand out to her. "Besides, I'm going to have to learn more about you if we're trying to convince people we're a real couple."

She sighed. Looking a little sad and—dare I say, regretful?—she shook my hand. "Fine, but you're not allowed to order vanilla."

I gave her a dark look. "Vanilla's not my flavor, Annie."

Shit, if only she knew.

Fifteen minutes later, we were sitting on a park bench eating our ice creams. Annie had ordered one scoop of chocolate and one scoop of pistachio while I'd gone for a cherry chocolate combination. She watched me expectantly as I brought the ice cream to my mouth and licked it. And yeah, okay, I might have groaned a little at how good it was. I hadn't had sugar in a long time, maybe a year. Annie smiled bigger than I'd ever seen her smile, looking satisfied.

"You can wipe that smug look off your face," I said, eyeing the handful of paparazzi who were hovering across the street, snapping shots of us. "Otherwise, I may have to kiss it off."

"Smug, *moi*?" she asked, happily licking away. The sight of her pink tongue sneaking out past her lips did great things for my filthy imagination.

"You know you are. Now, I think it's time I got my side of the bargain. First question." I hesitated, made sure she was looking into my eyes, and kept my tone carefully respectful. "What was it like growing up in foster care?"

Annie furrowed her brow. "Lonely. Frightening. Disappointing."

"Why frightening?"

"Isn't it obvious? You're this little kid at the mercy of strange adults, strange kids. It's like roulette. You could get nice people, or you could get bad ones."

Thinking of her as a little girl being sent to live with bad people made me angry, and it made me want to tuck her away someplace safe and take care of her; but I didn't let her see that. I was also careful to keep pity from my expression. "And why disappointing?"

"Because you get your hopes up, and then people decide they don't want you anymore," she practically whispered before her voice turned steely. "That's why I never let my happiness or survival depend on others. It means I eliminate the disappointment."

A light bulb went on like a fucking lightning strike, and understanding hit me.

Annie kept herself closed off from people, from relationships, so they couldn't reject her. It made me wonder if she'd ever allowed herself to be in a relationship at all, which prompted my next question. "When was your last boyfriend?"

"I do believe you've had your three questions, Mr. Fitzpatrick."

"The second two were follow-ups. Not real questions. Answer me."

She sighed, pursed her lips to show me she was dissatisfied, but answered anyway, "A little over two years ago. His name was Jamie. We...dated all through college."

I wasn't sure why, but I actually felt a bit disappointed with her answer. The possessive side of me wanted her never to have been with anyone. I was the kind of man who needed ownership, and that need had never been satisfied in my relationship with Brona. I never really felt like she was mine; she was sweet and unassuming at first, but soon she felt like an obligation, unable to take care of herself without my constant praise and reassurance. I also sensed she was always on the lookout for the next best thing.

"Follow-up question: Why did you break up with this Jamie person?"

"Follow-up? No, no, no. I fell for that once already."

"Fine. Then tell me because you want to tell me."

She considered me for a moment, licking the ice cream off her lips then sighed. "Fine. We weren't in a very traditional relationship. We were exclusive, but…." She shook her head, frowning.

"What? He wouldn't commit?"

"No. More like the other way around," Annie muttered to her ice cream cone. "Anyway, he wanted something more substantial. I wasn't amenable to his terms. So when I moved to New York, I saw no reason to continue our agreement."

"Agreement?"

"Uh, relationship."

I narrowed my eyes at her. "What was his story? Not very smart?"

"Oh, no. He was in medical school at Penn State and is probably in residency by now at Harvard or someplace equally impressive."

"Oh, so a troll? Ugly?"

She laughed a little but then caught herself before she could full-on giggle. "No, nothing like that. He was quite handsome."

I was putting the pieces together. She'd had an emotionless relationship with some good-looking, successful doctor guy, and she'd been the one to break it off after several years. She hadn't been lying earlier when she said she was a bit of a mess and had severe abandonment issues.

I wanted to ask her more about Jamie, but I didn't want to push my luck or use my final question. It wasn't even a very important one; but—maybe it was the horny caveman in me—I wanted to ask her about sex, suss out her likes and dislikes, and this was the perfect opener for that.

"Okay, so, last question. When did you lose your virginity?"

Annie shook her head and turned to stare at me. "Why do you want to know that?"

"Because I'm nosy. Talk."

We were both finished with our ice creams now. She folded up her napkin and took the end of my cone from me before walking to the bin to dispose of them. There was something surprisingly comfortable and intimate about the gesture. She came back, sat down, and smoothed her dress over her legs. I sat close, my arm resting along the back of the bench. I imagined the paps were getting some good shots of us.

"I was sixteen; he was eighteen. We'd been going out for a week or two, and then he took me to prom. That was the night we did the deed."

"*And*," I probed, "was it good, bad, mediocre?"

She thought on this for a while, mouth drawn into a slanted line. "It wasn't...good. Mostly it was just sore, and I wanted it to be over with."

"So he didn't make it romantic for you? Sounds like a right arsehole to me."

"Show me a teenage boy who cares about romance. And yeah, he was an asshole, as it happens."

I grinned down at her, moving my body closer so that our thighs pressed together. Annie froze for a second, so I nodded subtly toward the photographers. "Just making things look right for our audience."

"Oh, my God! I didn't even notice they were there."

I gave her a wide grin. "That's probably because you've been so enamored by my potent manliness."

This elicited a cute little laugh from her and a sarcastic, "Oh, yeah, that *must* be why." She paused and considered me a moment. "So, how about you? When did you lose yours?"

Her question caught me off guard. But still, I didn't mind answering. "I was fifteen."

"Wow, that's young. And who was the lucky girl?"

"It was young, I suppose, but I was a horny little bastard." I glanced down at her and winked. "Not much has changed there. The lucky girl was Trina. She was just fourteen. We'd been going out for a couple of weeks and decided to take the next step."

Annie moved closer, curious. "And?"

I shrugged. "And it was good. Well, as good as it can be between two kids who hardly know what they're doing. We quickly got the hang of it, though, and couldn't keep our hands off each other. A couple months later, we had a little pregnancy scare. She freaked out while I tried to be the big man and asked her to marry me." I paused and chuckled. "I was fifteen and ready to sign my life away, thought it was the honorable thing to do. It turned out her period was just late, and my proposal was unnecessary. She was so spooked by the whole thing that she broke up with me. I was heartbroken for a while before I really began dipping my toes into the world of sex again."

Annie's eyebrows rose. "Oh?"

"Yeah, I had a bit of a promiscuous phase in my late teens. Sex was a stress reliever for me. I probably over-indulged because my tastes got a little... kinky."

Annie's expression was a mixture of surprise and curiosity. I could tell she was about to ask me to elaborate on what I meant by "kinky," and I wasn't ready to go there yet; so I quickly changed topics.

"I almost forgot. We need to take a picture for my Instagram account. It's been left lonely and disused since Gerta opened it for me."

Annie looked up and bit her lip. "Oh, right, you want me in the picture with you?"

"Of course. We're a couple now," I said and pulled her close as I found the camera function on my phone.

"Yes, but there are quotation marks around 'couple,' remember?"

I gave her a fake scowl. "Like you'd let me forget." Raising the camera in front of us, I quickly turned in and laid a kiss on her cheek as I was taking the shot. She squealed when I did it, but it was already taken.

"That was sneaky!"

"I'm just trying to make us seem genuine, Annie dearest." I smirked and brought up the picture. "Wow, we look good together. And look at you," I went on, nudging her playfully. "Absolute stunner. Those eyes. Fuck."

"It's a nice picture," Annie admitted, grudgingly.

A naughty idea came into my head, and I couldn't help but vocalize it. I ducked down and brought my mouth close to her ear, my voice low and husky. "Yeah, and imagine how good we'll look when I'm inside you."

Annie's eyes met mine, and I saw her pupils dilate. A little breath escaped her, and her throat moved as she swallowed. Our gazes remained locked for a long moment before she drew away and tried to compose herself. I could practically feel her withdrawing.

"Please know this, Mr. Fitzpatrick, the only reason I'm not walking away right now is because there are photographers watching."

"Don't like the idea of my penetrating those walls you've built?"

She swallowed thickly, her hands balling into fists. "You like to make things hard, don't you?"

"No. You make things hard, Annie."

Her face flamed red and hot, and her breathing was uneven. "Please stop." Annie's eyes lifted to mine, and they held a desperate edge. "You think you're being cute, that you can be aggressive and flirt shamelessly and that it doesn't mean anything, that your words don't…affect me. But they do. You need to stop pushing—you need to be respectful of my wishes."

Shit, she was kind of sexy when she was scolding me.

With that, she stood and gestured for me to follow her. I did. But I also grabbed her hand and held it as we walked. We made our way back to my car in silence, and the return drive to the city was similarly conversation-free. I should have been pissed off at myself for ruining things, but I wasn't.

What I'd said had more than interested her. I'd seen it in her face and the way she'd clenched her thighs together. She'd even admitted that I affected her. She'd practically been humming with arousal. Yeah, she wanted me bad, and the challenge would be *respectfully* encouraging her to let go of her inhibitions.

I was determined to make it happen. I could be respectful…and still aggressive.

When we reached her apartment building, Annie was all business as she organized for us to go running together in the morning. It would save us both time, she said, as it meant we could be seen together and also get our daily exercise in. She barely gave me a second glance as she exited the car. I was back at my building, parking the car, when I noticed she'd forgotten her phone. It must have fallen from her handbag because it was lying on the floor.

Picking it up, I was about to tuck it in my pocket when it buzzed.

Yeah, I could have ignored the buzz, but I didn't. Instead I glanced at the screen and saw that it was a notification from her Twitter account. Except it wasn't *her* Twitter account. And I nearly dropped the phone because the handle in the notification wasn't @AnnieCat.

The handle was @Socialmedialite.

ELEVEN
ANNIE

New York's Finest
Blogging as *The Socialmedialite*
March 17
It's always sad when someone forgets to wear green on St. Patrick's Day. So, imagine how depressing it was for me to see Dara Evans this morning wearing a ghastly gray trench coat. I'm not sure who told her Disney was holding auditions for Cruella De Vil in the East Village, but a memo must've gotten lost someplace (or maybe she doesn't know how to read...?). Why else would she be wearing an ankle-length, baby seal fur coat on a warm March day? She might as well take out a billboard in Times Square to announce her supervillain status. At this point, I think I'd be surprised if she allowed one of her henchmen to club the baby seals. You know how much she loathes those ostentatious baby animals, spreading joy and happiness everywhere they go. The little cute bastards. Who do they think they are???
Hide your puppies and kittens, New York. Cruella, aka Dara Evans, is looking for a new sweater, and your little Fido is the perfect shade of innocent to match her baby koala mittens.
<3 The Socialmedialite

I took a cold shower when I got home. Then I took another cold shower in the middle of the night after having a wonderful and frustrating dream about éclairs and fellatio and Ronan and a bed with a mirrored ceiling.

I would never look at an éclair the same way again.

I was losing my mind, and it was all because I wanted him. I wanted him very, very badly. My desire felt like a vise around my heart, a ball and chain around my ankle. It weighed me down, made it hard to breathe. I was having hot flashes.

Hot flashes!

I was a mess.

Things went from bad to worse when Gerta emailed me early in the morning to tell me that Ronan had canceled our appointment to go running in the park. He'd emailed Gerta, not me. He didn't even cc me on the message.

Nor had he texted me; at least, I hadn't heard my phone chime. Feeling adrift and depressed that I wouldn't be seeing Ronan at all that day and, therefore, disoriented by my disappointment, I searched for my phone—just to make sure he hadn't texted me.

I couldn't find my phone. It wasn't in my bag, in the basket by the front door, or next to my workstation. I couldn't find it anywhere. After a half hour of frantic searching, I forced myself to stop, pause, and think.

The last place I remembered checking my phone was in my office, after the meeting, before Ronan had come to find me. Just that realization was enough to throw me for a loop. I'd gone over twelve hours without looking at my phone, checking in with my Socialmedialite blog. It had to be a new record.

Deciding that the phone must be at the office, I emailed Gerta back and asked her to check my desk for the cell.

Then I took another cold shower.

When I was finished but before I was dressed, I checked my Socialmedialite email account from my desktop PC, hopeful that Ronan had sent The Socialmedialite a message. I wasn't disappointed. He'd sent two.

The first was composed early in the day on Monday, just five hours or so after I'd sent my message warning him about Brona's claims of abuse. It read:

March 17

6:12 a.m.

Thank you for the heads-up.

You're right. I'd like to do something crazy; I'd love to retaliate, but I won't. Instead I'll do something completely out of character and let my "publicity people" deal with this shite.

Just so you know, because I feel like I need to defend myself to someone (even if it's some dude with a mermaid tat), she pissed me off any number of times; and she'd lash out during our rages and hit me all the time, but I never reciprocated. I would never hit a woman in a violent way. I would never do that. That would make me scum.

I'm used to fists against my face. You haven't played a match of rugby if you aren't bleeding by the end of it. When she hit me, it didn't faze me. But her lies and dishonesty sure as fuck made a dent.

My heart constricted, and I pressed my fingers against my sternum, trying to massage away the uncomfortable, leaden heaviness that had settled in my chest. If I ever came face to face with Brona O'Shea, I was going to…well, I didn't know what I would do. Part of me wanted to make her suffer for what she was doing to Ronan, what she was putting him through.

The other part of me *really* wanted her to suffer. So, if you're keeping score, all of me was in favor of making Brona suffer.

I also thought about how sadly ironic his email was because I was, right this minute, lying to Ronan.

I wanted him but not enough to change. That was the truth…mostly.

If I could be guaranteed that he wouldn't leave me, if I could be certain that I wouldn't be abandoned, I would have jumped through hoops lit with fire to have a chance with him. Basically, if Ronan was a member of a boy band, say One Direction, he'd be the Harry Styles. He was far too gorgeous and lusted after to be trusted to stay faithful, not to be stolen or have his head turned by the next sexy young thing who came along. I saw it happen all the time in my line of work.

But really, it wasn't just the lust and the intangible chemistry between us. Although, at present, the lust had a lot to do with it.

Really, it was him. His aggressive teasing and shocking suggestiveness; how assertive he was; how dedicated he was to his family; how smart and strong and capable he was; how focused he was on his profession, how driven and ambitious. I understood his drive and ambition, and I lauded him for it…even though I wanted to see him eat ice cream and lose some of his puritan control. Secretly, I wanted to be the one he broke his own rules for. I'll admit, it made me feel special, like I mattered.

And I knew that line of thinking was twisted and wrong and unhealthy. I mattered independently of whether Ronan Fitzpatrick desired me. I mattered regardless of whether he wanted me enough to settle down and give me stability and security and ice cream.

I kept Jamie at arm's length, and he didn't seem to mind. Well, he didn't mind at first. And when he did mind, when he wanted intimacy beyond the physical, I ended things. I ended things because life came without guarantees. Jamie had broken his own rules for me, but that hadn't mattered. Yes, Jamie was smart and handsome, but he lacked some intangible spark that Ronan had in spades. Maybe it was passion that Jamie lacked. Whatever it was, I was never in any danger of falling for him.

Not like Ronan. I couldn't stop thinking about him. Maybe Ronan would stick around long enough for me to lose myself in the promise of something concrete and lasting.

I shook my head, squeezing my eyes shut, and rubbed my forehead. Just considering this—a real relationship with Ronan Fitzpatrick—was madness. We'd known each other for such a short time. Granted, I'd let him in closer than anybody. I'd volunteered details about my past; I'd never done that with anyone before.

Ronan could no more promise me forever than my adoptive parents could. Maybe he'd last longer than the six months they'd given me before they got pregnant with their real child and returned me to the state.

I pressed my lips together, rolled them between my teeth—because my eyes were stinging, and I refused to cry about a distant memory that no longer mattered, about people who wanted me because of how adorable I was as a seven-year-old but loved me no deeper than the surface of my skin.

I cleared my throat and blinked away the moisture in my eyes, clicking on Ronan's second email. It was sent late Monday night, after I'd gone to sleep but before my second cold shower. It read:

March 17
   11:47 p.m.
   Funny thing about lies, lying, and liars—the truth always has a way of coming out. I wanted to thank you again for all your help. I do wonder, why are you helping me? What's in it for you?
   -Ronan

I frowned because the message was strange. I read it back several times then read his first email again. I searched for some clue as to why his second email was so terse, his tone truncated. I knew better than to read emotion into written words, so I tried my best not to fret over the note.

I tried and failed.

The words looked angry.

I went back to my room and changed, contemplated how to answer his message as I dressed. I spent the rest of the day—between work and eating my feelings and trying not to think about Ronan—periodically clicking back to his emails and studying them, working myself up into ball of stress. In the end, I decided that honesty was the best policy.

March 18
   4:10 p.m.

Dear Ronan,

I agree, the truth always comes out. I'm so glad you didn't do anything rash. She doesn't deserve your time and attention (or energy).

I was surprised by your questions in the last email, regarding what I'm getting out of helping you. The answer is quite simply this: I am getting the pleasure of your correspondence. I wonder if anyone has ever told you this before, but you are very charming and likable. You're very clever; your emails make me laugh. I like you.

-SML = Someone (who) Maybe Likes (you)

I scanned it a few times for typos then hit "send." The Socialmedialite was so much braver than Annie Catrel. I sorta had a girl-crush on my alter ego.

Approximately two hours later, still a ball of stress, I was just getting ready to log off of my work profile and start working on some blog posts when I received an email from Gerta.

March 18

6:46 p.m.

Hi, Annie.

Lost and Found recovered your phone. I have it here and will send it via courier before I leave today.

Also, Mr. Fitzpatrick stopped by. He apologized about having to cancel today and rescheduled your appointment for Thursday morning at 7:00; he indicated that you knew the address/location.

I took the liberty of moving your phone conference with Becky and the team regarding the Starlet to Friday afternoon.

See you tomorrow, Gerta

I cringed. I'd sacrificed Dara Evans, aka The Starlet, on my blog on St. Patrick's Day in an effort to draw attention away from Brona's lies. Now I'd pay for it, and poor Becky would likely bear the brunt of the fallout from The Socialmedialite's "baby seal" article.

At least I could look forward to a Thursday morning date with Ronan, even if it was all pretending for the cameras. The problem was I was pretty sure my pretending to be smitten with Ronan was more honest than all my forceful denials that we couldn't be together. Fiction had just become truer than reality.

* * *

I was early, but Ronan was earlier. I caught sight of him when I was about twenty yards away. He was hard to miss. Though he wasn't especially tall, he was cut like a marble statue. Presently he was wearing a white long-sleeved Under Armor running shirt that left none of his torso to the imagination, and black spandex running pants.

At some point I would have to talk to him about the spandex, but it wouldn't be today.

I was too busy being grateful for the advent of spandex to bother with trying to save him from his poor fashion choices. His thick, muscular thighs—rugby thighs—made my head swim as I approached. I had to force myself to look away even as I ached to take a picture of him, something I could keep for myself and look at later when I was feeling lonely.

…like a creeper.

Ugh! I was gross.

Ronan hadn't tried to call me, and he hadn't responded to the Socialmedialite's email. I missed him. Add to this my latest exchange with WriteALoveSong,

@WriteALoveSong to @Socialmedialite: THE WORLD IS ENDING!… I thought Ronan F. was the cocky jock who sent you the douchiest email ever. Why are you suddenly friendly with him on Twitter? Did he apologize? Or are you mesmerized by his… toe shoes.

@Socialmedialite to @WriteALoveSong: I'm trying to help him navigate social media. He's not a bad guy, he was just having a douchey moment.

@WriteALoveSong to @Socialmedialite: Maybe he should put that on a T-shirt "Watch out for random douchey moments" You're too nice to people, I can't believe you're helping him.

@Socialmedialite to @WriteALoveSong: He's actually really cool! You'd like him.

@WriteALoveSong to @Socialmedialite: I think you mean, 'He's actually really hot!' This is why I can't cover mainstream showbiz, it's the pretty people who are always forgiven.

I wondered if she was right. I was more than physically attracted to Ronan; I was desperately in lust and infatuation. Yet it was so much more than what he looked like. If all I wanted was handsome, I would have hooked up with my neighbor Kurt the King of Moisturizers.

As I neared, I saw that his skin was flushed and his white shirt was damp, sticking to the sweat covering his chest and back and sides. Obviously, he'd already done at least one lap around the park. My steps faltered. Soon I would be close enough to touch him...to talk to him. I thought about turning around and leaving, but I couldn't. I really, really missed him, the way he made me feel reckless, the way he looked at me like I was the only person in the room, on the street, in the world.

"Shelly sells shitty sea shells by the shitty sea shore...." I mumbled nervously, letting my anxiety get the better of me and giving into my compulsion to curse. I ground my teeth and continued forward.

Ronan was stretching, using a bench for balance. His gorgeous back was to me, and therefore he didn't see me approach. I cleared my throat loudly when I was about six feet away. This caused him to still and glance over his shoulder; I lost my breath a little when our eyes connected.

He wasn't smiling. He wasn't frowning, either. He was just looking at me. Then he wasn't just looking at me, he was smoldering at me.

Two days without my Ronan fix and now I was seized, caught in the web of his...Ronan-ness.

I had the distinct sensation that I was falling into his eyes; they seemed to have their own gravitational field. Without my intending to do so, my feet carried me forward as he straightened and turned completely around. I stumbled over nothing, and he stepped closer, his hands coming to my waist even though I was in no danger of falling to the ground.

"You look a little dazed," he said, giving me a crooked grin.

The rumbly cadence of his voice called to my inner—and thus far dormant—vixen. I was surprised to find that I had one and that I liked how vulnerable and exposed I felt under the beautiful burden of Ronan's stare.

But I hated that he was so handsome...and smart...and quick-witted...and perceptive....

Especially perceptive.

"I'm—I'm fine."

He nodded once then bent to kiss me. I closed my eyes and moved more completely into his arms, but then the kiss was over. It had just been a simple press of his lips against mine, and it left me feeling unfulfilled and cheated.

My lashes fluttered open, and I gazed up at him; his eyes felt distant, guarded as they moved over my face. He lifted a single eyebrow.

"I think that's a good enough show for the paps."

"The paps?"

"Yes, the paparazzi."

"Oh. Oh, yes." Remembering myself, I stepped away and looked at the still-brown grass under our feet. "Right."

I felt his eyes move over me, and I wondered if he saw the acute disappointment I felt at the impersonal nature of the kiss, meant only for show. I hoped he didn't. I did not want to be that girl, the one who sends mixed signals. Maybe it was already too late for that. Maybe I was that girl. But I couldn't help it. I liked him. I liked him more than I should.

This thought helped me regain my composure and focus on putting emotional distance between us, if not physical distance. Ronan reached for and held my hand in his then tugged me toward the trail.

"I've already gone once around the park. Do you want to run, jog, or walk?"

"I usually just walk." I glanced at nothing—a gazebo, a bench, a tree—just as long as it wasn't him.

In my peripheral vision, however, I discerned he was looking at me. "If we walk, then we might have to talk to each other. Are you sure you wouldn't rather jog?"

My attention darted to him; his statement surprised me. "You don't want to talk?"

He shrugged and gave me a small smile that didn't reach his eyes. "What's the point?"

I winced at his question, my heart twisting with a dull pain, and I lowered my eyes to the trail. We walked in silence for several minutes. I felt winded, my chest heavy, even though we weren't walking very fast.

Then abruptly he said, "Unless you want to tell me why you're doing this."

I tried not to flinch at the hard edge in his voice. "Doing what?"

"This." He paused then added, "This. Pretending to be my girl. I'm actually very curious. Will it help you with your career? Move up in the company?"

He sounded bitter. I gave him a sideways glance and found that his expression was clearly bitter as well, his lovely brown eyes rimmed with jaded sorrow. It reminded me of the first time I saw him, when I thought he was that Irish actor, and I wanted to embrace him and soothe away his troubles. Instinctively, I shifted so that I was walking closer, moved my hand to his elbow, and tucked myself close to his body.

"No, Ronan. It's not going to help with my career," I answered honestly, watching his profile. It wouldn't help me with my career because I had no plans to move beyond my current position, and it certainly wasn't helping my peace of mind.

His jaw ticked. "Really?"

"Yes. Really. I like what I do. I have no desire to…to be in charge of a group of people, be a manager. Right now I'm talent. I provide content, expertise, and guidance to the team. This is what I want to do. I have no ambitions to move up. If I could stay doing exactly what I'm doing forever, then I would do just that."

"Then why don't you explain to me what's really going on? Why are you doing this?"

"Because…." I began then stopped. My feet also stopped which forced him to stop. I pulled on his elbow until he was facing me.

Honesty, I told myself. *Be like The Socialmedialite…just be honest.*

I swallowed with difficulty because he was staring at me, and I could feel myself getting caught in his gravitational field.

"Because I want to help you," I blurted. My eyes darted away, but then I forced myself to look at him again.

He didn't believe me. I could tell.

"I don't get it, Annie." He shook his head. "One minute you don't want anything to do with me—"

"I never said that."

"'I don't want you, Ronan.'" He repeated the words I'd said to him in the bakery on Monday, making me cringe. My hand on his arm tightened as he continued, "One minute you don't want me, and the next you agree to go along with this farce that we're a couple. Why would you do that? To save face?"

"No! You know that I was about to tell Joan the truth on Monday—you know I was about to tell everyone the truth. But then you cut in and said that we had planned the whole thing, and I saw...I saw that I could help you."

What I didn't say, what I didn't admit, was that I'd jumped at the chance because it meant I would get to spend time with Ronan; I would get to talk to him, touch him, be with him without risking my feelings or growing attached. Because it was fake—or at least, I could pretend it was fake.

"You're doing this because you want to help me." His tone was flat, and his usually vibrant eyes were dull, guarded.

"Yes. I did...I do. I think what she did—what Brona is doing—is unfair to you. And if I can help, then I want to help. If I can make her lies go away...." I glanced over his shoulder, frustrated by my lack of ability to communicate. My tongue felt heavy in my mouth, and I gathered a deep breath, tried to ease some of my frustration, and closed my eyes as I continued, "I saw how that hurt you. I don't want you to be hurt—I'm not making sense."

He was quiet for several seconds, and I felt my face flush. I'd said too much, admitted too much, and my words were clumsy. This was precisely why I should only interact with the world via infographics.

"You're making some sense," he said, his gentle tone catching me off guard.

I opened my eyes and peeked at him. His gaze had softened, and I saw that he was studying me. I met his probing stare, relieved that the bitterness had been replaced by speculative warmth.

At length he shifted a step forward, entering my space. I lifted my chin to maintain eye contact and successfully fought the urge to back away.

Once he was basically crowding me, Ronan whispered, "Why do you care if I'm hurt?"

"Because...." I began, stopped, closed my eyes again, and gathered a deep breath.

"Look at me, Annie."

I didn't. Instead, I bit my lip and shook my head.

I felt one of his hands cup my cheek; his thumb pulled the flesh from my teeth then swept over my bottom lip.

"Look at me." This time it sounded a bit more like a command.

I opened my eyes. I looked at him. I told him the truth. "I lied to you."

I saw a flash of something behind his gaze, and he appeared to be holding his breath. "I don't like liars."

"I know, I know, I'm sorry."

"What did you lie about?"

"I want permanence," I said stupidly. "I want guarantees and stability."

"What? What does—"

I interrupted him, my words tumbling from my mouth. "I like you. And more than just in the biblical sense. I like *you*. I like that you're Mother Fitzpatrick with your team, but you flirt dirty with me. I like how you take care of your family and how h-h-honorable you are. And I want…." I tried to shift my gaze from his, but he wouldn't let me. Ronan lifted his other hand so that he held my face between his palms, forcing me to maintain eye contact.

"What do you want?"

"When I first saw you, do you know what I thought? I thought you looked sad. And even though I didn't know you, I wanted to do something to make that go away."

His gaze narrowed. "You mean in the break room? You thought I was sad?"

My eyes widened as I realized my mistake. As far as Ronan knew, the first time I'd laid eyes on him was at the office in the break room. "Y-yes, I mean, no—of course, I mean that—listen, it doesn't matter. What matters is that I saw you, I saw sadness. I wanted to help."

"But you don't want me?"

My frustration doubled. I gripped his wrists, steadying myself. I stared at his neck, irritated that I was so bad at this, and blurted on an exhalation, "I do want you, for some crazy reason I want to trust you; but I am *so* afraid." The last part of my sentence came out as a whisper.

He seemed to release the breath he was holding, and with it, I felt his relief like a tangible thing. The weight I hadn't precisely realized he'd been shouldering fell away. Ronan pressed a quick kiss to my forehead before saying, "Don't be. You don't need to be afraid of me."

"I can't not be. You don't know. You don't know what I'm like."

"I know you're gorgeous."

My eyes cut to his, and I frowned, fear making my throat tight. "See, that's it. That right there. That's the problem."

"What? It's a problem that I think you're beautiful?" He was truly perplexed.

"You'll change your mind. You'll find someone else."

Ronan stared at me like I'd grown wings and horns and eight legs. "What are you talking about?"

"I've worked really hard for stability, for security. Things are good now. I'm safe."

His thumbs caressed my cheeks and jaw, his eyes growing fiery and fierce. "You don't think you're safe with me? You think I'd hurt you?"

I sighed, knew my eyebrows were moving in all sorts of directions on my forehead as I struggled for the right words. In the end, I didn't make a conscious decision to tell him about it; I was speaking, and before I knew it, I was halfway through the story.

"Let me explain it this way—and I'm not using my background to gain sympathy. I don't want sympathy. Let me just tell you what happened. It will…it will make more sense, I think."

Ronan nodded his encouragement.

"When I was six, my mother left me. I told you this. But what I didn't tell you was that when I was seven, I was adopted by a family. They thought I was so cute. And, um…they liked how quiet I was, how sweet. It took me a while to come around, like, four months before I started to open up and be myself." I lowered my gaze to his neck, not wanting to see his expression when I told him the rest.

"Then she got pregnant, and they didn't want—they didn't want me anymore. So they gave me back to the state. And then my caseworker put me back in those adoption picnics again, where potential parents come to pick out kids, because I was still considered a good candidate. But I wouldn't talk to anybody, and I wouldn't look at anybody because, even at seven, I would rather be alone than be left again." I exhaled, closing my eyes briefly then returning them to his face.

He looked horrified, and there was no mistaking the pity in his eyes.

"Don't. Don't feel sorry for me. I didn't tell you this so that you would feel sorry for me."

"Screw that. Of course I feel sorry for you. How could I not? That's a shite story, and those people were arseholes; and if they were here right now, I'd fuck them up—well, I'd fuck him up. But I'd give her a stern talking-to."

I exhaled a little laugh and shook my head, trying to refocus on the reason I'd started telling him the story to begin with. "My point is I can't date. I can't be someone's girl. I can't be yours; I can't—"

I didn't get to tell him what else I couldn't do because he kissed me, and this time it wasn't a staged and chaste press of his lips to mine. This time he was ferocious. His hands dropped from my face, and he wrapped me in his arms, crushing me to his chest. His tongue invaded my mouth, stroked me, demanded that I respond.

I did.

I melted against him and grabbed fistfuls of his shirt, not caring that he was damp with sweat. Despite his earlier run, he smelled like sweetness and spicy cologne and something uniquely Ronan.

When it ended and my mouth was thoroughly loved, I was a lot dizzy.

"Now, you listen to me." Ronan nipped my jaw, still holding me close. He whispered hotly against my ear, tickling me and making me shiver, "This is happening. You and I are happening, and this is real. I like you—and more than just in the biblical sense, whatever the hell that means. I love that you're brilliant and generous and gorgeous and real. I like *you*."

He took this opportunity to tongue my ear, sending shocks of delight and pleasure racing down my spine.

"Ah…." I arched my back, instinctively pressing my body to his.

"I don't give a shite about your abandonment issues because I'm not going to abandon you. They don't matter. Don't let them matter."

He sucked on my neck, his hands roaming, massaging my back and bottom through my exercise clothes.

"You're just going to have to trust me. And tomorrow I'm taking you out and showing you off; not just because I really fucking like how you look, but because you're smart and good and genuine…."

I rubbed myself against him, made a little wild by his commanding aggressiveness. Therefore, I was wholly disoriented when he gripped my upper arms and held me away. He glared at me until I blinked at him and was able to bring him into focus.

Seemingly satisfied that he had my undivided attention, Ronan ended his suspended thought with a low growl. "…and now you're mine."

TWELVE
RONAN

@Jenny0989: @RonanFitz Men like you make me sick. You deserve to be hung, drawn, and quartered #manwhore #teambrona
@RonanFitz: @Jenny0989 Hang and draw me all you like, but go near my quarters, and we'll have a problem.

March 18th
4:10 p.m.
Dear Ronan,
I agree, the truth always comes out. I'm so glad you didn't do anything rash. She doesn't deserve your time and attention (or energy).
I was surprised by your questions in the last email, regarding what I'm getting out of helping you. The answer is quite simply this: I am getting the pleasure of your correspondence. I wonder if anyone has ever told you this before, but you are very charming and likable. You're very clever—your emails make me laugh. I like you.
-SML = Someone (who) Maybe Likes (you)

It was Friday morning, and I was re-reading The Socialmedialite's last message for the umpteenth time as I rubbed at my temples. My head was officially wrecked. Now I knew who the faceless person was on the other end of the emails.

I'll admit, when I first found Annie's phone in my car, I was furious. I felt betrayed and beyond angry. I couldn't believe that I'd yet again been taken for a fool by a woman. The doorman who worked in my building, Jeffrey, who I'd built up a friendly and amiable rapport with, had asked me how my day had been, and I'd responded with a frighteningly manic: "WONDERFUL, JEFFREY, JUST CUNTING WONDERFUL!!"

So yeah, Jeffrey and I were now on the outs.

When I reached the penthouse, I went one too many rounds on the punching bag in the gym. I didn't wear any protective gear, and my hands were abraded and raw by the time I was done. Fortunately, my temper had simmered down enough that I could bring myself to steep them in some warm water, disinfect them, and wrap them up for the night.

I thought I might be having an emotional meltdown, like a wife who just found out her husband of twenty years was cheating on her. On the periphery of my mind, I was aware that my betrayed reaction was way over the top. It brought me to the stark realization that I was far more invested in Annie than I'd thought.

I knew I wanted her physically, but it was becoming plainly obvious I had feelings for her that ran deeper than that. She'd woven her way into my affections, fucking up my steady plan to keep life simple. I was supposed to be going out and having no-strings sex, yet here I was, allowing myself to get involved. There were so many strings it wasn't funny, and we weren't even having sex yet.

But back to my most recent discovery. I tried to put things into perspective.

Yes, she had been lying to me, but I'd only known her for a short while. It wasn't like I'd done anything to earn her loyalty. After I'd worked myself to exhaustion, I collapsed on my bed, staring at the ceiling. My body was dog-tired, but my mind was a flurry of activity. I tried to imagine myself in Annie's shoes. I mean, the woman had difficulty putting herself out there at the best of times. I guessed that admitting her secret famous online identity to the likes of me would be a scary prospect. It was understandable she'd kept it to herself. In fact, if she had come right out and told me, I might have been suspicious. It would have been way out of character.

Still, I was pissed, mainly because she'd kept up the correspondence with me and not admitted she already knew me. She allowed me to believe she was a stranger I could confide in, someone far removed from my everyday life. It was one thing to simply *not* tell me she was The Socialmedialite—that was the part I expected—but it was another entirely to write to me day after day, pretending to be someone else. That part took effort and secrecy and a certain level of duplicitousness.

These were my thoughts up until I met her in the park yesterday for a run. She'd spilled her guts to me, and I couldn't help but be heartbroken for her, wrap my arms around her, and let her soft body sink into mine. I wanted to be angry, but I just couldn't hold onto it.

I understood Annie's reasons for being the way she was too well. And then I had another epiphany. I thought that maybe, just maybe, Annie wasn't being duplicitous by keeping her secret. Perhaps this was the only way she could truly be herself and get to know me without her anxiety getting in the way. She needed the veil. The distance. The electronic safety net.

It went without saying that my conversations with The Socialmedialite were far more open than my dealings with Annie in person. So, after I left her to go to work yesterday, I made a decision. I would allow Annie her safety net for a while longer. I wouldn't tell her I knew her secret just yet because that way we got the best of both worlds. We'd still have the electronic avenue of communication, the one where she was confident and spoke her mind. And then we'd also have the in-person avenue, where I could delight in being around her and teasingly coax her out of her shell.

Speaking of Annie's "electronic" life, I've been finding myself reading her blog more and more, working my way through her back catalog like it was a book I couldn't wait to reach the end of. Reading her posts made me warm to her that much more because, despite my original impressions, Annie's articles weren't the same as most of the celebrity gossip trash out there. They were witty and intelligent; they poked fun at egos and hypocrisy instead of weight gain and tawdry personal lives.

In one article earlier this year, she wrote about a hip hop artist buying himself a $40 million gold-plated car while at the same time advocating a campaign to raise money for the victims of natural disasters. Annie asked, *why not just donate the pointless, garish excuse for a motor vehicle to the victims before pleading with everyday working people to give up their hard-earned cash? Take that money in your mouth, and set a good freaking example!!!*

And then late last year, a celebrity phone-hacking scandal had hit the headlines, and the world's media was condemning a number of actresses and singers for saving racy nude pictures and videos to their phones. Annie stated, *Anybody, anywhere, at any time, should be allowed to save whatever the hell they want to their phones without those files being stolen and showcased to the entire world. I don't care if you're an Oscar-winning actress or a fry-cook at McDonald's, nobody's personal privacy should ever be invaded like this, never mind spread across the Internet to be picked apart, criticized, and condemned. Is it possible, just this once, to *NOT* blame the victim?*

Reading all this was confusing. Not only did I think she was beautiful and remarkable in real life; but behind her quiet façade she was insanely clever, and she had the balls to stand up for what she believed in. She had principles, and they were the kind I respected immensely. I admired her.

So now, I stared at the screen displaying her last message to me as The SML and deliberated on a reply. The stream of conversation between us had gone silent for the last few days. I needed to figure out just the right way to start it back up. Her coming out and admitting that she liked me made me preen like a bloody peacock. I began to type.

. . .

March 21
    9:45 a.m.
    Dear SML,
    First off, my apologies for the radio silence. As you can probably guess, I've had a lot on my plate the last few days. I'm trying to be less impulsive, less easily drawn into anger, so it took a lot to sit back once Brona's story came out. Anyway, I'm trying not to fixate on it.
    So, you like me, huh?
    I'd like to say I'm surprised, but it's obvious that your previous insulting messages were a prime example of a schoolyard crush. Ma always said that the girls only called me names because they fancied me ;-)
    Unfortunately for you, my affections lie with another. However, if you'd like to win me over, you're welcome to send some racy pictures (even if they're only of your boobilicious mermaid tat.)
    Don't be a stranger.
    Ronan

I hit "send," wondering how Annie would reply.
    She still thought I had no idea who The SML was, so I made it clear there was somebody I liked. As well—though I'd liked The Socialmedialite and had enjoyed our exchanges—since meeting Annie in person, seeing how adorable and beautiful she was, I had eyes and thoughts for no one else.
    I should have been clear earlier with her online persona, but I'd always been a flirt when I wasn't dating someone. However, now I took pains to make certain The Socialmedialite—and therefore Annie—didn't think I was chasing her in the real world while trying to get my jollies with some anonymous online bird at the same time. About a half hour later, I got a response.

March 21
    10:22 a.m.
    Ronan!
    How have you been? If it weren't for the fact that you and your new squeeze have been splashed all over the Internets, I might have thought you fell down a well or something. Because that happens all the time, right? Lol. When I was a child, I used to think that getting struck by lightning was one of the main causes of death amongst humans.
    So, you and this Annie girl, eh? I have to say, despite wanting you all for myself, I'm liking her, and from what I've read, everybody else does, too. Some-

times the public can be overly critical of the non-famous girlfriends of celebrities, because you know, jealousy *and all that. So it's a really good thing that people are embracing her. I read an article today on a very popular site questioning Brona's story, since she hasn't brought forth any evidence of her claims. I think you're well on your way to being in the clear.*

And not to worry about my little crush. I will harbor it with both grace and zero hard feelings.

Your chum,
The SML

P.S. I saw those pictures of you and Annie kissing in the park yesterday. Holy shit, they were hot! My mermaid may have had some happy time in the shower after seeing them. Enjoy the visual.

I was grinning like a fool by the time I got to the end of her message. Annie had a wicked side, I'd give her that. Still, the body of her message had been too casual and friendly, and I craved something more. This was why I pulled out my phone and typed a message to the real Annie.

> RONAN
> I miss your taste. Come over.

Her reply was almost immediate.

> ANNIE
> I'm working. You'll see me tonight.

Oh, no way was she getting off that easily. I went into full-on sext mode.

> RONAN
> I want to make you come with my mouth.

> ANNIE
> Ronan! I'm at the office and Gerta is RIGHT BESIDE ME!

> RONAN
> Gotta say, that kinda makes it hotter.

> ANNIE
> *squints eyes* Do you have a thing for Gerta?

Ha! I knew she didn't like how friendly I'd gotten with her assistant.

> RONAN
> Jealous, love?

It took a while for her to answer that one, and I liked to imagine she was cursing how transparent she'd been.

> **ANNIE**
> No.

> **RONAN**
> Good, because it's not Gerta's tits I fantasize about coming all over.

Another long pause. She'd seen the message, but she wasn't typing back yet. Then finally her response came.

> **ANNIE**
> Please stop texting me. Gerta thinks I might be coming down with the flu. Your last text caused a coughing fit.

> **RONAN**
> Got you thinking, though, didn't it? ;-)

> **ANNIE**
> Yes. Too much. You're too much.

> **RONAN**
> I've actually been told I'm just the right amount :-D Admit it, you're missing me as much as I'm missing you.

> **ANNIE**
> Maybe. Just a little.

> **RONAN**
> Tell me what you miss about me.

There was an even longer pause this time. I could just imagine her fretting over whether or not to indulge me.

> **ANNIE**
> I miss how you smell. How your body feels against mine.

Okay, I had not been expecting her to play along. And yeah, I was already hard.

> **RONAN**
> You gonna let me inside you tonight, love?

I could just imagine her blushing.

ANNIE

Isn't that more of a fourth or fifth date kind of thing?

RONAN

I'm Irish. We don't adhere to that shite.

ANNIE

I have to get back to work now, Ronan.

RONAN

Okay, then. See you tonight. xxx

RONAN

Keep thinking of me.

RONAN

I can't stop thinking about you.

    When it was finally time for me to get ready for my date with Annie, I put an inordinate amount of time into my appearance. In fact, I don't think I'd ever put this level of effort into looking good before. In the end, I settled on a fitted white shirt and a pair of dark blue trousers from some designer or other. Aside from the fact that you could kind of see my tattoo through the shirt, I looked pretty fucking respectable.

    I was addicted to the way Annie's eyes drank me in whenever she saw me, and I wanted to encourage more of it. I'd insisted I be the one to pick her up, and she'd grudgingly provided me with her address. She lived in a nice building in a very upper-middle-class area. It wasn't over-the-top fancy—which I imagined she could well afford, given the extra income from her blog—but it was cozy. I found myself smiling. I liked it before I even stepped inside the building.

    I wasn't smiling for long because when I knocked on Annie's door, she wasn't the one to answer. Instead, some blond prick stood before me, one eyebrow raised as he assessed my appearance. In my opinion, no man should be assessing the appearance of another man unless he bats for the penis squad.

    "Can I help you?" the man asked, arching a brow.

    "No, you're all right, mate. I think I have the wrong apartment," I replied and turned to try the next door when Annie called out. "Ronan, is that you? Come on in."

    Her voice sounded a touch strained, and I noted she was calling me Ronan rather than Mr. Fitzpatrick. Stepping past Mr. Peroxide, I walked into the lovingly furnished apartment, taking it all in. It was so warm and lived-in that I felt like staying here with Annie for the evening rather than taking her out as planned.

    Fuck, it smelled faintly of her perfume, too.

It was so perfect that I almost forgot about the arsehole standing behind me. I ignored him and turned to Annie, who was wearing a knee-length midnight blue dress that fit her perfectly, highlighting her little waist and generous breasts, though I wished it didn't flare out and hide her shapely legs and thighs. But it did dip attractively at her cleavage, displaying her gorgeous creamy skin to perfection. Her long hair was down, and she'd put on a small touch of makeup. I stepped up close to her and took both her hands in mine, noticing her nervous swallow. I rested them on my chest and rubbed my thumbs along the inside of her wrists.

"You look beautiful, love," I murmured.

Mr. Peroxide cleared his throat, and I turned my head to him, feeling a scowl coming on.

"This is my neighbor Kurt," Annie began, her voice faltering. She seemed to be having a hard time with this situation for some reason, so I kept rubbing her skin with my thumbs in an effort to relax her. "Kurt, this is m-my, my…my Ronan."

Her eyes widened; she looked like she wanted to facepalm, but her hands were unfortunately otherwise engaged. My grin spread wide across my face.

"Fuck yeah, I am."

"I mean, he's my…."

"I'm her boyfriend," I finished for her before she started to ramble.

"Kurt lives next door. He just came over to borrow some sugar. We were laughing at the fact that we've lived next to one another for so long but only met recently. It's crazy living in a city this big. You never get to know your neighbors, you know? Anyway, enjoy the sugar, Kurt."

I chuckled quietly. God, this woman was going to kill me, she was so cute. I wanted to see her get all flustered like that when I tied her to my bedpost, wanted to see how quickly she'd shut up when I put my mouth on her.

"Yeah, Kurt, enjoy the sugar. Wouldn't want you suffering a cup of unsweetened tea, now, would we?" I added and then gave him a wink that said I found him adorable. His posture grew stiff, and his mouth formed a thin line. I knew exactly what this fuck was up to. Sugar, my arse. Such an obvious ploy to try to wheedle his way into Annie's apartment. In fact, it pissed me off to know she'd let a man she barely knew into her home. I might have to punish her a little for that one.

"I'm actually having a dinner party tonight and needed it for a dish I'm preparing," he replied smoothly.

"Well, don't let us keep you," I said, my expression hardening now.

A silent staring contest ensued. He was the one to look away first, ignoring me and focusing his attention on Annie. "I'd love for you to come over later. It's just going to be me and a few close friends. Good food, good wine, intelligent conversation." His sharp blue eyes flicked to me for a second, and I swear to

God, I was ready to deck him. He was clearly insinuating I wasn't capable of the latter.

"We actually have plans," Annie answered, giving him a small smile. "But maybe some other time."

Kurt looked like the cat that got the cream, smiling back at her lasciviously. "Yeah, I'd like that. Another time then." Shooting me one last hostile glance, he turned and left the apartment. The moment the door clicked shut, I began walking Annie backward until her back met the wall.

"Some other time?" I said, cocking an eyebrow.

"I was being polite."

"You smiled at him."

"Yeah…he's my neighbor."

My tone was tender but firm when I replied, "Annie dearest, forgive me for being blunt, but he wants to fuck you. Something you'll need to understand about me—I won't tolerate men like that, especially not in your apartment. You're mine. I told you this. This is the way it works."

Her voice was tiny but distinctly outraged. "Are you fucking serious?"

I was surprised by how easily she'd cursed and how natural it sounded slipping from her lovely lips; it seemed my Annie had a dirty mouth. But being this close to her, having her smell surround me and her pliant body flush with mine, it wasn't a surprise that I grew aroused.

I pressed the evidence of this hard into her thigh, and she let out a little gasp.

"Let go of the righteous indignation, Annie. We're together now, and there are going to be rules. I don't want other men alone with you in your apartment, but it goes both ways. I won't have women at my place, either. Shit, I don't even want to look at any other woman but you. I feel…very protective of you. Irrationally so? Yeah, maybe. But it's just the way it has to be. I promise you, once you realize all I want to give you, you'll like it. Hell, you'll love it. This is us, and this is permanent."

Something in her melted. I could feel it in the way her body lost all tension. She sank into me, her hand pressed firmly into my chest. I didn't want to talk anymore, so I brought my mouth to her swan-like neck and licked a line all the way to her earlobe. She trembled and gripped my shirt. Grabbing the back of her knees, I easily pulled her up, and she wrapped her legs around my waist. It was the perfect position for me to grind my erection right into her sweet spot.

"Ronan," she sighed right before I captured her lips with mine, plunging my tongue into her soft, wet mouth. I began to move my hips back and forth rhythmically as I devoured her with my teeth, my lips, my tongue. She was so warm and soft I felt I could get lost in her for hours, days. I didn't know how long we'd been kissing when her phone began to vibrate loudly over on her coffee table.

She loosened her legs and dropped down, breathing heavily and resting her face in the crook of my neck. "God, what are we doing?" she murmured as though to herself. When I took her chin between my fingers and lifted her face to me, she seemed overwhelmed. I was going way too fast, but I couldn't seem to help it. There was something about Kurt's presence that made some ridiculous caveman part of me need to stake my claim.

By the time the phone stopped buzzing, Annie seemed to have collected herself.

"Let's go—grab your coat."

She nodded, though she appeared to still be dazed as she walked to the closet; but then she suddenly turned back to me. "Oh! I almost forgot."

"Forgot what?"

"I…." Her eyes lifted to mine then fluttered away to the table behind me. "I got you something."

"What?"

She walked past me, giving me a little smile, then retrieved a black unmarked bag. "It's not on the market yet, but it's supposed to be much better than the latest model; and I noticed you don't have a watch, so I just thought… here." She shoved the bag into my hands.

I studied her. "You don't need to buy me anything."

"I know. I wanted to do it."

"Why?"

"Because…." She shrugged, tucking her hair behind her ear self-consciously. "Because, honestly, it felt good. It felt good to think about you and what you might want, what you might need…." Her voice trailed off, and she looked nervous and uncertain.

Her answer was alarming, and I wasn't sure why it unsettled me. Nevertheless, I tried to give her a reassuring smile as I reached in the bag, pulling out a very sleek, high-tech watch in futuristic-looking packaging.

"It's a watch," I said. By the looks of it, it also appeared to be a very expensive watch.

"Yes. But it's more than that. You can use it to track your calories—both intake and calories burned, and you can enter diet data directly—and distance is recorded via the GPS tracking. And it also lets you send and receive tweets and take pictures which you can upload immediately to social media. It's 4G, and you're already connected. So you can do it all anywhere, anytime." She was smiling at me, a big, hopeful grin. "I thought it might make your online interactions a little easier, plus the fitness tracker…."

Being connected all the time sounded awful; but I saw that she'd put a lot of thought into the gift and was excited about it, so I did the only thing I could.

I said, "Wow, thank you, Annie. This is…really great." I even sounded like I meant it, probably because I did mean it.

Just the fact that she'd bought me a present blew me away. I was on her mind; she was thinking of ways to make me happy. That was the real gift.

* * *

I HELD HER hand as we made our way outside to hail a cab. I took her to Tom's for dinner because she seemed to really like the food there. Thankfully, tonight was Tom's night off, so I wouldn't have to sit through Annie fangirling him again.

Instead of sitting opposite her at the booth, I sat right next to her. After what happened at her place, I felt the need to be as close as I could possibly get.

I hadn't planned on drinking, but strangely, when the waitress came to take our order, I found myself asking for a beer. These feelings I had for Annie, the intensity of them, shit, it was no surprise I needed something to take the edge off. Annie ordered a glass of red wine, and I couldn't stop staring when her full lips curved around the edge of the glass. I could see in her eyes that she knew exactly what I was thinking.

I asked her lots of questions about her life now, her childhood, the kinds of things she liked to do. She was a tough nut to crack for most of it, only giving me quick, close-ended answers. I wanted to know about the things she'd been through as a kid. Just call me a masochist because I knew hearing about it would piss me off, but I still had this fierce need to know it all, somehow exorcise those demons for her.

She turned the conversation back on me and seemed more than content to listen as I talked about myself. In fact, she ate it up. I saw genuine interest with each new story; it didn't matter if I was talking about pranks during college or a particularly vicious rugby match, her eyes were bright, watchful, engrossed. She was enthralled, hung on my every word.

She made me feel like I was the king of fascinating blokes. It was a heady feeling, seductive, did wonders for my ego. It confirmed that she genuinely liked me.

"You're a great storyteller." Her words were a little slurred, and I smiled warmly. "This was nice," she went on as she gazed up at me from beneath her thick lashes. She was on her third glass of wine, her cheeks growing rosy, and I'd just finished my second beer. The waitress came and set the bill on the table.

"It's not over yet," I replied, rubbing my thumb over her bottom lip. I felt her breath sweep over my skin in a rush.

"No?"

I shook my head, my lips curving in a smile. "I'm taking you dancing."

Her eyes got big and round, and she seemed surprised. "You dance?"

I nodded. "Relatively well."

It wasn't long before we were being papped making our way inside a flashy nightclub in a stylish area of Manhattan. Truth be told, Tom had suggested the place. I knew no more about flashy Manhattan nightclubs than I did about open heart surgery. With my hand firmly on Annie's lower back, I ushered her to the bar, where a tall, slim woman wearing a belly top took our drinks order.

"Oh, my God! You're Ronan Fitzpatrick, aren't you?" a female voice squealed from behind me. Annie got a hunted look on her face and focused intently on the glass she was holding. It was moments like these that I realized just how unused she was to being around people. Obviously, she wasn't sheltered, but she'd kept herself away from social situations for so long that she was no longer equipped to handle them. I turned to find three women wearing tight little dresses and sky-high heels smiling at me like I'd just told them they'd won the Lotto.

"It is him!" another said. "Could you please sign something for us? We've been following your romance this week in all the magazines, and we are just obsessed with the both of you." They all gave Annie encouraging smiles, but she just stood quietly next to me as though frozen. I signed some napkins for them and let them take some pictures, and they gushed a little more before finally leaving us alone. The barwoman tapped me on the shoulder then and handed me a card.

"We've got a private VIP section upstairs if you'd prefer," she suggested.

I took the card, thanked her, and then slid my hand into Annie's.

"Did you notice how those women didn't talk about Brona?" said Annie. "This is good. It means people are focusing more on our relationship than her story."

"True, but it doesn't surprise me," I said tenderly. "One look at those big brown eyes of yours and the public probably fell head over heels."

Ignoring my compliment, she asked, "Are we going upstairs now?"

"Yeah, soon, but first I want to dance with you," I replied, leading her to the busy dance floor. The DJ started playing "Nightcall," and the heavy electronic beat sank into my bones. I brought my arms around Annie's waist and pulled her close, moving our bodies to the hypnotic song. I stared down at her the entire time, admiring how her lashes cast a dark shadow over her cheekbones. She refused to look at me, instead keeping her gaze fixed firmly in the vicinity of my neck. Frustrated, I brought my hands up to her face and cupped her cheeks, tilting her head so that she'd finally give me her eyes. Her skin felt warm and soft beneath my sport-roughened palms.

Our hips began to move in unison—a slow, sensual rhythm—and now that our gazes were locked, it felt like neither one of us could look away. I stared deep into her eyes, and even though we were surrounded by dozens of strangers, it felt more intimate somehow than if I were inside her. I felt like I was trying to see right into her soul. Right then I knew that this woman had the power to destroy me. It was a frightening prospect. She was way, way deep under my skin. I could hardly fathom what adding sex to the equation would bring, especially if she was open to doing things my way.

"I feel like I could lose myself and find myself in you, Annie," I murmured close to her ear.

She swallowed. "Don't say things like that."

"I can't help it. Believe me, I've tried. You make me feel *everything*."

Her body seemed to sink further into mine at that moment, and before I knew it, I was leading her upstairs to the private section the barwoman had recommended. A man in a suit led us to a little half-crescent alcove with plush, expensive-looking seating. Annie made a move to sit down, but I pulled her arm and twirled her so she fell onto my lap. I knew that fourth glass of wine was taking its toll when, instead of protesting, she let out a little giggle. God, she was so fucking sexy. Frenzied, I fisted her long, silky hair in my hand, yanked gently, and then brought my mouth over hers. I heard a small muffled moan as she strained to get closer, her breasts pushing into my chest deliciously.

Letting go of her hair, I grabbed her hips and lifted her so that she was straddling me. It was such a small movement, but it made *all* the difference. I knew Annie could feel it, too, when she sighed my name.

"Ronan...."

"Can you feel me, love?" I asked darkly, trailing my mouth down her neck, across her collarbone, and over her lush cleavage. I dragged my lips over the tops of her breasts and felt her quivering. Using one hand, I gripped her neck and could feel her pulse fluttering against my fingertips.

"Yeah," she finally answered, all breathy. "I need more."

She didn't have to ask twice. I suddenly appreciated that the skirt of her dress was long and flared rather than close-fitting because it meant I could slide my hand under without it really looking like we were doing more than kissing. Slowly, I ran my palm up her silky thigh before slipping it between her legs and cupping her over her lacy underwear. I didn't think I'd ever been this turned on in my life. Every little sound she made, every movement, made me feel like I might come without her even needing to touch me.

"Oh, God," she moaned, seeking my lips eagerly. I sank my tongue into her mouth at the same moment I slid my hand under the lace and felt her for the first time. Fuck, she was wet. She was getting loud now; but the music in the club was blaring, so I was the only one who could hear her. There was something exciting about that, about the fact that one of the workers could come by and discover what we were doing at any moment. I think Annie felt that excitement, too, because her skin was damp and had goosebumps where I was still holding tightly onto her neck. That was the sign that I was the one in control, the one leading her, even though she was on top.

I sank two fingers inside her and felt her pulse all around me. Jesus, I didn't think I'd last much longer. Groaning, I sought her clit with my thumb, rubbing circles while my fingers moved in a rhythm inside her. She was lost to me then, and I was lost to her. She owned me, and she didn't have a clue. I broke our kiss because I wanted to see her when she came. I knew she was close because her entire body felt like a coiled spring. Leaning back against the seat, I stared up at her, my hand still working beneath her dress.

Her long hair hung to the side of her face, her lips plump from kissing and her cheeks pink. Her chest rose and fell, making me wish we weren't in public so I could strip her bare. My body was covered in a layer of perspiration, I was so worked up, and then she came with a sharp, keening cry and tremors that lasted and lasted. She collapsed into my arms, and I was completely done for. Her face was in my neck, mouth planting kisses and murmuring indistinct words.

"That's it, Annie, that's it," I said, my fingers still inside her. I caressed her cheek with my other hand and whispered in her ear. "Come home with me."

"I shouldn't…."

"But you want to. For once in your life, let yourself have what you want."

She looked at me then, biting on her bottom lip, and replied with that sweet little word, "Okay."

The entire taxi ride to my building, I kissed her. I could have kissed her for hours. You know, those lazy afternoon sessions on the couch when just kissing is enough? Well, I could have done that every day with Annie and never tired of it.

In the lift up to the penthouse, my hands were all over her, in her hair, squeezing her arse, molding her breasts. Hers were all over me, too. She was finally letting go of her inhibitions. When she pressed her hand against my cock, I wanted to bite her, it felt so good. I kissed her so fiercely her lips were probably going to be sore in the morning.

In my mind, I searched through my memory of what I had in the penthouse. I hadn't brought very much with me, but there had to be something I could use to tie her up. Then I remembered the welcome basket that had been there for me when I arrived. It had silky red ribbon wrapped all around it. It wouldn't be great, but it would do for now.

Managing to slot my key in the door and still keep my mouth on hers, I pushed it open and pulled her inside, slamming her back against the wall and lifting her leg so that I could press my hard-on into her core. I heard somebody clear their throat just before a voice I recognized well said, "Um, I'm sorry to interrupt you two, but yeah, this is awkward."

Annie gasped in surprise, and I sagged against her.

Fucking. Hell.

I sighed, my hands fisting in frustration, and clenched my jaw.

"Lucy," I muttered under my breath. I took a moment to gather myself before I straightened and turned around to see my sister grinning and my mother wearing a small frown.

Sighing, I squeezed Annie's shoulder and with no small amount of reluctance said, "I guess this is the perfect time for you to meet my family."

THIRTEEN
ANNIE

The Fake Selfie: *When one pretends to be taking a picture of oneself, but is instead actually taking a picture of a person in the background. This method differs from the "Creeper Selfie" in that none of the photographer's face or expression is present in the picture.*
Best for: *Situations where taking a selfie wouldn't be unusual/draw attention, e.g. while alone at a tourist attraction or during a sporting event/concert.*
Do not use: *In restaurants or near mirrors.*

It was a banner week for me, a real doozy, a landmark of atypical Annie-isms.

First, I'd opened up to Ronan about my past, and, as much as I was able, I'd admitted to having feelings for him. I trusted him, or at least I was starting to.

Then I flirted with him via email; granted, it was as The Socialmedialite, and the lewd references all involved my fictional mermaid tattoo.

Of course, I couldn't neglect to mention the sexting—or as close as I'd ever come to sexting—on Friday that got me so hot I'd had to go to the bathroom and run cool water over my wrists and place a wet paper towel on my neck.

Oh, yeah, and then there was introducing him as my boyfriend to my bossy and persistent neighbor; ambiguously giving in to Ronan's demands about how I spent my time and with whom; the caveman dry-humping against the wall in my apartment; the orgasm in the dance club; and the make-out marathon in the taxi, in the elevator, in the hallway, and against the door of his apartment.

Ah, yes, and how could I forget meeting his mother and his sister immediately afterward? Or how I'd practically sprinted out of the apartment after introductions were made?

Lovely. Just lovely.

At least I hadn't spat tea in anyone's face…yet. Just my boyfriend's.

Ronan…my boyfriend.

He was my boyfriend. We were a *we*, an *us*. I was part of a couple; I was more than just a one. I tried to ignore the way my heart thundered whenever I thought about it, how excited just the thought of seeing Ronan made me, of belonging with him.

As well I tried to suppress thoughts of our future, asking myself whether we would live in Ireland or in New York—I hoped Ireland. I wondered whether Joan would mind if I telecommuted from overseas, whether Ronan already had an apartment in Dublin or we'd pick one out together. I didn't honestly care. Of course, getting shots of celebrities in Dublin might be an issue. But that didn't really matter. I would give up the blog in a heartbeat if it meant being with Ronan….

I was completely mad, made insane by physical human connection.

WriteALoveSong had even commented on "Annie and Ronan's connection." I received a message from her early this morning with a fuzzy picture of Ronan and me at the bar last night.

@WriteALoveSong to @Socialmedialite: I know you've got a little crush on this rugby guy, so prepare yourself. He's dating some hottie with a body and an epically pretty face. It looks very serious. One of my club contacts sent me the picture…If you need a shoulder to cry on, I can send you a blow-up doll. Just pretend it's me.

I'd looked at the picture entirely too much, liking how we looked together entirely too much. It was genuine and serious and happening entirely too fast, but I didn't care.

I was in desperate *like* with a real person. I couldn't remember ever liking someone as much as I did Ronan. I liked him so goddamn much; I thought about him all the freaking time. It was more than just how epically sexy he was. He was fucking charming as hell, and funny, and smart, and sweet, and brave, and determined, and honorable….

"Debbie downer does Dallas, dammit," I muttered under my breath, pushing these thoughts away before they started running away from me. I kept my eyes on the gravel path. How much I liked Ronan flustered and worried me, but I liked him more than giving into the temptation to worry. I wanted him. I wanted him so much it hurt.

And now, on this sunny and unusually warm Saturday morning in March, I was wearing makeup for the second time in two days, on my way to properly meet and spend time with my boyfriend's family. I was twenty-three, but last night was the first time in my life I'd ever met the family of someone I was dating; and I was sure I'd made a terrible impression.

Well, I reasoned, *at least I can't sink any lower in their estimation. I have nowhere to go but up.*

As well, I was wearing the necklace Ronan had given me. It felt warm against my skin, a gentle touch that made me think of him.

They were all there when I arrived even though I was five minutes early. My eyes were immediately drawn to Ronan, and my ability to hone in on his location even in a crowded restaurant was disconcerting. I took a moment to survey them from my spot by the front door.

Ronan's sister, Lucy, had rainbow hair, meaning she'd dyed her hair in sections. The front was red and then came orange, yellow, and green. Blue, indigo, and violet merged to form an amorphous bluish-purple at the back. Currently, she wore it in a long and loose French braid down her back.

She was sitting in profile and shared Ronan's attractive bone structure, but her features were exceedingly refined, elegant, and delicate. It was like his face but softer and feminine. Also, I remembered last night being startled by her eyes because they were cornflower blue.

Really, she was beautiful. But more than that, she had a friendly, carefree, spirited energy about her. During our very short introduction, she'd struck me as joyful, and I could see it now as she spoke to her brother. Her hands were animated as she talked, and her smile was enormous.

I shifted on my feet, allowing myself to lurk for a moment longer as I brought my attention to his mother. She was…well, she was beautiful. But hard. Even from this distance, I recognized in her a sort of kinship, a woman who'd had a difficult life, had been dealt an unfair hand.

She had the same blue eyes as her daughter, but—other than their coloring—Lucy and Mrs. Fitzpatrick looked nothing alike. Where Lucy was delicate, Ronan's mother was exotic, her features sharp. Her hair was blonde; her lips were cushioned and full; her cheekbones high, leaving a hollow above her jaw. She was stunning.

But hard.

She held herself away from her children even as she sat at the table with them. She wore a smile like people wear a coat or a scarf. It looked foreign and bulky on her features.

I wondered briefly if I looked like that. I wondered if a smile and joy and happiness looked like transitory visitors on my face rather than like they belonged there.

…or was I like Lucy?

No, I thought sadly. *I am not like Lucy.*

A cold sensation slithered over my skin, a blanket of sorrow, an inkling that maybe Ronan deserved someone less messy, less reticent—because he still had joy. Yes, at times his eyes were sad, but he still had a brightness in him, one he couldn't contain or hide. It was a part of him, and I loved it.

"Can I help you, miss?"

I started, turning my attention to the hostess who stood at my elbow. She was young, likely in her first or second year of college, and exceedingly pretty. Her eyes moved over me with solicitous curiosity.

"Oh, yes. I—uh, I see my party. They're right there." I pointed to the table where Ronan sat with his mother and sister.

The hostess's gaze followed where I'd indicated, and I heard her murmur under her breath, "Lucky you…."

I should have smiled at this and chuckled. A normal person likely would have agreed, *Lucky me.* Instead, I felt cagey and irritated. This was how it would be with Ronan. Other women looking, liking, coveting. I didn't have any desire to be waging a constant war against taller, sexier, slimmer, prettier girls. I felt a bit lost, in over my head. I didn't know what I was thinking, what I was doing here.

Who did I think I was? That I would have a chance with this guy? I was living in a fantasy, one that would leave me abandoned—again—and heartbroken.

These were my cheerful thoughts as the hostess unnecessarily guided me to the table. Her steps were hasty, leaving me several feet behind. I noted how she touched Ronan's shoulder and bent near him, whispered in his ear, how close she stood, how she lingered.

His eyes lifted as she spoke and fell on mine. Then he smiled.

And it was like the clouds parting.

I saw his joy, witnessed the happiness in his features shining like a beacon. He stood abruptly and must've not realized the hostess was still there because his chair hit her in the legs, and she stumbled back. He turned briefly to offer a hasty apology and then darted around the table to meet me.

He was…eager, excited, even. His excitement was palpable, contagious, and I found myself smiling broadly as he approached.

I opened my mouth to say hi, but he stopped me with a quick kiss, his hands sliding into my open coat and squeezing my bottom. I was glad the coat was long and hid his handsy liberties.

"I like your necklace." His eyes were warm, told me that he was pleased. Then he added against my mouth, "I missed you."

"It's only been ten hours." I smiled up at him, tilting my head back so I could see his face.

"It's been ten lonely, painful hours." He lowered his face to my neck. "I needed you last night. I had to be content with remembering how wet and soft your pussy felt when you came on my fingers." Ronan's voice was low as he whispered in my ear.

I shivered, my eyes half closing. I caught my lip between my teeth, unable to speak. I was panting and abruptly primed for anything he wanted to do to me.

"Ronan, don't be rude." Mrs. Fitzpatrick's voice cut through my arousal like a bucket of ice water. And lilting though it was, it held a granite edge.

He pulled back, a devilish grin curving his mouth as he examined the effect his naughty words had on my composure. His roguish brown eyes lit, fiercely ablaze. He looked like a mischievous boy who was quite pleased with himself for getting caught, looking forward to receiving punishment for plotted misdeeds.

I narrowed my eyes at him and endeavored to bring my body under control. Meanwhile, he winked at me and then turned back to his mother and sister, lacing his fingers through mine and pulling me after him.

"Sorry, Ma." He didn't sound sorry.

Ronan led me to the vacant chair next to his and his sister, Lucy's; his mother was directly across from me. I smiled at both Mrs. Fitzpatrick and Lucy in greeting, noted that Mrs. Fitzpatrick looked more assessing than welcoming, and allowed Ronan to help me out of my coat. He pulled out the seat, made sure I was settled, then claimed his spot again.

"Good morning," I said to the table. I was fighting with myself; I wanted to make eye contact but couldn't manage more than quick glances at either woman. "I hope I'm not late."

"Nah, we're early. I was starving. My stomach thinks it's dinner time." Lucy grinned, angling toward me, giving me all her attention. "I'm so glad you came."

I met her eyes directly and returned her friendly overtures with a broad smile. "Me, too. Thank you for inviting me."

Lucy's stare moved over my face, and she breathed out, "Goodness, you're gorgeous."

My attention dropped back to the table, and a surprised flush crawled up my neck. "Oh, thank you. That's...you're very kind."

"Don't embarrass her, Lucy," Mrs. Fitzpatrick said, though to my ears it sounded more like, *Don't embarrass me, Lucy.*

Lucy, ignoring her mother, addressed her next statement to her brother. "You said nothing, you tart. We've talked on the phone every day for the last month, and here you've lured the most beautiful woman in New York up to your lair." She *tsked*, and I saw her shake her head. "My brother is a sneaky and saucy wench."

"Can't blame me for wanting her to myself, can you?" I heard the warmth in his voice, the affection for his sister. He leaned forward and placed a hand on my thigh, sliding it under the hem of my skirt but no higher.

I swallowed thickly and reached for my water because my mouth was dry.

"I knew once I told you about Annie you'd be over here in a flash, wanting to braid her hair and dye it chartreuse or some such nonsense."

Lucy giggled. "I wonder, Annie. Have you ever thought about going blonde?"

"Don't you dare." His eyes widened with warning, though he looked like he was trying to keep from laughing. "Don't change a thing about her. My Annie is perfect just as she is."

This compliment quadrupled my blush, and I closed my eyes briefly. I was bad with compliments that weren't specifically about my work quality. I wasn't used to them, not real ones. Not compliments that came from a place of sincerity and fondness.

Yes, I'd been complimented on my looks before—but always with heat, never with warmth.

"Look, you're embarrassing her!" Lucy admonished him then covered my hand, capturing my gaze with hers. "My dearest Annie, stick with me. I'll make him stop torturing you."

"She likes my torture," Ronan muttered, squeezing my thigh, and reaching for his water glass.

Lucy made a face at him then glanced back to me. "He's rough around the edges, and he thinks of himself a bit too highly; but inside he's all mush. Did you know he likes show tunes?"

Ronan choked on the water he'd just sipped.

Lucy took advantage of his inability to speak to list all of the plays he'd taken her to and how they sometimes sang along to the soundtrack from *The Phantom of the Opera* while in his car back home. By the time he'd recovered from his coughing fit, the two siblings were sparring back and forth, seeing who could one-up the other with embarrassing details.

I watched their interaction with fascinated delight. They were so open. There was so much love, respect, and history between them. I was drawn to it and relaxed as I witnessed their banter. This went on for quite some time and was often paused when the three of us lost ourselves in a fit of laughter.

It was during these times—when Lucy, Ronan, and I laughed—that I was most cognizant of Mrs. Fitzpatrick. She didn't laugh; though her smiles were appropriate, both in size and duration, they never seemed to reach her eyes.

Breakfast came. We ate. Lucy skillfully tricked me into talking a few times about myself. She was charming. Ronan's hand remained on my leg but traveled no higher. I realized it was meant to show support, and when he stood and excused himself to the restroom, I found I missed his touch.

Lucy smiled at me once Ronan was out of earshot and then leaned forward conspiratorially. "Now then, quick before he gets back. How did you meet? Was it love at first sight? When are you coming to Ireland? Will you come out with me? What kind of music do you like?"

I grinned at her question assault, knowing with certainty that not loving Lucy was impossible.

"Yes. Let's hear the story," Mrs. Fitzpatrick drawled, her tone flat.

I glanced at her, found her examining me, her fingers steepled in front of her, her eyes anything but friendly.

"Oh, well…." I cleared my throat and fiddled with the rim of my half-eaten plate of eggs benedict. "We met at my office—"

"No, dear." Mrs. Fitzpatrick shook her head, her mouth both smiling and frowning. "I want the real story. This must be like hitting the jackpot for you." Her eyes flickered over me, holding disapproval and contempt. "How long did you plot all this before making your move?"

"Mother!"

"Shut it, Lucy. You don't get to have an opinion about this. Ronan isn't your son."

"He's my brother, and—"

"Yes." Mrs. Fitzpatrick's glittering eyes slid to her daughter. "And who has put a roof over your head and food in your mouth? I have. Your brother has. And you are a talentless burden to both of us. I know what's best."

Lucy winced, seemed to shrink in her seat and fold in on herself. I thought I saw a flicker of regret pass over Mrs. Fitzpatrick's gaze, but it was quickly stifled, replaced with a diamond-like sharpness as she refocused on me.

"You think you've got him? You think you matter to him? You are so wrong. Ronan is like his father—even when trapped, married with children, he wanted his freedom. I understood that. Brona didn't. That's why he never married her. They were together for years, and it never once occurred to him to settle down. Ronan won't settle down, and that's why she's gone off her rocker now. He's a shameless flirt. He's a philanderer. He uses people. It's who he is. It's in his blood. If you think you're anything but a dalliance, then you're living in a fantasy."

I tried, but I couldn't look away. Her uncanny ability to touch on the heart of my fears held me entranced. Mrs. Fitzpatrick leaned forward slowly, her movements measured and lithe, like a cat. When she spoke next, her voice was soft, gentle, beseeching, like she felt sorry for me and was trying to let me down easy.

"Who are you? Nobody. Nothing. Ronan is a Fitzpatrick. As such, he might enjoy what you offer him for a time, but…dear, you won't hold his interest for long. I know my son. He isn't perfect, but I love him. And I am telling you this because you seem like a nice person…."

She stared at me for a beat, holding me in suspense; even so, I wasn't prepared for her final words, smoothly and elegantly spoken.

"Ronan likes playing with his toys…." Her eyes lowered to the chain around my neck and the Celtic pendant as she added, "But he never notices when they break."

Nothing, no words, no sentiment could have been more effective. I sucked in a sharp breath. My eyes stung with unshed tears. Dumbly, I stood from the table and stared at it. My heart beat a steady rhythm in my chest, seemed to chant, *get out get out get out get out* between my ears.

I was so stupid. I knew better. I *knew better.*

I reached for my coat and bag with shaking hands, muttering, "Thank you for the lovely breakfast. But I have…I need to be someplace."

Lucy reached for my hand. I flinched away from her and didn't miss the reproachful glare administered by her mother. "No! Don't lis—"

"Let her go, Lucy. She has a lot to think about."

I didn't waste time pulling on my coat. I tucked it over my arm and made a beeline for the exit, stumbling a little in my haste, the need to escape choking me. Unfortunately, I had the worst timing in the world because Ronan was just leaving the hall leading to the bathrooms, and our gazes tangled as I made it to the hostess stand.

I winced, tore my eyes away, and swiftly bolted through the doors.

"Annie!"

My shoulders bunched at the sound of my name. He was behind me; he was coming after me, and he would catch me. There was no point in trying to outrun him. I stopped, grinding my teeth, my eyes closing as I put my feelings to the side, readied myself for what would come next.

He reached me in about five seconds, tugging on my arm and turning me to face him. I met his gaze briefly then yanked my arm out of his grip, pretended to be absorbed in putting my coat on.

"Where are you going?"

"I have someplace to be."

"Where?"

I lifted my eyes then and glared at him. "None of your business."

"None of my business?" I could see he thought I was joking at first. When he realized I was not, his features darkened, and a severe frown pulled his eyebrows into a sharp "V." "Everything about you is my business."

"No. It's not."

"I thought you understood how things are. We're together now, and there are rules—"

"We're not together," I whispered, my eyes stinging again. I firmed my lips, willing myself not to cry.

"Like hell we're not." He reached for me, and I stepped to the side, evading him.

"Don't touch me."

He moved like he was going to reach for me again, and I stiffened, adding more force to my voice. "Don't touch me; I mean it."

That seemed to do the trick because he reeled back like I'd struck him, and he looked equal parts surprised and hurt.

"What happened?" His eyes searched me as though he were looking for a sign, an injury.

He wouldn't find the injury because I'd never let him see it.

"I have to go."

"Dammit, Annie. What the fuck is going on?"

"I promised Kurt we'd spend the day together." It was such a low blow that even I flinched as I said the words. "I don't want to keep him waiting. He doesn't like that."

Ronan winced, his eyes half blinking. Then he stared at me. He reminded me of a gathering storm, imminently threatening. He was so strong, so big, so powerful. But it wasn't his body that was dangerous. His words, his looks and touches, his laughs and smiles…his lies.

And he looked hurt. His face told me that I'd hurt him. I felt myself soften toward him; my chin wobbled, but I quickly caught the instinct to soothe and comfort before I gave into it, into him and these feelings I had no right feeling because I knew better. I ripped my gaze from his and stuffed my hands in my coat pockets.

"I have to go," I whispered.

"Go then." His tone was flat, and he took a step back as though giving me a wide berth, showing me he wasn't going to stand in my way.

I nodded, knowing with certainty that I was going to start crying in the next sixty seconds. I would cry all the way home. I was going to be that mad, insane crying woman, walking the streets of New York, sobbing like a fool.

Because there was nothing else to say, I left.

And I cried.

FOURTEEN
RONAN

@RonanFitz: My phone keeps whistling at me. Anybody know how to shut it up?
@Irenelovesrugby: @RonanFitz If I were your phone, I'd be whistling at you too, sexy ;-) :-* <3 :-P
@RonanFitz: @Irenelovesrugby Something wrong with your keyboard, darlin. Shitload of nonsense at the end there.

"Loooook, darling brother, I brought you a gift," Lucy singsonged as she came into my room and draped a blue and green scarf around my neck. I took a glance at the label and saw it cost over two hundred dollars.

I let out a low whistle and said, "Pricey. What's this for?"

She perched on the edge of my bed and crossed one leg over the other. "I thought a gift might cheer you up."

I was sitting in a chair by the desk at the window, pathetically reading through all of the emails I'd swapped with Annie, aka The Socialmedialite, and trying to find a clue as to why she might've withdrawn. In other words, I was moping.

"And I thought you believed that happiness can't be found through material possessions," I countered, arching a brow.

Something passed over her face, but it was gone in an instant. Now she was smiling. "Ah, that's true, but it doesn't count for gift giving. Studies have actually proven that we derive far more happiness from buying things for other people than we do buying for ourselves."

"Yeah, well, a scarf isn't going to make me feel better," I said and ran a hand down my face. "I really thought I'd made a breakthrough with Annie, and then she just rushes off like that during breakfast." In all honesty, it was taking every ounce of my willpower not to go over to her place because thinking of her spending even a second with that overly coiffed dickhead of a neighbor made me want to break something, preferably his smug face.

Lucy sucked in a deep breath, and her words came out in a hurried, whispered tumble. "You know, I couldn't say anything in front of Ma at the restaurant earlier, but I don't think Annie's rushing off had anything to do with her feelings for you. It wasn't your fault. Ma was an absolute cow to her. She first insinuated that Annie was with you for the money, and then she...well, she made it sound like you're not...."

I held my breath; I didn't even blink. When Lucy didn't continue, I pressed, "Like I'm not what?"

Lucy huffed, "Like you have 'commitment issues,' like you don't believe in monogamy."

I got up abruptly from my chair, jaw clenching, temper rising.

"She did what?" I asked, my voice low in disbelief.

"I'm sorry, but it's what she said. You're always away, whether you're travelling with the team or coming to New York for a break. You don't spend time with Ma the way that I do. You get her in small, palatable doses." Her voice grew sad as she looked down at her hands in her lap. "Besides, you're, like, her favorite person, so obviously she's going to be nice to you. You don't see the side of her that the rest of us see."

Frowning, I walked toward her and placed a hand on her shoulder. "Has she been giving you trouble?"

Lucy scoffed, but it seemed forced. "Hardly. Her remarks have just gotten worse the last few years. Before then, you were always around to temper her moods."

"That's not on. I'm going to have a word with her."

"No, don't...."

Lucy grabbed my wrist to try to pull me back, but I was already marching from the room. I found Ma in the lounge going through a bunch of shopping bags she'd just brought back. She and Lucy had spent the day enjoying some retail therapy. When they'd arrived the other night, Ma had said she was desperately worried about me over the whole Brona thing, and that's why she'd dropped everything to come see me. Now I was beginning to wonder if she'd just wanted to enjoy the shopping opportunities New York provided and stick her nose in my business with Annie.

"What do you think you're playing at, talking to Annie like that?"

She didn't look up from her treasures as she asked, "Has Lucy been telling tales?"

"What exactly did you say to her?"

When she did glance up, she gave me a placid look like I was being overdramatic and took her time setting the Louis Vuitton bag aside before answering me. "Oh, Ronan, come sit down. I only have your best interests at heart."

"No, you obviously don't. If you did, you'd be treating Annie like a queen rather than sniping at her behind my back. That girl is everything to me, so you're going to have to accept her. Jesus, the shit she's been through, and you go and pull a stunt like this." I was wracked with worry, furiously running my hand through my hair, trying to figure out a way to apologize to Annie.

Ma scoffed and rolled her eyes. "*Please,* I'm sure whatever she's told you is a web of lies concocted to solicit your sympathy. Girls like Annie see men like you coming from a mile away. Believe me, I know."

"Girls like Annie?"

"You know, the ones that rely on their looks and their horizontal talents."

Something in me snapped. "God give me patience, you haven't a clue. So in future, you can keep your mouth shut and your nose out of it. I'm going out. If you want dinner, you can order something in."

I grabbed my shoes from where I'd left them by the door to the room and pulled them on, giving her my back.

I heard her sniff then take a shaky breath.

I ignored her dramatics and continued, "Oh, yeah, and take it easy on Lucy, would you? She's your daughter and the only female friend you have, so quit giving her shit all the time. She's a great girl."

I made the mistake of glancing toward her. My mother's eyes were watering, and she looked at me like I'd struck her, like I'd betrayed her.

Just. Fucking. Fantastic.

I didn't want to apologize. Hell, I had no reason to apologize. So I turned from her watery gaze and marched to the door. I was just about to leave when she spoke up, and I could hear the falling tears in her voice. "I'm sorry—I've been missing you, that's all," she called after me, her words ending on a sob.

I loved my mother to pieces; but she was a master manipulator, and I knew the crying jag was her way of getting me to feel sorry for her. No matter how angry I was, I couldn't walk away from her when she crying; I just didn't have it in me.

"Fuck," I swore and walked back to her, flopping down beside her and pulling her in for a hug. "The next time you're around Annie just be nice to her, okay? She's an amazing woman, and I really think you'll like her once you give her a chance."

"I'm sorry," she said again, and I patted her on the back before standing up. "I really don't know what I could have said that upset her so much."

I ignored this statement because it sounded false. "I really need to get out for a while. I'm going stir-crazy sitting in this place all day."

She nodded, and I gave her once last reassuring look before I left. I'd hardly made it to the street before my phone started ringing. I pulled it out immediately, hoping it was Annie. Disappointment struck when I saw it wasn't a number I recognized. I answered, and Joan began talking down the line immediately.

"Okay, so I've just been in a video conference with your people back in Ireland. As you're probably aware, the Sportsperson of the Year Awards are taking place in Dublin next weekend, and the organizers would like you to go and present an award. As well, we've arranged several additional public appearances. You'll be there for three weeks at least. Apparently, they're on your side in relation to the bad press surrounding your ex. Rachel and Ian have been working around the clock finding ways to discredit her. We have quite a laundry list compiled. No need to thank them—Brona has made it quite easy. Also, the ceremony will be a great way for you to initiate your return to the team, get your picture in the magazines and such. I'm going to arrange for Annie to accompany you. You'll leave on Thursday morning and fly back to New York on Sunday. That gives you a couple of days to prepare. Sound good?"

I laughed. "Did you even breathe during all that, Joan?"

"I'm a busy woman," she replied, a smile in her voice. "Now, are you on board for this or not?"

"Yeah, I'm on board," I answered. I didn't relish the idea of going home so soon, but several weeks alone with Annie all to myself was too good an opportunity to pass up. She clearly didn't want to be around me right now, but I didn't think she'd say no to Joan. After she passed on a few more details, I hung up and typed out a message to Annie.

> RONAN
>
> Lucy told me what Ma said to you. I'm so sorry. She was way out of line. We need to talk. I'm going to call you in a minute, so please pick up.

I crossed the street and walked inside the park, finding a bench and sitting down. Then I dialed Annie's number. No answer. I tried again twice, but there was still no answer, so I sent another text.

> RONAN
>
> Please tell me you were lying about Kurt. I'm going crazy here. I can't stand the thought of you with him. With anyone. Please pick up. I never beg, but I'll beg for you, Annie.

After several more attempts to call her, I hung up. She was shutting me out.

I ended up taking a cab to Tom's. The place was crowded and busy, but he made time to sit with me and listen to my woes. For the second day in a row, I found myself drinking; and it's embarrassing to admit because I certainly didn't look like a lightweight, but I was tipsy by the time I got to my second beer. I'd been living so clean, putting my health and fitness first, that my body wasn't used to alcohol. Tom had to take my phone off me when I tried to drunk-dial Annie.

It wasn't like she was going to pick up anyway.

Later on he brought me back to the penthouse, and Ma looked horrified to see I'd been drinking. I'd be lying if I said I didn't take a small amount of pleasure in that. She'd screwed things up for me with Annie, so I wasn't feeling so warm toward her right then.

The next morning I woke up with a thumping headache. It was safe to say this was the first time I'd experienced a hangover in a long while. Even after all the drama of my breakup with Brona, I never hit the bottle. I was being ridiculous. After some exercise and a nourishing breakfast, I decided to try a different tack and emailed The Socialmedialite.

March 23
10:07 a.m.
Dear SML,
Here lies the message of a desperate man.
I need your advice. It saddens me to admit that I'm having woman troubles. I'm crazy about Annie, but she's not taking my calls. We were getting along great, but then my mother showed up for an impromptu visit and said some harsh stuff to her, all of which was complete bullshit. My mother can be possessive and overprotective, but that doesn't excuse her behavior. In a nutshell, Annie's feelings were hurt, and she ended things. I need to make this right, but I have no idea what to do. You're a woman—tell me how women think, what they need.
Your suggestions are much appreciated.
Ronan

After stewing for a minute or two, I hit "send" and waited. And waited. And then waited some more. Deciding that a watched pot never boils, I went and took a run around the park. I was going overboard with the exercise, but it was the only thing that channeled my restless energy. I had REO Speedwagon blaring on my iPod in an effort to drown out my thoughts.

I spotted a group of college guys playing a game of rugby and offered to join in. A couple of them actually recognized me and were over the moon to have me take part. All of Annie's teachings must have been rubbing off on me because I took the opportunity to take a picture with them and posted it to Instagram.

@RonanFitz: Saw these boys in the park. Decided to join them for a match.

I felt weird and stilted in the way I wrote the caption, but I just didn't know how to insert my personality into the post. Still, after only a couple of minutes, the picture had thousands of "likes," and people were commenting on how they wished they could be there. A bunch of people who were in the area even came by to watch. It surprised the shit out of me. I'd never tried anything like this before, never knew the influence a single picture could have. I mean, people who had seen the picture came to watch the game, and they were actually nice to me, offering compliments and words of support.

We all got very excited to have an audience, and things got a little overenthusiastic between me and the boys. I walked away with a couple of bruises, but for the first time in a long while, I felt good about the sport. I'd been so angry about what the fame had brought into my life that I'd almost forgotten how much I loved to just play, be a part of a team, enjoy the sense of competition and camaraderie.

And, to be completely honest, I loved the brutality of it. Though it was a match, it was real in a way real life isn't. You hit, you scrum, you fight, you kick and punch and beat the living shit out of each other, and it's glorious. Everyone knows the point. Everyone knows the goal. There's no second-guessing, and there are no pulled punches.

After the match, I signed a bunch of autographs and talked to the people who'd shown up. I declined going to the pub for an obligatory beer. By the time I got home, I was exhausted but in a good way.

"Where have you been all day?" Ma asked when I arrived at the penthouse. There was a hint of annoyance in her voice that said she was looking for a fight, but I wasn't going to engage her.

"Out," I replied shortly and walked down the hall to my room.

"Well, that's you told," Lucy chuckled from where she'd been lounging on the sofa reading a magazine.

"Shut up, you," Ma snapped, and I heard her heels clicking on the wood floor before the front door opened and shut, signaling her departure.

I opened up my laptop to find a response from The SML.

March 23
5:22 p.m.
Hi, Ronan,

I don't remember ever telling you I was female. Still, if you want my advice, here it is:

If Annie needs space, give her space. From the stories about her so far in the press, she sounds like a sensitive girl, and perhaps cooling things off for a while could be a good thing. Maybe your relationship was too much too quickly.

Perhaps the harshness from your mother was a bit of a wake-up call, a good reminder that you belong to a lot of people—and not just your family. Think about it. She's a normal girl living a normal life. She's not used to people with cameras following her everywhere she goes. Perhaps it's not that her feelings for you have changed, but more that all of it—meeting your family, dating a celebrity—is just overwhelming.

I don't have much more to offer than that.

Of note, I'm going to be away on vacation for the next ten days, so I'll be out of touch.

Yours,

The SML

P.S. I saw you've been a bit of an Instagram sensation today. I think it's safe to say you're officially embracing my way of life. Well done! Plus, you must not be so brokenhearted. People were posting lots of pictures of the game in the park, and it looked like you were having a fantastic time :-)

Okay, so she was definitely being passive-aggressive with that last bit. And now I really regretted ever having played that game today. I must have been experiencing a moment of stupidity when I neglected to realize that Annie, being the online wizard that she was, would see the picture I'd posted.

I wanted to write something in reply, but I didn't see the point. My entire plan had backfired. I'd futilely hoped that Annie would reply with some suggestions on winning her back like, I don't know, showing up outside her place and butchering a love song or something.

Her advising me in a roundabout way to back the fuck off was not my desired outcome. Also, the idea that she was overwhelmed by the media circus that was my life hurt. I wanted her by my side, but I didn't want her to feel harangued.

So I moped around for the rest of the evening. Lucy tried her best to cheer me up, but it was a hopeless mission. I was wallowing like a lovesick fool. When Ma got home, she was clearly in a huff with me because she went straight to the guest room without so much as a word.

The following morning, while I was sitting by the counter eating breakfast, my phone buzzed with a text. My heart thudded when I saw it was from Annie.

> **ANNIE**
>
> Joan wants us seen together today. Gerta is forwarding you details on where to meet me for lunch. It's a health food café, so I'm presuming you'll be able to eat what's on the menu.

Her text was so cold and businesslike, and the underlying message was clear as day: *This is all for the cameras.* My gut sank, but I didn't allow myself to lose hope. The fact that she was agreeing to see me at all was a good sign.

A few hours later, I was dressed in a dark grey shirt and a nice pair of jeans.

"Where are you off to?" Ma asked as she sipped on her coffee where she sat in the lounge area.

"I'm meeting Annie for lunch. I'll see you later," I replied, and she started getting up from her seat.

"Oh, great, I'll come with you then. I'm starving, and it'll give me the chance to apologize."

I held up a hand. "No, Ma, you can't come. You can, however, apologize to Annie, but we'll plan for that another time."

Before she could say another word, I was out the door.

* * *

I SAW ANNIE as I approached the café. She was sitting in the outdoor section as she waited for me, her long hair down and tossed over one shoulder. I noticed she was wearing one of her older baggy brown cardigans covering a pretty flower-print dress beneath. The fact that she was wearing the cardigan made me think she wasn't feeling so special. She didn't want to be noticed today.

Fuck, there was no way I'd ever not notice her. I thought back to our first meeting and how I'd lasciviously planned on making her a new notch on my bedpost. A temporary though very lovely distraction. It was almost like some higher power was playing a sick joke on me because now I couldn't imagine my life without her.

"Hey," I said, hardly recognizing my own voice, it was so tentative. I couldn't believe it, but I was nervous. I was never nervous. She stood when she saw me, and I leaned forward, placing my hand on her shoulder and kissing her lightly on the cheek. She smelled incredible. I'd missed her so badly that it was almost too much to be this close to her. "You look beautiful," I murmured in her ear, trying to ignore the gaggle of photographers across the street snapping shots.

Annie cleared her throat. "Thank you."

We sat down then, and I didn't know what to say. This was my opportunity to apologize for my mother, and I wanted it to be perfect. I scanned the menu for a minute, and then the waitress came to take our order. Once she was gone, I leaned across the table and placed my hand over Annie's. Her skin was soft and warm, so lovely. I missed the feel of her. My body practically hummed with the need to touch her everywhere all at once.

"I'm only letting you keep your hand there for the cameras," Annie said quietly, dragging her teeth anxiously across her lower lip. I ducked my head to catch her eyes.

"How are you feeling, love?"

For a second, she seemed taken aback by the tenderness in my voice. If she thought I was pissed at her for staying away, for not answering my calls, then she was dead wrong. I could never be angry at her. I was too infatuated to be angry.

"I'm okay. Busy with work and all," she answered and reached for her glass of water to take a sip.

"And Kurt, right?"

I knew I wasn't imagining things when I saw her wince. "I think we both know I'm not interested in Kurt."

I squeezed her hand in silent thanks, knowing it took a lot for her to say that, to give me that small consolation. Then I let out a long breath. "I need to apologize for my mother's behavior," I said and began rubbing my thumb across her skin. "She was way out of line talking to you like she did. I've already set her straight, and she's sorry. She wants to apologize in person, too...."

"I'd rather she didn't." Annie lifted her eyes to mine and stared at me for a long moment; I felt and saw something like steel, a stern resolve in her expression as she continued, "I don't wish to be rude, but your mother is...well, I don't believe it's possible for us to reach any kind of friendly understanding. I have a hard time being around people like her. I've organized my life to avoid confrontations, and I have no desire to meet or see her again. Anyway, it was probably for the best, what she said. It helped me realize that what's been going on between us could never work."

I opened my mouth to disagree with her, but she held up her hand.

"P-please, just let me speak. The real issue isn't what your mother said or whether it is true. The point is that we come from entirely different worlds. I mean, I don't mind being your temporary fake girlfriend for a couple of weeks, but I couldn't handle it forever. I don't know what I was thinking. I need to return to normality eventually. Everyday encounters with people are difficult for me. I wouldn't survive living in the spotlight. I'm not strong like you. I thrive on anonymity."

I tightened my grip on her hand, my voice laced with emotion. "Don't do this. How often do people find a connection like we have? I'll protect you. I'll keep the press away. Hell, I'll even give up playing rugby if it means we can be together."

Her lips parted, and she blinked at me in surprise. I'd startled her. It took her a moment to recover, and when she did I could see that I'd rattled her cage. "Y-you love what you do. I would never ask you to give it up."

"Just because I'm not playing professionally doesn't mean I can't play at all. Anyway, I'm getting old. I'm almost at retirement age now, you know," I joked and mustered a smile. "Please, Annie, just give us a chance."

"It's better this way." Her eyes cut to the table, and she shook her head as though convincing herself. "At least if we go no further, then we'll never know what we're missing. We avoid the pain."

I flattened my mouth, my tone turning serious. "I know what I'm missing, Annie. You are singular to me, exceptional. You're brilliant and adorable and so fucking real. I care about you. And I haven't been able to get the taste of you, the feel of you, out of my head since we first kissed."

Shakily, she withdrew her hand and put it on her lap under the table. She closed her eyes for a second, obviously mustering the courage to say something. The moment was broken when the waitress arrived with our food. Unsurprisingly, I had no appetite whatsoever.

Annie dug into her sandwich, not meeting my eyes. I took the opportunity to study her. God, she was so beautiful that it was almost a physical sort of torture not to reach out and kiss her. There was something extremely closed off about her today; and disappointingly, I knew a breakthrough wasn't on the cards, so I decided to let it go for now. I needed to just be content to be spending time with her. Leaning back in my chair, I nudged her foot with mine to get her attention then asked, "Has Joan told you about Dublin?"

She nodded but didn't speak, chewing on a bite of sandwich.

"Are you going to come?"

Again, all I got was a nod, but it filled my chest with relief. All I needed was this opportunity to get to her, convince her to let her walls down. Once we got to Dublin, I'd have to pull out all the stops.

She gave me a sad look then, her deep brown eyes downturned. Obviously, spending time with me was painful for her. She wanted me, but she wasn't going to let herself have me. Her look was like a punch to the gut. I hooked both my feet around hers legs and drew her thighs between mine under the table.

"Hey, I'll behave on this trip. I promise. You don't have to worry." Lies. Lies. Lies.

She swallowed, breathing sharply. "Thank you."

For the rest of the meal, I kept her legs between mine, but she didn't tell me to stop. She craved the closeness just as much as I did. We ate in quiet companionship, and then too soon we were saying our goodbyes. I didn't want to let her go.

Therefore, before I could think too much about it, I pulled her against me and brushed my mouth against hers, just a soft touching of lips, really, a whisper of something. In comparison to our previous kisses, it was extremely tame. But when I leaned away, my eyes hungry for her reaction, I wasn't disappointed.

Annie stared up at me, her cheeks flushed, her eyes bright, and her hands white-knuckled fists gripping the front of my shirt. It took her a moment to realize that my hold was undemanding, that I'd basically let her go. Remembering herself, she stepped away, gathering an unsteady breath.

She hesitated.

I waited.

Then she shook her head and walked away.

I watched her go for as long as she was still in view, until she'd turned the corner. It was only Monday, and I couldn't stand the thought of not seeing her until Thursday. Life was going to be agony.

* * *

Life was agony, and I was verging on pitiful.

I filled the days with workouts and spent the rest of my time with Lucy. There was still a bit of a frosty atmosphere between Ma and me. Lucy was completely taken with New York, her blue eyes alight with wonder at every new thing she saw. She even proclaimed that she was going to live here one day, ever the dreamer. But I had no doubt she'd make it happen.

She went out of her way to cheer me up, every evening presenting me with new gifts like ties and aftershave and novelty socks. When Thursday morning finally came around, Annie texted me saying she'd meet me at the departure gate. I was disappointed because I'd been hoping to share a cab with her to the airport. I said goodbye to Ma and Lucy, who both had one more day in New York before their flight home, then made my way to JFK. It felt like it took forever to get through security, and when I finally did, I spotted Annie sitting by a window watching planes take off and land out on the runway. She was holding a steaming paper coffee cup in both hands, her ever-present mobile phone sitting on her lap.

She was chewing on her lip when she saw me coming. Not even waiting for me to say hello, she blurted out, "I've never been on a plane before."

I took the seat beside her, eyebrows raised. "Never?"

She shook her head. "Never. Any long distances I've had to travel have always been by bus or train. I'm kind of terrified."

"Do you think you'll be a nervous flyer?"

"Honestly, I have no idea." She sounded distracted.

"Well," I said, blowing out a breath, "I'll just have to keep you occupied, then, so that you aren't thinking of it. We'll play some games, like Twenty Questions or I Never. It'll be fun." I reached out and softly squeezed her thigh. Her gaze fixed on my hand until I moved it away. We were booked in first class, which was good since Annie had the look of a rabbit caught in the headlights this morning. Trying to be a gentleman, I asked her if she'd like to sit by the window, but she fervently shook her head no.

I took her hand in mine during takeoff, and she didn't protest, squeezing her eyes shut the whole time. I watched her closely, ready to calm her at the merest sign of panic. I knew some people went a little bit crazy on airplanes. When she opened her eyes, we were in the air. She glanced past me and out the window.

"Wow," she breathed, leaning closer and marveling at the clouds and blue sky beyond. You could see the city drifting away beneath us, the buildings tiny in the distance. She was practically sitting on top of me, but I wasn't complaining, mainly because her breasts were pushing into my arm. I closed my eyes for a moment, savoring her scent and the comfort of having her so close. For a brief moment, I forgot about our emotional distance and just enjoyed being near her.

"Sorry," she said then and drew away.

I opened my eyes. "No apologies needed, love. You sure you don't want to sit by the window?"

Unlike before, now she seemed positively elated by the idea. "Yes, please, if you don't mind," she enthused, and I grinned, undoing my seatbelt. Our bodies brushed briefly as we switched seats, and she blushed, keeping her gaze on her shoes. For the next hour, Annie was glued to the window, marveling at the sky. It was probably the most charming thing I'd ever witnessed and made me fall that little bit harder for her.

I busied myself with a book and let her enjoy her window-seat view.

Some time elapsed before she got up and excused herself to the bathroom. And yeah, I'm not going to lie, I got a nice look at her arse as she went by me. Today she was wearing jeans and a purple knitted jumper. She didn't have any makeup on, and her long hair was braided into a side plait. She looked so incredibly natural and fuckable. It was such a sweet torture.

For several short seconds, I was wracked with indecision. I'd told her I'd behave on this trip, but the temptation to follow her was too much. I rose from my seat, smiling amiably at the air hostess as I passed by and made my way to the restrooms. I waited patiently until Annie was done, and then, just as she was stepping out to leave, I got in her way and moved forward, leaving her no other option but to retreat back inside. A moment later I'd flicked the lock, and we were alone.

"Hey," I murmured as she leaned into the sink and I crowded her space. There was no way to *not* crowd her space; the toilet was the size of a postage stamp.

She swallowed and moved her lips, drawing my attention to her mouth. It seemed redder and even more plump than usual. *Such* a temptation.

"What's going on?" Annie asked, eyes on my shirt collar rather than my face.

"I miss you so fucking much," I said, my words almost choked, pained. I brought my hands to her hips and slid them around her waist then down to her bottom. She sucked in a quick breath before exhaling. When she finally looked up at me, she was flushed—but not from displeasure. Her eyes were practically glowing.

I drew air in past my teeth before asking, "Oh, Annie, what am I gonna do with you?"

FIFTEEN
ANNIE

The Companion Fake Selfie*: When two or more people pretend to be taking a picture together, but are instead taking a picture of a person in the background.*
Best for*: Situations where taking a group selfie wouldn't be unusual/draw attention. This method, unlike the "Creeper Selfie" and "Fake Selfie," can be used in restaurants. However, caution should be used if the waiter/waitress is overly helpful and might offer to take the picture instead.*
Do not use*: Near mirrors.*

I was hot, and it had nothing to do with my sweater. I was hot because I had a war raging within me. I hadn't yet reconciled what I knew was safe with what I wanted.

I miss you so fucking much.... That's what he'd said.

He had no idea.

No. Idea.

I ached for him, for that fleeting sensation of belonging with him. I ached for being seen and known by him. I ached for our connection, for enjoying him, being with him, listening to him. I ached for how he touched me; his dirty, shocking words; his skilled hands; how he commanded a response from my body with just a look or a whisper.

I ached for Ronan.

It was physical, and it was painful; and resisting him felt like being sawed in half with a dull, rusty blade.

"Ronan." I shook my head, squeezed my eyes shut; I was trembling. When I spoke next, I wasn't surprised to hear myself beg, "Please don't do this. Please…please."

I felt him shift, hesitate. I held my breath: waiting, wanting him, and hating myself for being weak and yielding where before I'd always been resilient and constant.

Eventually I heard Ronan mutter, "Christ, Annie. Come here." He slid his hands from my bottom to my back and then my shoulders. He pulled me against him, tucking my head under his neck and against his chest. He squeezed.

He gave me a hug.

I released an uncontrolled and watery sigh, closer to a choked sob than an exhalation, and wrapped my arms around him, returning his embrace. I buried my face in his neck and held on tightly. I didn't know how I was going to let him go, both figuratively and literally.

People who grow up with families, with a guardian or a parent or both parents, often take hugs for granted. I could count on one hand the number of times I'd been hugged since my adoptive family returned me to the state. It was the hugs that I missed the most, being held and touched with affection—even if the affection was only skin deep.

I often wished afterward that I didn't know what it was like to be held. I wished they'd never hugged me. I resented them for showing me what I was missing. I was growing to resent Ronan for similar reasons, but it was much worse.

Ronan's affection for me wasn't just skin deep. He'd admitted as much to The Socialmedialite. Additionally, if I'd been experiencing any lingering doubts, they were erased when he made his impassioned speech during lunch several days ago, when he offered to leave rugby so we could be together.

After gaining distance "from the breakfast of spite," as I'd started calling it, and his mother's detestable statements (and doing some digging into her past), I realized her claims about Ronan's fidelity were all lies, misleading half-truths at best, clearly meant to drive a wedge between us.

Part of me hated that I'd rolled over and given up so easily. But my need for self-preservation endured above all else.

Ultimately, Ronan's mother provided the wake-up call I'd needed. I knew it was for the best. Self-preservation demanded that I stay ignorant regarding the workings of a real loving relationship, one based on mutual admiration, respect, and a potentially soul-deep connection.

I had to be strong. I had to redouble my efforts. I couldn't bend or yield.

But first I let myself hold and be held. I'd shared too much. I'd trusted too much. I'd given too much. I'd let him in and allowed myself to think about Ronan and Annie in terms of a "we" and an "us."

And I was very afraid that I'd already fallen in love with him.

***

THE HOTEL WAS beyond swanky, but I was only peripherally aware of its opulence. My eyes were on the marble floor and ornate Kashmir carpets. I was tucked under Ronan's arm, held close to his chest as he navigated the lobby; I followed him blindly. This was for several reasons.

First, I was jetlagged.

After the bathroom hug that lasted well beyond ten wordless minutes, Ronan led me back to our seats, holding my hand. Again he gave me the window seat. However, this time he also spent the rest of the flight touching me, but it was nothing overtly sexual, just affectionate. The touches warmed me, made my blood simmer, and went a long way toward melting my resolve. He brushed my hair away from my cheek, and his hand lingered on my neck; or he'd place his hand on my knee to get my attention and keep it there for several minutes, his thumb drawing light, slow circles on my kneecap.

At one point he picked up my hand and massaged it. He didn't ask permission; he did it absentmindedly while staring at my fingers.

"Go to sleep," he said. So I did, feeling both safe and at risk of falling deeper but too weary to care.

The plane touched down at 7:30 a.m. Dublin time, which made it 2:30 a.m. New York time. Ronan woke me with a soft kiss, first on my lips then on my forehead. My brain felt stuffed with cotton and cobwebs and maybe maple syrup. I just wanted to sleep.

The other reason I was following Ronan blindly was because of the photographers. As soon as we passed through customs, we were basically accosted. I'd been stunned by the sheer number; I tried to estimate but quit counting when I got to twenty.

I thought the paparazzi in the States were aggressive, hiding behind bushes and trailing us around the city. I'd been so wrong. So very, very wrong. The "paps" in Ireland didn't seem to understand the concept of personal space, nor did they see anything amiss about touching me or telling me how much they appreciated the size of my breasts.

It was at this comment that Ronan wrapped his arm around me possessively and pressed me against him, caging me within his strong arms. He said something to the photographers, but I didn't understand the words—either because I was too stunned or because Ronan was speaking another language, I had no idea. Then he navigated us both to the relative safety of the first-class lounge.

When we got to the lounge, he looked like he was ten seconds away from murdering someone. He was so angry. He kept asking me if I was okay; meanwhile, he was grinding his teeth, his heart beating a hundred miles a minute, and his grip on my shoulders was just shy of painful.

Without letting me go, Ronan walked to the bar, flipped open his phone, and placed a brief call. At the bar he ordered me a Bloody Mary and a soda water for himself, all the while administering "fuck off" glares to anyone who dared make eye contact. He waited until our drinks arrived before moving us away. Still under his arm, I stumbled where he led, which was to a corner behind a floor-to-ceiling panel, hiding us from the glass windows facing the rest of the airport.

A big, leather couch sprawled under dimmed lights; he settled himself on one end and then situated me so I was next to him. He told me to drink the Bloody Mary. So I did. Then he told me to put my head on his lap and sleep for a bit. So I did. His arm rested along my body, his hand on my hip.

Some indeterminate time later, Ronan woke me with another kiss, framing my face with his big palms. I was informed that his security team had arrived and they would make sure that we made it to the car unmolested.

He added under his breath, "And they'll keep me from killing those fuckers...."

The security team did more than that.

They took us out of the airport through a series of tunnels, thereby avoiding the paparazzi all together.

Yet Ronan kept me tucked against him the entire time—when we walked through the tunnels, when we finally made it to the car, during the ride to the hotel, when we walked from the car to the hotel through another sea of photographers, and finally when we checked into the fancy schmancy Merrion Hotel.

Once we boarded the elevator, Ronan barred the way, letting no one else on, and instructed the bellhop to take the next lift. No one argued. I glanced at Ronan's face as the doors slid shut and found that I would not have argued, either.

"Ronan...are you okay?"

He glanced down at me, his handsome face marred by a frown of concentrated frustration. I was surprised to see that all his irritation was directed inward.

"I am so sorry, Annie. They had no right to touch you or talk to you like that. Those motherfu—" He didn't finish the insult. Instead, he clenched his teeth and glanced away, huffing a bitter laugh. "No wonder you don't want to be with me. No one is worth putting up with all that shite."

His words caused an acute stab of discomfort in my chest near my heart. Looking at him intensified the hurt. Maybe it was because I was jetlagged, or maybe it was because of the Bloody Mary; but I couldn't let that statement stand unchallenged.

"You're absolutely fucking crazy if you think you're not worth putting up with those wankers."

The hard line around his jaw softened, and his eyes widened in surprise. I didn't take too much time to process the abrupt change in his demeanor because I'd just realized that my words were somewhat slurred. I scrunched my face as I tried to concentrate on willing the cobwebs away, but it was no use. I was not a person who could function well on less than six hours of sleep.

Therefore, I pressed on, hoping to make my point as clear as possible even in my unsteady state. "You're worth…going to graduate school again; you're worth writing a master's dissertation with Professor Perkins as a mentor."

"Who is Professor Perkins?"

"Now, *she* is a motherfucker. Just be glad you'll never meet her." I shook my head, found the movement made me dizzy. I stopped shaking my head but continued my rant, which was quickly turning into a tirade. "You are worth so much more than the hassle of a few asshole paps. It's not your fault that they acted like a pack of crude douchebags. You're smart, and kind, and…just fucking wonderful. Never doubt that. Never."

I let my head loll to the side as I gazed up in his big brown eyes. I loved his eyes. They were so big. And brown. And dreamy. And they were smiling at me. In fact, his whole face was smiling at me, his eyes sparkling as they perused my features.

"Annie dearest, are you feeling okay?"

"Mm-hmm." I nodded dreamily then added, "But I'm a little tired…I think."

His mouth was pulled to the side in a delicious slant. I wanted to lick the curve of his bottom lip, but I didn't, mostly because the doors to the elevators slid open to our floor just as I seriously considered lifting on my tiptoes to make it happen.

He stared at me for a beat, not immediately exiting the lift, like he was waiting for me to say or do something. Eventually, tearing his gaze from mine, Ronan guided me down the hall to the room. I didn't take note of the room number as we entered, nor—for that matter—did I know what floor we were on. Neither did I think much of the facts that our suite was huge and beautiful, but had one bedroom, and that one bedroom had only one king-sized bed.

Now that I'd made my point with Ronan and he seemed to be sufficiently calmed down, all I could think about was sleep. When I saw the bed, I stepped out from beneath the safety of Ronan's arm, stumbled toward it, and let myself fall face first into its feathery embrace.

"Oh…this is heaven," I groaned as I swam up the length of the soft duvet, caressing the satiny texture with open palms. "I never want to get up."

I felt the bed depress next to me and then Ronan's hand on my back; he shook me a little. "Annie, you shouldn't sleep anymore until tonight. You need to stay up, or else your body won't get used to the time difference."

I turned and lay on my back. The movement caused my sweater to ride up and bare my midriff; Ronan's hand now rested on the skin of my stomach. The sensation wasn't sobering. If anything, it made me feel delightfully warm and cozy. I wanted him to keep it there. I had his touches on the plane to blame for my level of comfort with his touch now.

I wanted him to curl up on the bed and spoon me. I'd never been spooned—I'd only been forked and knifed.

"I don't care." I tried to open my eyes so I could look at him and show him that I was serious; I failed. My eyes would not stay open. So I covered his hand with mine and administered an ineffectual tug, trying to get him to lie down as well. "Come lie down with me; sleep with me. You know you want to."

Ronan huffed, or growled, or some combination of the two. "You're making it really hard for me to be good."

I reached blindly for him, already succumbing to the gentle promise of sleep in a luxurious bed. "So what if we don't" …*yawn*…"adjust to the time difference" … *yawn*… "what's the worst…" *yawn*… "that could…" *yawn*… "happen?"

Ronan's voice sounded far away when he answered; but his hand was still on my stomach, and my hand still covered his. "The worst that could happen is that we'd be up all night."

"So?"

"Do you want to be up all night with me, Annie?"

"Mmm…."

That was a delicious thought, much more delicious than an éclair; and it was with that thought that I fell completely and pleasantly asleep, dreaming about all the things I wanted to do to Ronan that night.

* * *

I WAS WOKEN up by the sound of a phone ringing, but it wasn't the normal light trill of my cell phone. It was a meaner noise and sounded less like a ring than an oscillating buzzer. I lifted my head and tried to get a handle on where I was and what time it was and what the hell was going on and *am I in my underwear?*

The ringing stopped abruptly. I blinked at the side table where the phone now lay silent and then glanced around the room. The morning's events came back to me but not in a rush. More like a sporadic leaky faucet. I remembered the plane landing and customs and the rude paparazzi and…the bar at the airport. The rest was a little fuzzy, but I did recall leaving a car and entering the hotel lobby, Ronan checking us in, and flopping down on the bed as soon as we walked into the hotel room.

I glanced down at myself. I was under the covers of the bed, and I was dressed in my underwear, bra, and the T-shirt I'd been wearing under my sweater. I thought about my state of undress for several seconds and realized Ronan must've taken off my jeans and sweater when I passed out; he must've also tucked me in and closed the drapes. I spotted my clothes folded into a neat pile on the foot of the bed.

The phone rang again, causing me to jump and my heart to bounce around my ribcage. I pressed my hand against the spike of anxiety in my chest and grabbed the phone, mostly to stop the infernal sound.

"Yes?"

"Ms. Catrel, this is O'Hare, the concierge. Mr. Fitzpatrick left instructions to wake you at noon. It is now noon. I am also to remind you of your appointment at two." The voice on the other end was impossibly polished. It did more to clear my head than the ringing phone.

"My appointment at two?"

"Yes, ma'am. In your room. Massage, facial, pedicure, manicure, hair, and makeup…for tonight's event."

I swallowed a sudden weird sensation in my throat. "Oh, right. Thanks."

"No trouble at all, Ms. Catrel. Your lunch is on its way up now, and may I suggest the complimentary bathrobe in the closet should you not yet be appropriately attired to receive guests?"

As if on cue or by magic, a knock on the suite door sounded at just that moment.

"Thank you," I said absentmindedly to the elegant voice, searching the room for the aforementioned closet.

"No trouble at all, Ms. Catrel. Again, my name is O'Hare should you require any assistance during your stay. Patricia's has been assigned to you and Mr. Fitzpatrick for the duration, and I hope that you will not hesitate to contact me or Patricia should you need anything at all."

"Oh, okay. Thank you." I scrambled to the edge of the bed and jogged to the nearest closet.

"No trouble at all, Ms. Catrel. Enjoy your lunch."

And, with that, O'Hare clicked off. I tossed the cordless phone to the bed and yanked open the closet door, finding a beautiful woman's paisley blue silk bathrobe hanging next to an equally lavish black and gray striped man's bathrobe. I quickly tugged off my shirt and pulled on the robe, tying it as I jogged to the front door of the suite.

A pretty older woman stood in the doorway. She was dressed in a business suit, and her graying red hair was tied back in a severe bun. She was smiling at me.

"Good day, Ms. Catrel. I'm Patricia." She reached her hand forward, and I took it, shaking it automatically.

"Nice to meet you. Please call me Annie."

"Yes, of course. We have your lunch here as well as several items for your afternoon appointment." She shifted to the side, indicating with a wave of her hand the food cart behind her, five burly-looking bellhops or waiters, three youngish maids or beauticians, and various contraptions set on luggage carts. "May we enter?"

Inwardly, I shrank at the sight of the crowd outside my door, but I was too surprised to think much about their presence. Ultimately, my desire to avoid confrontation won out over my fear of interacting with people.

"Yes—yes, please come in," I stammered and stepped out of the doorway. They filed into the room very much like a parade; the food cart and shiny brass luggage carts were parade floats.

Patricia administered orders to the group of them, telling them where to put what. Then she turned back to me. I was still hovering by the entrance, watching the bustle with some fascination.

"Mr. Catrel, I see you have not unpacked." She motioned to my luggage, where it lay stacked by the sofa. Patricia crossed to me, slid her hand into the crook of my elbow, and then guided me away from the door and toward the bedroom, where the food cart had just been wheeled. "Please allow me to unpack your belongings while you enjoy a soak. Your lunch is in here, next to the sitting area within your room. I will be pleased to draw you a bath."

"I-I can draw my own bath."

"Of course you can, but it would be my pleasure," Patricia said, her voice level and kind. She brought me to a comfy chair and deposited me there and then motioned for the bellhop—or was he a waiter?—to arrange the cart in front of me.

She disappeared into the bathroom while the waiter lifted the elegant silver coverings, revealing china laden with an assortment of delicious-looking salads, little sandwiches with no crust, a piping-hot bowl of lobster bisque, a big basket with fresh berries, a carafe of yogurt—which he noted was made at the hotel—and a tray of various Irish cheeses.

Also revealed was a steeping teapot and glass-topped tea box with loose-leaf teas; I had my choice of everything from prosaic peppermint to exotic oolong. And last, but certainly not least, he lifted the top off a platter of delicate petit fours, three of which were miniature éclairs.

My mouth was watering.

I felt like I was in one of those rags to riches movies from the 1960s and '70s, where the insignificant orphan is suddenly faced with everything she ever wanted—namely, lots of beautiful little desserts.

When the waiter was finished announcing my lunch, he made a short bow, asked if I needed anything further, and then—when I shook my head—left me to my food.

I stared at the lot of it, not sure where to start. My stomach rumbled in protest at my indecision.

I'd just decided to begin with the soup when Patricia re-emerged from the bathroom and strolled toward me with smart steps. "I've taken the liberty of adding rose and lavender essential oils to your bath." She stopped at the edge of my table and began spooning peppermint tea into the steeper. "Please don't hesitate to call upon me during your stay, Ms. Catrel. Our team's sole purpose is your comfort while you are here with us. Since you're traveling without your own team, please think of me as your personal secretary."

"Uh, I have no…team."

"That's no matter." Patricia gave me a warm smile and a little nod. She then turned and exited through the bedroom door, calling as she left, "I shall return in a half hour to unpack your things and then again at two for your appointment."

A few minutes later, I heard all of them file out of the suite and the door close with a soft click.

Then, feast before me, warm bath next on the agenda, I was alone.

* * *

I DECIDED I could really get used to being pampered even if that meant having to endure increased levels of human interaction. I stuffed myself. It was shameful. But I wanted to try everything, and everything tasted so good. The only item I finished was the yogurt. It tasted more like a custard than yogurt, and I feared I would go into withdrawal when I returned to New York.

After gorging myself, I sent a quick message to WriteALoveSong. Before I'd left New York, I told her I was going to be out of town for a few weeks for work, but I promised to message as often as I could. So I fired off a fast note.

@Socialmedialite to @WriteALoveSong: I just arrived and ate my weight in breakfast foods. You may not hear from me for the next week as I digest all these waffles.

I was surprised when she quickly responded:

@WriteALoveSong to @Socialmedialite: Ohhh… waffles! What did the hipster glass of water say to the ice cube?
@Socialmedialite to @WriteALoveSong: …oh no… what?
@WriteALoveSong to @Socialmedialite: I'm you before you were cool. Have fun on your trip!

I rolled my eyes and chuckled despite myself, typing out a speedy, *Farewell for now*. After switching off my phone, I waddled to the bathroom and disrobed, climbing into the most luscious bath of my life. Really, there was no other word for it. It was luscious.

The water was still hot, and I discovered why when I was fully immersed; the porcelain was heated. As well, the bubbles were miraculous and never seemed to diminish or fizz out.

Patricia knocked on the bathroom door to announce her presence and alert me to the fact that she was unpacking my bags. I thought about sending her away, but the luscious bath and sumptuous lunch made me feel lethargic and amenable to being spoiled. So I called my acknowledgment and relaxed.

It was in the bath that my thoughts invariably turned to Ronan. I wondered where he was, what he was doing, when he would be back. I also realized the ramifications of the single-bedroom suite and the single king-sized bed.

A surge of anxiety at the thought of sharing the bed with Ronan was followed by a surge of something else, something altogether more pleasant and dangerous. This, of course, made me think about Ronan undressing me as I slept this morning, his large, powerful hands pulling down my jeans as I lay limp beneath him....

I closed my eyes, indulging myself in the fantasy of Ronan undressing me completely; in the fantasy I was still limp, but I was awake. I touched my breasts lightly as I imagined him slowly slipping the straps down my shoulders, unhooking the clasp at the front, and revealing the expanse of my skin to his eyes. I imagined him lowering his mouth to me while the back of his fingers caressed a light path from my ribcage to my stomach then lower, into the waistband of my pink lace underwear.

My hand served as a substitute for his, and I touched myself, enjoying the slippery softness of my skin, feeling myself and knowing that this was what he would feel, wondering if he would be pleased with the slopes and curves of my body and all its secrets. I imagined his eyes on me, devouring the sight of my nakedness as he left a trail of wet kisses between my breasts, lower to my belly button, until finally—

My musings were cruelly interrupted by another knock on the door. I yanked my hand away, splashing water and some of the miraculous bubbles onto the marble floor then sat upright in the tub.

I glanced at myself; everything below my shoulders was still neatly hidden beneath a layer of white foam. "I—uh—come in. I'm nearly finished."

My exhale was unsteady, my heart beating excitedly, and I knew I was flushed with the evidence of my almost orgasm. Hopefully, Patricia would assume the blush was caused by hot water and not hot thoughts.

But it wasn't Patricia at the door. It was Ronan.

And he wasn't exactly dressed. He was wearing a towel around his narrow hips, a glimpse of swim trunks visible, and nothing else.

I gawked at him—this being my first time seeing his body live, in person, and not in the static pages of a magazine or pixelated on the Internet—and knew nothing virtual or imaginary could come close to the reality of that chest and torso. He was all rigid muscle and sharp angles. A tribal tattoo of some sort snaked up his hip, originating from beneath the towel and spiraling up to his ribcage and chest. I wanted to trace it with my fingers, the curling lines. I wanted to press my mouth against it and taste his skin. He looked like he'd be hard to the touch, but I knew he'd also be warm.

"Annie?"

I blinked, startled and mortified to realize I'd been staring, and snapped my mouth shut. With an effort, I lifted my gaze to his and set my jaw, fighting the urge to return my attention to the perfection of his body and the mystery of his tattoo.

"I—um—yes?"

Ronan shut the door behind him and stalked closer. His eyebrows lifted as he drew near, and his gaze moved over my face, dipped to my shoulders, detoured on my mouth.

"Enjoying your…bath?"

His eyes reminded me of chocolate in that moment, velvet dark chocolate, the kind used in succulent desserts, hot and silky, the kind you dipped strawberries in and savored as the juice from the berry and the sweet bitterness of the chocolate danced a euphoria over your tongue and down your throat….

I squirmed, my breath coming short, my arousal making me feel unsteady and lightheaded.

"Yes." The word emerged as a breathless whisper, drawing his attention back to my eyes.

"You look uncomfortable. Is the bath too hot?"

I shook my head.

He hovered for a moment, surveying me—him and his epic torso—then sat at the edge of the tub and dipped his fingers into the water.

"What—what are you doing?" Again, my voice was breathless.

Part of me hoped he was going to say, *Finishing what you started.*

Another part of me hoped…oh, hell. Who was I kidding? Every part of me hoped he would say, *Finishing what you started.*

Instead he said, his lips twitching with poorly hidden amusement, "Just checking the temperature. You look flushed." The back of his fingers brushed against my thigh, and I jumped, an inelegant squeak escaping my throat.

This was met with the rumbling sound of Ronan's laughter and a rather obnoxious smirk. "You need to relax. Maybe you should take a nice, long bath."

I glared at him and his grin, bringing my legs to my chest and wrapping my arms around my calves. Nothing of my body was visible besides my shoulders, but I felt suddenly quite *seen*. "I was…I am perfectly relaxed."

"I could help, you know." He nodded at this assertion, his hand still in the water, his fairytale body and warm, silky chocolate eyes filling my vision. "I could give you a massage…or a rubdown."

I gritted my teeth and shook my head, but I said nothing. Because if I spoke, I would undoubtedly say yes.

He thought he was so clever. And he was. He was entirely too clever. I could see that he knew exactly what I'd been doing, or about to do. Doubtless he'd even realized that he was the sole inspiration for my dirty daydream.

"It would be no trouble at all. I promise you'll like it." His hand in the bath moved to my shoulder, and he brushed the back of his fingers against my collarbone, leaving a wet trail of sliding bubbles from the top of my sternum to my shoulder.

I rolled my lips between my teeth to keep from panting.

"Loosen your arms, and open your legs for me," he said, his voice growing both solemn and soft; it was a command. His fingers slid down my arm to my knee, and he covered it with his palm, squeezing gently.

My eyelids drooped, and I half blinked, my heart hammering and hopeful. Everywhere he touched went lax. My arms fell to my sides, and my legs relaxed, opened as he nudged them apart. Then he skimmed his light caress between my thighs, and I held my breath.

His chocolate gaze grew fierce and demanding, a contradiction to the feather-light ministrations of his middle finger at my entrance. He stroked me, opening me, entering me. As well, his words were serene and hypnotic.

"Spread your legs, all the way. Let me touch you; let me help you feel good…that's it. Oh, Annie dearest, you're so fucking soft and tight. You feel like heaven."

I swallowed the building thickness in my throat and instinctively reached for him, gripping the towel at his waist. My other hand moved to my breast, and my head fell back against the rim of the tub. I moaned.

"Shhh…." He leaned forward, briefly covered my mouth with his to silence me, and then whispered against my lips before pulling away, "Your Miss Patricia is in our room unpacking your things. You have to be quiet."

My breath hitched, and I nodded, whimpering a little but not loud enough to be heard. His index finger joined his middle finger, stroking me while his thumb danced little rhythmic circles over my clitoris. I bit my lip to keep from moaning, and I squeezed my eyes shut.

"No, no. Look at me," Ronan demanded, his voice still calm and commanding. "Look at me when you come."

I opened my eyes and found that he was skimming the top of the water with his free hand, pushing the bubbles out of the way so he could see me, where he entered me, where I cupped my breast. His eyes, avaricious and focused, moved over my body.

"You are magnificent." His tone was dispassionate and removed as he studied me, as though he were an observer and not a participant.

My lungs were bursting with fire, and I couldn't seem to breathe deeply enough, my inner walls grasping covetously as he moved in and out, filling me. But it wasn't enough; his movements were too temperate. I needed him. I needed more than his tender fingers. I needed him to be harder, firmer. I needed him everywhere.

"Ronan," I panted, reaching for his wrist between my legs, pushing his hand more firmly against my center. "Ronan, I want you. I need…. Please, please."

"Hush," he said, his touches still lithe and gentle, far too gentle. They were teasing. He was driving me crazy, and he sounded like he knew it. Looking at him, at the set of his jaw and the brutal gleam in his eyes, I had the distinct impression I was being punished.

I whimpered again.

He *tsked*, his fingers leaving my body to spread my arousal over the lips framing my clitoris, more teasing. "Such a greedy girl."

"Please, please," I begged, mindless, desperate.

"Are you going to leave me again, Annie? Are you going to walk away? Rip me open? Make me beg?" Though his tone was tender, his words stabbed at my heart.

"Ronan…."

"Do you trust me?"

I nodded and spoke the truth. "Yes. Yes."

"Are we together? Are you mine?"

I bit my lip, and despite his earlier command, I squeezed my eyes shut. I wasn't too far gone to make promises I didn't know if I could keep. Without the carved perfection of him filling my vision, I was able to gather several sobering deep breaths. I reached again for his wrist, stilling his movements and pulling him away—though it felt like I was removing a part of myself—and I closed my legs and twisted them to the side, away from him.

I let go of the towel around his waist and used my arms to cover myself. I was shaking, though the water was still hot and so was my body, my insides molten with unfulfilled longing.

I heard the faint splash of his hand leaving the water and then nothing. I pressed my lips together to keep my chin from wobbling. I was such a mess. I wanted him; but I didn't want to lie to him, and nothing had changed. I knew he was watching me, waiting; I felt his eyes sure as a hand sliding over my body.

At last he said, "I see."

The air shifted. I knew he'd moved. I dared to open my eyes into slits and caught sight of his back just before he opened the door.

"I'll be back to pick you up. You need to be ready at five." His tone was unruffled, verging on bored. It did terrible things to me, like force two tears past the barrier of my eyelids.

And then he was gone.

SIXTEEN
ANNIE

New York's Finest
Blogging as *The Socialmedialite*
March 29
You know what I both love and hate about New York? Toplessness.
In case you didn't know, going topless in New York City (for both guys and gals) is a-okay. That's right—New York is all for equal-opportunity torso ogling. Last week, Marta Duvall and her fiancé Eric Harper, went topless while hanging out (pun intended) on the chilly lawns of Central Park.
Even though I've blacked out both Marta and Eric's nipples in the picture above, I fully support NYC's topless policy…except for the unavoidable tattoos of regret which are often revealed.
Take the following picture, for example. This is a shot of Eric's back. As you can see, because of how I've enlarged the area and added the helpful red arrows and circles, Eric has a very awkward caricature of his ex-girlfriend (actress Temaya Garrison) on his right shoulder blade. Ironically, in the tattoo, Temaya is also topless.
Perhaps instead of paying for the removal of Temaya's hooters, Eric is planning on donating the saved money to today's highlighted charity! All donations received today will go toward "Tit for Tat," a program that helps breast cancer survivors (with breast reconstruction) by providing expertly tattooed nipples.
<3 The Socialmedialite

I was on my fourth glass of champagne when Ronan came back. Granted, I'd had four glasses over the course of an hour and a half, but it was four glasses nevertheless.

I was sitting on the least comfortable chair in the suite, all trussed up and trying not to move for fear I would wrinkle or smudge or flatten something. My afternoon of beauty treatments was…interesting. The entire team had been women. I'd never had a facial or a massage before. Both were actually quite nice, soothing, especially after my frustrated fantasy and bathtub encounter.

The hair and nails and makeup portion, however, was aggravating. I didn't like being poked, prodded, and painted. Patricia, who I suspected was my fairy godmother, must have noticed my grimace because she was the one to suggest and pour the champagne. It helped.

She was also kind enough to fill the silence with tales from her past. She'd been a Rockette at Radio City Music Hall for four years before joining a traveling Broadway company. Her past was colorful and shocking, and she was completely engaging. Her stories, plus the champagne, went a long way toward taking my mind off what had happened earlier.

But Ronan never completely left my mind, how he'd touched me with such gentleness and care yet looked at me with an unforgiving harshness, like I'd betrayed him.

And now I was sitting on the wooden chair at the desk, trying to concentrate on work emails and checking the comments on my blog, all the while trying to ignore the constant throbbing ache between my legs and how I missed his smile.

He entered the suite, and I glanced up, found him wearing a tux that looked custom cut for his frame. I swallowed a mouthful of lust. He didn't look at me as he entered. Instead, he strolled to the bedroom, opened and closed a few drawers, and then reemerged. His attention was on his watch.

"We have to go," he said, opening the closet in the entryway and pulling out my coat and an umbrella. "Are you ready?"

"Yes, all set." I was proud that I sounded so completely normal because I didn't feel normal. I felt jumbled and unsteady and saturated with self-doubt.

"Okay, then let's go." He glanced at me and indicated the door with a tilt of his head. I felt something bend and then snap painfully behind my ribs as his eyes met mine. His were flat, disinterested.

He looked distracted.

He'd never looked at me that way before. Never. I was anyone and everyone. I didn't matter.

I nodded, tearing my eyes from his and closing the programs on my computer, hiding the shaking of my hand by gripping the mouse tighter.

I was being stupid.

We weren't together.

How many times of my pushing him away did I think it would take before he'd stop pursuing me? This was what I wanted.

I closed my laptop and stood carefully in the stilettos. Patricia had helped me practice walking once she realized I was a high-heel novice. I felt almost proficient, except for the fact that my stomach was a mass of tangled unhappiness knots. I didn't want to see the ambivalence in his eyes, so I kept mine averted—to the floor, to my bag on the table by the door, to my coat as I took it from him and shrugged it on.

I lifted my hair out from the collar and preceded him out the door without further instruction or discussion. I felt him behind me, heard his steps echo mine as we neared the elevator. Silence and melancholy were my companions on the ride down.

As we neared the lobby, Ronan fit his hand in mine and pulled me closer. I glanced at our joined hands then at his profile. He was watching the display count down the floors. He almost looked nervous.

"There will be photographers in the lobby and on the street. Stay close, okay?"

I nodded and actively held his hand rather than passively allowing my hand to be held.

He misinterpreted the tightness of my grip and slid his eyes to mine; they flickered over my face. "Don't worry—they won't get close this time. I'll keep you safe."

"I know." I gave him a little smile, nodded again. "I trust you."

His gaze hardened, and he flinched; it was almost imperceptible, but I saw it.

I frowned at his reaction to my words and blurted, "Ronan, I am so sorry."

He glared at me until the doors opened, his jaw ticking as he withdrew inside himself, and I heard him mutter as we left the elevator, "So am I."

* * *

He was right.

There were photographers in the lobby and on the street. Everyone knew my name and called to me. It was disconcerting, but he shielded me with his body until we were in the limo. We sat on the two sides of the bench, Ronan putting the length of the back seat between us.

He spent the entire time on his phone, his knee bobbing up and down in an uncharacteristic display of nerves, and I stared out the window, thinking about the irony of the situation. The first time we'd gone out to lunch together—which felt like a lifetime ago but was really just over month—he'd scolded me for checking my phone.

When we arrived at the event, there were even more photographers. But this bunch was more professional and obviously present to document the comings and goings of the sporting elite.

Ronan exited first then held his hand out to help me from the car. He then tucked my hand in the crook of his elbow and led me to the red carpet.

Once we were clear of the limo—flashes going off in every direction—Ronan leaned down and whispered in my ear, "If you can manage a smile, that would be great. Also, we're about to meet a few of my mates. You'll want to look them in the eye as you shake their hands, say hello—you know, talk to people. Otherwise, they'll think you're a stuck-up American bitch."

I glanced at him as he retreated, and he held my gaze, smiling at me like he'd just said something charming and expected me either to laugh or blush.

His words were nasty, mean, unlike him. He seemed…off.

And again, the irony of the situation struck me. Ronan was giving me advice on how to behave, what to do, what to say. This was the real world, his world of beautiful people and fame. My world was the virtual world of avatars and words. My currency wasn't traded in this forum. Nevertheless, his words were condescending and unnecessary, and his aim was perfect.

I smiled at him, as big and brilliant as I could manage. Then I punched him in the shoulder with all my might, hoping it looked like a love tap.

His grin doubled, and he laughed, though it sounded a bit sinister. "Ouch, darling. Trying to hurt me?"

"Of course not." I shook my head in a playful manner, my smile plastered on my face. "I would never assume hurting you was within my power."

I didn't know why I said it, but I felt a surge of bitter satisfaction when his grin waned and fiery anger flashed behind his eyes. Hopefully the photographers mistook it for passion.

I tore my gaze from his and smiled at the flashing bulbs. I smiled at the attendants who met us and showed us where to stand. I smiled as Ronan was interviewed—both at Ronan and the interviewers. I smiled as he skirted questions about our relationship and told everyone I was here as his friend with practiced smoothness. I smiled as we entered the event.

And I smiled as I was introduced to his mates.

My cheeks hurt like a bitch, and yet I still smiled.

Strangely, I found the smiling helped. It helped a lot. It felt like a mask for me to hide behind. No one expected me to actually speak, only to smile and nod and drink champagne and look pretty and laugh at the appropriate times. It was the opposite of my comfort zone—behind the computer, sharing my thoughts with the world and being valued for what I did and wrote, not what I looked like —and yet…and yet it was fine.

I was fine.

I'd been so twisted up about Ronan and my feelings for him that I'd forgotten to obsess about the event, or freak out about the plunging neckline and high hem of my dress, or wallow in my social phobia. Now that I was here, surrounded by the conversation of strangers and on the arm of the man I'd stupidly fallen in love with, it was my fake-as-fuck smile that won the day.

No one noticed.

After another glass of champagne, I stopped noticing, too.

Well, that's almost the truth. I stopped noticing until I felt Ronan's hand grip mine like a vise and his body turn rigid next to mine.

We were approaching our table near the front, and he was moving through the crowd; I was indulging myself by watching him move. He was so graceful, adroit. Being next to him made me feel more graceful. I'd managed to keep from tripping over my own feet all night, which was a huge achievement in and of itself.

So when Ronan stopped suddenly and I collided against him, I figured my luck was up. But he moved quickly, his strong arm slipping around my waist, keeping me upright. He turned toward me, but he wasn't looking at me. His eyes were frustrated and unfocused; he was glaring at some inconsequential spot beyond my head.

"Shite," he breathed through clenched teeth. "I was hoping they wouldn't come."

Unthinkingly, I placed my hand over his chest and searched his expression for a clue. "Who? Who is it?"

His gaze sliced to mine. "My grandparents."

I frowned, not understanding why this was upsetting news for ten seconds. Then I realized he was referring to the Fitzpatricks, the family who'd never claimed him as their grandson, the family who thought of him and his sister and his mother as a stain on their good name. I finally understood why he'd been acting so anxious. I thought it was because of me, because I'd angered him. Maybe my rejection earlier had contributed to his foul mood, but the Fitzpatricks and the possibility of their presence at the ceremony was the root cause. Turning my head just slightly, I caught sight of the elderly couple, arm in arm, both well-dressed and silver-haired, graciously mingling with their peers. They were the picture of old money.

I felt sad for Ronan and wished I could take his unhappiness away. On a complete whim of instinct, I leaned forward and kissed him lightly on the mouth, cupping his cheek with my hand then smoothing it down to his neck and shoulder.

Then I whispered against his ear, "Ronan, you are worth ten thousand Fitzpatricks and their self-important douchebaggery. Their stupidity is their loss, not yours."

I gave his shoulder a squeeze of reassurance and then leaned away so I could see his face.

He was smiling at me. It was a small, quizzical smile, like I was maybe a little weird but maybe also a little wonderful.

"You don't have to say that kind of stuff. No one is around to hear you."

"I know I don't have to." My eyes fell away under his steady stare. I was frustrated by my ingrained instinct to look away.

But soon I bested my innate desire to shrink under the weight of his penetrating gaze. Clearing my throat, I lifted my chin stubbornly and firmed my resolve, meeting his probing eyes with determination. When I continued, I did so because I wanted to bolster Ronan's confidence with the truth. But also, I wanted to prove that I could be strong for someone, be resilient and a source of courage for someone other than myself.

"But the words are true, Ronan. They needed to be said. You needed to hear them, and I wanted to say them."

His gaze narrowed, searched mine. "Why?" he pushed.

We were standing very close, but I felt like we were still a great distance apart.

Not having anything to lose, I told him the truth—well, part of the truth. "Because I c-care about you, Ronan. You mean s-something to me."

He considered me, his eyes no less examining but growing a good deal less aloof and guarded.

Abruptly, he leaned forward and kissed me. He released my hand and scooped me up, moved both his arms around my waist, wrapping me in the strength of rock-solid man.

It was terribly inappropriate for a formal ballroom. I didn't really notice. But when he finished, I did notice his smile was self-satisfied, charming, and completely genuine.

He administered a quick up-down sweep of my body then sighed. "Holy fuck, you're gorgeous tonight. I've been trying not to think of how satisfying it would be to take you from behind in that dress."

My mouth opened in shock, and I felt a flaming blush creep up my neck to my cheeks. "Ronan!"

He shrugged as though this were perfectly polite conversation. "I've wanted to tell you all night" —he paused just long enough to give me a small peck on my nose and then continued as he turned away and tugged me toward our table — "but I wasn't sure if you'd punch me in the shoulder again."

* * *

"How is your sister, Ro? She still coloring her hair to look like a rainbow?" Bryan Leech, one of Ronan's teammates, asked this question from the far side of the table. He was one of the only guys present who didn't bring a date. As such, he was one of the only guys present who didn't have a woman on his lap.

Everything had gone swimmingly. I was Ronan's smiling date. He'd ignored his extended family with polite indifference. Then he'd presented the award and done a great job. Everyone wanted to talk to him after dinner. He was a perfect gentleman, introducing me to each new person as his "good friend" from New

York. Then, as the evening was winding down, we were waylaid by six of his teammates who insisted on buying us a round of drinks.

This was ridiculous because all the drinks at the event were free.

Ronan didn't consult me, not even with a glance. I thought for sure he would beg off as he must've been exhausted.

But no, he surprised me by accepting the invitation immediately and pulling me along to a table in the corner. It was mostly hidden from the rest of the grand ballroom due to the opportune placement of three tall faux shrubberies.

Ronan ordered me champagne, water for himself, and was mercilessly teased for his choice in beverage. Just as I was about to claim the seat next to his, he grabbed my hips and placed me on his lap.

And, as such, there I happily sat—just like all the other ladies with their husbands or boyfriends or dates—and my head was lying against Ronan's shoulder. I was playing with the open bow tie at his neck, trying to tickle him. My playfulness alone was evidence that I'd had far too much to drink. Not to mention Ronan kept giving me these tender looks that made me feel entirely intoxicated.

"My sister is none of your business," Ronan said, his arm around my waist settling me more firmly against him, his hand on my thigh edging under the hem of my skirt.

So yeah, I was drunk.

Well, I was mostly drunk.

Okay, I wasn't precisely drunk. But I was too tipsy to care about much other than how lovely Ronan's arms felt around me.

"I'd like to see what's at the end of that rainbow," Bryan called back, eliciting several jeering shouts from those gathered—even some of the women—the comment obviously intended to ruffle Ronan's feathers.

"You shut your fucking mouth before I break your jaw." Ronan laughed as he said these violent words, and so did Bryan and everyone else in our party. They all obviously thought this threat was hilarious.

"Ah, Mother Fitzpatrick, we've missed your ugly mug." Tevan Flynn, another of Ronan's teammates, raised his beer in Ronan's direction then added before taking a big gulp, "Here's to Ronan, ugly as a sheep's arse, and yet he finally managed to find himself a looker. May she always be blind to your hideousness."

This was met with a few noises of agreement and chuckles.

"American girls like them ugly," Bryan called from his spot, still stirring the shit. "It's the accent they like."

"That's a load of crap, Bryan Leech." Marta Goodwall, a transplant with her husband from Australia, gave him a teasing sneer. "Your voice is like nails on a chalkboard, son. Good thing you have such a pretty face. Listen to old Marta." She leaned forward and patted Bryan's hand yet still managed to keep her seat on her husband's lap. "It's in your best interest to say as little as possible when women are around. You ruin everything as soon as you open your trap."

The entire table erupted in uproarious laughter; and Bryan chuckled along with the lot of them, though I noted his cheeks above his red beard were tinged a slight shade of pink. I even giggled a little from my spot, though I dared not laugh too hard. Otherwise, my atrocious guffaw might draw attention.

Meanwhile, Ronan's chest vibrated against my cheek, and he threw his head back as his laughter filled the air, the sound curling around me. I closed my eyes to savor it and snuggled closer, placing my lips against his neck so I could feel, hear, and taste his delight.

He sucked in a startled breath, and I felt him stiffen which made me stiffen; and I worried that I'd gone too far.

"Sorry," I whispered, pulling away slightly as I listened to the laughter taper off around us.

But Ronan wasn't looking at me. He was looking beyond our little gathering, and his grip had tightened possessively on my body. His fingers moved a full two inches up my skirt. I blinked at his steely, stoic expression and then followed the direction of his gaze.

There at the periphery, just behind Marta Goodwall and her husband, David, stood none other than Brona O'Shea and Sean Cassidy—Ronan's ex-girlfriend and the teammate of Ronan's she'd cheated with.

A hush fell over our group, and eyes moved back and forth between Sean and Brona, and Ronan and me. Brona was looking at me…sorta. Rather, she was looking at Ronan's hand where it gripped me immodestly beneath my skirt. Her pale blue eyes were flashing thunderbolts of malice at his hand and my thigh.

I didn't know quite what to do, so I smiled, hoping the mask I'd abandoned earlier would slip seamlessly back into place.

Sean spoke first. "Hey, room for two more?"

All eyes swung to Ronan. His jaw ticked. I was sad to see that his earlier happiness had evaporated, leaving only disdain and suspicion.

Yet, a part of me—a very big, but as yet very silent, part of me—was pleased to see that Ronan didn't look at all jealous.

"Of course." Ronan nodded once, affixing an imitation of a smile to his face; his voice was hard and cold. "Always room for you, Sean."

I glanced at Sean, found him looking unaffected and placid. He was taller than Ronan by two inches at least and had that rich-boy aura, like he was perpetually bored and plagued by ennui. He was very, very pretty—not handsome but pretty—and I wondered how someone so pretty could play rugby. Wasn't he afraid of ruining his pretty face and pretty hands and pretty everything?

Brona moved to sit on his lap, and he lifted his hands up to give her space, to steady herself without his assistance, like he didn't care where she sat just as long as she hurried up. I noticed that her eyes didn't stray from Ronan's hand up my skirt until she was settled, and then her glare lifted to mine. I got the distinct impression she wanted to cut me.

Ronan's arm around my waist shifted to my shoulders, and he pulled me toward him, bringing my ear to his mouth so he could whisper, "You want to leave?"

I turned so that I could see his face and gave him my newly discovered smile mask. "Do you want to leave?"

His eyes darted over me; he seemed to be studying my expression, looking for a hint. He frowned, concern flickering over his features.

At length he said, "You finish your drink, and then we'll leave. I don't want those fucks thinking that what they do matters."

"Aren't you going to introduce us to your stunning date?" Sean's cheerful voice cut through our impromptu powwow, bringing our attention back to the table.

Ronan grumbled something under his breath that no one but I could hear; he said three words, and none of them should be repeated.

"What was that?" Sean pressed; he lifted his hand as a waitress approached and pointed to Tevan Flynn's glass of whiskey. "I'll have two of those, top shelf. What do you want, Bunny?"

Bunny?

My smile mask slipped.

Brona was still tossing kitchen knives at my face as she ordered, "I'll have champagne, top shelf."

Sean shifted in his seat, huffed a condescending laugh. "No, Bunny. There's no such thing as *top-shelf* champagne."

She squirmed, her expression turning pale. "She knows what I mean. I want something expensive, the good stuff, yeah?" It was clear that he'd embarrassed her.

The server gave Brona a tight smile and nodded as she backed away. "Of course. I'll be right back."

Bryan cleared his throat, bringing the attention back to himself. It was obvious that he cared about Ronan and was trying to lighten the mood.

"So where did the nickname *Bunny* come from? You don't look like a rabbit, Brona. Do you like carrots?"

Brona opened her mouth to respond, but Sean beat her to it. His tone was dry and droll and perfectly polished as he said, "Oh, that's because we fuck like rabbits."

Several of the wives at the table gagged while several others rolled their eyes. No one laughed. Brona looked like she'd just swallowed a tablespoon of vinegar. I almost felt sorry for her.

Marta piped up with a disapproving head shake. "Really? Sean Cassidy, was that entirely necessary? Didn't your mother raise you with manners?"

He chuckled. Again, his chuckle sounded condescending. "Please accept my apologies if anything I said was untoward." Then he turned his pretty face back to Ronan. "But I would point out that Ronan here has yet to make introductions, which is also quite rude."

Again, Ronan muttered those three words. Again, they weren't quite loud enough to be heard.

"Sorry, what was that?" Sean leaned forward, turning his ear toward us.

Ronan lifted his voice, saying, "I said, 'Go—'"

But before he could finish and repeat *go fuck yourself* for a third time, I straightened, blocking Ronan from view.

"I'm Annie Catrel."

"Ah...the lovely Annie speaks." Sean grinned, cocking his head to the side, his eyes conducting a slow once-over of my body.

I clenched my teeth and readied myself to fight against the instinct to withdraw, but it never came. I was too angry. This guy was an asshole.

"Yes. I speak. Quite well," I said flatly.

"Hmm...well, Annie who speaks quite well, what do you do? I mean, other than Ronan?"

I felt Ronan stiffen, ready to pounce. Brona—not at all helping matters—gave a tittering laugh once she caught on to the joke.

"Fucking hell, Cassidy...." Tevan shook his head, throwing his teammate a disapproving glower. "Why do you always have to be such a dick?"

"What? She claims to speak quite well. I'm giving her a chance to prove her *speaking* abilities." Then he turned his attention back to me, "Tell us about yourself. Did you graduate, let's see, what's it called in the States? High school?"

I nodded. "Yes. I was valedictorian. In case you don't use that word here, it means I...." I hesitated, not wanting to say *top of the class* because I felt certain that would be used against me. Therefore, I said, "It means I had the best grades out of all the students in my graduating class."

"Oh, my, that sounds very important. And you went to university?"

I nodded, absentmindedly stroking Ronan's hand where it rested on my hip. "I did."

"And where did you go? What was your area of study?"

"I went to the University of Pennsylvania and majored in statistics."

Sean blinked, his expression altering by the tiniest fraction. I'd surprised him.

I continued, wanting to clarify, "But that was undergrad. For postgrad I went to Wharton and graduated—again as the class valedictorian—with a master of science in statistics and marketing."

"A master of science?" Sean's frown was disbelieving, as was his tone.

I nodded and added, "Yes. Of science. The title of my thesis was *Info-*

graphics as a Means to Effectively Transfer Knowledge Reducing the Bias of Consumer Interpretation."

Sean stared at me. In fact, the entire table stared at me. I felt myself wilting under the attention, so I reached for my champagne merely to have something to do. It almost tumbled from my grip, but I saved it at the last minute and finished it in three gulps.

Then Ronan chuckled.

Then Ronan laughed.

Then Ronan laughed so hard he seemed to have trouble drawing breath.

I turned to look at him, confused by his joviality, found his eyes bright with amusement and moving over me with raw tenderness.

"Oh, Annie," he whispered affectionately, "what am I going to do with you?"

I heard someone release a low whistle, followed by Marta asking from her spot, "Isn't Wharton one of those hoity-toity schools in the States? Really hard to get into? And you graduated top of the class?" She sounded impressed.

Ronan smiled at me for a beat and then leaned to the side to address the table. "No, no, Marta. They don't have hoity-toity schools in the States." He paused, and I realized later it was for effect when he added, "It's *top shelf*."

SEVENTEEN
RONAN

@Joshblue93: @RonanFitz Why u such a dickhead?
@RonanFitz: @Joshblue93 Got too big a dick/I get too much head. You choose.

My ex didn't have much in the way of brains; however, she did have enough cop on to know that I was mocking her. I'd always hated when people pretended to be something they weren't, and Brona was a prime example of that. I was willing to bet she thought she could upwardly mobile her way into an engagement with Sean, who, unlike my good self, had the full backing of his well-to-do family and would inherit a shit-ton of money and property when his parents died.

And, big shocker, Brona was all over that.

I didn't think there was a single person at the table who believed these two were a love match. Shit, I didn't even get the sense that they liked each other. Brona was currently taking a break from shooting daggers at poor Annie in order to focus her arsenal on me. Her lips looked more *enhanced*, shall we say, than the last time I saw her, and she wore a tight red dress that barely covered her tits. I couldn't believe I'd stuck my cock in that. Repeatedly.

Perhaps I'd been suffering from low self-esteem.

The biggest surprise of the night, though, was how little all this crap was affecting me. In fact, I was finding it kind of hilarious. With Annie close, her perfectly round arse pressing into my more than welcoming lap, the whole world was looking pretty fucking rosy. I wasn't even bothered that my grandparents were pretending I didn't exist, as per usual.

"Oh, Ronan, you look like you've been enjoying your time off from the team," Brona chirped from her place across the table. "It must be great to be able to relax now and not to have to worry about eating right and training all the time."

Was she insinuating I'd let myself go? Annie glanced at me, a look of bewilderment on her face like she'd just come to the same conclusion. Brona was clearly angling for a reaction because I hadn't been in such good shape in years. I was too much of a stubborn bastard. Throw me off the team? Fine, go ahead; I'll come back better and stronger than ever before. Brona knew I had a short temper, and she was playing on that weakness. I gave her nothing.

"Pretty much," I replied casually, stroking my hand back and forth over Annie's thigh and pressing a soft kiss to her bare shoulder. "But I have other ways of keeping fit nowadays."

Brona pursed her ridiculous lips and barely managed to contain her sneer.

"I'll drink to that," Bryan put in cheerfully, lifting his pint.

Marta began to steer the conversation in another direction, and the table filled with chatter. I was quite happy to remain sitting there with Annie on my lap, even with sausage lips and fuckface across the table. I had a keen eye on Annie's fresh glass of champagne because, as soon as she finished the last mouthful, we were out of there. Unfortunately, she was listening with interest to the conversation around her and seemed to have forgotten her drink.

"God, this party is so *boring*," Brona complained loudly, and I saw Sean roll his eyes behind her back. The spoiled little shit deserved everything he got with her. He must've thought that, just because she was my girlfriend, she was some kind of prize. He met my eyes then, and I smirked at him. Yeah, enjoy that fucking prize, dickhead. I should probably thank him. Prick did me a favor. Just thinking of the difference in how Annie made me feel and how Brona did, I realized just how much I'd been missing out on.

"Bunny, some of the ladies are dancing out on the floor; why don't you go join them?" said Sean with false affection. "I know you love to dance."

Brona frowned and then pouted as she twisted in his lap. "Are you trying to get rid of me?"

"Of course not, Bunny. You know how I love to watch you put on a show for me," he said, voice dipping low to convey the double meaning.

Annie had just been bringing her glass up to her mouth for a drink and choked a little on the liquid. I rubbed her back. "You okay?"

She nodded furiously, her eyes watering like she was trying not to burst into laughter. I could tell she was tipsy because I didn't think she meant to reply so loudly. "I'm fine. It's just that Bunny as a nickname cracks me up, and he won't stop saying it." She smacked her hand off my knee in delight. Okay, maybe she was more drunk than tipsy.

"Fuck, they all heard me, didn't they?" she gasped, covering her mouth with her hand.

I couldn't have been more in love with her in that moment.

"You're a little bitch," Brona hissed, getting up from the table with a look of outrage on her face. Then she leveled her eyes on me. "Looks like you had to sink pretty low to find someone who'd put up with your *proclivities*, Ronan." She let out a harsh laugh. "Then again, fat girls don't have very high standards, do they?"

Annie might have been drunk, but she comprehended Brona's insult loud and clear. She grew tense in my lap. I balled my fists to keep from lashing out. No way was she going to talk to Annie like that.

"Bitter, are we, *Bunny*?" I asked, channeling all my disgust into my words. "We all know you had to write to Santa for those knockers."

I squeezed Annie's thigh to soothe her; but her cheeks had grown red, and her lashes shaded her eyes. She was upset and embarrassed.

"Can we leave now?" she whispered.

I was already standing. "Absolutely."

Brona looked like she'd won, her chin raised high as she watched us leave. I had to resist the urge to bark out a laugh because she hadn't won a thing. In fact, I'd won just by the fact that I wasn't with her anymore. I'd won by the simple fact that I had Annie under my arm instead of her. I led us outside and into a waiting taxi. She stared out the window on the drive, her voice quiet when she said, "I don't understand how you could ever be with someone like that. She's horrible."

I ran a hand down my face and tugged her closer. "Don't let the shit she said in there get to you. You're beautiful, and she's jealous." I paused, letting out a tired sigh. "She wasn't always so horrible, but yeah, the seed must have been there. I was just too blind, too preoccupied perhaps, to see it."

"People aren't always what you think they are," Annie murmured, her head lolling to the side. She was exhausted, and it wasn't surprising. She'd been through so much in the last twenty-four hours alone.

Her words piqued my interest, and I wondered if she was referring to her secret identity as The Socialmedialite. My heart pounded. Would this be the moment when she came clean?

"No?"

She shook her head. "Human beings are really good at hiding stuff. You shouldn't blame yourself for not seeing through Brona in the beginning."

So maybe she wasn't going to come clean, but at least she didn't think I was an awful person for having been with someone like Brona. When we arrived at the hotel, I paid the taxi driver and tipped him handsomely. By the time we got to our suite, Annie looked just about ready to keel over from exhaustion. I fervently wished she wasn't so exhausted because seeing her dolled up like she was tonight, wearing a dress that showcased her body to perfection, had me worked up like a sailor on his first day of leave.

I lifted her into my arms and strode through the suite, entering the bedroom and laying her down on the mattress. Tiredly, she thanked me before resting her head on the pillow and closing her eyes. A moment later, I heard her breathing deepen in slumber. Well, it didn't look like I'd be getting any action tonight. Not that I would have gotten any even if she was awake. Annie was always a tricky one. You never quite knew if something was going to make her scurry away or open up like a flower. Visions of her in the bath filled my head, how soft and silky and deliciously slippery she'd felt in my hands. How pliant she'd been to my demands, and how it had taken the willpower of a saint not to have her right there and then.

I was no saint, though.

The main reason I didn't take her was because I wanted the first time I sank inside her to be perfect. I'd been fantasizing about it for weeks.

A little sigh escaped her, her long mahogany hair spread across the pillow like a dark halo. I sat down on a chair beside the bed, rested my elbows on my knees as I leant forward and just watched her. I let out a long, distracted breath. She was so beautiful, so perfect it was painful. I loved her thick, dark lashes, the delicate curve of her lips.

I loved her pale, flawless skin. I loved the way her eyes crinkled and lit up when she smiled. I loved her soft, rounded belly and her lush, curvaceous thighs. I loved the musical cadence of her voice when she spoke.

Shit, I just loved her.

Loved. Her.

I was in love with her.

And I was fucked.

Time passed as I imagined a hundred different ways of telling her how I felt. And every single time I saw her withdraw. I saw her tuck herself away into a tiny square of paper that I could never unfold. It terrified me. Then I thought of how much braver she was online. How she never minced her words or beat around the bush. How she was still Annie, just with the fear subtracted.

With trembling hands, I stood and walked out of the bedroom and into the lounge. My laptop sat on the desk waiting for me with all its potential for both creation and destruction. I opened it and began to type. I wasn't even sure if I was going to send the message; it just felt freeing to get the words out in some way.

March 30

3:24 a.m.

Dear SML,

I know you're away on holiday right now; but I need to talk to someone, and you seem like my best option. I'm all mixed up. If you've been following the "news," you probably already know that I'm back home for a couple of days. Annie came with me. It's been crazy. The press are twice as nasty and far more in your face over here, so it's been really hard to keep calm. It's been even harder for Annie. This isn't the life she chose, and yet she's doing it all for me. I'm not sure if I deserve it. She's handling this shit better than I ever have—even though I know it must be twenty times more difficult for someone who's unaccustomed to the limelight. And it's a revelation because she's actually so much stronger than I am. She's handling it all so gracefully.

I'm in awe of her.

But here lies the rub: she's all I think about. She's the only person I want to spend time with. I'm fascinated by every little thing she does.

And the fact of the matter is, I'm in love with her. Heartbreakingly, soul-wrenchingly, earth-shatteringly in love with her.

It's nothing like I've ever felt before. And I need her to love me back more than I need to take my next breath. I can't imagine a greater agony than this big, pulsing, fierce love I have for her being unreciprocated. I would rather take a hundred blows to the head out on the field, suffer a thousand concussions, than not have her beside me for the rest of my life.

You probably think I'm being melodramatic. I'm not. I've always known what I wanted from life. I don't have a single indecisive bone in my body. And I know with all my heart that I want Annie. I need to make her happy.

But how do I tell her? How do I explain to her the extent of my feelings without frightening her away?

I am a ship out on the ocean seeking a compass for guidance. Be my compass, SML; otherwise, I might screw this whole thing up spectacularly.

Yours,
Ronan

I read over the message several times, my finger circling the mouse, the cursor hovering over the "send" button like the ultimate test of courage. I was running on too little sleep to tell whether or not this was the move of a duplicitous fuckwad or the most ingenious idea ever. I thought that if I could give Annie advance warning that I was in love with her—give her some time to digest it and come to terms with it—then maybe she'd allow herself the chance to discover that she loved me back. I knew that she did. She just didn't know it yet. I also knew from past experience that she would lie to herself instead of stepping off the cliff with me.

So, this was it. I hit "send." I just hoped I wouldn't regret my decision.

When I returned to the bedroom, Annie was still fast asleep, still fully dressed, too. Taking my time, I removed her strappy heels and her gown. I was oh, so careful not to wake her. She mumbled a little in her sleep; and I thought I heard my name pass her lips in a sigh, but I couldn't be certain. Still, it made me hard enough to cut steel. Once I had her under the covers, I hovered. I knew sleeping on the couch was the gentlemanly thing to do, but I just couldn't tear myself away from her. Her body was so warm and soft and welcoming. The couch was a dried-up old rice cake, and she was a filet mignon. Finally decided, I undressed in record time and slid under the covers with her. When I wrapped my arms around her, she rolled over, her body instinctively sinking into mine. It felt right. It felt perfect.

And it was like this that I fell into the most peaceful sleep I'd had in a very long time.

* * *

When I woke up, I got a feeling that someone was watching me. I couldn't feel the warmth of her skin anymore, so I knew that Annie must be awake already. Blinking a few times, I turned my head to see her lying on her side, holding herself up on her elbow as she stared at my exposed torso. I must have thrown the blankets off in my sleep, because I was completely uncovered.

I shot her a lazy grin. "Enjoying the view?"

Her gaze snapped to attention. It was clear that she'd been so intent on studying my body that she hadn't even realized I'd woken up. And yeah, I took a certain degree of satisfaction from that. I loved her eyes on me, looking at me like I was an éclair she wanted to sink her teeth into.

She cleared her throat, her cheeks growing pink. "I was just admiring your tattoo."

I looked down at the thick black script that spelled *Mo teaghlach, mo chroí* from one collarbone to the other.

"It's handy that's there, isn't it?" I smiled and shifted closer. "Otherwise, you would have had to admit you were ogling."

I put my hand on her shoulder before gliding it down her arm to her hip. She was wearing a baggy blue T-shirt that I distinctly remembered *not* putting on her last night—which meant she'd gotten up and put it on herself. I didn't like that she felt the need to cover up.

Her brows knitted together, but the hint of a smile played on her lips. "I wasn't ogling. I don't ogle. I was wondering what the words meant, if you must know. Sorry if you mistook my wonderment for oglement."

I took her hand in mine and brought it to my chest, placing her palm flat to my skin. "First off, 'oglement' isn't a word. And second, my tattoo is Irish for 'My family, my heart.'"

She sucked in a breath and nodded. "So you got it for Lucy and your mom?"

"Well, I sure as shit didn't get it for the Fitzpatricks." I chuckled derisively.

"I told you last night. Not knowing you is their loss, Ronan."

"Fuck yeah, it is. Family isn't always the one you're born into. Sometimes it's about people who get into your blood, inside your heart, and under your skin all on their own." I stared her intensely, gripping her hand tight. She blinked, like she'd been in a trance for a moment, and drew her hand away. When I realized she was about to scamper, I wrapped my arms around her waist and pulled her back into the bed. She struggled a little—which ended up with me hovering over her, her wrists bound together above her head.

Her breathing grew rapid, which caused her breasts to move up and down, pressing them into my naked chest deliciously. She twisted this way and that for a moment before giving up. Her body went limp, and I sank myself into the space between her thighs. I rotated my hips just enough so that she could feel how hard I was. Her gasp was muted by the sound of the main door to the suite opening and Patricia's voice calling, "Don't mind me. I'm just leaving your breakfast out here, Annie."

"I ordered food," Annie whispered and bit her bottom lip. "I hope that's okay."

She seemed nervous, like ordering food was taking liberties or something. I put my thumb to her mouth and pulled her lip from between her teeth. "You never have to ask permission. Okay? Not unless I'm fucking you—then you always ask permission."

Her eyes got big, but she didn't breathe a word. I left her then, staring after me curiously. I was still hard but knew that if I stayed in that bed a second longer, I'd be inside her in no time. Everything about her was made to be fucked, pleasured, worshipped.

So yeah, I needed a minute.

I saw Patricia's form retreating out the door just as I entered the lounge. It was a good thing, too, because all I had on was a pair of boxers, and I was still sporting some serious wood. I didn't want to give her an eyeful. She'd left a cart of food by the table. Every item you could possibly wish for first thing in the morning seemed to be provided. I wheeled the cart into the bedroom, where Annie was still lying on the bed, a flush to her cheeks that told me she was still thinking about what I'd said to her.

Did the idea of asking permission during sex appeal to her?

God, I hoped so.

"Tea or coffee?" I asked in a cheerful voice that made her giggle, but I noted she was careful to stifle it.

"Are you my manservant this morning?"

"If that's what floats your boat," I replied, grinning. "So, what does the lady desire? Toast? Eggs? Sausage?"

On the last option, her eyes inadvertently wandered to my crotch, and I knew I had her. Come hell or high water, neither one of us was leaving this suite today, and I planned on playing dirty.

I let out a bark of laughter and winked. "Sausage it is then, you naughty little thing."

"You're so, so...." she began but couldn't seem to find the word.

"Dashingly handsome? I know, it's such a burden."

She scowled at me playfully, crossed her arms over her chest, and leaned back against the headboard. "I was going to say big-headed."

"Well, that's also true." I waggled my eyebrows at her. Seriously, there was no way she was going to win with me today. I poured her some tea, set it on the dresser beside her, then filled a plate with sausage and eggs. She brought the teacup to her mouth, taking a sip as she watched me climb onto the bed with the plate in hand. Yes, I was going there, and there was nothing she could do to stop me.

"Um, I can come over; you don't have to...."

Silencing her with a look, up on my knees I straddled her thighs and sat, digging the fork into a piece of sausage and bringing it to her mouth. Her eyes traveled from the fork to the sausage to me in blatant disbelief. She seemed to have a moment of indecision before she finally leaned forward to take a bite.

Playfully, I withdrew the fork. "First, take the T-shirt off."

I saw her throat bob as she swallowed. "I don't see why that's necessary."

"You don't make the rules. Take it off."

"Ronan...."

I put the plate down, braced my hands firmly on either side of her head, and bent down so my mouth was a whisper away from hers. "Take. It. Off."

Her lip quivered, and I saw the surrender in her eyes when her hands went to the hem of the T-shirt and lifted. I'd be lying if I said I didn't enjoy her defiance. I liked a little bit of a fight before the inevitable surrender. And if Annie's expression was anything to go by, she was enjoying this just as much as I was. Her pupils were dilated as fuck.

The shirt was gone a moment later, her peachy pale skin and lush breasts hugged perfectly by the black lacy bra she was wearing. I picked the plate back up and lifted the fork to her mouth again. This time I let her have the sausage. I didn't even really know where all this had come from, but I did know that I derived a strange sort of pleasure from watching her eat. I guessed it made sense when I thought about it. I was a kinky fucker, simple as that.

I watched her chew and swallow with the same amount of rapt attention I'd give to her hand between her legs bringing herself to orgasm for me.

With the plate between us on the bed, I continued to feed her with one hand while the other traced the curve of her breasts. I could see through the thin fabric of her bra that her nipples were rock hard, and when I pinched one, it elicited a strangled sound of pleasure from deep in her throat.

"You are pure pornography, Annie Catrel," I said, my voice low and husky.

"Do you know that? Do you know how much every single thing you do tortures me?"

"Oh, God," she moaned.

Moving the plate aside, I ran my knuckles down her stomach until I reached the hem of her underwear. The material was light and flimsy, and she sighed when I began rolling it down her thighs. She wanted this, too. This was my first time seeing her properly, stark sunlight streaming through the windows, and she was absolutely exquisite. I had to take a steadying breath in order to continue.

She grew rigid as I moved my body down the bed so my face was between her legs. I rubbed the inside of her thigh tenderly.

"Relax," I whispered, bringing my mouth to her wetness, and then licked.

"Ahhh," she cried out, clutching a handful of my hair. I chuckled and went at her in earnest. She was so soft and silky beneath my tongue. I met her gaze from below and came up for air, ordering, "Bra off."

She didn't even hesitate this time, reaching around to undo the clasp and revealing her perfectly full breasts tipped with tight, pink nipples to my greedy eyes. I saw her fist the sheets in her hands, her hips rising up off the bed when I sucked her clit into my mouth and flicked it with my tongue. I added some fingers to the equation, savoring the hot, tight feel of her.

"Please," she murmured. "More."

So I gave her more. I gave her everything. Before I knew it, she was touching her breasts, pinching her nipples as I devoured her, and I swear I could have come from the sight. She was simply glorious. When she came, it was with the most beautiful sounds I'd ever heard, all quick, shallow breaths and sweet little sighs. I couldn't hold back any longer, my balls drawing tight as I emptied myself onto the bed sheets.

Chest heaving, Annie looked down at me, her eyes full of such tenderness and affection that I felt breathless for a moment. She seemed curious.

"Did you...."

"Yeah, you're just too sexy," I replied with a wink and a ragged breath. I had only woken up, and already I was exhausted but in the best way possible. She giggled and stroked my hair away from my face as I rested my head against her thigh.

"What are we doing here, Ronan?" she asked, still stroking. Despite her question, her voice was lazy with post-orgasm chill.

The smile I gave her was devilish. "I'm enjoying you, Annie. And you're enjoying me enjoying you."

"And when we go home?"

I nuzzled her thigh and felt her shiver. "You forget, I am home. And you know, I'm kind of considering not letting you go now."

"I have to go back," she said past a sigh.

"Yeah, I know. And I'll be going with you. And when we get there, we can enjoy each other some more. And maybe, just maybe, I'll feed you some more sausage, because we both know how much you like that."

Her lips twitched as she said, "You know, it doesn't always have to be sausage...."

Her sassy response caused an unexpected burst of laughter as I lifted myself up off the bed and went to the breakfast trolley. All this talk of food was making me hungry. Everything was either greasy and fried or loaded with refined sugars.

"Ah, fuck it," I said and picked up a Danish, taking a big bite.

Annie's eyes glittered as she watched me. "So good, right?"

"Too good," I replied then pointed the Danish at her. "Not as good as you, though."

She blushed. "Ronan."

"Annie," I said, mimicking her scandalized tone. "I've just had my mouth on your vagina. All embarrassment is no longer allowed."

She glanced at me from beneath her lashes. "Okay."

"Good. Now, on to the next item on today's agenda. Bath or shower?"

"Um...."

"I'm thinking a shower," I teased. "Sure I've already seen you in the bath—which, by the way, I've been meaning to ask you about. What in the world were you doing in there with all those bubbles and nothing but your hand?" My chuckle was devious. And then, if I ever had any doubts that I loved this woman, her next words blew them all to shards.

"Thinking of you," she whispered bravely. I almost dropped the Danish. She glanced to the side and continued talking. "I'm kind of obsessed with your body. I mean, it's easy for most women to be sexy. They were born with boobs and bottoms, and that's what men like. But men have to work for what women like. That 'V' thing and the six-pack and, man, those thighs. You have to kill yourself with exercise and eating right to look like you do. I respect the hell out of that. And well, the least I can do is pay you the compliment of looking after all your hard work."

She gave me a wicked little smile, and I was done for. She was literally holding my heart in her hands, warming it with her honesty and her openness. I strode toward the bed, and she squealed when I picked her up and threw her over my shoulder.

"For that little speech, love, you get a bonus orgasm."

EIGHTEEN
RONAN

@Pixiefacecarla: Saw @RonanFitz out and about today. He looked at me for a second and now I think I'm pregnant. #swoon #sexybastard #icandiehappy
@RonanFitz: @Pixiefacecarla Fairly sure that was @Tomsouthernchef. He's a notorious eye impregnator. Bet you a tenner the baby comes out ginger.
@Tomsouthernchef: @RonanFitz Jealous of my superpower?

"You, me, and a couple of the lads for a game down at Old Wesley, what you do say, Fitzy?" Bryan asked through the phone. I'd put him on loudspeaker. "My brother and his mates play there. They'd sell their grannies for a chance to meet you. Come on. It'll be fun."

I'd just finished up in the shower with Annie and hadn't wanted to leave the hotel suite for the rest of the day. Now Bryan was nagging me to go and play a match with a bunch of pimply teenagers. I knew which option was more appealing, but I felt bad saying no. I glanced at Annie, who was standing by the window toweling her hair dry. She gave me an enthusiastic smile and a thumbs-up to show she thought it was a good idea.

"Is Cassidy going to be there?" I asked.

"Ah, shit, probably. He's not an intentional fuckwit. He was just raised that way. You know what his family's like. Just ignore him if he shows up."

"It's difficult to ignore a cock when there's a cock in your face, Bryan."

"Can we leave the cocks out of it? I've just eaten breakfast," he said, chuckling, and I gave in. In all honesty, I missed the boys. It'd be nice to play a game, get back to what I enjoyed for a while.

"Fine. I'll be there. See you later."

"Later," said Bryan before hanging up.

"So, it looks like I'm playing a match today," I said, looking to Annie. She was all wrapped up in a bathrobe, and the sight was a serious test to my willpower. "You don't have to come. You could stay here and enjoy some more spa treatments if you like."

"No, no," she said fervently. "I'd seriously love to come see you play."

I smiled. "That's what I like to hear. Listen, I have a few things to take care of first. I'll be back in an hour, and then we'll head out." She nodded and continued toweling her hair. I loved how she looked right then, so fresh and clean and pretty. Walking over to her, I took her chin in my hand and tilted her head so that I could kiss her. "You are distractingly beautiful, do you know that?"

Her only reply was a sweet little smile.

"Okay," I said, backing away. "I'm going to go now. Otherwise, I'll never leave."

She laughed, and I threw on some clothes before heading out. I was in between living arrangements, so I didn't actually have a permanent address. Brona and I had been renting an apartment together, but after things blew up with her, I had all my stuff moved to Ma's. Well, technically it was my house since I'd bought the place for her. Anyway, it was where I was keeping my cars, and I wanted to go pick one up. Being such an avid driver, it killed me to have to take taxis everywhere.

I knew Ma and Lucy were back from New York because I'd gotten a text from Lucy last night. Ma was still licking her wounds; and I didn't have time for a confrontation, so I hoped she'd be out. I didn't get my wish, and as soon as I slotted my key in the door, I heard her footsteps coming down the stairs.

"Ronan," she said as she took me in. "You look good. How was the ceremony last night?" There was a hesitancy in her voice.

"It went well. Annie and I both had a great time."

She frowned and pursed her lips when I said Annie's name, and I let out a long, irritable sigh. I really wasn't in the mood for this.

"Yes, well, that's good to hear. Though I can't understand why you're staying in a hotel. You're my son, and I have more than enough room to put you up here."

I arched a brow. "Oh, yeah, because that would be a barrel of fun. I'm sure Annie would just love having to deal with your digging into her every chance you got."

"I told you I wanted to apologize!" she exclaimed.

I was cynical. "Do you, though? Do you really want to apologize, or is it simply a case of keeping your friends close and your enemies closer?"

Her voice grew heavy with emotion. "Is that how you think of me? You think I'm some sour, calculating bitch? Sometimes parents have to make hard decisions when it comes to their children, and believe me, I have always had your best interests at heart. I just don't want to see you being taken advantage of by another cheating, money-hungry gold-digger. It broke my heart to see how you were after Brona."

My entire body sagged as I went to sit down on a step. After a moment she came and sat beside me, and I could tell from the silent way she was wiping at her eyes that she was crying. I didn't think these were stage tears, either. She was genuinely upset. And she genuinely thought I was going to get taken for a fool again. I had to explain to her that Annie was a million miles away from Brona.

"Remember how you used to tell me about the Fitzpatricks and how after Dad died they tried to take me and Lucy from you? They wanted to pay you off to disappear and never see us again, and if you didn't take the money, they'd completely disown us and never acknowledge either of us as their grandchildren."

I looked down to see her face etched in sadness at the memory. "Yes."

"And what did you say to them?"

A hint of a smile returned to her face. "I told them to go shove their money up their arses. That I'd never allow anyone to separate me from my children. That I'd raise you and Lucy better than they ever could, even though I hadn't a penny to my name."

I put my arm around her shoulder. "I was always so proud of you when you told that story to Lucy and me. You were a lioness protecting her cubs, and it gave me a sense of complete belonging to know my parent loved me so much she'd live with nothing in order to keep me. Now, imagine if you hadn't loved us like you do. Imagine if you'd taken that money and abandoned us, two little kids all on their own in the world."

She shuddered. "It doesn't even bear thinking about."

"No, it doesn't," I said. "And that's exactly what happened to Annie. Her mother left her on the steps of a fire station when she was six years old and was never seen again. All through her childhood she was in and out of foster homes. Just like Lucy and I might've been, Annie was alone in the world, only it was worse because she didn't even have rich grandparents. She had no one, which makes it even more amazing how she's transformed her life. She has a career, a top-class education, and a home; and, believe it or not, the woman doesn't need a penny from me. She's got more than enough money of her own."

Ma stared at me, her eyes wet, and brought her hand to her mouth. In that moment, I knew I'd broken through to her. She was thinking of Annie; she was thinking of her as the little girl with no one rather than the money-hungry gold-digger she'd imagined her to be.

"God, that poor girl," she whispered, and I reached over to wipe away a few of her tears. She swallowed and focused on me. "I'm so sorry, Ronan. This life, you know, it's made me hard. I haven't been the…kindest mother—to you or to Luce—I've had to be that way to protect you. And ever since Brona almost destroyed your career, I've been on the defensive, looking out for anyone who might try to take advantage of you again."

I took her hands in mine and looked her in the eyes. "I know, and I love you for it; but you have nothing to fear with Annie. I learned my lesson with Brona, and I made a promise to myself not to put my trust in a woman again. But then Annie came along and turned my world upside down. I knew deep in my heart that I could trust her." A long silence ensued before I added, "I'd like you to get to know her. Give her a chance. I promise, once you do, you'll see exactly what I see."

She shook her head sadly, "The things I said to her. God, Ronan, even if I do give her a chance, I'm not sure she'll want to give me one."

"She will," I said soothingly. "Just give it time."

* * *

WHEN I FINALLY opened the garage and was greeted by the sight of my lovingly restored 1970 red Dodge Charger, I felt like Odysseus arriving home to Ithaca after twenty years of struggle. I ran my hand over the hood, my body humming with the need to get behind the wheel. I grabbed some training gear from the house and then hopped in the car. And okay, maybe I was a little late getting back to the hotel because I took the scenic route. I needed some alone time with my baby.

Fuck, that drive was almost sexual. Driving in New York had been fun, but coming home just felt right. When I finally made it back to the suite, I found Annie sitting on the bed, her laptop open in front of her and a look of consternation on her face. She was so absorbed by what she was doing that she didn't hear me come in. I stood in the doorway for a minute, soaking up the sight of her long hair hanging over one shoulder, the figure-hugging cream blouse she wore, and the long vintage-looking purple skirt that swept attractively over her thighs.

"Hey," I said, throwing my keys up into the air and catching them. "You almost ready to go, love?"

Her eyes shot to me, and for a brief moment she looked like a deer caught in the headlights. I watched her swallow, scratch her wrist, and then straighten out her blouse before it hit me. The email I sent last night. She'd been reading it. She knew.

I swear I could feel my heart trying to pound its way out of my chest.

Now I was the one who felt like a deer caught in the headlights. Every feeling of doubt and insecurity I'd ever had flooded me all at once. *Love me back*, I begged. *Please, if there's any mercy in the world, make her love me back.*

I cleared my throat and nodded to the laptop. I hardly even recognized my own voice when I spoke. "Anything interesting?"

She looked away and shut the computer down. "Oh, just the usual work stuff."

She sounded shaky. I stood there, frozen, not knowing what to say or how to act. Then she got off the bed and walked toward me with some kind of determination.

She's going to pull away, I thought. *She's going to run again, make up some excuse to leave and get a flight home early.* And the scary thing was that I wasn't sure I could let her go. I'd kneel at her feet and beg her to stay because I belonged to this woman heart and soul, and I needed her to belong to me, too. When she was less than a foot away from me, she stopped. Her big, bottomless eyes never left mine, both of us asking silent questions but receiving no answers.

I saw her hands trembling when she reached up and settled them on my chest.

"You're nothing like what I expected you to be, Ronan Fitzpatrick," she said, her voice barely above a whisper.

I drew in a breath in the exact same moment that she leaned in and pressed her lips to mine. At first I didn't react at all; perhaps I was in too much shock. I just stood there as her lips caressed me, her soft tongue sliding into my mouth and licking along my own.

She wasn't pushing me away.

When the realization finally sank in, I gripped her neck and slid my arm tight around her waist, pulling her body flush to mine. I kissed her back. I kissed her with everything I had inside me until she was needy and hot and whimpering. We only came up for air when my phone started ringing. I knew it was Bryan or one of the lads, wondering where I was. I was only irritated for a second before I realized it was the perfect distraction. Annie knew that I loved her now, and the hotel suite felt too small, too close. We needed to get out and let it all sink in.

"That'll be one of the lads," I said, smiling down at her tenderly. "We better make a move. Looks like we're already late. It's good to know you can hardly stand being in the same room as me without jumping my bones, though," I teased and gave her a light pinch on the bottom. She yelped then laughed, her eyes shining brightly, and something inside me relaxed. We needed to be silly for a while. Things were turning too serious.

On the drive to Wes, I kept catching her watching me from the corner of my eye. Her body was turned to me, her cheek lying on the headrest. Her face bore a perennial blush, and there was a dreamy look in her eyes. My little distant Annie was coming closer; her icy exterior was thawing, and all because she now knew I loved her. I could have high-fived myself for having the idea to write to her Socialmedialite account. She could hold the knowledge of my love without having to admit any of her own feelings, and I didn't mind. I wanted her to know that I was fully committed. Just like I'd told The Socialmedialite in my email, she was "it" for me.

Every time I let go of the gear stick, I put my hand back on her thigh, loving the feel of her beneath my palm. When we arrived at the pitch, I saw a couple of the wives and girlfriends hanging out on the sidelines, drinking coffees, and chatting.

"Come on, I'll introduce you," I said to Annie, taking her hand in mine. Her expression told me the last thing she wanted to do was meet yet more new people, but she let me lead her over nonetheless. Marta was there, alongside one or two of the women Annie had met last night, so it wasn't so intimidating.

A loud wolf whistle rang out, and I recognized Tina, Desmond McAleer's wife, as the culprit. I'd known Tina for years. She was flirtatious and loud-spoken, but it was all in good fun.

"Looking hot, Fitzpatrick," she called as we approached. "When are we going to see you back on the field, eh? I'm sick of looking at the same old arses. You've been well missed."

"Tina, it's a pleasure as always. And you'll get a good look at me today. But first I'd like to introduce you to my girlfriend, Annie."

It was the first time I'd introduced her as my girlfriend since we'd arrived in Dublin. I didn't see the point in pretending anymore. She was mine, and I wanted the whole world to know it. It took Tina less than a second to tuck Annie under her wing and begin introducing her to the other ladies she didn't know. I gave her a soft, lingering kiss on the mouth which elicited several sighs from the women.

Then I headed to the clubhouse to change into my gear. Much to my irritation, Sean was there in all his blond pretty-boy glory. Somebody seriously needed to smack the self-satisfied look off the bloke's face because the bashing I'd given him obviously hadn't worked. I'd gotten myself suspended from the team, and he was still walking around looking like he'd just pissed in everyone's cornflakes and was thoroughly delighted by the fact.

Someone was obviously trying to stir up shit because it turned out that Sean and I were nominated to pick teams. In the end each side had an even mix of professionals and amateurs. And in the end my team wiped the floor with Sean's team. Yeah, Tevan came away with a bloody nose, I had a whole host of new bruises, and one of the young lads elbowed Sean in the face. It was apparently an accident, but I had my suspicions. And those suspicions had me grinning like a bastard.

I strode over to Annie at the end of the match, slid my hand around her neck, and kissed her with everything I had in me. She drew away, breathless, and her eyes had that dreamy look in them again. God, I couldn't wait for her to look at me like that when I was inside her.

"You're all dirty and sweaty," she said, laughing and fixing her hair in place.

"Occupational hazard. Besides, there's nothing wrong with getting a little dirty." I winked.

"I like it," she threw back as I was walking away, and I shot her a simmering look over my shoulder.

After I'd showered and dressed, I was sitting in the changing rooms pulling on my boots when Sean sauntered in. He had a towel tucked around his waist and wore a pair of designer flip-flops. He stood in front of me, and I cocked an eyebrow while he let out a long sigh that only the truly pampered and jaded can do justice.

"So, long story short, how would you like to get Brona back in your bed?"

I barked out a laugh. "Long story short, are you high?"

"I've grown bored, Fitzpatrick. Unfortunately, Bunny is quite like a roll of cellotape. She sticks. And now she's been throwing around words like 'wedding' and 'engagement ring.' Quite frankly, I think it's time I moved on. So, if you still have a thing for her, I could arrange for her to go running back into your big, strong, working-class arms. Call it a peace offering, a way for us to mend our bridges."

I pointed to my face. "You see this look? This is my 'go fuck yourself' look. So, go fuck yourself, Cassidy."

He tutted. "So aggressive. There's no judgment here, Ronan. If you want her, you can have her. Even I can admit that she sucks dick like a Dyson. And I've had a lot of fellatio in my time. *A lot.*"

Seriously, this prick didn't even know what he sounded like, did he? He was such a cliché I almost felt sorry for him.

"You must really be missing that hospital bed because you're five seconds away from a return visit. I suggest you leave now. Otherwise, I can't be responsible for fucking your shit up. Again."

He raised his hands in the air. "No need for violence. I'm offering you an olive branch here. Let's not allow a pair of plastic double-Ds to get in the way of our friendship. We have to put the team first."

I shook my head at him and couldn't help but laugh. "We were hardly best buds before all this. But seriously, if you're so concerned about the team, then why did you even sleep with her in the first place?"

He shot a look toward the ceiling, shrugged, and then looked back to me. "I was drunk and horny. She saw an opportunity. There's nothing very deep about it."

"Well, no surprise there."

He narrowed his gaze fractionally at my response. "So, do you want her back or not?"

The look I gave him said it all. "I've got a girlfriend who I'm very much in love with. And I'd rather stick my penis in a blender than go anywhere near that poisonous brat ever again."

He sucked in a long breath then exhaled. "Fair enough. And I must say, congrats on the new bird, man. She is *smokin'*."

"So much as look at her, and you'll regret it," I warned.

He threw his hands into the air. "Touchy, touchy. But okay, I guess I deserved that. Oh, and a word to the wise, you're doing well in the press at the moment, whereas Brona's looking like a twisted attention whore. However, I suspect she has something up her sleeve. Just a feeling. You may want to get your people on the case. Don't say I never gave you anything," he finished and then strode off.

I sat there, staring at the tiles on the floor and wondering if he was trying to fuck with my head. Something up her sleeve? I tried not to dwell on it because she was probably just going to do another interview with some trashy gossip mag.

A little while later, in order to evade the paps, a small group of us made the drive up to the Dublin Mountains to have dinner and drinks in a cozy little pub off the beaten track. The whole time Annie was snugly tucked under my arm, sipping on a glass of Baileys, looking rosy-cheeked and thoroughly relaxed.

This is the life, I thought to myself.

She'd put her hair in a loose ponytail and strands fell messily over her neck and shoulders. I wanted to grip that ponytail in my hand while I took her from behind. My quick and dirty orgasm today had definitely not been enough to keep me satisfied. In fact, it had kind of made matters worse. Getting a taste of her had only made my hunger grow even fiercer. I wanted to make love to her; but with everything going on and us staying in a hotel room (where seemingly Patricia felt she had the freedom to come and go as she pleased), it just didn't feel like we had the required privacy. We were constantly surrounded by people, and I just wanted to be alone. Nobody else but me and Annie.

When she stood to go use the bathroom, I watched her smooth her skirt down over her thighs and walk away. Bryan had the good nature to rib me about it.

"Can't take your eyes off that one," he said. "You've got it bad, Fitzpatrick."

"Leave him alone," said Tina, who sat with her husband Desmond on the other side of the table. "I think it's lovely. You can practically feel how badly they're into each other. Makes me a little jealous, if I'm honest."

Seriously, they were like a bunch of clucking hens. We'd finished our food, and Annie's glass of Baileys was empty. I thought this was as good a time as any to make a move. Just as she returned to the table, I stood and helped her on with her coat and handbag. She seemed surprised that we were leaving already but let me lead her outside nonetheless. We said our goodbyes, and it felt good to get back behind the wheel. I knew that soon enough I'd be back in New York amid the traffic and the people and the stress, so I decided to make the most of the moment.

"You mind if we go for a drive before we head back to the hotel?" I asked Annie as she settled into the passenger seat.

She did a cute little yawn. "Not at all. I'll warn you, though. I'm exhausted, so I may fall asleep along the way."

"Get in the back and lie down if you like," I suggested. The idea seemed to appeal to her because she climbed between the seats, giving me yet another spectacular view of her arse. I had to resist the urge to lean forward and give it a little bite. She lay down in the back, and I sat there for a moment, looking at her through the overhead mirror. Such a fucking temptation.

I had a feeling this was going to be the best drive of my life.

In some places the roads weren't lit very well, and it seemed like I'd gotten my wish because it really felt like we were all alone. We talked a little along the way with Annie explaining some of the stuff about her job I didn't know. Seriously, the woman was so intelligent when she was relaxed enough not to be anxious that it made me feel dumb in comparison. Yeah, I was educated, but Annie just had this natural flair for what she did that I was in awe of.

All the while she talked, I had my eyes flickering between her and the road. She sat with her feet up on the seat, her body strewn in such a way that she was almost lying down, with her head resting against the edge of the window. It was kind of a high, having her all to myself like this. I started to fixate on how she hadn't put on a seatbelt and how those seatbelts hung next to her body. It would be so easy to strap her down. I could be pretty creative when the mood took me.

When I saw a little turn off the main road, I took it until we came to a secluded nook surrounded by tall trees. I parked the car. I was still staring at her through the mirror when she sat up, asking, "Why have we stopped?"

I exhaled and tapped my fingers on the steering wheel. Was I actually considering doing this? I mean, depending on what she preferred in bed, I could scare her off for good. Then again, from the very moment I'd met her, I had the distinct feeling that we were compatible, unnervingly so. Somehow, I just knew she'd be perfect, that we'd be perfect.

"Taking a little break," I replied as I turned off the engine. I left the keys in the ignition so that the radio could stay on. I'd found a station during the drive that was playing some nice, relaxing chill-out music, and I thought silence might make Annie uncomfortable. Her eyes flickered when I began climbing toward her into the back, and all of a sudden she was sitting up straight, watching me warily.

"Hey," I said.

"Hey."

It was crazy how she could go from relaxed to uptight in a heartbeat, and strangely, I kind of got off on her uptightness because it was so much fun helping her unwind. I let out a low, dark chuckle and pulled her into me; the moment my lips met hers, her tension melted away. Her hands gripped my shirt, her body straining against mine. I cupped her cheeks as I slid my tongue into her mouth, a hard, probing invasion. She allowed it with a sigh, and I began to ease her into a reclining position.

She was heaving and breathless when I broke our kiss to whisper in her ear, "I'm going to try some stuff, okay? I promise I won't hurt you, but I'd really like it if you let me. You can tell me to stop any time if you feel uncomfortable."

"Some stuff?" she asked, aroused yet perplexed.

My hand wandered under her skirt, between her legs, and straight beneath the fabric of her underwear. I fingered her soft, silky flesh, finding her wet. Perfect.

"Yeah," I answered, my voice pure gravel. "It's better if I just show you. Telling is no fun."

She nodded, lips plump from our kissing, and her breath escaped her all in a rush. Kneeling between her thighs, I took her hands and raised them above her head. Then I took the strap of the seatbelt and carefully wrapped it around her wrists. She stared at me, mouth parted, pupils gigantic, as I made a little knot and secured her in place. The way the seatbelt was installed meant that when I let go, it tightened further.

"Is that comfortable?" I asked tenderly, running a hand along her trembling collarbone.

She swallowed and whispered, "Um, yes. It's not uncomfortable."

"Good." I took the middle seatbelt then and wrapped it just as firmly around her waist.

She didn't sound upset, only curious, when she said, "I don't understand why you're doing this."

I raised myself above her, staring down as I replied, "I'm doing it because it's what I like." Then I kissed her again, and I knew I had her. Her mouth was soft and welcoming, and the little moans I swallowed told me she was enjoying this game. I rolled my hips, letting her feel just how much she was affecting me. Minutes passed, and she was panting, a blush painting itself red over her bosom. I pulled away and began to undo the buttons of her blouse.

"This isn't fair," she whined, voice needy. "I want to touch you."

"Not tonight, love. Tonight, you're the one who gets touched."

Luckily, the bra she was wearing unclipped at the front, and in no time I had her breasts bare and begging for my mouth. I sucked one nipple and then the other while she undulated beneath me, opening up just like a flower. Her thighs hugged my hips in a vise-like grip, and I started to push her skirt up until it was bunched at her waist. My fingertips dug hard into her skin as I pulled her knickers off and tucked them in my pocket. She'd already slipped off her shoes during the drive, and I could feel her heels digging into my thighs. I caressed her needy flesh, my chest moving up and down rapidly, my erection outlined starkly in my jeans. Everything felt too tight, and she was too beautiful. I was drowning in her.

I rose on my knees and stared down at her, savoring the sight of her bound and restrained. It set off some kind of chemical reaction in my brain because my entire body hummed with satisfaction. I loved seeing her like this. It was exactly what I needed. I was improvising the fucking seatbelts in my car as restraints, and now I couldn't picture our first time happening any other way. I could only imagine what she must be thinking.

I circled her clit with my thumb at the same time I slid a finger inside her. She cried out, and I hummed in appreciation. Her startled, pleasured noises were completely gratifying. I'd been at her for less than a minute, and already I felt her orgasm building, hurtling toward the finish line. I knew it had to be the restraints. She got off on them just as much as I did.

"Ronan," she gasped, "I'm going to come."

"Come then, beautiful, come for me."

Her eyes snapped open, and she gasped loudly as she bucked and came on my hand. I kept stroking her, drawing out every last wave.

Not quite recovered, she blurted, "That was…."

"Intense."

"Yeah."

She was so wet now that it was impossible for me to wait any longer. Annie twisted and turned her body, clearly desperate to touch me. I loved it that she couldn't. Loved that I was torturing her because it meant, when I finally gave her all of me, it would feel like so much more.

The fact that I didn't have a condom had been at the back of my mind the whole time, but I'd been trying to ignore it. Still, it was troubling. I trusted Annie implicitly and wanted her to trust me back.

"You want me inside you now, love?" I purred as I pulled myself free of my pants.

Her eyes ate me up as she nodded and licked her lips. I allowed my gaze to trail over her body before I leaned forward and ran the tip of my cock over her folds. She whimpered, and I bit the inside of my mouth because fuck, it felt too good.

"Please, Ronan," she begged, opening her legs wider, voice breathless.

"I don't have protection," I admitted.

A flicker of hesitation passed over her face before she rose forward slightly to kiss me. "It's okay. I trust you."

And damn, was that exactly what I needed to hear. No sooner had the words passed her lips than I was sinking myself inside her. I did it slowly, savoring every inch, until I was buried deep. She moaned and sighed my name. I loved the sound of it, remembered back to the time when she'd only call me Mr. Fitzpatrick. Now all the formalities between us were gone. She was mine, and I belonged to her. I didn't think a time would ever come when I didn't want her this badly.

I began to move my hips in a slow rhythm, fixating on the belt secured snugly around her belly. It was such a sexy look. And wow, the feel of her around me was incredible. I'd never felt anything like it. Had never made love to a woman I felt such a fierce, soul-deep attraction to.

I rested my forehead against hers as I started to increase the speed of my thrusts. "You cannot imagine how unbelievable you feel, Annie. I don't ever want to leave."

"I don't want you to, either," she breathed. "I feel so surrounded."

I rose then, unable to contain my need to fuck her senseless any longer. My hips jutted in and out almost violently, and she took it all, soaked me in and let me back out again, gave me something that I didn't ever want to forget. She absorbed me. She was everything in that moment. All I could see.

"You drive me crazy," I said and then let out a string of select swear words.

I could feel myself getting closer, closer to the divine heaven of coming inside her perfect, beautiful, celestial fucking body. I stared at her face, her eyes big and taking everything in. She was still all tied up; and I saw how not touching me was painful for her, yet she was getting off on it. I thrived on that pain. I was still thrusting in and out, her thighs holding me in place, when I ran my hands from her neck down to her breasts and all the way along her torso.

She arched, straining for my touch, "Ronan, oh—oh God...."

Annie came apart, swift and fierce, saying "please" over and over, begging me. She shook from the force of her orgasm but was unable to reach for me.

I had all the power, and she had nothing. I could do anything to her, and she was simply there to enjoy the ride. A willing, submitting participant in this game for two. This was the dynamic I'd craved my whole life, but I had never found a partner as perfect as my dear, sweet, gorgeous little hermit.

In the next second I came with a deep, strangled groan as I melded my mouth to hers and thrust my tongue inside. I'd never climaxed so hard in my life. I felt empty, drained in the most wonderful sense of the word. I drew away and cupped her face in my hands, planting tiny, worshipful kisses on her cheeks, her mouth, her forehead, her eyelids, and murmuring desperate declarations. "You're perfect. The feel of you. Can't get enough. I'm addicted. I love you."

I was still kissing her, working my way down her neck and nibbling on her earlobe, when I realized I'd said that last part out loud.

NINETEEN
ANNIE

New York's Finest
Blogging as
The Socialmedialite
April 11
It's time for everyone's favorite blog post! That's right—it's time for DILFs!
Sometimes "DILF" stands for "Dudes I'd Like to Flip Off."
Sometimes "DILF" stands for "Dogs I'd Like to Fix" (I think everyone remembers the prodigious leg-humping incident of 2014).
And sometimes, "DILF" stands for "Donalds I'd Like to Fire" (spoiler alert, it's always Donald Trump).
But I think everyone's favorite kind of DILF post is when it stands for "Dads I'd Like to Fuck" ☺
It may be crass. It may lower me in your eyes. You may object to the fact that I'm looking at these dads with lustful intentions and licentious lewdness. But—come on—if our society has MILFs, then we need to have some DILFs for the ladies.
Amiright, ladies?
So, feast your eyes on the pictures below, my sisters in avariciousness. Today I've included a record-setting 36 desirable, drool-worthy dads.
You're welcome.
<3 The Socialmedialite

I didn't say it.
    Not in the car on the drive back.

Not when we made love again that night in the shower…although I almost said it then. I said a lot of things in the shower—like telling Ronan he was a sex god, and that I needed him, and begging him to make me dirty so we could take showers and baths together eight times a day—these things made me blush scarlet every time I thought about them once the sex haze had cleared.

I didn't say it when he woke me up the next morning by blindfolding me and trailing ice cubes over my bare skin, promising me pleasure only if I could lie still and silent.

Nor did I say it over the next two weeks as we went from event to event or when we came back to the hotel every night.

He didn't say it again, either.

However, regardless of where we were—a charity garden party fundraiser, a visit to a public school for a photo-op, a youth rugby match—he always found a way to show me how he felt. He made sure that I was served special peppermint tea at the garden party. He introduced me to the kids at the school as his fairy princess. He gave me his coat at the youth rugby game and rubbed my arms to keep me warm.

At night he showed me by tying me up, taking me how and when he liked, always being in control, initiating lovemaking that was both terrifyingly tender and tenderly terrifying.

I loved it. I loved how he surrounded me. I loved how ceding control made me feel safe and protected. I loved begging him, following his rules. I loved the freedom I found in complete capitulation.

And yet…I didn't tell him that I loved him, even though I did.

He must know, I thought, staring blankly at my computer screen. I was reading through the latest comments on my DILF post. People's reactions ran the gamut of appreciative to shocked to *Hey! That's my husband!! Woot!!*

I noticed that WriteALoveSong responded with a photo comment of a very, very nicely built male member of the military dressed in a bluish camouflage uniform holding the hand of an adorable little boy. The boy had brown curls and rosy cheeks and couldn't have been older than four. She'd added beneath the picture, *Add this to your next DILF post (and you're welcome).*

The charity I was highlighting along with the post was for veterans who were also parents. It helped them train and find work after discharge from the military. I'd tried to include as many dads in uniform as I could, but of the thirty-six, only fifteen were service members.

I was also avoiding my phone. Ronan's sister, Lucy, had called and left a message; she wanted to go shopping and out to lunch. I didn't know what to do. Since the rugby match, I'd gone out for coffee with a few of the team member's wives and girlfriends. It was like a club, and I had automatic membership as long as Ronan and I were together. There was camaraderie, but it also felt like a no-pressure group. They were happy to let me be the quiet one.

But with Lucy...Ronan loved Lucy. And I wouldn't be able to blend in when it was just the two of us. I wanted her to like me; I wanted us to be friends—really, really good friends—but I had no experience with real-life friendship.

I didn't want to fuck it up.

I was startled by the sound of the suite door slamming shut, followed by Ronan's loud footsteps approaching. Just his footfalls alerted me to the fact that he was upset, and this flustered me; so I quickly shut my laptop just as he stormed into the bedroom. My attention snapped to his as he entered.

"Annie...." he said, like he intended to add something more but didn't quite know what to say. Though he looked angry, he also looked aggravated about his anger.

I stood, watched him with wide eyes, and then prompted, "Is there something wrong?"

"No! Of course not! Everything is just *cunting wonderful*!" he thundered and then turned away and stomped out of the room.

I stared at the spot he'd just vacated for a few seconds, wracking my brain for what I might have done to upset him. I wondered if the source of his fury was my lack of verbal reciprocation of his feelings. My heart tugged painfully at the thought because I did love him.

Bracing myself, I hurried out of the room, found him splashing Scotch into a glass at the wet bar. It was only 10:00 a.m.

"Hey...so, I think I know why you're upset." I twisted my fingers in front of me, stopping just four feet from where he gulped his drink.

He set the empty glass back on the bar, his eyes cutting to mine as he refilled the glass.

"I doubt that," he said, shaking his head once.

"Is it because of... When you said—when you told me—"

"Nope. And I don't regret telling you, either, so you can stop fretting I'm going to take it back."

I shifted on my feet, feeling a little unsteady. "Is it because I haven't...I haven't said—"

"Nope. I figure you'll tell me when you're ready." He studied the liquid in the cut-crystal tumbler then took another swig.

"Oh," I breathed, feeling equal parts relief and confusion. "Then what did I do? Because you're obviously upset with me about something."

Ronan set the tumbler back on the bar and shut his eyes, exhaling a laugh that wasn't completely devoid of humor. We stood there for several moments, so long I thought he might not respond.

Then he said in a rush, "I'm the jealous sort. I know that, and I think you do, too. I don't like sharing what's mine."

I frowned at his words, not understanding and saying the only thing that made any semblance of sense, "Ronan, I would never cheat on you."

His brown eyes opened, but they remained on his empty glass. "I know that. But I don't even like you looking at other guys."

This statement only served to deepen my frown. "I honestly don't understand where this is coming from. Of course I'm not going to ogle other guys in front of you. That would be completely disrespectful. Just like I wouldn't want you to do that in front of me with other women. But…."

"But," he echoed, a small smile tugging his lips to the side.

"Yes, there is a 'but.' But of course I'm not blind, and neither are you. Of course we're both going to continue to notice other people, even if we don't act on it."

He sighed then laughed again; this time it sounded self-deprecating.

Ronan said to himself, "Ah, I am so screwed," as he turned toward me, abandoning his glass on the bar and wrapping me in his arms. "You're going to force me to grow up, aren't you, Annie? I'm going to have to stop picking fights with all the boys who give you a second look. You're going to make me *mature*."

I smiled against his neck, snuggled closer as I returned his embrace. "I hope not too much. I kind of like your dirty mind."

"I'm beginning to think I'm not the one with the dirty mind," he mumbled, somewhat cryptically.

Before I could question this remark, he bent forward and captured my mouth. Soon all thought—or ability to think coherently—was driven from my aforementioned mind and replaced with a delightful series of completely dirty thoughts.

* * *

I WAS WAITING for Joan. We were set to have a call about the progress of my projects, not just Ronan's.

If Ronan were my only project, then I would deserve five stars, a big bonus, and a standing ovation. He had entirely ingratiated himself to the public. Not quite a reformed bad boy, he continued to be something edgier, more elusive.

Really, he was the ideal image sketch I'd drafted plus something entirely his own, something I never could have designed or defined, and people loved him. They loved that he was a blue blood with white-collar mannerisms. They loved how unrepentantly ambivalent he was about fame yet how much he obviously loved his sport. They loved his raw talent and his dedication to excellence.

He did nothing by halves.

I thought about the latest letter he'd written to The Socialmedialite, about how he loved me, and it made my silly heart do a happy jig and then cry in the corner of despair.

I felt guilt. Ronan had written to The Socialmedialite thinking of her as an impartial third party, asking for advice, baring his soul. I'd read his private thoughts, I'd been lying to him, and I hadn't yet responded. His words were so beautiful, so moving, so exactly what I'd needed to push me over the edge. Every time I read the letter, I became lost to my feelings—of swelling love and anxious despondency—and my mind blanked. I didn't know how to respond.

I had to tell him the truth—both about who I was and how I loved him—but I feared losing him. I knew it was partially the fear that kept me silent on both accounts. The other part was giving up my anonymity. Being The Socialmedialite was my outlet. Until Ronan, it was the only avenue where I could truly be myself. If I told Ronan, if he knew, then he would have power over me, and I would never be anonymous again.

The sound of my computer notifying me of a call pulled me from my thoughts. I blinked at the screen and saw Joan's avatar—which was just a picture of her giant leather office chair—flashing insistently. I took a deep breath and accepted the video call, straightening in my seat and hoping my attention would follow.

As soon as she came into focus, she started to talk. "Annie, we need your help with The Starlet. She's tossed out our summer plan and wants us to start from scratch. Beth sent her an email, and Dara responded that she's not used to having to read actual words. I blame your infographics. You spoil the clients."

"Hi, Joan." I gave her a half smile, feeling strangely nostalgic for my comfortable life in New York.

"Have you opened the file I sent? Let's modify it while I have you on the line. I can call Beth in here if needed…."

We settled into our client discussions, no pleasantries, just like old times, and I actually found myself relaxing as we went through the details and proposals. This felt like solid ground. This was my area of expertise, not falling in love with an infamous bad-boy sex symbol on the precipice of dominating the world stage while deceiving him about my secret identity.

All was well—relatively speaking—until the hotel phone started to ring. I ignored it. It stopped, and then it rang again. After the fourth call back, I glanced at my cell phone and found no messages. Whoever was calling via the hotel phone didn't have my cell number. Joan could tell my attention was split.

"Just, would you get that? They're obviously not going to stop."

Relieved, I reached for the receiver. "Hello?"

"Ms. Catrel, this is O'Hare, the concierge. You have a visitor."

"Uh, well, I'm in the middle of a work call. Perhaps my visitor could leave a message?"

"Ms. Catrel, your visitor is Ms. Brona O'Shea, and she is quite insistent that you'll be very interested in an envelope currently in her possession."

My face must've betrayed my confusion and surprise because Joan's voice was shrewd and her glare sharp as she demanded, "What? What is it? Who is that?"

My gaze flickered to the computer screen, where Joan was leaning forward in her chair, and I said into the phone, "Please send her up."

"Right away, Ms. Catrel. Patricia will escort her to your apartments and will be happy to serve tea while the two of you have a…visit."

"Thank you, O'Hare."

I held the receiver to my ear for a full five seconds after the concierge had clicked off, my eyes on the glass top of the desk, going through the likely scenarios of what Brona had brought with her in the envelope. Obviously, the most likely answer was that Brona had been bluffing to gain admittance to our rooms and start trouble.

But if she weren't bluffing and the envelope actually contained something damaging to Ronan, I would need to separate myself from my feelings for him. Whatever it was she'd brought, Ronan was my client. Regardless of what he'd done in his past and how that might influence my rage levels as his girlfriend, I needed to converse with his ex-girlfriend as though I were merely part of Ronan's publicity team, as his advocate.

"Annie, who was on the phone?" Joan's impatient question pulled me from my internal pep talk.

I replaced the phone on the charger and lifted my eyes to my boss. "That was the concierge. Brona O'Shea is downstairs and wants to speak to me."

"I bet she does," Joan scoffed.

"She has an envelope with her and informed the concierge that it contains something that I will find very interesting."

"What's in it?"

"I guess I'll find out when she gets here."

"No. *We* will find out. Keep me plugged in and angle your screen toward the door. It's a shame I can't be there in person to negotiate this…Let her know as soon as she walks in that you're in the middle of a work call with Ronan's publicity team. She'll see it as an opportunity. Also…."

I nodded, mostly listening to Joan's strategy, clicking through my open tabs on my laptop and closing several windows. If Brona would be talking to Joan via my laptop, I didn't need her to see my Socialmedialite email account or the blog post draft I'd been writing.

Joan detailed her plan while I prepared to face Ronan's ex with as little outward emotion as possible. However, just as the knock sounded on the suite door, Joan surprised me by saying, "…and of course you might need to play the role of jealous current girlfriend—good cop, bad cop—then I'll make her think I'm on her side."

I'm sure I looked a little startled and a lot confused as I squinted at Joan. "Wait, you want me to be the bad cop?"

She nodded. "That's right."

"But I'm not bad cop. *You* are bad cop."

"No, you're confusing reality with fiction. In real life, I'm always the bad cop, and you're always the good cop—which is why we switch roles when we're playing our parts. The good cop is *always* pretending to be the good cop, and vice versa."

I opened my mouth to respond, but the knock sounded from the door again, firmer this time, followed by Patricia's voice saying, "Ms. Catrel, I have your tea."

Resigned to the oddness of this situation and anxious about its outcome, I angled my laptop toward the room as instructed and crossed to the entrance. After inhaling a steadying breath, I opened the door.

Patricia was standing in the doorway. Behind her was a cart with tea and lovely sandwiches and petit fours. And behind the cart, with two serious-looking hotel security guards on either side, was sour-faced Brona O'Shea.

I opened the door wider but stepped to block Patricia from entering. "Thank you, Patricia. I can bring the tea in. Ms. O'Shea and I would like some privacy."

"See, Patty. I told you, you're not needed." This came from Brona. From the way she spoke to Patricia, I surmised the two women were more than acquainted.

Patricia's gaze was laced with worry, and she shifted a half step forward so as to whisper, "Ms. Catrel, I am very discreet. Send security away if you must, but please reconsider. I've...had the *distinction* of acting as Ms. O'Shea's liaison while she stayed with us in the past. I must advise you against—"

"She said leave, Patty. Now take your goons away, but leave the fancy tea. I'm parched." Brona said this as she elbowed her way past the guards and to the suite entrance. She gave me a pinched look as she brushed past, lifting her chin in the air like I was beneath her notice. I did see that she had a manila envelope tucked under one arm. It was bulky, and I guessed it contained something more than papers.

I allowed her to enter and turned a calm smile to Patricia. "All will be well. I'll call when we're done with the tea service. Thank you."

Patricia looked like she wanted to protest again but instead handed the tea cart over to me and then closed the door. I wheeled it into the sitting area.

But before I was quite finished relocating the tea, Brona said, "I like my tea with lemon, milk, and sugar."

"How nice for you."

Brona whipped her head toward where my laptop sat on the desk and the sound of Joan's voice, laden with sarcasm and disdain. Brona turned her attention to me, then the laptop, and then to me. Her big blue eyes gave the impression they might pop from her head.

"What...what's this? Are you recording me?"

"No," I said softly.

"Maybe," Joan teased at the same time. "Ms. O'Shea, allow me to introduce myself. I am Joan Davidson from Davidson and Croft, the firm responsible for Mr. Fitzpatrick's public image and general well-being."

Brona stepped closer to the desk and opened her mouth to speak, but Joan cut her off.

"No need for chitchat. Here is how we're going to do this: you are going to tell me what you want, and I am going to do everything in my power to give it to you, assuming it's within reason and assuming that whatever you've brought in that envelope is worth the price. Now, what do you want?"

"I don't—I mean—I want—"

"Please, dear. Hurry up. I have a meeting in fifteen minutes, and I won't be made late."

Brona lifted her chin, her eyes flashing fire. "Fine. I want money, a million euros—no! I want five million euros. And I want a recording contract with one of the big labels."

Joan gave her a sideways look. "Ooookay—"

"And I want to record a song with Beyoncé."

Joan smiled then suppressed it, clearing her throat. "Sure. That's all very doable. Now, what am I buying?"

Brona curled her lip, gave me a smug, hateful glare, pulled the envelope from under her arm, and began to spread the contents on the nearest table. "It's photos, see? And a tape of Ronan…and me…having sex."

My stomach twisted uncomfortably as Brona used her pregnant pauses to show Joan and me several eight-by-ten photos and then a mini-DV tape.

It wasn't precisely jealousy that I was feeling, more like an echo of jealousy that Ronan had ever been with someone else. It was irrational and silly. And yet it made some fierce, shadowy part of me roar with outrage. I wanted to burn the tape. I wanted to slash the photos. I wanted to claw her eyes out.

Instead, I gritted my teeth and returned my attention to Joan.

"Come closer to the monitor. I need to see the pictures."

Brona did so happily, showing each of the pictures to Joan one at a time and pausing significantly between each.

Then I heard Joan say, "Meh."

"'Meh'? What do you mean, 'meh'?" Brona huffed.

"I mean *meh*. So what? Who cares?"

I saw Brona's back stiffen as she straightened with surprise. "He's got a spreader bar on me! I'm gagged and tied up, and there's a collar and leash, and—"

"Yes. My eyes work quite well. I can see all that. I just don't see why these pictures would be worth five million euros to anyone, least of all Mr. Fitzpatrick. I assume the tape is more of the same?"

I tried to school my expression, but my heart was thundering in my chest. As nonchalantly as possible, I crossed to the couch and sat on its arm. *A spreader bar? A leash? What the hell? Is that what he likes?*

"But—but…uh…." Brona stuttered.

Joan's voice lifted. "The fact of the matter, my dear, is that a sex tape and dirty photos like those will only help Mr. Fitzpatrick's sex appeal and our overall campaign. You see, he's in the dominant position. He's holding your leash, not the other way around. Meanwhile, they'll make you look weak and pathetic. They'll kill any aspirations you might have of becoming a pop princess because parents don't want their little girls to grow up to be submissives in dog collars. You see, you can sell those photos and that tape to some filthy tabloid, and they'll fetch you about five hundred thousand euros; but that would be the end of your singing career, wouldn't it?"

Brona turned slightly away, giving me her profile. I saw that her face had drained of color and her hands were balled into fists.

Joan *tsked*. "Poor dear. I'll tell you what we'll do. How about I give you two hundred thousand euros, and you give us the photos and the tape? But really, that's my only offer."

Brona's bottom lip quivered, so she flattened her mouth into a stiff line. "What assurances do I have that you won't just release it?"

"We have our plan. It's been working quite well so far. I see no need to throw a sex tape into the mix. So, you have my word that we won't make it public for…oh, let's say two years. Tick tock, tick tock. I've got that meeting, and I really must dash."

"Fine!" Brona shrieked, turning back to Joan and using the back of her hand to wipe away two tears. "Fine. When do I get my money?"

"Are there any other copies?"

"No. It's all here. I've got media arseholes breaking into my apartment all the time looking for shite. They've taken my computer twice. So I kept this in a security deposit box. There are no other copies."

"Well, good. Just leave those with Ms. Catrel, and she'll have the money transferred into your account."

"Today?"

"Actually, she can do it right now. Write your account number down, and have some tea. You'll have the money in less than twenty minutes."

Brona was losing steam; her shoulders slumped. Her gaze flickered to mine, and I saw her eyes were rimmed red with unhappiness and exhaustion. I almost felt sorry for her.

"Fine." She pushed the envelope and pictures away from her, sending several photos to the floor.

"Good. Well!" Joan clapped her hands together, her smile very shark-like as she added, "It's been a pleasure, Ms. O'Shea, but I really must be going."

And without a goodbye or another word, Joan clicked off.

*   *   *

Brona didn't stay more than a half hour, just long enough to confirm that the money had been transferred. Nor did we talk…at first. After I placed the call for the bank transfer, I poured myself tea. She sat quietly on the desk chair, holding her face in her hands, and not looking at me.

All her earlier pomp and venom was gone. She looked tired.

This was not the first time I'd had to pay someone off on short notice. The Starlet—Dara—had assaulted a woman and her children at a florist just two blocks from my apartment. I had to run down to the scene and negotiate a payout before the woman took the story to the press.

But this felt very different.

I hadn't yet studied the photos. I'd only overheard the conversation between Joan and Brona. In my mind, I was imagining the worst-case scenario—Ronan hitting Brona with a whip or chain or riding crop while he held her down, her legs spread by a spreader bar, her mouth gagged so she couldn't scream, a tight collar around her neck.

I shivered, and my stomach churned. I didn't want that. I didn't want someone hitting me and getting off on it. I might love Ronan, but I wouldn't love that. I'd narrowly escaped abuse my entire life; there was no way I would succumb to it willingly now that I was an adult.

Frustrated, I pinched the bridge of my nose and closed my eyes, tried to sit very still.

I was psyching myself out.

I needed to look at those pictures, but I couldn't, not yet. Not while Brona was in the room.

"I'm not stupid, you know."

Her voice was watery but firm, like she was trying valiantly not to cry. I opened my eyes and gave her my attention, keeping my face passive, patient.

"I'm not stupid. I had a plan." She was sitting upright in the chair, her arms crossed over her chest. She was inspecting me as though trying to determine what my plan might be.

"A plan?"

"Yeah, and it was good; it was working. But Ronan, he's just so fucking stubborn. I finally, *finally* figured out a way to get that ring on my finger and that fucker, he wouldn't set a date. He kept putting me off."

"He asked you to marry him and then wouldn't set a date?"

"Nah. I just bought one and started wearing it, let the press make up the rest. And it worked. Except…it didn't. Because he flat out refused. Said he'd always take care of me but that we weren't getting married. He gave me an allowance, like I was a child, like I was his responsibility or something. Fuck that. I was good enough to tie up, but I wasn't good enough to have my name on his bank account."

I considered her for a moment. Her frustration was a tangible thing, giving her an aura of electric instability. I decided silence was probably my best recourse.

But she continued unprompted, "So what was I supposed to do? Huh? That money is as much mine as it is his; I earned it! I supported him through everything, let him use me for his sick fantasies, put up with his bitch mother and annoying sister."

"You never loved him," I said, more to myself than to her. Despite my decision to stay quiet, the words slipped out, my heart hurting a little on Ronan's behalf.

"What? Love him? *Love* Ronan? He doesn't want love. He wants a fuck toy. He's messed up. All he wants, all he's ever wanted, is just someone to play with, to control, boss around. He said he wanted to take care of me, but what he wanted was to control me. Of course I didn't love him."

My phone chose that moment to chime. I held her gaze for a beat, her words distressing me for so many reasons. I didn't even know where to start. So I turned my attention to the screen.

"You can check your bank balance. The funds have been transferred." I was impressed with how composed I sounded.

She stood abruptly, pulled a glittery pink thing from her glittery pink purse and began tapping away at the screen. She also continued speaking—mumbling to herself, really—though I wished she wouldn't.

"You know this already. I don't have to tell you how sick he is, how he won't touch you unless you can't touch him. But maybe you like it, maybe you're just as messed up as he is...."

Mercifully, she was finally quiet. I saw the exact moment she read her bank balance because her eyes brightened. She sniffed, wiped her hand across her nose, and then actually smiled.

"Well, screw all of you. I'm about to be a star, and you can all go to hell."

Without even a backward glance, she strolled to the door and left, slamming it on her way out.

I waited maybe three seconds then bolted for the pictures, sending a few skidding toward the wall in my haste. I forced myself to calm down, again gritting my teeth, and then flipped the first one toward me. Every muscle in my body was tense as I consumed the image.

Then I frowned at it, confused, because for all of Brona's ranting about how sick Ronan was, I didn't see anything all that objectionable. If this was her Hail Mary pass, if this was what she'd been threatening Ronan with and ranting about for months, then it won the award for most anticlimactic blackmail moment in the history of the world.

Yes, she had a collar on, but it looked like one of those fashion collars. There was a leash or a strap attached to it, but Ronan held it almost absentmindedly around his wrist. It wasn't tight. She wasn't being choked.

She was bent over the arm of a chair, wearing a black leather bustier with feathers, and her hands were tied with what looked like the same material as the leash, likely a leather strap, and her legs were cuffed to a spreader bar, holding them open. She wore nothing else. Ronan was behind her. His eyes were closed, his hands were on her hips, and he was taking her from behind.

I checked the rest of photos, and they were basically time-elapsed images of the same thing. I then searched the photos for other things like whips or implements of pain. I found none. I noted in one of the pictures you could see clearly that Brona had a scarf or silk tie over her mouth, but it looked loose. She'd hardly been gagged.

Feeling both relieved and oddly excited, I was struck by the anomalous irony of the situation. I was looking at photos of Ronan having sex with another woman, and rather than jealousy I was picturing myself in her position, with my legs held apart and my hands bound as Ronan used my body for pleasure.

"I saw Brona on my way out."

I stiffened, straightened, sucked in a sharp breath, and my eyes flew to the door.

Ronan stood just at the entrance, his eyes wary but intent as they searched my face then dropped to the pictures in my hands. He stepped all the way in and shut the door with a soft click.

"She said you were sick, just like me." His words were teasing, though they carried an edge of something that sounded a lot like hope. He stalked toward me, looking painfully delicious in a charcoal grey suit.

I gathered a deep breath then let the pictures fall to the desk, arranging the images so he could see them as he approached.

"Joan convinced her to sell them plus a tape of the two of you."

He nodded absentmindedly, glancing at the pictures. "Have you watched the tape?"

"No. I don't have a mini-DV player."

He turned his gaze to mine, ensnared it. He looked cautious; his stare was probing. "But you would have? If you had a player for it?"

I met his stare and gave him honesty. "I don't know. I don't think so. The pictures paint a pretty clear picture on their own. Ronan, do you think…?" I paused, trying to figure out how to ask my next question. At length I blurted, "Do you think there is anything else? Do you think Brona might blackmail you with something else? Or is this it?"

"This is it." He indicated the photos with a tilt of his head. "As far as I know, this is the worst of it."

"The worst of it…." I echoed, scanning the pictures.

"And what do you think? Of the pictures."

"I think...." I swallowed with effort, tilted my chin up to fight my instinctive urge to look away. "I think I don't like seeing pictures of you with someone else."

The corner of his mouth curved upward, and he took the top picture and turned it face down. "Don't look at the pictures then."

I pressed on before I lost my nerve. "I also think that we should maybe talk about how you—I mean—what it is that you...." I licked my lips nervously. Again, I didn't know how to ask the question.

Just how kinky was Ronan?

Just how kinky was I?

"Go on," he said, the beginnings of a smile now melting some of his caution, his gaze turning warm and curious. He reached for my hand and then began pulling me while he walked backward toward the bedroom.

"What I mean is, do you like the collar? Do you want to...leash me, too?" My voice broke on the last word, making me cringe. I wasn't good at communicating about sex because I'd never done it. Everything I'd done prior to being with Ronan was vanilla to the extreme and hadn't required any discussion.

He shook his head as we crossed over the threshold into the bedroom. The curtains were open, and sunlight served as the only light source.

"No. The collar was Brona's idea, as was the leash, and we used them only once. I think now, now that I've seen the pictures, she must've done it only for the sake of the camera."

"And the spreader bar?"

"Oh, now I'd like you in that very, very much. And maybe later, once you've grown used to the bar, we could use a sling." His gaze darkened as he led me to the bed. Ronan guided me to a sitting position at the edge of it, but instead of sitting next to me, he backed away until he was standing at the wall, next to the dresser, putting at least five feet of distance between us.

"So...." I stared at him, feeling dichotomously aroused and worried by the idea of a spreader bar or a sex sling. What we'd done so far, what we'd been doing with restraints and ice cubes, that felt entirely normal to me—frisky but well within the confines of normal.

Ronan was the first guy who'd ever wanted to tie me up during sex. Even though we hadn't actually discussed it beforehand—or after—it felt... right. It was good.

But toys? A collar and leash? Leather and feathers? Full-on kink?

His left eyebrow lifted, very slowly, as he watched me struggle for words, his lips twisting a bit to the side.

Finally he prompted, "Annie, what do you think we've been doing so far?"

"I guess—I guess I thought we were—" I sighed, blinking at a spot over his shoulder. "I thought you just liked things to be intense during…and I like it, too. But I wouldn't call tying me up or blindfolding me BDSM."

"It is and it isn't. What we've been doing is what I like—restraint, dominance, and submission. I'm not keen on sadomasochism. I don't get off on hurting people, but I do like to be in control."

"Dominance and submission?" My voice cracked again, and I felt a little breathless, excited by the labels.

"Yes." He inclined his head, studying me thoughtfully. I watched him with wide eyes as he nonchalantly plucked my scarf from the dresser and strolled back over to where I sat perched on the edge of the bed. He hovered above me for a long moment, his dark eyes hot as they unapologetically stared down the front of my shirt. My insides did a somersault and heated, rearranging themselves, burning beneath his suggestive stare.

Ronan took a deep breath then knelt, situating himself between my legs. His hands slipped under my skirt, inching upward and spreading my thighs, still holding the scrap of fabric. He tickled me with it. The silky softness sent a shock of goosebumps along my skin, spreading heat up my chest and neck and searing arousal between my legs.

"I like," he whispered, his gaze holding mine. "I like deciding what happens and when. I like having control and being responsible for your loss of control. I like taking care of you, all of you. I like your trusting me, implicitly and explicitly."

Ronan's thumbs were rubbing light circles on the skin of my thighs just below my apex. Instinctively, I inched closer, my legs opening wider. I reached for his shoulders and tried to pull him toward me. I needed his touch a few inches higher, but he retreated. He withdrew his hands, his fingertips skimming my bare skin, sending a shiver to my center.

"Do you trust me, Annie?" He leaned back, his eyes still holding mine as he unbuttoned my shirt and meticulously pushed it down my shoulders, all the while holding my scarf.

"You know I do."

"What if I tied you up?" Ronan discarded my shirt and then unclasped my bra. His question was soft, curious.

"You've done that." I helped him by withdrawing my hands from the bra straps. "You know I-I like that."

"But what if I tied your legs, too, spread them, and you were face down on the bed? What if I blindfolded you? What if I used toys?"

I blinked at that, instinctively covering my chest with my arms. "T-toys? What kind of toys?"

"Only toys that would make you feel good." Ronan took one of my hands, then the other, from where I crossed them over my chest; he looped the now-twisted scarf around my wrists and tied a secure knot, his thumb and gaze lingering on the vulnerable skin.

"Would it hurt?" I managed to whisper.

His eyes darted back to mine, and he answered immediately, "No. Like I said, I crave submission, control. I'm not a sadist. I don't like hurting people, and I would never want to hurt you. I want your surrender."

I exhaled an unsteady breath as Ronan pulled off his tie, his fingers moving to the underside of my knee, the barest touch; but it initiated spikes of heady, aching longing between my thighs. He slid them down the back of my calf to my ankle and gently, reverently slid my foot out of my terrycloth slipper. I thought he was going to wrap the tie around my ankle, but instead he brought my foot to his mouth and ran his tongue along the base of my toes, making my leg jerk and spasm.

It was ticklish, but it was more than that. It was carnal. Sinful. Overwhelming. My sex pulsed, and my bound hands balled into fists.

I cried out, "Ah, Ronan!"

His grin was devilish, pleased, as he lowered my leg and knotted his fancy tie around my ankle.

"Will you submit to me, my darling? Hmm?"

"I'm not sure what I'm supposed to do."

"You say yes and you say please and you beg me for more."

I blushed a little as I pointed out, "I already do that."

"So you do." Ronan nodded, looking dangerously pleased, and added, "But if we're going to really do this, if you're really going to give up control, you'll need a safe word."

My mouth parted in alarm and surprise; I stared at him for a moment. "A safe word?"

"Yes. How about 'peppermint'?"

"To make you stop? If I say 'peppermint,' then you'll stop?"

"That's right. I can't take control you're not willing to give." Ronan unbuckled his belt, slid the leather strap from his waist.

"But...." I struggled to form a coherent thought now that I was faced with a belt. "What are you going to do with that?"

He took my hands and looped the belt through the knot made by the scarf. "Get on your stomach, face down on the bed, and lift your arms over your head. I'm going to secure the belt to the headboard so you can't move."

I licked my lips, thinking this over, then asked, "How are you going to restrain my other leg?"

His eyes moved between mine, and his mouth widened in a slow smile. "If you must know, I have another tie"—he nodded to the closet—"in there."

"And you're going to tie me to the end of the bed? So I can't close my legs?"

"Yes. So you're open to me. So I can touch you however I like, for as long as I like, wherever I like."

I stared at him, my heart racing, but I knew I was going to do this. If I enjoyed it half as much as I loved the idea of it, then I was pretty sure Ronan Fitzpatrick was going to ruin me for all other men.

Ronan stood smoothly, his mouth twisted to the side in a faint smile, and offered me a hand. I placed both of mine in his, and he helped me stand. I hesitated for a fraction of a second and then turned and walked on my knees to the middle of the bed. I lay down and did as he instructed, my arms over my head, reaching for the headboard.

"Such a good darling," he praised me. I felt the bed depress behind me and realized he was straddling me. He looped the belt into the headboard and tugged, making sure it was reasonably sturdy. Then I felt him move behind me and tie my ankle to the footboard.

He bent over me, his hot breath against my neck. "Don't move."

I nodded, blinking at the drapes and the comforter and wall filling my vision.

He left, but then I heard him return at once. I closed my eyes, and he secured my right ankle as he'd done my left. I felt my skirt hike up the back of my thighs as he opened my legs to tie me to the bed.

"Oh, wait, my skirt. Shouldn't I—?"

"Shh…." He cut me off with a soft hush, the tip of a single finger sliding from my heel, along the back of my leg, to just under the hemline. "From this point forward, you are only allowed to say four things: 'yes,' 'please,' my name, and 'peppermint' unless I instruct you otherwise. Do you understand?"

I nodded and acquiesced quietly. "Yes…Mr. Fitzpatrick."

He stilled, like I'd surprised him. But then I heard him chuckle, his finger drawing my skirt higher up my legs. "Oh, this is going to be fun."

He used just his mouth at first, biting me, tasting me, licking and devouring the bare skin of my neck, shoulders, back, and legs. It felt divine, and I was melted, became rubber. He was still fully dressed, yet somehow that made it even hotter.

Then I heard a buzzing sound, and I stiffened, my eyes opening wide with alarm. His hands moved beneath my skirt, lifted it slowly until my white lace panties and bottom were exposed. The buzzing became louder; and I tried to press my knees together, but I couldn't because my ankles were tied. A spike of fear, but also anticipation, pulsed through me.

He bent over me, tongued my ear, and then whispered in a fall of hot breath, "This will be one of your favorite toys."

The next thing I knew, he'd lifted my hips slightly from the bed so my bottom was in the air, and he pressed a vibrating something to my center. He moved it back and forth over the lace panties with aching slowness, from my clitoris to my opening, and I cursed the scrap of fabric separating my body from his mystery device.

"Oh...." I rocked my hips, arching my back, straining, loving the exquisite torture.

He moved the delicious vibration away. "Ah, now. Say 'please.'"

"Please...."

"Say my name."

"Please, Mr. Fitzpatrick."

I heard him give a short growl of appreciation, and then the toy was back. This time he moved my panties to one side and entered me with his fingers while he pressed the vibrator to my clit.

I sucked in a sharp breath, my hips bucking and pressing backward, needing him to be harder, needing the vibration higher. But he continued to tease me. He bit my bottom then licked the spot, tracing his tongue from my left butt cheek to my lower back.

"You're so wet for me, Annie. You want me to fuck you, don't you? You want my big cock inside you. You want me to surround you and fill you up." He removed his fingers and his toy, and I cried out, my sex clenching with no purchase.

"Yes, please, Mr. Fitzpatrick." My breath hitched; my body was on fire and fighting the bonds. I needed him, his bare skin. I needed the contact and his silky heat. I was so empty.

"Then you'll be mine. Say you're mine, Annie." I heard his zipper and then the soft sound of his pants falling to his knees. The bed depressed behind me, between my spread legs.

"I'm yours; please, I'm yours."

I felt him grip the waistband of my panties just before I heard the distinct sound of his tearing them in two. I felt the head of his erection against my entrance, and I tried to push backward. He chuckled, though it sounded strained.

"Tell me I'm yours."

"I—I'm yours."

"No...." He moved himself so that his thick head drew a circle around my clit, spreading my arousal over both of us.

I groaned, arching my back until it was almost painful.

"No, say, *Ronan, you are mine.* Say it."

"Ronan, you are mine; you are mine." I swallowed the last word then bit my arm, needed to feel something. This limbo between sensual teasing and full-on fucking was making me crazy.

He pushed into me then, and I whimpered. He felt amazing, necessary. Ronan leaned forward, and I felt his chest—still clothed in his suit—against my back. For some reason, the fact that was I bare to him except for the skirt around my waist and he was still mostly dressed made me even hotter.

I could barely move except for tilting my hips back to meet his thrusts. He surrounded me, pinning me down, hovering over me, filling me. I didn't last long, and I came with a strangled cry, saying his name, saying *please* and *oh, God* and *yes*.

"Perfect, my perfect girl. I love the way you come on my cock."

I felt him lean away before I was quite finished, fitting one of his hands between my stomach and the mattress and lifting my hips. He fit the vibrator between my legs, dancing and tapping it against my clitoris, as he pumped in and out.

Then I came again, and it hurt so very, very good. It rocked me—it was an explosion of white heat and stars under my skin, streams of ecstasy and pleasure and pain rushing through my veins. It felt wild, blazing hot, and uncontrolled; and I had no choice but to abandon myself to it, my bound hands gripping fistfuls of the comforter, turning my face into the mattress to stifle my loud cries as tears leaked from the corners of my eyes.

I hadn't recovered, tremors still wracking my body, as Ronan collapsed on top of me with a strangled groan of his own, my name on his lips.

Our heavy breathing mingled. I felt the thudding of his heart against my back. It matched mine.

I loved him.

I loved what we'd just done.

I wanted to do it every day. I wanted to wake up with him every day, see him, touch him, hear him laugh, listen to his stories, be shocked by his dirty mouth every single day.

He was worth losing my anonymity. I wanted to share everything with him.

I had to tell him the truth.

I was going to tell him the truth.

I just didn't know how to tell him the truth because I didn't want to lose him.

TWENTY
RONAN

@RonanFitz: My girlfriend is so pretty.
@Anniecat: @RonanFitz Hush now.
@RonanFitz: @Anniecat Come back to bed, love.

All I wanted to do was lock myself away in the hotel suite with Annie. Unfortunately, the more people became aware that I was in the country, the more shit I got asked to do. Honestly, it was exhausting having to meet and greet and be sociable when all I wanted was to tie Annie to my bedpost and tease her body until she begged for release. But such was life. I wanted to get back on the team as soon as possible, and smiling for the cameras was the only way to speed the process along. When we went outside, we always had an audience of at least thirty photographers. It felt like living in a goldfish bowl.

We were on our way back from our final engagement, a charity dinner, and the organizers had hired a limo to take us to and from the hotel. It was only six thirty, but we'd shown our faces; and as eager as I was to be alone with Annie, I also wanted to sleep for at least ten hours. So, an early departure it was. She checked out the drinks cabinet and reclined back on the long seat, emitting a weary little sigh.

We stared at each other for a moment, smiling in contentment. I didn't think I'd ever get over her smile. Her face. She was in my dreams and my thoughts. I was completely overrun by this woman, and there was nowhere else I'd rather be.

I leaned forward, resting my elbows on my knees and letting my eyes trail down her body. She looked just as exhausted as I was.

"What's wrong, love? Is the day having trouble with what the night got up to?" I teased.

She let out the most adorable yawn I'd ever seen and pretended to scowl. "You're a stupid sexy slave driver, Ronan Fitzpatrick. And my wrists hurt."

I chuckled. "That's Sir Ronan Fitzpatrick to you. Come here—I'll give them a rub."

She stuck her tongue out at me and grabbed a small bottle of liquor from the drinks cabinet to examine the label. I gave her a reprimanding look before she finally crawled across the seats and into my lap. I took a deep breath and wrapped my arms around her tight. There was a thoughtful expression on her face before she said quietly, "I like being here with you. You seem, I don't know, more yourself in this country than you did back in the States."

"It's got nothing to do with geography, Annie. It's just you. Being with you makes me calmer than I've ever felt. Being inside you feels like home," I said, whispering the last part huskily.

I saw her shiver at my words before she brought her nose to mine and nuzzled. The affectionate gesture made my heart squeeze. God, how I loved her.

Taking both her wrists into my hands, I started to massage them, noticing that I had been a little bit rough with her last night. I'd have to learn more control. Normally, I was the definition of controlled in the bedroom, but with Annie I tended to lose it a little. It was like I'd been waiting my whole life for the ideal partner, and now that I'd found her, it was impossible to hold back.

By the time we arrived at the hotel, Annie was resting her head on my shoulder, her body limp and relaxed as I soothed her with my fingers. I'd be content to stay like that for hours, and I felt the urge to tell the driver to do another loop of the city; but we both needed sleep. And yeah, sleepy sex with Annie before we both finally drifted off also sounded appealing.

Thankfully, there were only a handful of photographers hanging about when we left the limo. I led her to the lift, and we stood facing each other as other people got on and off. I couldn't stop smiling at her, telling her with my eyes all the things I planned to do with her when we got to our room. There was only one more floor until ours, and finally we were alone in the elevator. She gave me that look I love, the one where she glances up at me from beneath her lashes, and in the moment I felt too full of emotion. I was so in love with her I was drowning, and the overflow of water came out in my words. I barely even had to think about it. I just said it. I knew it was what I wanted. She was all that I wanted.

"Marry me."

She stared at me, eyes growing larger by the second as my words hung in the air.

"What?" she whispered, and before I could hesitate, I slammed my hand on the button to stop the lift and got down on one knee. Taking her hand in mine, I said it again, eyes blazing, heart hammering. "I love you, Annie, and I want you to marry me."

"You're…you're…get up, Ronan."

"Not until you answer me," I said firmly, seeing a thousand "yeses" written all over her face, but not a single one of them left her lips.

Her entire body began to shake, and I stood, taking her face in my hands and kissing her cheeks, her nose, her chin, her eyelids, every part of her that I adored.

"I think I need to sit down," she said just as the lift creaked into movement again. Someone had obviously overridden my command to stop it. I took her hand in mine and led her off, eyeing her the whole time and trying to read what she was thinking. I'd just put my entire self out there for her, and her hesitation was killing me with every second that passed.

When we got to the suite, everything looked normal at first. I opened the door with my keycard, and Annie stepped in, slipping off her shoes and coat. I noticed a couple of cushions had been strewn on the floor, and the drawer to one of the desks had been pulled wide open.

"Oh, shit!" I heard her shout as she entered the bedroom. I was heavy on her heels and found her standing with her hands to her mouth in panic. The place was trashed, our suitcases open and clothes tossed everywhere. Every single drawer and the closet were wide open, too, and it looked like someone had tried to break into the safe but had been unsuccessful. There was a massive dent in the metal, but it remained shut tight. That was a relief because that's where I'd stored Brona's sex pictures.

Once Annie had taken a moment to collect herself, she dove forward, frantically searching through her things and muttering panicked expletives to herself. I picked up the phone and immediately made a call down to reception to inform them of the break-in. O'Hare sounded absolutely appalled by the news, and I got the feeling this sort of thing didn't happen here often. It was a five-star hotel, and I knew the security was top-notch.

It could have been thugs looking for valuables, but why would they only break into one room? No, this felt like someone searching for information, and what with all the paparazzi following our every move, I wouldn't put it past one of them to try something like this for an exclusive.

When I looked back to Annie, I saw that there were tears streaming down her face as she wrung her hands. "Ronan, my laptop is gone. Somebody's taken it."

I strode toward her and took her hands in mine, rubbing the inside of her wrists with my thumbs in an effort to calm her.

"The police are on their way. And don't worry about the laptop. I'll buy you a new one. Do you have everything backed up?"

She started shaking her head furiously. "No, you don't understand. It's not about replacing it. It's about the information that's on it. Shit, Ronan, I can't...." Words failed her as she began to sob, and I pulled her tight to my chest, surrounding her with my arms.

All of a sudden, the cause of her panic struck me. She obviously had all of her Socialmedialite files on her laptop. If somebody broke into it, they'd be able to expose her as the anonymous blogger. Not to mention the fact that she still didn't know that I knew. Something twisted inside me, something sharp and horrible. I didn't like feeling that I was deceiving her, and I'm sure half of her alarm was down to the prospect of my finding out.

"Hush, love; everything is going to be fine. I'll sort this," I murmured just as there was a knock on the door.

Settling Annie on the edge of the bed, I went to answer it and was greeted by O'Hare and two policemen. I made sure to voice my dissatisfaction with their security measures loud and clear. O'Hare grew frazzled, assuring me that the price of our stay would now be complimentary. I wasn't mollified by that, and I think he knew. I thought of the clusterfuck this could've been if the thieves had gotten Brona's pictures and clenched my fists.

Thinking of someone taking Annie's things pissed me off even more. I didn't want the world to know who she really was just as much as she didn't. She might have been thrust into the world of celebrity by being my girlfriend, but it would be a whole other story if her identity as The Socialmedialite became known. She was the Internet's best-kept secret, and I'm sure those working in the media would sell their left kidneys for the exclusive.

I wanted to protect her so badly, and the fact that this was out of my control was hard to handle. I felt like wrecking the world just to keep Annie from exposure.

Making a concerted effort to calm down, I told the officers how we'd found the place, and O'Hare went to look for the security footage of the corridor outside our room. Patricia trundled in with tea and sandwiches at one point, disappearing into the bedroom to talk to Annie. I noticed her shut the door after a minute and wondered what they were discussing. Despite all this drama, my proposal was still at the forefront of my mind, and I knew that if Annie was uncertain about saying yes before, now she was positively terrified. The break-in couldn't have come at a worse possible moment.

About a half an hour later, I was standing in the hotel's monitoring room watching a lone male walk right up to our suite on the screen, fiddle with the lock, and then disappear inside our rooms. He was wearing a peak cap but no balaclava, and though the footage was grainy, I recognized the prick immediately. He was one of the more aggressive paps I'd dealt with and had been following Annie and me nonstop since we arrived in Dublin. I even knew his name because I heard another photographer call him Gavin once. After the police left to search for him, I thought about returning to the suite, where I knew Annie was still in turmoil, but my guilt and apprehension kept me away.

I didn't want her to say she wouldn't marry me, but I also needed to tell her that I knew she was The Socialmedialite. Before I did that, though, I needed a fucking drink.

At the bar, I acted completely out of character by knocking back three shots of whiskey all in a row. I noticed some women sitting close by eyeing me and grew irritated by it for some reason, so I didn't stay long. I left right after the third shot of liquid courage and took the lift up to our suite. When I got there, Patricia was gone, but the rooms had been tidied. I found Annie sitting in bed with a cup of peppermint tea in her hands and a bathrobe on. Her hair was wet, and her eyes were red, indicating she'd been crying. In fact, by the looks of it, she'd been crying *a lot,* and I wanted to punch myself for not being there to comfort her.

"We have a lead on the thief," I told her softly, standing in the doorway. She was staring out the window, not meeting my gaze. "I'm almost certain it's one of the paps who's been following us. Total shithead. There's a good chance we'll get your laptop back in one piece."

Her eyes flickered to me then, and I saw her swallow. "You don't understand. The first thing he'll do is download my entire hard drive. It's the information that's valuable, Ronan, not the laptop." Her voice went really quiet then as she whispered, "They'll use it against me."

Seeing her like this made me ache. I wanted to share her burden, tell her everything would be all right, but I couldn't. I balled my fists and gritted my teeth.

"We'll figure it out together, Annie. You're not alone in this," I tried to reassure her.

Her eyes were watery again, more tears building, and the look she gave me made my heart crack in two. "You won't be saying that once you know the truth. You won't want anything to do with me then." A pause, before she continued under her breath, "Especially not marriage."

I took three long steps into the room and sat down on the edge of the bed. This was it. She could tell me now, and it would all be out in the open. I'd never have to admit I already knew. "What truth?" I murmured. "What are you talking about, darling?"

Our gazes locked, and the look of pure terror on her face told me she was never going to admit it. "Nothing. It's just client information. It could cause trouble for them if the press gets its hands on private documents."

"You're lying," I said. "Annie, don't ever think there's anything you can't tell me. I love you. You know this. Nothing can change that."

"I'm not lying," she croaked.

Frustrated, I climbed to the center of the bed and took her face in my hands. "You are. Don't be scared, love. I'm not going anywhere."

"You can't know that."

"Yes, I can. Tell me."

I felt her pulse flutter against my fingertips, her breathing growing panicked. She was like a small bird trapped in a cage, desperate to break free. I hated putting her in the cage, so I decided to take the bullet instead. It felt like all the air went out of me as I exhaled heavily and said, "Look, you don't need to worry about anything. I already know."

Time slowed. Annie frowned. I swallowed. Every muscle in my body clenched tight, and comprehension lit in her eyes.

She moved away as far as she could go, which wasn't far, and I hated how she was looking at me in that moment. She was looking at me like I was a stranger. Suspicion laced her words.

"You know what, Ronan? What do you know?"

In a heartbeat, the tables had turned, and now I was the one panicking. She tried pulling away from me again, but I gripped her shoulders, pinning her in place. "I know about your blog," I said, trying to sound strong and confident and failing miserably. My voice was all scratchy and uneven. "I know that you're really The Socialmedialite."

Her eyes flickered back and forth between mine in disbelief for what felt like forever. When she finally spoke, it was just one word.

"No."

"Please let me explain."

She squeezed her eyes shut. "This isn't happening." One second she was weak, distraught, but the next second, that all changed. She opened her eyes and glared at me. "How long have you known? How did you find out?"

"Your phone," I confessed. "That time you lost it. You left it in my car. A tweet came on the screen from your Socialmedialite account. I put two and two together."

Her chest rose and fell in anger, but I didn't let her push me off. "That was weeks ago! You…I…we…we've exchanged emails since then. You pretended…."

"You pretended, too," I said, cutting her off. "You pretended for longer; but I forgave you, and now you need to forgive me."

"Get off me," she fumed.

"Don't run away from me," I begged.

"I said, 'GET OFF ME!'" she yelled, and my body went limp. I let go of her immediately, and she climbed from the bed, feet stomping on the carpet as she paced the room. I was shattering into tiny pieces as I felt her emotionally sever all ties. I couldn't handle this. I was in too deep, and if she left me now, I'd never recover.

"I'm so sorry, love; please come here, and let me explain. Let me explain why I lied," I said, sounding like a desperate man. She was the only woman I would ever be desperate for. I had to make this right.

She stopped pacing and turned to face me, speaking in stops and starts like she was putting pieces of a puzzle together in her mind. "You manipulated me. You wrote me emails looking for romantic advice, and you knew it was me all along. You wrote that email saying you loved me knowing I'd be the one to read it. You can't just…." Her voice broke as tears took over. "You tricked me, Ronan!"

"I wasn't trying to trick you. It was the truth!"

"The truth? Was it? Or has this all been a game? Did you send that email just so I'd let you fuck me?!"

Okay, now I was pissed. I stood from the bed and walked toward her, backing her up and slamming my hands into the wall behind her. I faltered a little when she flinched. "I don't play games, and I've only ever been real with you, Annie. I sent those emails because I wanted you to know how I felt, but I knew that if I told you in person, I'd scare you off. Writing it down and letting you read it without having to respond gave you safety. No matter what you might think, you always come first for me. And I asked you to marry me because I want you to know I'm all in. You have me, body, heart, and soul."

She closed her eyes when she spoke. "Please, stop. Just stop…."

A lump formed in my throat as I stepped away. Turning her head, she glanced at me then looked to the floor. Her voice was tiny when she spoke, staring at her feet, "Can't you see? I feel…violated and exposed having you know, having anyone know."

"Am I just anyone to you?"

She didn't answer me. Instead, she shook her head and continued as though I hadn't spoken. "Blogging…blogging has always been my biggest secret. This is probably going to sound crazy, but it's the only place I can be free and completely happy—it's the only place where I can be my true self without fear. If people know it's me, then it's not my escape anymore. You took that freedom away from me, Ronan, and I'm not sure if I can forgive that."

I wasn't a crier. In fact, I could count on one hand the number of times I'd actually cried in my life, but right then I felt a tear leak out. She was so, so damaged by her experiences, and writing was her way of escaping. But it had to be anonymous. That's the only way it worked. And now she felt like I'd ruined it.

"I'd never tell anyone," I began; but she cut me off, and her passion returned as she threw her hands out in anger.

"That's not the point! That thief has my laptop. Soon he'll know my secret and will sell it to the highest bidder. I'll be hounded. My life will never go back to the way it was. It had been safe and comfortable, and though it might have been lonely, it was perfect for me. I wish I'd never met you! If I hadn't, then none of this would have happened!"

My heart fell to the floor. I could literally hear the awful, bloody thump. I was done for. Her words cut into me like a knife. I must have looked completely miserable as I stood there, staring at her, begging her with my eyes not to do this.

She did it anyway, barely looking at me when she said harshly, "Do you have somewhere else you can stay? I'd like to be alone."

"You're angry. I get that. But if I go, will you talk to me in the morning? Give me a chance to explain?"

"Okay, fine."

She wouldn't quite look at me, but her words gave me a small piece of relief. I could fix this. After she'd had some time to let her anger dissipate, she'd hear me out.

"All right then. I'll go," I said sadly and began moving toward her. I needed to kiss her cheek, hug her, anything, before I left, but the look she gave me as I approached told me no. She couldn't give me anything right then. I felt like a dying man as I walked out of the suite, barely enough strength to go down to reception and get another room for myself. The woman at the desk gave me an odd look, so I lied and told her we didn't feel comfortable staying in a room that had been broken into. After I said that, she was practically falling over herself to offer me another suite.

Despite my exhaustion, I didn't sleep a wink. Instead, I sat up watching mindless television and trying to resist the urge to return to Annie and force her to listen to me. I tried to convince myself that giving her space was the best idea and that forcing things with her had never worked before.

At six thirty the following morning, I took a shower to try to wake myself up and put on the same suit I'd worn to dinner the previous evening. Finding O'Hare at the concierge's table, I asked him if the police had reported back about the theft. He smiled proudly and told me he'd just been about to come find me. They'd caught the thief and had returned the stolen belongings, which consisted of both mine and Annie's laptops, our travel itinerary, and Annie's tablet.

For the first time since yesterday, I felt like smiling. Annie would surely be over the moon to have her things back and might even be less angry with me. Carrying our stuff up to the suite, I wore a stupid, hopeful grin on my face, thinking I was going to make everything better. I threw open the door and called out her name. Receiving no answer, I called again and opened the bedroom door slightly, thinking she might still be asleep. My heart skipped a beat when I peeked inside.

The bed was empty. And on the dresser was a small piece of paper with a note.

. . .

Ronan,
I'm catching a flight home early. I can't stay here anymore.
I'm sorry.
Annie.

* * *

I had my things packed and was organizing a flight within seconds of reading her note. No way. There was no fucking way I was letting her end things like this. Fifteen minutes later, I was outside and in a taxi headed for the airport. I tried calling her a bunch of times, but her phone was turned off which made me think she was probably in the air. I wondered how many hours I was behind her. Had she left early this morning, or had she simply gone the moment I left her last night?

Shit, I never should have left her. I couldn't believe she left me. She said she would give us a chance to talk. But she didn't. She lied, and that was the rub.

It didn't take long for me to check my luggage and go through customs. I hadn't eaten since yesterday, and my stomach was starting to tell me all about it by the time I arrived in the VIP lounge. It was unnerving. I never forgot to eat. Never. This thing with Annie was messing up my head big time.

I was just about to go in search of food when I stopped dead in my tracks; sitting at a table by the window were my paternal grandparents, Mick and Marie Fitzpatrick. They sipped on coffees and nibbled on breakfast muffins, barely talking to one another, with the silent urbanity of the upper classes.

Seriously, the world was shitting all over me today.

I wasn't sure what it was. Perhaps I was cracking up after everything that had happened with Annie because I'd long ago given up trying to be a part of their lives, but I felt the urge to confront them. They'd never wanted anything to do with Lucy and me, and I'd always been angry about that, saying fuck them and their money. And for a long time I'd been holding onto that anger, letting it fester and make me feel like I was never quite good enough. That I could never reach whatever ridiculous standards these people had set for themselves.

They were probably jetting off on one of the many luxurious holidays I was sure they took every year. I stood for a moment and watched them as they started to bicker with one another about something. In that moment, I realized just how unimportant they were. How my anger over all those years, especially when I was younger, had been so pointless.

Without thinking, my feet were moving, and I was walking toward them. It had been a long time since I'd engaged them, and I'd been hurt by their rejection back then. Now I was looking at them with brand-new eyes.

I didn't give two fucks about them anymore, and it was absolutely liberating.

"Ah, Gran and Granddad, how are ya doing this fine morning?" I chirped and pulled a chair up to their table. Marie startled comically, looking like a terrified owl, and Mick began to fidget uncomfortably in his seat.

"Ronan, this is unexpected," he said, sitting up straight and looking over my shoulder—I was guessing for some sort of excuse to leave. He was old now, and I was in the prime of my life. He glanced at me warily, like he found my size unsettling. I took a small piece of pleasure from that. Once there was a time when I was weak and he was strong. Now the tables had well and truly turned. Reaching over, I snatched a bit of muffin from his plate and took a bite. Not because I wanted it but because I wanted to make him as uncomfortable as possible. The fucker had it coming.

"So, where are you off to this time? Wait, let me guess; it's Mykonos again, isn't it? You always were fond of the old Mykonos, Mick," I said, taking the piss and giving him a nudge with my elbow. "They've got some *fabulous* nightclubs there, I hear. Great for when Gran wants to kick back with a good book and you can head out on the tiles, eh? Meet some like-minded male company."

Marie was starting to become embarrassed, her eyes pleading with her husband to somehow get rid of me. Other people were starting to look, and if Marie Fitzpatrick hated anything, it was a scene.

"You're being distasteful," said Mick. "And my wife and I would appreciate it if you left."

I slammed my hand down on the table hard, and he full-on jumped in his seat. It was hilarious, and I was a little bit drunk on the power. I didn't need his approval anymore. Why hadn't I realized this years ago?

"I'll go when I'm good and ready," I said, voice hard, making sure he heard the threat.

"Mick, call airport security," said Marie, all high-pitched and squeaky. "This is harassment."

"If this were harassment," I began, my tone quietly sinister, "you wouldn't still be sitting comfortably in your seats. Pair of fucking cowards, the both of you. You're so preoccupied with what other people think that you've lived empty, lonely lives, and you've missed out on knowing your grandchildren. It's your loss. Do you hear that? You lost."

Mick had his phone out of his pocket now, fumbling to search for the number to the airport's security department. I laughed and loudly pushed my chair back. "Relax—your scumbag grandson is leaving now, so you can go back to arguing and silently hating one another. I used to hate you. Now I just pity you."

And with those parting words, I went.

I still had no clue what I was going to do when I got to New York. I had no clue what I was going to say to Annie when I saw her. I was so goddamn angry with her for giving up, for running away, for not trusting me, for lying about giving me a chance.

It wasn't like with Brona. I respected Annie, I'd wanted to marry her, I was well and truly in love with her, and she'd thrown it all back in my face. She'd given up on us without a fight, like we didn't matter.

But I did know that if by some miracle we found a way to get past all our shite, together we would never be anything like Mick and Marie Fitzpatrick.

TWENTY-ONE

ANNIE

The Mugger: *When one bumps into the subject, quickly snaps a picture, and runs away.*
Best for: *Close-up shots when the digital zoom on the phone's camera will not suffice, low light.*
Do not use: *If the person is faster than you. You'll never get away with it.*

I was a coward and a hypocrite.
    But mostly a coward.

I couldn't quite manage a full breath or a complete swallow, not even when I walked through the doors of my building and on to the elevator. I thought for sure I'd start feeling better once I got home, less hunted. I didn't.

Instead I felt…empty. And desperately alone. And foolish. And hypocritical. And cowardly.

I'd never had a problem with my cowardice before. Being a coward always felt like the smartest course of action; it felt like the surest path to sustained and guaranteed safety. But now that I'd been brave—even if it had only been for a few short weeks—being a coward felt like choosing to live underground instead of soaring through the air. I'd voluntarily given up my ability to fly.

I'd betrayed Ronan by lying to him and then judging and condemning him.

I'd betrayed myself by fleeing and not making every attempt to work through our—really, my—issues.

And I had no one to talk to about it because I was a fucking hermit!

My first instinct was to message WriteALoveSong and ask for help…but I couldn't do that. I had pseudo-friends, people who commented on my blog, but no real-life confidants. No friend to call. No mother to have over. No gay BFF to cry to while he made me fabulous martinis. I'd started interacting with some of the wives and girlfriends of Ronan's teammates while in Ireland, but I couldn't call on them now, not about this.

I was alone with my cowardice and crazy internal monologue.

"Damn, dammit, dickless Donald Duck," I mumbled, unzipping my suitcase, trying to sort through my hastily packed clothes while at the same time trying sort through my hastily stuffed feelings. Both were in complete disarray. Everything was wrinkled and tangled, and I was probably going to cry.

Then my home phone rang, and I jumped at the unexpected shrill sound. I blinked at it, recalling that my cell phone was still on airplane mode from the red-eye. My heart leapt, thinking that it might be Ronan, so I ran and grabbed the phone without checking the caller I.D.

"Hello? Hello?"

"Annie?"

My leaping heart fell to the rocks below, bruising itself. I stiffened and held my breath because the person on the other end sounded exactly like Ronan's mother.

"Hello? Are you there?" she asked, and now I was certain it was her.

I closed my eyes to gather any semblance of mental armor I had left and cleared my throat before answering, "Yes. I'm here. Hello, Mrs. Fitzpatrick. How can I help you?"

She was silent for a long moment. I thought I heard a door open then close. She blurted out, "I am so sorry, Annie. I am so sorry I was such a…well, such a cunt."

I half choked, half laughed as my eyes flew open; I reached for the table behind me for balance. "Uh—I—um…I—" What does one say to a woman who's just called herself a cunt with complete sincerity? Eventually, I managed, "Mrs. Fitzpatrick, I don't know what to say."

"Then, please, just listen." She took an audible breath before continuing, "First, I am sorry. What I said to you, it wasn't right. I had no right. My son…he is just like his father in so many ways, but he is also very different. I didn't have the easiest time with his dad. I never quite belonged, and I think he knew it; but I loved him very much."

"Mrs. Fitzpatrick, you don't need to tell me this. I don't want you to feel like—"

"But I do. I do need to tell you—because you love Ronan, and he loves you. Most of the shite printed by the media is just that, shite. But pictures don't lie. The way you two look at each other, I can see it. It's obvious to everyone that you care about him deeply."

I rubbed my forehead with my fingertips; this was not a conversation I was ready to have. "I can't—"

She interrupted me again. "He told me about your past, about how you grew up."

I had no response for that, though I sat down and released a quiet sigh. Unaccountably, my chin began to wobble.

"I know something about feeling unworthy, Annie. And I'm sorry if I made you feel that way."

I shook my head. "You were right. He deserves better. He deserves better than me."

"No, he really doesn't." She laughed lightly. "The way you've taken care of him, helped him, put yourself out there in the public eye. I'm not sure there is better than you. And, anyway, he wants you. He loves you, Annie."

"I know," I half sobbed.

"Then let's start over. Let's be friends."

I was crying now but silently, and I hiccuped ungracefully as I said, "Friends?"

"Yes. Friends. I'm a shitty mother—poor Luce will tell you that—but I think I can be a good friend."

I sniffled, "Oh, Mrs. Fitzpatrick—"

"Please, call me Jackie."

"Jackie, if you knew what I—"

"None of that. Just promise me you'll think about it, okay?"

"But—"

"Please, promise me. Please. For Ronan's sake?"

I took a calming breath and forced my voice to be firm. "Yes. For Ronan's sake, I would do anything. But also…I want to start over, too."

"Good! It's settled. Luce will be so happy; she…well, she's a good girl. We'll be back in the States next week, and I know Ronan is on his way now. We'll all get together." Her tone shifted, and I felt certain she was anxious to end the conversation—likely not wanting to push her luck.

"Wait, Jackie, you should know that…I don't know how to tell you this, but—"

"Tell me on Thursday. Listen, I've got to run. I'll ring you when we arrive. Talk soon!"

"Wait—"

It was too late; she hung up, leaving me feeling like I'd just been tossed about by a hurricane. I shook my head and pressed the "off" button. A great, giant swelling of remorse filled every inch of my chest and radiated outward, numbing my fingertips and buzzing behind my ears.

Then the phone rang once more. This time I checked the caller I.D. The display told me the call originated from Davidson & Croft. I figured it was Gerta, so I answered.

"Hello?"

"Annie. You're back."

It was Joan.

"Uh, hi, Joan, I know I wasn't supposed to be back until—"

"Well, we have lots to discuss! I'm taking you off the Fitzpatrick account."

I didn't say anything for a few seconds because my mind couldn't quite comprehend the words Joan had just spoken.

"Annie…?"

"Uh, yes. Sorry, I'm here."

"Did you hear me?"

"No—I mean, yes. At least, I think I heard you, but I don't understand what you mean."

"We're assigning Beth as the primary liaison for Mr. Fitzpatrick. You'll take back The Starlet. Also, feel free to keep the clothes, but please do dress as you like. Obviously, I don't really care one way or the other…."

I rubbed my forehead with my fingertips again, feeling acutely frazzled, and tried to make sense of what Joan was saying. She was prattling on about my pink cardigan and how it was a shame that I should choose to wear navy blue and brown when red and jewel tones suited me so much better.

The gist of her one-sided conversation was as follows: I was being taken off Ronan's campaign. It didn't matter what I looked like or how I dressed; she valued my brain. However, it was important that I understood non-summery colors suited my complexion best. Yellow was a complete disaster.

…I am being taken off Ronan's campaign.

My brain hurt.

"Wait! Wait a minute, just—just stop talking," I shouted at the phone and the inside of my apartment. I was greeted by Joan's sudden silence as I closed my eyes and rubbed the center of my chest with my fingertips, trying to find the right way to ask my next question.

I decided there was no right way to ask the question, so I demanded, "Why am I being taken off the Fitzpatrick account?"

I heard Joan clear her throat, could see her in my mind's eye straighten her spine and purse her lips. She didn't like it when people were demanding.

At length, no longer able to handle the suspense of her cool silence, I added in a much calmer tone, "I'm sorry, Joan. I'm sorry. I shouldn't have…shouted. I apologize. I'm just very surprised that I've been removed from Ronan's team. I've worked very hard on this account, and I would like to know why I'm being excluded."

Her softened, measured tenor surprised me as she explained, "Mr. Fitzpatrick called this morning. He asked that you be removed from his team. Furthermore, he requested that the relationship we've doctored for the media end immediately."

"He…he did what?" Now my brain and my heart hurt.

"Obviously, I told him that he is making a mistake. You are the best in this business, I told him. Your ideal image sketch has become a reality much faster than we could have foreseen, largely due to your timing strategy, the social media campaign, and your involvement as his *faux* love interest. Public perception is just as you've designed. I further explained that we couldn't just end things between the two of you. We'll have to phase you out of the public eye and phase someone else in who is equally relatable and likable. Otherwise, we risk making him look flighty and unfeeling. Side note here, I'd like your input as to appropriate candidates."

"Phase me out?" I choked. "Candidates?"

"He eventually ceded that point. You're off the account, Annie. But you're still on girlfriend duty for the next four to six weeks—but don't worry, it's just a few public appearances. Becky has been sketching out the schedule since I got off the phone with Mr. Fitzpatrick. She'll send you the draft this evening."

"The schedule?"

"Of obligatory public appearances."

I was mostly quiet for several long moments, but I abruptly became aware that I was breathing heavily and clutching my forehead with stiff fingers.

Ronan wanted me gone.

He wanted me gone.

He didn't want me.

He didn't even want to see me.

I'd left last night, and I'd ruined everything; and I had no idea how to make things right. Maybe there was no way to make things right. Maybe I'd left one too many times.

"Annie? Are you…are you all right?"

"No," I blurted, shaking my head and obviously feeling more afraid than sane, because I blurted, "I'm not all right. I'm all wrong. I've ruined everything. I'm in love with him, and I didn't tell him. Instead, I ran away when I found out something that I didn't know. I didn't know that he knew who I was. And when I found out that he knew, that he knew about who I was all along but loved me anyway, wanted me anyway, forgave me anyway, I panicked and left because his love felt like a manipulation. But it isn't, and his emails were the only way he had of telling me how he felt without me freaking out like a 'Freakout Francine!' And instead of admitting the truth and owning my part and accepting his feelings and trusting him, I turned and fled like a spineless asshole."

"Oh, dear."

"Yes. 'Oh, dear' is right. I'm totally fucked, aren't I?"

"Uh…."

"It's okay, you can say it. You can say, 'Annie, you are fucked.' I mean, what kind of person falls in love with Ronan Fitzpatrick but is too much of a hypocrite and coward to own up to those feelings, especially when I know—*I know* for a fact—that they're reciprocated! I know it, Joan! But not anymore because he wants me off the account!"

I might have been slightly hysterical at this point. I wasn't crying, but I was screaming at my boss.

"Annie, calm down."

"I can't! I can't calm down, Joan. I can no longer keep my shit together. You are the closest thing I have to a real-life friend, and you intimidate the crap out of me. I have no one. I had someone, but I threw him away, twice. Two times. I thought I didn't need anyone. I was wrong. I'm so very wrong…I'm a spineless asshole."

I was pacing the apartment, making contingency plans, because I was pretty sure I was about to be fired. My blog could support me, pay all my bills… assuming I wasn't about to be outed as The Socialmedialite by the dunghead who'd stolen my laptop. Then I would become a true hermit. A shut-in, finding photos for my blog from other sources. Maybe I would get a ferret. A cat just felt too benign. My kind of crazy deserved an ambiguously cute rodent with a penchant for biting.

Really, I had more money than I needed. Years of spending funds only on takeout, tea, and pastries had yielded a significant savings. Being miserly with my finances and feelings was about to pay off in the most tragic way possible.

"Listen to me—"

"I'm fired, aren't I? It's okay if I am; just tell me now. If I'm going to lose my shit, I might as well lose all of it at once and have a shit storm of shittiness."

"Annie, shut up and listen."

I snapped my mouth shut and sat down heavily on my couch, released a resigned exhalation, and bit my bottom lip to keep from saying anything else.

"Now…." Joan cleared her throat, and I heard some movement in the background. I thought I heard her snapping her fingers. She often snapped her fingers at people when she wanted their attention.

I prepared myself for what would undoubtedly come next, and tangentially I decided that I should have invested in a therapist years ago. Then I could have called her or him rather than committing professional suicide. Therapists always struck me as a hire-a-friend service. Therapists are to mental and emotional purging what prostitutes are to physical urges.

Amidst my meanderings about prostitutes and therapists and ferrets, Joan surprised the cuss out of me.

Of note, she didn't fire me.

Instead, she said, "Put on some tea. I'm coming over. And don't even think about having another childish fit and leaving the apartment. You might have given Ronan Fitzpatrick the slip, but I will hunt you down and make your life very uncomfortable until I am satisfied that you've learned your lesson. You can't run away from people who care about you and are invested in your success and happiness. It's a dick move, Annie. Don't be a dick."

Also of note, she used the word "dick."

"Uh…." *What?*

Before I could say anything, Joan abruptly hung up, leaving me staring at my apartment, wondering into what bizarre universe I'd just stumbled.

* * *

I DIDN'T RUN away. Instead, I did as I was instructed and put the tea kettle on, prepared two cups of Earl Grey, and changed into a black T-shirt and black yoga pants.

Joan arrived no less than twenty minutes later; she must've rushed, taken the company car. Maybe she flew on her broom…. Whether she was a good witch or a bad witch had never quite been settled. For now, I assumed she was a good witch with ruthless tendencies.

I opened the door and stepped back, my eyes wide as she strolled in—giving me the once-over as she passed.

"First of all, you're not fired, so you can wipe that look of panic off your face."

I shut the door and followed my boss into my apartment. She looked somehow shorter here. Maybe it was the lighting.

She continued as she scanned my place, inspecting books on my shelves and frowning at my desk in the living room. "I do not excel at this type of thing, so I'll just tell you what I think. Then we can sit on the couch and drink tea and do whatever it is that women friends do when one of them is having a crisis. Here is what I think: you're having a colossal overreaction. Mr. Fitzpatrick is on his way to New York as we speak. He took the first flight out of Ireland this morning—I imagine he did so once he discovered you'd left. When he called me, he sounded angry, yes. But he also sounded concerned about you, about your being forced into taking on his account, forced into a relationship for the sake of his career."

This news should have been a relief. Instead, it just made me feel more like a spineless asshole. "But he's not the problem. I'm the coward. I'm the one who left. I'm the one that overreacted when I found out…when he told me about the thing with the thing."

"The thing with the thing? Are you having a seizure? Suffering from aphasia?"

"No," I huffed, pulling my hand through my hair and scratching my scalp. "He found out who I really am."

"He found out about your home life? When you were a child?"

"No. Not that, I told him about that." I waved her question away. "He found out about who I am now, what I do when I'm not at work or working. Actually, he knew all along, and I didn't know. And now that I know that he knew...I just don't know."

"Annie, stop speaking in code. I can't help you see reason and get your shit together if you don't tell me what's really going on. Why is it that you left Mr. Fitzpatrick, the man that you supposedly love and trust?"

I peered at her from between my fingers and shook my head. "I can't tell you. If I tell you, then you will fire me."

Joan frowned at me, her gaze feeling remarkably penetrating and shrewd.

Then I felt the hairs on the back of my neck rise as she said, "Oh, I think I understand. This is about your stolen laptop and hobby blog, isn't it? You should know the laptop was recovered before it could be hacked—Ronan told me on the phone. Your secret is still relatively safe."

I straightened. My hands dropped as I held her gaze but said nothing. I couldn't speak. The news that they'd recovered my laptop before I was exposed should have eclipsed everything else. It didn't. The fact that Joan knew my secret was the only take-home message.

Her lips curved into something resembling a smirk, and she shook her head. "He knew all along, did he?" Then she added as though speaking to herself, "Ronan Fitzpatrick is smarter than I thought."

Again, and for the second time in a half hour, I wondered into what bizarre universe I'd just stumbled.

"Wha-wha-what do you mean?"

"*New York's Finest*. The Socialmedialite," she said plainly. "Well, of course I know. I've said it to anyone who will listen—you *are* the best. You've built a social media empire over the course of three years. Your contacts are invaluable. Your influence priceless. Why do you think I pay you so well? It's not for those irritating infographic emails, that's for certain."

"But...how? How did you—"

Joan interrupted me. "That's not relevant. And, just to ease your mind, no. No one else knows or suspects, as far as I'm aware. The issue here is that Ronan Fitzpatrick knows."

I swallowed mostly air. The fact that Joan had known my secret all along circled my head like chirping birds. I couldn't quite grasp it…. I seemed to be having this problem a lot lately.

"Although…." Joan's smirk flattened. "I was quite irritated by that Dara Evans article you published over St. Patrick's Day. I surmised you did it to draw attention away from Mr. Fitzpatrick. Nevertheless, Becky and Ian had a hell of a time convincing her to get rid of that infernal baby seal coat. You know what she said? She said seals sexually assault penguins and deserved to be clubbed. That woman is nuttier than a Snickers bar."

I snorted a shocked laugh and then clapped my hand over my mouth before I could completely embarrass myself. Joan's smirk was back. She looked...more human somehow. Not quite approachable but not the Wicked Witch of the West, either.

She twisted and glanced at the couch behind her and then took a seat, smoothing her black skirt as she sat. "Let's get to it. Ronan did what exactly? Why did you flee Ireland? It's such a lovely country, and the people are so accommodating."

I gaped at her, still overwhelmed by her recent revelations, but found myself talking regardless. "Nothing...really. You're right, I completely overreacted."

I proceeded to tell her about what had happened—the emails exchanged, how I'd kept the secret from him and he knew the whole time, how he'd told me he loved me but I hadn't reciprocated. I felt myself deflate as I spoke. Obviously, I left out the heavenly kinky sex part and the more intimate details. When I was finished, I found my voice steady and calm but tired, recent events coming into distinct focus.

She nodded thoughtfully and paused after I finished my tale, surveying me with squinted eyes.

I watched her for a bit then volunteered, "I guess I'm worried that he won't take me back. I mean, I made such a mess of things."

"Well, he shouldn't have emailed The Socialmedialite under false pretenses, though I certainly understand why he did it. That's a gray area. Also, I understand why you didn't tell him about your blog, but you shouldn't have been such a ninny about your feelings."

"But how could I tell him how I felt when I was lying to him?"

"Because the blog isn't any of his business, that's why. It is, in fact, your business. It's how you make a substantial amount of your income. It's not illegal, and your identity is a secret for obvious reasons. You weren't lying to him. Has he told you about all the ways he makes money? About all of his investments? Certainly not. What a silly thing to expect."

"Joan...."

"You know I'm right. But it's neither here nor there since he does know. As I suspected would be the case, he doesn't care."

"What if I'm too late? What if he doesn't want to marry me anymore? What if he won't take me back?"

"Do you want to marry him?"

"Yes," I answered without giving it much thought beyond how my heart swelled and danced and felt ready to burst.

She nodded thoughtfully. "Well, you'll find out tomorrow. You and he are scheduled to attend the premiere of *Accidental Assassin*."

I heaved a watery exhale, crossing my arms and letting my head fall to the chair behind me. "I'm so afraid."

"There is nothing wrong with being afraid, Annie," she said, standing and sighing. "But there is everything wrong with being *only* afraid."

* * *

Everything happened as I feared it would.

Ronan slipped into the limo, his face blank, his eyes hooded as he settled into his seat. He then took stock of the interior of the limo, his gaze moving over me with no trace of interest. I recognized this look from our first night in Ireland, how he'd inspected me before the Sportsperson of the Year dinner, except this time it felt more permanent, less premeditated.

"Ms. Catrel." He nodded at me. His tone wasn't aloof. It was polite.

Ugh.

I twisted my fingers and tried to swallow the building lump in my throat. "Ronan, can we—"

Before I could finish my question, Beth opened the opposite door and poked her head in, her efficient gaze sweeping over both of us.

"Oh, good, Annie, you're wearing the dress Joan picked out. Remember, at least three big kisses on the red carpet—at least—and hold hands the entire time, okay? Since the sudden separation in Ireland, you two really need to lay it on thick. Also, put these earrings on." Beth handed me a velvet box.

Ronan seem to be watching our exchange with bored indifference.

At a loss, I opened the box and glanced at the contents. Within were diamond studs, at least a carat and a half each. Expensive but understated. They would have been perfect for me, except—

"She can't wear those." Ronan leaned forward, grabbed the box from my fingers, and passed it back to Beth, who was still hovering outside the limo.

"Why not?" Reluctantly, she accepted the box.

"Because her ears aren't pierced," he added as he settled back into his seat, looking irritated and impatient. "Time for us to go."

Beth nodded, her eyes moving between us, then stepped away from the car and shut the door, leaving us in an odd, strangled silence. The car moved. We were on our way.

I stared at him.

He looked out his window.

I was afraid.

Fear clawed at my throat.

But for once, I wasn't only afraid. I was hopeful.

"Ronan, can we talk?"

"What about?" He didn't look at me. He sounded completely indifferent. I felt my hope shrivel a little.

"F-first, I n-need to apologize for…for s-so many things."

"Apology accepted."

I gritted my teeth and closed my eyes, resting my elbow on the window sill and holding my forehead in my propped-up hand. "Please let me say this; please let me—"

"There's nothing to say, Annie. You left. Again. After I asked you to marry me. And you didn't return my phone calls. That spoke volumes."

I cringed, glanced at him. "I didn't want to talk over the phone."

"Then invite me over for fucking tea." His voice was hard.

"Ronan—"

"No." The single word was steel, echoed in the limo. *It* spoke volumes. "No. I know what you're going to say, and I find that I don't have it in me to care. There are some things, some people, worth fighting for. You would be worth fighting for, you would, if you wanted me like I…like I want you."

"But I—"

He lifted his voice over mine, his bitterness a tangible third being in the car. "And I'm not just saying that because you're an excellent fuck, because you are the best lay I've ever had." He said this with an acrimonious laugh, and I winced at his harsh, vulgar words. He continued, "I'm saying it because you don't believe it. You're not invested, Annie. Not in me, not in yourself. And I can't fight that. I can't make you fight."

"But I am! I am invested—" I leaned toward him, and he flinched away when I reached out to touch him, causing a giant stab of pain to pierce through my heart and radiate up my neck, throb in my brain.

"Really?" His gaze slid from my outstretched hand to my eyes. "For how long? Until…what? My ma says something you don't like? I expect too much? No, no. I should have listened to you when you said you didn't want me enough to change. At least in that you were honest."

I pressed my lips together. I didn't trust myself to speak without crying, and I couldn't cry. We were about to walk the red carpet at a mega event. We would be photographed over and over. If I cried, then it would interfere with the image we'd been building for him. So instead I closed my eyes as he continued.

"I was mad, crazy, thinking we were suited. I see clearly now that you're always going to be too afraid to do anything meaningful that isn't anonymous. Your job—cleaning up arseholes' images? That's shite work. It's dishonest, and it's beneath you. But what you do on your blog is meaningful. The charities that benefit, the way you raise awareness about things that matter? That's meaningful. But you're too much of a fucking coward to take credit, to take the good that you deserve. I'm not going to waste my time trying to convince you of what you deserve. That's a losing battle. And I won't be with a coward."

My heart didn't shatter. It cracked. Then it just hung out there, all crumbling and ruined. He was right. I was a coward, and I didn't know how not to be. He was also right; I didn't know how to deserve him. I didn't know where to start.

The rest of the ride passed in silence. We arrived, and he helped me out of the car. He gave me the prescribed kisses, perfectly timed, very passionate, entirely for the benefit of the cameras.

We didn't speak again. Instead, I did what I knew was expected. I smiled.

What I wanted to do was the opposite. I wanted to frown. I wanted to cry and scream and push him around. I wanted to demand that he not give up on us, on me. As the evening wore on, I felt my smile grow more and more false until it slipped completely from my face.

* * *

HE PUT ME in the limo and muttered something about taking a taxi just before shutting the door.

Given our departing Ireland on two different flights, leaving in separate cars from the premiere, and my waning smile over the course of the evening, I knew someone would remark on the strained air between us. The ideal image of his I'd been working so hard to maintain would be tarnished.

Strangely, while I sat in the back of the limo watching but not seeing the lights of New York fly by my window, I couldn't muster up enough professionalism to give two shits about his ideal image.

When I arrived home, I stomped into the lobby, feeling oddly furious. With the fury came an unexpected bravery, and I realized belatedly that, on the ride to the event, I shouldn't have felt hope.

I should have been angry.

I should have pushed him. I should have yelled at him for lying to me and forced him to work things out between us.

I should have demanded it, for us, for myself.

Instead, I'd conceded because I didn't want to mess up his goddamn ideal image. In doing so, I'd proved him right.

By the time I entered my apartment, I was so beyond pissed, I was in a rage.

I thought about taking a taxi to his apartment, banging on his door, demanding that he open up and kiss me for real. I played the scene over and over in my head. I'd race up the stairs in my evening gown, scream at him to open the door, be a complete lunatic....

Yeah, maybe not so much.

I wanted to demand what I deserved, but I wasn't magically going to become loud where before I'd always been quiet. I couldn't change overnight. Not only that, but being a lunatic at 2:00 a.m. would prove nothing in the long run.

I needed to prove—to Ronan and to myself—that I was invested, that I could and would be brave.

And it needed to be something big. And I had to do it soon, like right now. Right this minute.

I spun around my living room, my eyes searching for something, anything—

a sign, a clue, a message from above. The fury was quickly giving way to frustrated despair.

But then my phone chimed, alerting me that someone had just messaged The Socialmedialite. It was WriteALoveSong.

I scanned her message which, strangely enough, had a snapshot of Ronan and me at the premiere from earlier in the evening.

@WriteALoveSong to @Socialmedialite: Are you back in town yet? I know you don't do the gossip stuff, but it looks like that rugby guy you like might be calling it quits with his girl. He looks pissed, and she looks petrified.

Quite suddenly, I knew what I had to do, and I found I had the bravery—or stupidity—to actually do it. Before I could lose my nerve, I responded.

@Socialmedialite to @WriteALoveSong: What if I told you that I'm Annie Catrel? What if I told you that I'm crazy in love with Ronan Fitzpatrick? What if I told you he already knows I'm The Socialmedialite, *but I freaked out when I found out he knew, and, petrified, I left him in Ireland? And now he's shut me out?*

I hit send then waited, pacing my apartment. WriteALoveSong, for better or for worse, was my closest friend. All my earlier reasons for not reaching out to her felt stupid. I suddenly wanted to know her, and I wanted her to know Annie. I was tired of hiding. I wanted a real relationship—with Ronan, with WriteALoveSong, with the world. I wanted to trust. My phone chimed almost immediately with her response.

@WriteALoveSong to @Socialmedialite: Haha, funny.

I growled my frustration as I messaged her back.

@Socialmedialite to @WriteALoveSong: I'm serious. I'm Annie Catrel. I work at Davidson & Croft. I graduated from Wharton School of Business. I'm still wearing the irritating formal dress from earlier, and it itches like hell. I AM HER! And I need your help. I need your help as my friend. What am I supposed to do? I love him. I want to fight for him. How do I fight for him? Tell me what to do.

Five minutes passed, and she didn't respond. And then five became ten, then twenty. I was staring at my phone, willing her to message me back. I was concentrating so hard that when my phone rang I jumped.

I blinked at the screen and saw that the number was reserved; nevertheless, I quickly swiped my thumb across the screen and answered.

"Hello?"

I heard someone shift in a chair or on a couch before a male voice asked, "Annie?"

I hesitated, frowning at the air in front of me, but then answered, "Uh, yes. Who is this?"

"Annie who is also The Socialmedialite?"

I tensed as the deafening sound of blood rushed between my ears, and I demanded, "Who is this?"

"It's WriteALoveSong."

Um…what?

"I…what?"

He cleared his throat, and I heard him shift again in the chair. "I'm WriteALoveSong."

I blinked at the air in front of me and blurted, "Oh my God! You're a man!"

He chuckled, "Yes. I'm a man."

"I thought you were a woman."

"I figured you did."

"But-but-but you're a man."

"Yes."

A smile laden with incredulity tugged on my lips, and I shook my head. "I-I can't believe—I can't believe I'm talking to you. How did you get my number?"

"I looked up Annie Catrel; she—I mean, you—have an unlisted number, which is smart. But I have a friend who can get me any number I need, listed or unlisted."

"Well, that's handy."

"Yes, it can be."

We were silent for a long moment, and my heart was acting all wonky, my internal temperature rising then falling. Somehow I needed to get Ronan's attention, convince him that I was all in. I needed my friend's help—I needed WriteALoveSong's help—and so I'd trusted that *she* would want to help.

But *she* was a *he*…and I didn't know if that changed everything.

Ronan had been so right. The physical—for better or for worse—mattered. It was part of the person, and it was diluted, changed by the barrier of online interactions. I'd known WriteALoveSong for over two years, but…did I really? Obviously not.

I inhaled, intent on apologizing for bothering him with my girl drama, but he spoke before I could. "Annie, we're friends, right?"

"Right." I pinched the bridge of my nose, feeling a lot ridiculous. This was so odd and awkward.

I heard him take a deep breath before he said, "You asked me for help; you asked me what to do, and I want to help you." He sounded solemn, like he was making me a promise. "If you really love this guy, then this is what I think you should do…"

TWENTY-TWO
RONAN

@ShellyKeeling08: @RonanFitz Have you read New York's Finest today??!?!
@Starryeyes: @RonanFitz I just read the blog post and my heart is bursting at the seams <3 <3 <3
@Jennybabes45: @RonanFitz If you don't love her back, I swear I'll punch you in the testicles.

I was going to end up wearing a hole in the rubber; I knew I was. The screen on the treadmill read twenty-two miles; the calories I'd burned were well into the thousands. I was even starting to feel lightheaded. I knew it was Tom when I heard the front door open and somebody step inside because he was the only one with a key. Ma and Lucy had long since gone home, and, despite the fact that Ma had been getting on my last nerve, I kind of wished they were still here. It would make my heart feel less alone.

My heart that Annie was destroying.

How a person could be so afraid of rejection that they'd give up the potential for true happiness boggled my mind. We were finished. I was done…but my fucking heart still held out hope, making every breath feel like someone was stabbing me with a thousand needles.

Tom came into the room and stood watching me for a minute. Then he walked up to the treadmill and told me I had five seconds to get off before he pulled the plug out. I didn't savor the prospect of face-planting on the rubber, so I reluctantly slowed my run and stepped off. My entire body was dripping with sweat, and my muscles spasmed in a way that said I'd overdone it. Tom handed me a towel.

"I have to be honest, mate—you look like shit."

"Not sleeping and an overabundance of lactic acid will do that," I deadpanned and went to knock back a bottle of water, emptying it almost all in one go. I'd been functioning on less than three hours sleep a night.

"And having your heart broken," Tom put in.

I scowled. "Piss off."

My phone pinged with yet another notification, but I ignored it. I'd been ignoring it for hours now, too stubborn to face the world. Annie didn't want me. Well, she didn't want me like I wanted her. That was the only fact I could handle right now. Any online bullshit could wait.

"Have you spoken to her?" Tom asked, wincing at my harsh response.

"Yes."

"And…?"

"And nothing. I'm moving on."

Now, if only I could convince my heart of that. This pain was worse than any injury or beating I'd ever had to endure.

"Moving on to what? Tying up women like Brona and letting them sell their story to the highest-bidding tabloid? You were famous before all this, but now everyone knows who you are. You can't go back to the way things were."

His tone put me on edge. "I never said I could. And why are you here anyway? Don't you have work?"

He paced and continued talking, ignoring my question. "I've even had photographers hanging around the restaurant, you know. It's verging on ridiculous. And I came because I give a fuck. Look what happened the last time you lost the plot—you nearly killed that prick Sean Cassidy. I'm here to make sure you don't go down the same road again."

"Jesus, Tom, that was a completely different situation. Who do you think I'm going to hurt? Annie?"

"That's not what I'm saying, and you know it."

I was about to throw back some cranky retort when my phone started buzzing and I recognized Lucy's ringtone. She was the only person whose calls I never ignored, so I went to pick it up.

"Lucy," I answered.

"Oh, my God, bro, have you been online yet this morning? Have you seen it?" Lucy began, her voice positively bursting with emotion.

"I'm taking a break from online, Luce. What is it?"

She let out a worried sigh. "So you haven't seen it. Okay. You need to go onto *New York's Finest* right now and read the latest post. Crap, why didn't you tell me about any of this? Why didn't you tell me who Annie really was?"

What she said had me moving through the penthouse at warp speed and searching for a computer. "There wasn't a right time.... How the hell do you know?"

"Quit asking questions, and just go read her post. Call me back when you're done." She hung up, and I finally found my laptop. My heart pounded, the anticipation killing me as I waited the fraction of a second for the page to load. Then it was finally on the screen, and I felt my skin prickle as I started to read.

New York's Finest
Blogging as *The Socialmedialite*
April 22
LADIES AND GENTS! I have an announcement!
You know that guy I featured on my blog a few months ago? The really, really hot Irish rugby player who plays the position of "hooker" in the RLI (Rugby League International)? The one with the anger management issues, the body of a gladiator, and the face of a movie star? The one with the questionable fashion choices, leading me to ask whether he was the lovechild of a leprechaun and a hobbit? Ronan Fitzpatrick? Yeah, that guy.
Well, I have a confession to make.... I'm in complete and total foolish love with this man. I love him more than Dara Evans loves stealing baseballs and candy from children, or clubbing baby seals and turning them into coats. I love him more than Sean Connery loves talking about Scottish politics while living in Southern California with a llama. I dream about him; I miss him when I don't see him; and I want to spend the rest of my life trying to get him to eat ice cream and ruin his diet.
I don't care if he wears toe-shoes...okay, that's a lie. I need to talk to him about the toe-shoes, but even if he did continue to wear the toe-shoes, I'd love him anyway. He is the strongest person I know—and the kindest, the bravest, and the most generous. And I've pushed him away because I was too afraid of being seen. I was too afraid of being known. I was too afraid of deserving and needing someone, but it's too late. I need him. I need Ronan Fitzpatrick. And fuck, damn, shit, hell—I deserve him.
I love him more than my fear. I love him more than my safety and my peace of mind. I love him more than I value my common sense. I love him more than being anonymous.
So...there it is. I've just committed social media suicide (and maybe professional suicide), but I don't care. I would rather crash and burn in the flames of courage than sit in the comfortable, lonely shadows of air-conditioned cowardice for another second.
<3 The Socialmedialite
AKA Annie Catrel

"Holy fuck," Tom swore as he read over my shoulder. "Your girlfriend has a pair of balls on her, that's for certain."

I was still in too much shock, the words on the screen blurring my vision; otherwise, I would have given Tom a wallop for insinuating the woman I loved possessed testicles. But okay, metaphorically speaking, she did have a pair. My heart beat faster than my brain was moving, and considering my brain was racing faster than Usain Bolt on steroids, that was saying something.

After everything that had happened, I'd lost all hope. I didn't think Annie was ever going to give us a real chance, and now I had one hitting me square between the eyeballs. That's what the article was about, wasn't it? It was her saying she was all in; she was saying "come and get me" in the only way Annie could.

I thought of the implications of what she'd just done. We'd narrowly escaped her being exposed as The Socialmedialite when her laptop was stolen, but now she'd come out of the proverbial virtual closet. She'd signed off as Annie Catrel, and the media was going to be all over it. All over her.

I had to find her.

Quick as a flash, I was out of my seat and pulling on my boots, rummaging in my coat pockets, trying to find my car keys.

"Hey, hold up, mate," said Tom, placing himself in front of me. "Where do you think you're going?"

"To find Annie."

"Not right away, you're not. Maybe sit down and take a breather for a minute, yeah?"

"I don't want a breather. I need to see her," I said and tried to push past him. Unfortunately for me, Tom was a tall fucker, and my head was all over the shop.

"This woman means the world to you—I can see that—but I'm sure she's feeling pretty delicate right now. Such a big confession will do that to a person. Maybe wait 'til you've both had time to process. Otherwise, you might fuck things up worse than before."

I lost some of my steam as his words took root, my brows furrowing in frustration. I *had* fucked things up with Annie the last few times I'd seen her. I'd pushed her. Then I pushed her away. And fuck if she didn't just push me back.

"And anyway, you need to shower before you go anywhere," he said and steered me in the direction of the bathroom.

Before I knew it, I was standing under the spray, drowning my need to see her in hot water and soap. What Annie had written was running through my head in a loop. I already knew that she loved me; the struggle was in getting her to admit it, both to me and to herself, and now she'd just told the whole world. I couldn't believe how much everything had changed in such a short amount of time. I was still wondering if this was a dream. Yesterday I was comatose, heartbroken and depressed beyond measure. Now I couldn't stop grinning as I punched my fist into the air in victory.

Yeah, that's right, I just victory-punched, butt-naked in the shower.

I just loved her so much I felt I was going to burst with it.

I'd been wrong. She was so fucking brave. I was going to kiss her all night once I got my hands on her just to show her how proud I was. Shit, I'd buy her a thousand roses and a shop full of éclairs in appreciation of her bravery. I knew it had taken everything for her to do what she'd done.

Screw Tom. I was going to find her right now.

Five minutes later, I was dressed and out the door, Tom calling after me to wait. He might have been taller than I was; but I was faster and sneakier, and I managed to make it to the elevator before he could catch up. Before I knew it, I was burning rubber on the road to Annie's. I found myself with one hand on the steering wheel, the other at my mouth as I chewed half my fingernails off with nerves.

The last time we'd spoken, emotions had been running high for both of us. I'd said things I shouldn't have said. I just hoped that what she'd written meant she'd forgiven me and it wasn't just some way of coming clean to the world about who she really was.

No, that definitely wasn't it. If it were, then she wouldn't have included all the stuff about loving me.

When I got there, I had to park across the road from her apartment building because there were vans and cars blocking half the street. Curious. I got out and strode across, only to see the paparazzi crowded around the door to the lobby when I got closer.

Fuck.

I was about to turn around and get back in my car because if I approached them I'd be swamped in seconds; but then I heard her, and my heart exploded.

"Please, let me by. You're crushing me," Annie demanded, and my feet were moving again, my hands balling into fists. Those fuckers had clearly caught her leaving the building and had pounced like a pack of ravenous wolves.

"Socialmedialite, tell us why you came clean?"

"Annie, have you spoken to Ronan yet?"

"Did you write the post to win him back?"

They all threw questions at her, one after the other in a never-ending stream, cameras flashing rapidly, the lights blinding. She must have been terrified, though she was hiding it well; she'd lifted her chin in defiance. There were at least thirty of the fuckers, all surrounding her. When I reached them, I began pulling them back one by one. It only took a moment for them to recognize who I was because seconds later the cameras were flashing at me and questions were being thrown in my direction.

They cleared back a little when they saw the murderous look on my face, and when I finally got to Annie, I found her against the wall, clutching her handbag, her eyes wide as she tried to hide her fear. They'd cornered her away from the door so she couldn't get back in after she'd left. The moment her eyes connected with mine, I saw a myriad of emotions flash across her face, the most powerful of which was relief.

"Ronan," she breathed as I took her into my arms, shielding her from the horde. I ran my hands down her face to her neck and then along her body, an all-consuming instinct to check if she'd been hurt.

"Are you all right?" I asked, my voice coming out in a growl since I was so pissed. One guy was hovering over my shoulder to try to get a shot, and I felt like hitting him, making an example to the rest of them to back the fuck up.

Annie brought her hands to my chest, and I looked down to see they were shaking, her eyes wide and flickering between mine as if to ask, *What have I done?*

She seemed a little bit out of it, so I repeated my question. "Annie, answer me. Are you all right?"

Swallowing hard, she finally found her voice. "I'm okay, just a little… surprised. I didn't expect them to find me so quickly." She sounded stronger than I expected, and it made me proud.

"Fucking parasites. Come with me. Just stay close, okay?" I said, ducking down to meet her eyes.

She nodded, the fear she'd been holding at bay starting to bleed through. "Okay."

Taking her hands, I pulled them around me so she was holding onto my waist. Then I placed her firmly under my arm and began leading her through the crowd.

"Back the fuck up," I warned any pap who dared get too close. They all did as I instructed.

A couple of minutes later, we were at my car, questions still being thrown at us about our relationship, about Annie being The Socialmedialite, about whether or not I knew all along. I reached across her and opened the door, using my body as a shield to keep them at bay as she climbed in. Once I had her secured, it was easier for me to get around to the driver's side, probably because I had no qualms about pushing and shoving people out of the way.

At one point, a short guy grabbed me aggressively by the shoulder, and I swung around, temper flaring as I gripped his collar with one hand and clenched the other into a fist, ready to punch. When I saw the look of sheer terror on his face, all my anger drained out of me. He was just a person trying to do a job. Yeah, he was a parasite, and he was going about it all the wrong way; but he didn't deserve a beating. None of these people did. I had zero respect for how they chose to make a living, but I wasn't going to waste a single ounce of anger on them anymore. It wasn't worth it.

I was sure there'd be some stories circulating the next day about how I'd manhandled a photographer, but I didn't care. My goal right now was to get Annie away from here and somewhere safe. They could crucify me all they wanted.

Their shouts were muted only when I climbed in the driver's side and slammed the door shut. Annie had her phone in her hands, scrolling through her messages. It looked like she was doing it as a means of calming her nerves rather than because she actually needed to check them.

"Joan called and asked me to c-come into the office," she said, her voice breaking up a little. "I didn't realize they were all outside until I'd already left, and then they blocked the door so I couldn't get back in." The final part was whispered, and something inside me snapped.

"Fuck," I swore and pulled her into my arms, kissing the top of her head. "That shouldn't have happened."

"It's my own fault," she muttered, her face pressed into my chest.

"No, it isn't. Anyone with a shred of human decency should know it's not right to corner a woman all alone like that. Those pricks could have really hurt you."

"I'm okay," she sniffed. "But I think I should maybe take some self-defense classes."

I laughed lightly and then let out a long sigh. "Look, I'm going to get us away from here. Then we need to talk. If I stay here any longer, there's a good chance I'll get out of this car and deck someone."

Annie only nodded silently in response, and I started the engine. I drove in the direction of Davidson & Croft, stopping a few streets away when I saw a rare parking spot. Once the engine shut off, silence filled the car, and I didn't know what to say first. I was still trying to find the right words when Annie broke the quiet.

"So, you read my post?" Her voice was so small that I almost didn't hear her.

I turned my body to face her. "Yeah."

It was clearly a struggle, but she forced herself to look me in the eye. I was surprised when her voice became demanding, fierce as she prompted, "And?"

"Hilarious, as always," I answered affectionately, and she frowned, biting her lower lip, looking upset as she glanced out the window.

I heard her mutter, "Crappity, crap, crapper. Fuck a duck and smack a rapper...."

Trying not to laugh, I leaned forward and caught her chin in my hand, bringing her attention back to me. "It was also the bravest, most honest thing I've ever read, and I don't feel worthy of the sacrifice."

"But I love you," she said far too loudly for the inside of a car, her eyes big, then rushed to continue, "I wanted to show you I was all in, and I didn't know how else to do that, to make you believe it. So I gave up my anonymity. There's no going back now."

I stared at her for a long time as a smile shaped my lips. "You sound so frightened, love."

"I am frightened. I'm terrified. But I'm not *only* frightened. I'm…I'm angry with myself for leaving you in Ireland and not giving you a chance, giving us a chance. You deserved better. We both did. And I'm angry with you for not giving me a chance to explain last night. But I understand why. But I'm still pissed. But I forgive you, and I want you so much. I love you."

This last bit made me smile like an idiot. "She loves me…."

"Yes. She loves you. And she wants to marry you, and part of her is still afraid you're going to change your mind—and now I'm talking in the third person because I've been going crazy and I haven't slept in over twenty-four hours."

"I'm not going to change my mind. That's not ever going to happen. After that stunt you pulled, you're stuck with me."

"Good." Her chin wobbled, and I saw her eyes were filling with tears. Her voice was watery as she added, "Because you're stuck with me, too. I deserve you, Ronan Fitzpatrick."

I laughed. "God help you."

She huffed then sucked in an unsteady breath, but her eyes didn't waver from mine. "And I deserve constancy and honesty. I deserve respect and love. I deserve unfailing devotion."

"You have all of that—you have all of me."

She nodded, and I was relieved to see her tears recede, though she still looked weary.

"Ah, my Annie. Love is terrifying, I know because I'm also terrified of losing you. But I know now that it's also amazing. And we're in this together. Never forget that." I murmured the last of these words as I bent and captured her lips softly. My hands found each of her shoulders and began to massage them. She was wound so tight, and I felt a powerful urge to relax her—not to mention my need to touch her everywhere was practically consuming me.

"I thought you were going to kill one of those photographers back there," she said in between my kisses as she took a rushed breath. I was planting them all over her face now, my hands cupping her neck, thumbs rubbing the little indents at the base of her throat.

"I almost did, but you know what? I'm learning to deal with it," I murmured in devotion. "There are always going to be paps, Annie, and there are always going to be journalists to write lies about me, about us; but I'm realizing it doesn't matter. None of it does. See? I'm *maturing*."

She hiccuped a little laugh.

I continued, "All that matters is that I have you. The rest is background noise. It's not worth breaking a nail over, never mind losing my temper. And if it means we get to be together, I'll take it all with a smile on my face because you and me, darling, we're the real deal. *You* are worth fighting for. I'm not letting you go now, not for all the tea in China."

Annie smiled and let out a nervous chuckle as I sucked her bottom lip into my mouth. "That's a lot of tea."

"Fuck yeah, it is." I laughed and kissed her properly, my tongue sliding against hers, tasting and exploring every inch of her soft, perfect mouth. Only this morning I thought I'd never get to do this again, never be able to drink her in and feel my heart getting bigger and bigger with all the love I felt for this beautiful woman that I wanted to possess until I was old and gray.

She clutched at my shirt as my hands traveled down her spine, reaching under to cup her arse. She gasped into my mouth as we fit against each other, and I pulled her closer to me, cursing the gear stick that separated us. I was mentally trying to figure out how to get her under me when somebody rapped loudly on the window. We broke apart, chests heaving, the sounds of our labored breaths filling the space as I turned to see a stern New York cop glaring down at me. I rolled down my window and was told we were parked in a handicapped spot and needed to move, pronto.

Annie groaned a little, fixing her top back in place, as I pulled the car back out onto the road. When we reached Davidson & Croft, I drove up to the entrance and let her out to deal with Joan while I went in search of somewhere to leave my car. I allowed myself a moment to soak in the sight of her arse as she walked off and was on cloud nine when she turned twice, smiling over her shoulder at me, looking braver each time.

Once she was safely inside, I drove away.

I couldn't believe I had this woman. This woman who seemed designed by some divine power specifically to be mine, and I was designed to be hers. One thing was for certain—as soon as she was done talking to her boss, we were going back to my place, and we wouldn't be leaving for a long, long time.

TWENTY-THREE
ANNIE

The Shameless Snap: *When all else fails, lift your phone, focus the camera, and just take the fucking picture.*
Best for: *Situations where being stealthy is not possible or necessary.*
Do not use: *If the subject of your photo is prone to violence, or has diplomatic immunity (or both).*

"I don't know how else to say this other than…I resign."

Joan blinked at me three times very slowly over steepled fingers and with a blank expression.

"I see…." she said.

I fiddled with the envelope and then placed it on her desk. We stared at each other for a long moment, her expression giving away nothing of her thoughts. She didn't take the envelope.

I was just about to explain myself when she continued, "Yes. I see. It's for the best. I was going to have to fire you. Dara Evans has already called about that article you wrote on St. Patrick's Day as well as your little coming-out article this morning. She wants to sue us. Your resigning makes sense for the company."

I nodded, firming my lips. I was disappointed. I think part of me hoped Joan wouldn't let me resign. I liked my job most of the time, especially when I was working with public figures who deserved the good reputation and ideal image I helped them achieve.

But I was also relieved.

Helping people like Dara Evans had always felt like trying to put a shine on poop.

"Thank you for everything, Joan."

I gave her a half smile, and her eyebrows lifted a notch, betraying a hint of surprise.

"Are you referring to when you lost your shit, or are you referring to all my excellent professional mentorship over the last year?"

"All of it. Thank you. You're a...you're a good friend."

"No, I'm not, but it's cute that you think so." She leaned forward suddenly and snatched the letter off the desk, held it lightly in her right hand. "Of course, I'm not going to let you off so easily. You have accounts of key clients still in your queue. I expect you to stay on in a consulting position for an indefinite period of time."

I blinked my surprise. "You want me—you want me to—you—"

"We'll pay you your hourly rate as a contractor. Rachel will send you the details tomorrow. Also, it would be best if you and Mr. Fitzpatrick got married at some point, had a few beautiful children that played rugby. Everyone loves a DILF."

I couldn't help but laugh. It was shocked, quiet and soft at first, but then it erupted into an uncontrollable fit of giggles. Joan's expression did change then. She looked both dismayed and diverted.

"Oh, my lord. What is that sound you are making? Is that...a laugh?"

I shook my head, then nodded, and then shook my head again, holding up one hand as I clutched my belly with the other.

Joan glanced at me askance. "For the love of God, don't ever laugh in public. No one will forgive you for it. You'll be ridiculed, Ronan will go on an assault spree, and then Ian will have a mental breakdown trying to clean up the mess."

***

GERTA CRIED WHEN I told her the news but then stopped crying when I told her I would be staying on as a consultant. I was surprised by the force of her reaction and found myself comforting her with an awkward one-armed embrace. She laughed at my lack of ability to comfort and pulled me into a full hug.

"Oh, Annie...." she sighed; I felt her shake her head against my shoulder. "Now we can be friends outside of work, too."

I was speechless. Friends. I was going to have friends. Ronan's mother Jackie, his sister Lucy, the wives and girlfriends of his teammates...these would be my friends. Being with Ronan would mean an instant circle of friends.

And then it hit me that all my online friends, the ones I'd made as The Socialmedialite, might now become actual, in-real-life friends. This thought felt a little overwhelming and a lot exciting. Being with me might mean an instant circle of new friendships for Ronan as well. Maybe WriteALoveSong and I would meet for lunch, or go to the movies, or hang out like real people.

Maybe he and Ronan would become good friends, too, especially after I explained that WriteALoveSong—whose real name was Broderick—had helped me understand that I needed to go public with both my feelings for Ronan and my identity as The Socialmedialite. Broderick's idea had been tamer, less risky than what I ultimately decided, but his original suggestion made me recognize that I needed to take a risk and now was the time.

Gerta left to find me some boxes, and Ronan appeared a moment later, bursting into my office with restless energy and a stern expression. Even so, my smile was immediate.

"Ronan." I beamed, crossing to him.

"You quit? You quit your job? Why? Did Joan make you? Because if she did, I swear to God I'm going to—"

"No, wait. Listen—it's not like that." I reached for his hands, needing to touch him. Our reunion this morning had been too short, and I was low on sleep. I needed the feel of him to prove that I wasn't dreaming while awake.

"Then what's it like? Because that fuckface Ian Shitforbrains stopped me in the hall and told me you were in Joan's office and you quit. You are fucking awesome at your job, Annie; and if they can't see that, then they're all wankers, the lot of them."

My smile widened as I rushed to explain, "It was my decision. I quit on my own, with no pressure from Joan. In fact, she wants me to stay on as a consultant."

His eyes narrowed. "She's not pushing you into staying on, is she?"

"No." Rather than laugh at his expression of suspicion, I pressed my lips together and added, "It'll be the best of both worlds. As a consultant, I'll be able to pick and choose which clients I work with. It'll be great. I'm very pleased."

"Hmm...." He surveyed me, searching for sincerity. Obviously finding it, his expression cleared. "Okay. Good. I guess this also means more working from home?"

"Yes. I'll be working from home all the time now. No more office visits." I glanced around my office and realized with a little pang that I was actually going to miss the three walls and window view. My days here, even though they were sparse, were the only times I had to leave my apartment. Now I would have nothing to force me from my home other than my own will.

I felt the weight of Ronan's stare and turned my attention back to him. He was watching me with a heated and focused longing that nearly stole my breath. Searching my gaze, his own growing almost devilish, he lifted his hand to my cheek, his fingers wrapping around my neck, and tugged me closer.

"It's a shame that we never christened this office…." he whispered against my mouth.

"Christened?"

"Fucked on the desk."

"Oh!"

He slipped his arm around my waist and crushed me to him, his mouth fiercely colliding with mine, his hands possessive. We hadn't been separated that long. Measured in time, we'd made love four days ago, but the emotional distance between us had been boundless—at least it had felt that way to me. His touch, possessive verging on desperate, told me he felt the same.

Peripherally, I heard Gerta's squeak, followed by the sound of the door clicking shut. Ronan's kisses grew softer, more loving, cherishing, even as he walked me backward to the desk. His deft fingers untucked my shirt and adroitly moved to the clasp of my bra.

I pulled my mouth away. My protests—though based in logic—were largely half-hearted. "Wait, we have—we have so much to talk about, to settle. I love you, and I want you to know that I—"

"Hush, Annie dearest. We have the rest of our lives to talk, and I promise we will; but we only have ten more minutes in this office."

"But…but I have no restraints."

Ronan pulled three inches away, his hands lifting to cradle my face as the back of my thighs met the desk. His dark eyes were foggy with lust, but there was a sweetness present, too, a welling of sincerity and emotion.

"My love…." He paused, kissed the tip of my nose, and whispered, "I don't always want you tied up. I want you free. I want you wild. I want you brave. I want you any way I can get you. I want you now, and I want you for the rest of my life."

I faltered, not knowing what to do, how to touch him. He must've seen the indecision in my eyes because he gripped my hands and slipped them under his shirt to the bare skin of his stomach.

"I want you to touch me, Annie. I want to feel your hands on me. Don't you want that, too?"

Really, his words were all the invitation I needed. I dug my fingers into the ridges of his stomach and around his sides, feeling a sudden sense of greedy urgency. I kissed him—*I* kissed *him.* He groaned his approval. All thought of living underground, giving up bravery for safety, fled and would never been seen again.

I absolutely could not stop touching him. He felt hot and smooth under my fingers, hard and delicious. That's right, he felt delicious, and I wanted to taste him, bite him, consume him.

Hurriedly, I pushed his shirt up to his collarbone and bent to lick and bite his chest, my hands moving to his pants. He made quick work of lifting my skirt and helping me step out of my panties. I half noticed he shoved them in his pants pocket just before I opened his belt, button, and fly and stuffed my hand down his boxer briefs.

We both sucked in a sharp breath, his palms coming to my breasts, kneading me through my bra. I stroked him, and he released a shaky breath and a "fuck." This was my first time touching him like this, and I felt like I might spontaneously combust with lust. He was thick and long and hard and male and hot and so fucking sexy. The power I felt, holding him in my hand, encircling his perfect cock with my fingers. I was powerful. I was in control.

I stroked him again, and his patience snapped. In one swift motion, Ronan lifted me to the desk, swatted my hand away, and stepped between my spread legs. He then buried himself to the hilt with a single inelegant, swift thrust.

My hands went to his bottom, my nails digging into more delicious skin, and I pressed him to my center. I threw my head back as he pumped in and out. He lowered his mouth to my neck, biting and sucking and licking, tasting me as I longed to taste him. I lifted my chin and caught his lips, my fingers moving to his back and then his shoulders.

I anchored him to me with my hands, by winding my legs around his. I couldn't get enough of his body, the friction and heat we made. I pulled back an inch and focused on his face, found him gritting his teeth, his jaw ticking, his eyes shut tightly.

My heart dropped, and I stiffened with disappointment. "Ronan, do you not like this? Should I not touch you?"

"No. God, no. It feels so good. You feel fucking fantastic. Don't stop." His head dropped to my shoulder, and he made a sound like a growl.

"Are you sure? Why-why are your eyes closed?"

"Because if I look at you while you're touching me like that and making those soft, sexy sounds and feeling wet and tight and like heaven around my dick, then I'm going to come in ten seconds."

My breath hitched, and I arched my back as he paired this speech with a sharp pinch to my nipple, sending a wave of coiling warmth to my lower belly. I was close, and his words pushed me closer. We were a tangled mass of limbs, and I was sitting bare-assed on my desk with my skirt hiked around my waist, and Ronan Fitzpatrick was fucking me, and it was uncomfortable and ungraceful and sexy as hell.

"Right now, Annie. Come for me now." He moved his thumb to my clit and rubbed, his entire body taut, straining; a bead of sweat trickled down the side of his face. The sight of him so close to losing control was all that I needed to push me cresting into completion.

Ronan released a string of nonsense which might have been a foreign language, his pace frantic, his eyes finally open as he followed me, watching me, finding his own end and lingering there inside me, the final rocking movements of our bodies meant to prolong our shared pleasure.

He was breathing hard as he wrapped me in his arms, crushing me to him. His skin was damp, his heart beat like it wanted to leap out of his chest, and he was still speaking in some unknown language.

"What—what is that? What are you saying?" My breaths were still labored.

"It's Irish, and I'm promising you forever. You have to marry me, Annie. Say yes."

"I told you in the car. Yes, I will marry you." I smiled against his hard chest.

"And it's not just the sex—but I'm not going to lie, the thought of not having sex with you again makes me want to die—it's you. It's seeing you every day, it's the way you look at me, it's watching you come into your own, it's how you touch me, it's your generosity, your beauty, it's you."

My smile turned soft, and I snuggled closer. "You like how I touch you?"

"Yes. It's addictive. Never stop."

"Does this mean you won't tie me up anymore?"

He paused, stilled, and then leaned away, searched my face. His eyes were bright with reverence and devotion. "You tell me."

"I like touching you. I like touching you a lot."

"Then—"

I hurried to add, "But I also like not touching you."

His gaze warmed with happiness and maybe a little amusement.

"Then we'll do both. My only stipulation is that I have a safe word, too."

My eyebrows jumped as I stared up at him, and I felt the stirrings of a quizzical grin on my lips. "*You* want a safe word?"

"Yes." He lifted his fingers to my now messy hair and tucked it behind my ears, his poorly suppressed smile claiming his features.

I crossed my arms over my chest and cleared my throat as I watched him expectantly. "And what will your safe word be?"

"Éclair."

"Éclair?"

"Yes," he said, his smile now enormous, his brown eyes bright with mischief and affection.

"Why éclair?"

"Because, love…." Ronan cupped my cheeks in his palms and tilted my head back as he lowered his lips to mine. He brushed a soft kiss over my parted mouth and then whispered, "I've always wanted you to eat me like an éclair."

He wanted me to react, be shocked at his lascivious suggestion—typical, wonderful, dirty-minded Ronan.

Instead, I ignored the intent of his statement and pressed, "But doesn't that undermine the purpose of a safe word?" His languid near-kisses were making me feel warm and fuzzy all over.

Ronan chuckled, nipped my bottom lip, made sure my eyes were on his as he responded, "Oh, Annie, I'll never be safe with you."

EPILOGUE
RONAN

Using my key, I opened the door to Annie's apartment and stepped inside. She sat in the living area wearing a loose top that hung off one shoulder, giving me a tempting and very sexy view of her silky skin. Her hair was in a bunch on top of her head while her fingers danced rapidly over the computer keys. Too fuckin' cute. I still couldn't get used to the fact that one day I was going to marry this woman. That I had her for keeps.

Her and all her oddball online friends.

At first it was strange meeting these people that she'd known as The Socialmedialite but now was free to interact with in person. I was surprised that I liked most of them, especially Broderick. He's the quiet sort, and I might have been tad jealous of their relationship when I found out about it. But I changed my mind about him pretty quickly. Added bonus, he could actually keep up with me in the park when we went running.

Hearing me come in, Annie glanced over her shoulder and gave me a warm smile, her eyes flickering with curiosity to the brown paper bag I held in my hand. I smiled back at her but said nothing, setting the bag on the entry table and going to hang up my jacket. I really liked Annie's apartment here in New York. It felt so much like her, like home, and I was dreading having to leave when I returned to the team next month.

We'd casually discussed trying out the long-distance thing for a while but hadn't managed to come to an agreement. In all honestly, I didn't want even a centimeter of distance between us, never mind a whole ocean. So yeah, I wanted to be away from her about as much as I wanted to put in for a hysterectomy. Annie told me she'd give up her blog to come live in Ireland, but I could see the reluctance in her eyes. The prospect of leaving it all behind pained her. I just couldn't bring myself to make her do it. She loved blogging. It was her joy, her passion.

So we were at something of a standstill.

Well, I was hoping to remedy that standstill today. I just hoped she'd go for it.

"What's in the bag, Ronan?" she called casually. I resisted the urge to snicker because I was intentionally misleading her with this one. I wanted to surprise her. The bag bore the stamp of her favorite Italian bakery; however, it didn't contain any of the usual sugary treats. After she'd put herself completely and totally at the mercy of the media by coming out as the creator of *New York's Finest* in order to declare her love for me, I wanted to give her something in return. Annie had made the absolute sacrifice; she had given up her anonymity to be with me, and though I wasn't sure I had anything quite so weighty to lay on the line, I wanted to give her something that meant a lot to me. Something that would show her how much she mattered. It was *quid pro quo*. If she could give up something for me, I could give up something for her, too.

"Nothing important," I lied as I stepped up behind her, swept some fallen strands of hair away from her neck, and bent to place a kiss just below her ear. She shuddered at the touch of my lips, and I grinned. Even the tiniest reaction from her was addictive, and I savored every one of them.

"Call Lucy on Skype, would you?" I murmured. "We both have something we want to discuss with you."

"Okay, but why am I calling your sister?"

"You'll see."

Perplexed, Annie did as I asked, and soon Lucy was smiling at us on screen, wearing a T-shirt with a psychedelic-looking My Little Pony on it, her multi-colored hair hanging in a long, loose plait.

"Hello, lovebirds, how's she cuttin'?" Lucy chirped, full of excitement.

I knew the reason why, but Annie didn't. Not yet. She gave me a confused look at Lucy's turn of phrase, so I explained, "It's Irish slang for how's it goin'."

"Oh," said Annie, eyes lighting with understanding as she turned back to Lucy and grinned. "She's cutting just fine, Lucy. And you?"

Lucy shifted on her seat with barely contained glee. "I'm great! Fantastic, actually."

"You seem really excited," Annie noted, suspicious now.

"I am," Lucy replied then glanced at me. "Have you told her yet?"

"No, I was waiting to do it with you."

Annie looked up at me. "Told me what?"

I took her hand in mine and began rubbing her wrist. "Lucy and I have a proposition for you."

"Okay?"

"So, you know how you want to move to Ireland, but in order to do that you'd have to give up your blog?"

"Uh-huh."

"Well, Lucy and I were talking, and we came up with a solution. Ever since her visit, Lucy's been dying for an excuse to come back here, so what we propose to do is this. Lucy will come live in New York and work for you, taking celebrity pictures, and you can come to Ireland but still write your blog, only with Lucy sending you the photos for your posts."

"It's a win-win. Plus, I've always fancied myself an amateur photographer," Lucy said to Annie with a wink.

She was quiet a moment, looking between both of us with an expression I couldn't quite decipher. I knew the verdict was a good one when a smile finally took shape. "That's a genius idea! I can't believe I didn't think of it myself."

She dove from her seat and threw herself into my arms. I pulled her close and kissed her softly on the mouth, nipping at her bottom lip. God, how I loved this woman.

"Ugh, okay, can you two wait until I'm gone to starting sexing it up, please?" Lucy's voice came through the speakers, and Annie and I both started laughing.

"I'm moving to Ireland," Annie whispered, eyes full of emotion and disbelief as she stared up at me. "We get to be together, and neither one of us has to give up our careers."

"It's a sweet fuckin' deal, right?" I said affectionately, running my thumbs along her jaw.

"And I get to come to New York," Lucy added, doing a little jig in front of the camera. "Big Apple, here I come, baby! Better get ready for Lucy Fitzpatrick!"

Seriously, my sister was a nut sometimes. I was a little apprehensive of her moving to a place this big, full of dangers and vice, but Tom had promised me he'd keep an eye on her.

"She's going to come over in two weeks so that we'll have a little time for you to teach her the ropes," I said to Annie after we'd said goodbye to my sister, who'd declared to us that she was going to find Jared Leto and lure him into marriage.

"Sounds good." Annie nodded and bit her lip. I recognized the flush to her cheeks well. Let's just say, my fiancée really, *really* liked me right now, and when she really liked me, she also liked for me to do the things I liked to her. I sucked in a harsh breath and ran my hand from her collarbone to the back of her neck, where I cupped her firmly. She gasped at my hard touch, her full breasts brushing off my chest as I turned her and led her across the hall to the bedroom, plucking the brown paper bag from the entryway as I did so. It jingled a little, and Annie gave it a curious glance. Baked goods didn't normally jingle.

I nudged her down onto the bed and set the bag beside her. When she moved to open it, I gave her a stern frown, and she withdrew her hand. Her breathing was shallow, her lips plump as she licked them, and I knew by the way her pupils had dilated that she was aware we were playing now. In the bedroom, both of our roles fit us like gloves, and it was a true revelation to finally be able to sate my desires. With Annie there was no fumbling or awkwardness; we both knew the mechanics that worked for us, and we complemented one another perfectly.

"Take your clothes off and turn over," I said, reprimanding her for looking in the bag without asking permission.

Eyes downcast, she did as I instructed, quickly slipping off her top and pants before lying flat on her stomach, her gorgeous round arse facing me. I soaked in the sight of her red lacy underwear, took two steps forward until my knees hit the bed, and bent over her. My breath hit the side of her cheek, my mouth at her ear when I said, "You have to remember to ask permission, Annie." Then, bringing my hand to her arse, I gave her a hard little spank, and she yelped then moaned into the pillow. The slap and the way I spoke to her had fired her up, I could tell. Rubbing her bottom to soothe the sting, I planted a wet kiss to her neck, licked, and then stood again.

"Now you have permission to look," I said, voice heavy with sexual promise.

I smirked when she dove for the bag with excitement, pulling out the pastry box and giving me a confused look. She shook the box, and again it jingled. Opening it, she pulled out the keys.

"Are these...."

"The keys to my Chevy," I said tenderly.

"But why are you giving them to me?"

"Because I wanted to give you something, and I remembered you once telling me how much you loved the Chevy, how you'd like to have a car just like it one day. Well, now you do."

When she looked at me, her eyes shone with emotion. "That's your favorite car. It's the first car you ever owned. You love that car."

"True, but I love you more. Now the thing I love most has something I love dearly," I murmured affectionately and brought a hand up to caress her cheek. I couldn't help but add teasingly as I brushed my lips across hers, "Plus, it's not exactly my favorite anymore. That honor now belongs to the Charger. It is, after all, where we first made love."

Annie let out an emotional giggle then began kissing me back, her breasts moving against my chest. "I never knew a man could be so romantic about cars."

"You haven't met many car enthusiasts, have you?" I asked.

She shook her head. "Just you."

I held her chin as I slid my tongue teasingly between her lips. She gasped for breath. "I don't even know how to drive."

"You'll learn," I said, my voice growing deeper as my arousal increased. "In fact, this evening I'm taking you out for a lesson, but first, we play."

"Wait, wait," she protested. "There's something else in the bag."

"Ah, yes, there is. I almost forgot," I said, pulling back.

Annie dipped her hand in the bag and pulled out the brochure I'd tucked in with the box. "A property brochure?" she asked, eyes alight with excitement.

"That's right. If we're moving to Ireland, we're gonna need a home, now, aren't we?"

I was taken completely off guard when tears started to fill her eyes, and I pulled her close.

"Hey, hey, what are the tears for?" I said, brushing away some of the wetness beneath her eyes with my thumb.

She sniffled and spoke so quietly. "I'm sorry. I'm being an emotional idiot. It's just that I love you. I've always been alone, and the idea of having a proper home with you is a little overwhelming. I feel like I'm going to wake up in a minute, and it'll all have been a dream."

I took her hand in mine and placed it over my heart. "That's not going to happen. This is real. You're my home now, and I'm yours. Nothing can change that. I won't let it."

The look she gave me took my breath away, like I was all she ever wanted and she couldn't believe she actually had me. That went for both us because I felt exactly the same way. I returned her look, and then my lids grew hooded. Being alone in a bedroom with my beautiful fiancée did that to me. My eyes trailed to her chest, where her breasts rose and fell with her breathing, and I slid my arm beneath her body, pushing her to the top of the bed. A tiny sigh escaped her when I climbed between her legs and captured her wrists in mine, pinning them over her head.

"So, love, silk rope or cuffs today, what will it be?" I purred and thrust my hips into her.

Her eyes glazed over, and a fiery expression came over her as she met my stare. "Or I could touch you."

A grin shaped my lips slowly as I thought of all the ways I was about to make her scream. "Why, Annie dearest, that's the correct answer."

* * *

New York's Finest
Blogging as *The Socialmedialite*
February 14

I don't care what anyone says to the contrary, Lumbersexuals are here to stay.

They're too delicious to be a fleeting fad. It's like everything you want in an actual lumberjack—the beard, the smoldering eyes, the well-muscled torso, the big hands, the flannel, the boots—but without the dangling food in the mustache, dirt on the floor, or any actual lumber (but don't worry, there's still plenty of wood *nudge nudge* *wink wink*).

Although, I admit that some of these Lumbersexuals take things a bit too far. For instance, my husband and his teammates. As you see from these stealthy pictures taken two nights ago, none of them have shaved for almost four months, not even a trim! They all look like wild beasts or Neanderthals.

Well, everyone but poor Sean Cassidy. Sadly, as you can see from the third picture down, his beard is uneven and splotchy, like a prepubescent with peach fuzz. It resembles some kind of Rogaine accident or beard Hair Club for Men subscription gone terribly wrong.

Aside from Sean's valiant (but failed) effort, these guys are all growing beards for a good cause, and I can't fault them for that.

Check out the link to the highlighted charity below to learn why Irish rugby players aren't shaving and maybe donate some cash to this worthy cause.

Till next time!

(Wedded in bearded bliss) The Socialmedialite

THE END

ABOUT THE AUTHORS

L.H. Cosway has a BA in English Literature and Greek and Roman Civilisation, and an MA in Postcolonial Literature. She lives in Dublin city. Her inspiration to write comes from music. Her favourite things in life include writing stories, vintage clothing, dark cabaret music, food, musical comedy, and of course, books. She thinks that imperfect people are the most interesting kind. They tell the best stories.

Come find L.H. Cosway-
Facebook: https://www.facebook.com/LHCosway
Twitter: https://twitter.com/LHCosway
Mailing List: http://www.lhcoswayauthor.com/p/mailing-list.html
Pinterest: http://www.pinterest.com/lhcosway13/
Website: www.lhcoswayauthor.com

    Penny Reid is the *New York Times*, *Wall Street Journal*, and *USA Today* bestselling author of the Winston Brothers and Knitting in the City series. She used to spend her days writing federal grant proposals as a biomedical researcher, but now she writes kissing books. Penny is an obsessive knitter and manages the #OwnVoices-focused mentorship incubator/publishing imprint, Smartypants Romance. She lives in Seattle Washington with her husband, three kids, and dog named Hazel.

Come find Penny -
Mailing List: http://pennyreid.ninja/newsletter/
Goodreads: http://www.goodreads.com/ReidRomance
Facebook: www.facebook.com/pennyreidwriter
Instagram: www.instagram.com/reidromance
Twitter: www.twitter.com/reidromance
TikTok: https://www.tiktok.com/@authorpennyreid
Patreon: https://www.patreon.com/smartypantsromance
Email: pennreid@gmail.com …hey, you! Email me ;-)

OTHER BOOKS BY L.H. COSWAY

Contemporary Romance

Painted Faces

Killer Queen

The Nature of Cruelty

Still Life with Strings

Showmance

Fauxmance

Happy-Go-Lucky

Beyond the Sea

Sidequest for Love

The Cracks Duet

A Crack in Everything (#1)

How the Light Gets In (#2)

The Hearts Series

Six of Hearts (#1)

Hearts of Fire (#2)

King of Hearts (#3)

Hearts of Blue (#4)

Thief of Hearts (#5)

Cross My Heart (5.75)

Hearts on Air (#6)

The Running on Air Series

Air Kiss (#0.5)

Off the Air (#1)

Something in the Air (#2)

The Rugby Series with Penny Reid

The Hooker & the Hermit (#1)

The Player & the Pixie (#2)
The Cad & the Co-ed (#3)
The Varlet & the Voyeur (#4)

The Blood Magic Series
Nightfall (#1)
Moonglow (#2)
Witching Hour (#3)
Sunlight (#4)

St. Bastian Institute Series
Foretold

OTHER BOOKS BY PENNY REID

Knitting in the City Series
(Interconnected Standalones, Adult Contemporary Romantic Comedy)

Neanderthal Seeks Human: A Smart Romance (#1)

Neanderthal Marries Human: A Smarter Romance (#1.5)

Friends without Benefits: An Unrequited Romance (#2)

Love Hacked: A Reluctant Romance (#3)

Beauty and the Mustache: A Philosophical Romance (#4)

Ninja at First Sight (#4.75)

Happily Ever Ninja: A Married Romance (#5)

Dating-ish: A Humanoid Romance (#6)

Marriage of Inconvenience: (#7)

Neanderthal Seeks Extra Yarns (#8)

Knitting in the City Coloring Book (#9)

Winston Brothers Series
(Interconnected Standalones, Adult Contemporary Romantic Comedy, spinoff of Beauty and the Mustache)

Beauty and the Mustache (#0.5)

Truth or Beard (#1)

Grin and Beard It (#2)

Beard Science (#3)

Beard in Mind (#4)

Beard In Hiding (#4.5)

Dr. Strange Beard (#5)

Beard with Me (#6)

Beard Necessities (#7)

Winston Brothers Paper Doll Book (#8)

Hypothesis Series
(New Adult Romantic Comedy Trilogies)

Elements of Chemistry (#1)

Laws of Physics (#2)

Irish Players (Rugby) Series – by L.H. Cosway and Penny Reid

(Interconnected Standalones, Adult Contemporary Sports Romance)

The Hooker and the Hermit (#1)

The Pixie and the Player (#2)

The Cad and the Co-ed (#3)

The Varlet and the Voyeur (#4)

Dear Professor Series

(New Adult Romantic Comedy)

Kissing Tolstoy (#1)

Kissing Galileo (#2)

Ideal Man Series

(Interconnected Standalones, Adult Contemporary Romance Series of Jane Austen Reimaginings)

Pride and Dad Jokes (#1, TBD)

Man Buns and Sensibility (#2, TBD)

Sense and Manscaping (#3, TBD)

Persuasion and Man Hands (#4, TBD)

Mantuary Abbey (#5, TBD)

Mancave Park (#6, TBD)

Emmanuel (#7, TBD)

Handcrafted Mysteries Series

(A Romantic Cozy Mystery Series, spinoff of *The Winston Brothers Series*)

Engagement and Espionage (#1)

Marriage and Murder (#2)

Home and Heist (TBD)

Baby and Ballistics (TBD)

Pie Crimes and Misdemeanors (TBD)

Good Folks Series

(Interconnected Standalones, Adult Contemporary Romantic Comedy, spinoff of *The Winston Brothers Series*)

Totally Folked (#1)

Folk Around and Find Out (#2)

All Folked Up (#3)

Three Kings Series

(Interconnected Standalones, Holiday-themed Adult Contemporary Romantic Comedies)

Homecoming King (#1)

Drama King (#2)

Prom King (#3)

Standalones

Ten Trends to Seduce Your Best Friend

Made in United States
North Haven, CT
26 January 2025